RE DEC 2016

NA SEP 2018

# THE LITTLE PARACHUTE

D09971836

# Also by J. Robert Janes

## The St-Cyr and Kohler Mysteries

*Mayhem*

*Carousel*

*Kaleidoscope*

*Salamander*

*Mannequin*

*Dollmaker*

*Stonekiller*

*Sandman*

*Gypsy*

*Madrigal*

*Beekeeper*

*Flykiller*

*Bellringer*

*Tapestry*

*Carnival*

*Clandestine*

## Non-Fiction

*The Great Canadian Outback*

*Geology and the New Global Tectonics*

*Earth Science*

*Rocks, Minerals and Fossils*

*Airphoto Interpretation and the
Canadian Landscape*
(with Dr. J.D. Mollard)

## Thrillers

*The Hunting Ground*

*The Alice Factor*

*The Hiding Place*

*The Third Story*

*The Watcher*

*The Toy Shop*

*The Sleeper*

*Betrayal*

## And for Children

The Rolly Series

*Danger on the River*

*Spies for Dinner*

*Murder in the Market*

**Also:** *Theft of Gold*

*The Odd-Lot Boys and
the Tree-Fort War*

# THE LITTLE PARACHUTE

## J. ROBERT JANES

MYSTERIOUSPRESS.COM

OPEN ROAD

INTEGRATED MEDIA

NEW YORK

All rights reserved, including without limitation the right to reproduce this book or any portion thereof in any form or by any means, whether electronic or mechanical, now known or hereinafter invented, without the express written permission of the publisher.

This is a work of fiction. Names, characters, places, events, and incidents either are the product of the author's imagination or are used fictitiously. Any resemblance to actual persons, living or dead, businesses, companies, events, or locales is entirely coincidental.

Copyright © 2016 by J. Robert Janes

Cover design by Mauricio Díaz

978-1-5040-3611-5

Published in 2016 by MysteriousPress.com/Open Road Integrated Media, Inc.
180 Maiden Lane
New York, NY 10038
www.mysteriouspress.com
www.openroadmedia.com

*This is for the librarians of the central branch of the St. Catharines Public Library who over the past forty-five years have stick-handled oft-curious, and at times demanding, requests. Had they not done so, where would folks like me be?*

# Acknowledgements

As with the St-Cyr and Kohler mystery series, there are a few words and brief passages in French or German. Jim Reynolds, of Niagara-on-the-Lake, very kindly assisted with both; the artist Pierrette Laroche, on occasion with the French. Should there be any errors, they are my own, and for these an apology is extended.

# Author's Note

*The Little Parachute* is a work of fiction in which actual places and times are used but altered as appropriate. Occasionally the names of real persons appear for historical authenticity, though all are deceased and the story makes of them what it demands.

# THE LITTLE PARACHUTE

*Parachute: umbrella-like device of cloth and harness used to retard the fall of a person or package from an aircraft; during wartime used to drop secret agents and clandestine wireless sets into enemy-held territory where things are seldom what they seem*

# 1

It was hot in the room and Angélique didn't know what to do. The Sturmbannführer Kraus-SS, ramrod stiff and very sure of himself, sat across the table from her, studying hers and the boy's papers. Tormented flies buzzed against the curtainless windows through which the late August heat of Paris streamed. Sweat beaded her underarms. Dark stains grew next to her belt where the flowered cotton print was pinched. There were stains down her back, stains under her breasts and around her neck.

The boy watched the flies. Now one, now another. Silently she asked, Are they Spitfires, Martin? Heinkels, Stukas or Messerschmitts? In the late summer of 1943 one still had to ask such questions.

'He's your son?'

They spoke in French. 'Yes, of course he is.'

'He doesn't look a bit like you.'

She shrugged. 'It's his father. Men like that always put their stamp on things.'

'But you're not married?'

'Since when did that mean anything to reproductive organs?'

Herr Kraus acknowledged this. He wasn't handsome, not

blond, blue-eyed and all the rest. He was brown-haired, brown-eyed, thin-faced, thin-lipped, sharp-nosed and, without the uniform, could well have been taken for a junior accountant in a shoe factory. Age about forty and passed over but now successful in his new line of work.

The chair, a sturdy wooden thing, much scraped and banged, had leather belts and buckles to tightly fasten the arms and legs, though hers were not yet fastened. Sweat stains marred the leather, which was really quite new, in spite of the shortages. There was blood. Old, dried and caked, the claw marks of fingernails. She could smell the excrement and vomit. Suddenly the room, bare but for the table, the two chairs, the lamp on its stand, and a copper bathtub—*Ah non*, why did they have one here?—gave up its stench.

Numbers 72, 76 and 84, the avenue Foch, were the headquarters of the SS in France, this the top floor of number 72, and *why* had they picked her and the boy up? *Why* had they been detained so long? For taking the train from Abbeville? For carrying sixty eggs, four kilos of butter, eight of ham, six of bacon and three freshly roasted geese all in two shabby brown leather suitcases?

The *marché noir*\* . . . Did they suspect her of planning to sell the stuff? If so, they were somewhat mistaken. Oh for sure, she had thought of it, who wouldn't? A little something for oneself, a little cash, but . . .

'Your name?'

How cold he was. 'It's on my papers.'

'Just give it to me.'

'Angélique Bellecour.'

'Age?'

'Thirty-six. Look, why don't you tell me what you want? The boy has to go to the specialist. For months we've waited for permission to leave the *zone interdite*.† He can't talk. He hasn't since the Blitzkrieg. The Messerschmitts, they . . . they

---

\* The black market
† The Forbidden Zone that was along the coast and extended at least 20 km inland

machine-gunned the road and killed a lot of people. Me, I . . .
I found him wandering in a field.'

'Then he's not your son.'

'*Ah, nom de Dieu*, monsieur, why such suspicion? Of course
he is. We all ran. What were we supposed to have done? Died
like the others?'

'Then where is his father?'

'I don't know. It's been three years now, hasn't it, since the
Blitzkrieg? Maybe he's been . . . well, you know. Maybe that's
why my son won't talk.'

Kraus passed smoothing fingers over their papers only to
hesitate at the *laissez-passer* that had allowed them to travel
from the Forbidden Zone. She was lying, of course. After a
while one got to sense such things. Perhaps it was the way she
studied the leather straps rather than look at him, perhaps
it was her anxiety over the boy whom she could only see by
turning, since her back was to the windows. What really is he
up to—is this what you're wondering, Angélique Bellecour?
Are you afraid this "son" of yours will betray you?

The sand-coloured hair that was thick and secured with
the double twist of a strong elastic band was not stylish, but
elastics like that were impossible to get these days. Still, she's
from the countryside, he reminded himself, and they might
have had a few, though he doubted it. The grey eyes were
widely set and earnest in alarm and uncertainty, the lips resolute, full and soft, not defiant yet. No lipstick too. Small,
enamel earrings—flowers of some sort and cheap—were worn
perhaps to please the boy. The bare arms were softly tanned
from being out in the fields in her off-hours. There was a
small scar, a cut that had been stitched long ago, on the left
side of the wide, smooth brow. The nose was freckled and
robust—solid peasant stock there. The cheeks were not thin,
the face a broad oval. A small brown mole marred the left
of a deeply cleaved chin. She had good breasts; good, strong
shoulders—the peasant ancestry again, he reminded himself.
A passable figure. Taller than most—yes, yes. Her head was
still held high. The eyebrows, wide and full, added further to
the worried gaze.

At once, a pleasant-looking woman, now well past her prime.

'It says here that you're a secretary.'

'At the hôtel de ville, which is also the Kommandantur. There are three of us secretaries, but the boy and I don't live in town like the others. We live at the farm of my uncle.'

'To the northeast of Abbeville?'

Angélique warned herself never to volunteer information, but said resignedly, 'Yes. It's about twenty kilometres from town. It's near Bois Carré but not too close. Some distance from the woods.'

She was making certain he knew it too. 'Do you gather mushrooms there?' he asked of the woods.

'Mushrooms? Ah! It's forbidden. All such things are, General. The trapping of rabbits, the fishing in our ponds and rivers, the taking of wild birds. All things, so we do not ever go to that woods even for the firewood we must not gather so as to heat our stoves to cook or keep warm in winter.'

One of the many rules of the Occupation that were far too often broken but which she obviously still hated. 'Boy, come here.'

'Martin, the major wishes to speak to you.'

First it had been "general", now "major". From flattery to the reality of working in the Kommandantur? wondered Kraus. And how was it, even then, that a French secretary could identify the collar bars and epaulets of an SS uniform? 'Boy, give me your name.'

'He can't.'

'Let him.'

'But . . .'

'YOUR NAME!' shrieked Kraus, causing them both to jump, the boy to open his mouth in panic, to try to say, *Martin . . . My name is Martin.*

'*There*, now are you satisfied?' she demanded, and reaching out, pulled the boy to her. 'It's all right, *mon petit*. The major didn't mean to startle you. He's just doing his job.'

The boy was thin and growing tall, thought Kraus. The sea-green eyes that were brimming with tears went with the dark reddish lights in the hair and the big ears. The angelic bone structure of the face—indeed, that of the arms and hands, too—didn't have the coarseness of the woman. There was sunburn—the skin was peeling. There were more freckles on the nose, the cheeks and narrow brow than on her. Had he been circumcised?

'Wait here.'

'But . . . But, *please*, we have an appointment at 4.00 p.m. The specialist.'

'You're among them.'

It was now nearly 3.00 and they had been kept waiting downstairs for hours. Just hours.

Pocketing their papers, Kraus left the room, left the door open into the corridor. They didn't hear him take the stairs or the lift, nor did they hear him go into one of the other rooms.

'*Chéri*, you mustn't worry. Hey, it's all right. You'll see. As soon as we can, we'll go to the clinic. A few tests, that's all. Your ears, your voice box—the doctor will look down your throat with a light. He'll tell us if there's any medical problem, but me, I don't think there is.'

Martin pulled away. He went back to the windows to watch the flies.

'We'll pay the doctor with the butter, *chéri*, and maybe the geese or the ham. He won't insist on everything. Doctors aren't like that. There'll be something left for the room. Some little hotel. Then tomorrow we'll go to the Louvre and I'll show you paintings and sculptures like you've never seen before. I think the Occupier must have put some of those back after it was emptied early in 1940 and lots had been stored away. It'll be our little holiday.'

He wasn't listening. He had "taken down his wireless aerial" and was concentrating on the flies. Several were gathered in a corner of the windowpane. They buzzed. They fought with one another and only as she drew closer to the tall French windows with their narrow balcony so high above the street did she see the handprint and realize the fingernails must have been pulled.

Bois Carré . . . The woman hadn't said *verboten* signs had been posted all around that woods or that there were sentries, felt

Kraus. She hadn't let on that the local villagers and peasants were terrified of what was going on there and tried to ignore it. Guilt-ridden perhaps, some of them.

The "son" wasn't hers—the boy couldn't be. He didn't look at all like her, but they could check for stretch marks. Had she any, this Angélique Bellecour?

Born 8 May 1907 in Tours, a long way from what she now called home. Not stylish. Not fashion-conscious. Not married. No curls, no waves. Not interested in men, or did she simply no longer care about her appearance? Three years into the Occupation, defeat and despair of its never ending had so disillusioned the French, many of their women had given up even worrying about what they looked like.

Not Jewish, not one of those, though a few of the non-French Jews were still left, still trying to hide out—he was certain of it, and those others would also be taken care of. Again he wondered if the boy had been circumcised. They'd have to check, but did she spend time in that uncle's *potager* when not needed in the fields, or was she working for the *Banditen*, the so-called *Résistance*, the terrorists?

Probably. Vegetable gardens were a means of survival.

What lay before him in the crowded suitcases was not survival but riches beyond most Parisians. Illegal, too, of course. Though many did, it was still forbidden to forage the countryside farms and return with food. There were ration tickets, alcohol-free and meatless days for that purpose, and every one of the French were supposed to obey the system even if it wasn't working properly and was being constantly abused by themselves.

Survival—yes, yes, but the food in these suitcases could be survival of a far different sort. 'These things could simply have been brought for her to admit, if stopped, to the lesser charge of dealing on the black market,' he said aloud and to the others. 'That would have landed her a few weeks in the Petite Roquette.* We'd have sent the boy home to that "uncle" of hers. She would know this, too, and that the boy is also good

---

* The women's prison

cover. Always travel *à deux, n'est pas*? Always look as if you're simply going about your normal routine.'

He held up one of the geese, but the prisoner, Henri-Paul Doumier, land surveyor, didn't understand. Battered nearly senseless, his eyes swollen shut and blackening like overripe plums about to burst, Doumier sat in a stupor. His nose was broken, a tooth still clung to a lower lip that had been split. The rounded shoulders had collapsed so that the neck craned forward, begging for the blessed release of the floor.

Blood dripped from his nose to lose itself among the greying black pubic hairs and spatter the limp penis with its foreskin. A father of four grown children, two boys, two girls, the boys "lost" in the war—this had been claimed. There was evidence of it, but were they really in England and just waiting to come back?

'I think so,' said Kraus, not bothering to explain his thought trend to Doumier or the others, the musclemen, the *gestapistes français*. 'That bitch down the hall is a part of it, isn't she? The three of you took the same train. You left quite early in darkness. Straight up the Somme to Amiens and then the *rapide* to Paris, arriving at 9.05 a.m., a four-hour trip, a delay on arrival of only five minutes. That's pretty good but we couldn't let you slip away, could we? You were the only ones in from Abbeville today. She and that boy of hers travelled third class while you sat in comfort in the second-class coach. You were her lookout; she covered your back. You were afraid you'd be followed—of course I can see that. Either one or the other of you is the courier, or the both of you. I think you should tell us. We'll get the names of your contacts here in Paris from her.'

There were two others of the SS in the room, both specialists in this game of prying secrets. Fritz-haired giants. Blond, blue-eyed Aryans. Dead-cold about their jobs and ruthless, but with the help of those others, the French Gestapo.

Kraus gave them a nod.

The tooth was spat. '*Non! Non, idiot!* She has nothing to do with this. *Nothing!*' shrieked Doumier.

He coughed blood. Perhaps he panicked at the thought

of what they would do to him, perhaps he revelled in the thought of getting that bitch out of harm's way.

'There . . . there was no one with me,' came the broken cough. 'Me, I was alone.'

'That's what they all say, but we knew you were coming,' said Kraus. 'We had word of it. Ah, please don't look so dismayed. Betrayal is so typically French, it's become the usual. I think the reward was four kilos of white sugar. I can't be sure. Sufficient in any case.'

The head was yanked up so that the plum-black eyes had to squint into the glare of the light and the blood ran down the back of the throat.

'Crush his testicles. Let her hear him scream.'

'They're badly swollen, Sturmbannführer. The shock might kill him. The heart, you understand? He's very weak. He's old.'

'DO IT!'

Martin felt her take him by the shoulders, and when Angélique pulled him against her, the warmth and the sweat made their bodies cling and he thought he could hear her heart beating. Ever so slightly her hands shook just like they did when she washed his neck and back. She liked to feel the softness of his skin—he knew she did—but that it always made her tremble as if she never knew when he'd vanish and was afraid to hold on to him for fear it would be the last time.

She spoke quietly, urgently. 'Martin, listen to me. Don't draw your little parachute for them. You mustn't, *chéri*. They wouldn't understand. They won't think of it as your way of telling people how you came to be with me in France. They'll think of it as something else, something very bad. They'll beat me, Martin. They'll pull out my fingernails just like they did to the one who left this. They'll never let me go if you do.'

Shaking his head, he felt the soft, round firmness of her breasts beneath the thin cloth of her dress and that of her slip and brassiere.

Satisfied that the warning had registered, she let him watch the flies as they buzzed and fought furiously with one another to get at the bloodied handprint. She touched his neck and ran a finger through the fine, damp hairs, smelled the gentle musk of him, said, 'You're so like your father. Every day you remind me of him.'

Every day she "ached" for his father and prayed for him to come back when it was safe and the war was over, but why does a woman "ache" like that? he wondered, concentrating on the flies. There had been a lot of flies on the road that day in June of 1940. After the Messerschmitts had machine-gunned the road, squadrons and squadrons of bluebottles had come racing in from the nearby farms to feed on the dead and lay their eggs in the wounds, the eyes, the nostrils, the gaping mouths of children, the guts that had spilled out of one man's stomach like coiled and bloodied snakes becoming sticky in the sun.

There hadn't been a sound except for that of the flies. All the cars, wagons and lorries that had been piled high with suitcases, mattresses, blankets, chests, chairs, birdcages even, the prams, carts and wheelbarrows too, had been strewn in a huge line of wreckage that had extended as far as the eye could see. Fires too, and dead horses, a mongrel with its tail between its legs. No one but himself had been standing. Even the wounded hadn't cried out. Even *they* had waited a moment.

Slowly the people had begun to pick themselves up in the fields, and slowly they had come back to the road as if they still couldn't believe what had happened.

'Martin, I loved your father with every part of me. In spirit, if not in the flesh, you are mine. Please don't tell them I'm not your mother. It's our little secret, *n'est-ce pas*? Just you and me.'

Impulse is a terrible thing, but he knew he had this hold over her, and in the dust of that window near the handprint, he deftly drew his little parachute and silently said, That's me, isn't it, Angélique? I've been dropped from the sky by para-chute. That's how I got here.

Angrily she hissed, 'If you feel *anything* for me, you will erase that immediately!'

It was a nice little parachute but was not of white silk, thought Martin. No, this one—his—was of dark blue, almost black silk but with silver stars and clouds and shooting stars and a big yellow moon. And as he had sailed down from the skies above at night, he had guided his parachute by pulling on the lines and letting the air either fill a part of it or spill out.

'Martin, *please*! It's too dangerous.' How could he do this to her? If she erased it, he would only draw another. The Sturmbannführer could well ask him to write his name. Martin had both pencil and paper for this purpose and would do so and then, as so often, out of perversity, would add his little parachute, his special sign, and with himself dangling from the straps. It was his way of explaining why he wasn't home in England with his mother but was here in France with his father's lover.

But of course the Germans wouldn't know it was Martin hanging from those straps. They'd think it was someone else entirely, a clandestine wireless operator from England, sent to help the *Résistance*.

'Martin, I can't undo what I've done to your mother and her marriage but if you leave that there, they will kill me and what will God say to you when you have to answer at Judgement's door?'

She always used this threat when things weren't going well. She had even got old Father Benoît, the village priest, to force him to write down his answers and pass them under the grille during confessional so that God would know the truth and that Father Benoît would at least *think* he did.

She prodded him sharply. He held back. He wanted to shout at her, I DIDN'T WANT TO COME TO PARIS, DID I? IT WAS ALL YOUR IDEA. YOU WERE FEELING GUILTY ABOUT HIDING ME AWAY LIKE THAT. YOU HAD FINALLY DECIDED YOU HAD BETTER DO SOMETHING!

Lights down his throat, the secrets of his voice box revealed to the prying eyes of some "specialist". The throat would have to be sliced open, an operation with ether, much ether poured onto a pad of surgical cotton and clamped over the nose and mouth, the struggles, the panic, the need to breathe . . . Giselle and André and all his other "cousins" at the farm had said that the specialist would have to install a mechanical talking box with a *key* to wind it up. There'd be a hole in his throat. A *hole*! The specialist would have to make a little wooden door for it. A *door*!

The scream from down the corridor began on a broken note but it caught in the air and it made the heat vibrate. It brought the beads of sweat out on her brow and face, her underarms as Angélique stiffened in panic until she felt as if she was drowning in sweat and cried, 'Martin, *please*!'

The sweat was like ice on her burning skin. It made her shiver uncontrollably. It made her urinate—'*Ah non!*' she wept but nothing could stop the flood that now filled her shoes and left its evidence on the floor.

Martin smelled its sourness but only as in memory of the road that day, for the scream was like others he had heard then. Unbidden the images came rushing at him: the flashes, the roaring, the hammering of bullets, the smashing of glass and metal, the cries, the shrieks, the screams, the stench of his pee . . .

The Messerschmitts had come back. They had timed it perfectly. Everyone who had been left alive had returned to crowd about on the road. This time a man's head exploded in a shower of blood and brains. His eyes flew apart. A little girl's back was torn to pieces. Her mother couldn't reach her. The father had tried to save her mother and the baby by lying on top of them. There hadn't been room for the girl, but the cannon shells had had no mercy and had found them, too, and gone right through the father to explode underneath, ripping the baby from its mother's breast.

Again there was silence after the Messerschmitts had left. Again, after a long, long time, people began to pick themselves up.

When Angélique found him, Martin flung himself against her and buried his face in her dress, the sour stench of urine then, and now too, of his own and hers.

Kraus saw the two of them clinging to each other next to the windows. They were caught against the light, the heat and the flies. A woman of thirty-six; a boy of ten she claimed was her son. A reddish-brown-haired, green-eyed, fair-skinned, freckled boy with big, troll-like ears and teeth that were too big for the rest of his face.

'Come here,' he said. 'Sit down.' And when she had, Kraus noticed everything about her including the dampness of her shoes and white ankle socks. 'Your name?' he asked.

Had Martin erased the parachute? 'Angélique Bellecour.'

'Age?'

'Thirty-six.' He had better have.

'Date of birth?'

'8 May 1907.'

'Parents?'

Martin let them talk. He turned away to watch the flies. One of them was crawling over his little parachute. Had it been later on that same day in June of 1940 that he had seen a British pilot bail out of his two-winged fighter only to have his parachute burst into flames?

It must have been. That's why he had made his out of asbestos cloth, but with the dark blue silk and the stars and moon on either side so that it would be invisible too, against the night sky.

He had come down in a field in France and in darkness and now here he was, three years later, in Paris with her. *Friday, 27 August 1943.* Fridays were *never* her best days. There had been no sign of his father after the Messerschmitts had come back. 'He's gone,' she had said. 'He had to leave us, Martin. He had to get away while he could.' But had she lied to him, and to herself?

'Where was the boy born?' asked Kraus.

'Near Tours, at Saint-Étienne-de-Chigny. There's a convent. My parents didn't want others to know I was giving birth to an illegitimate child. As soon as we could, I went to live and work in Orléans. I wanted to finish my studies but it was impossible. As it was, I had just enough money left over each week to pay a woman to look after the child while I was at work.'

'Her name?'

'Madame Marie-Léon Jeannôt.'

'Address?'

'Look, it was a long time ago. She'll have moved. She wasn't young. She was an old woman.'

'There's no need to get angry. Address?'

*Ah, merde alors!* '72 rue de la Bretonnerie, apartment 10. She was on the floor below mine. It was really very convenient. Possibly the best situation I've managed.'

'That's near the Palais de Justice.'

'*Ah oui, bien sûr.*' Did he already know that she had lived there once, alone and childless? 'Look, I really must get the boy to the specialist. Appointments like that are very hard to arrange.'

'How long were you in Orléans?'

It would go on and on. 'Two years. Martin was just learning to walk when I answered an advertisement for Aix-en-Provence. We went there for his health and mine. The chest. Neither of us are very good in the cold, damp weather. Last winter's flu was terrible.'

She had said it and he had let her do so knowing that every word would have to be repeated *exactly* as she had first given them. Time and again they would demand these answers.

'Aix,' he said.

'Yes. A notary.'

She tried to find the will to smile at the memory but failed and said with a shrug, 'Actually a widower who was looking for a wife and housekeeper as well as a secretary. It didn't work out. I was doing all the work and he was doing all the complaining.'

'And then?' he asked.

He didn't bother to grin at her little joke or to ask the notary's name and address. He would come back to those later. Angélique knew he would. Again she worried about the little parachute. Was it still there on the window?

'And then?' he reminded her.

'Nice in the spring of '35, an export-import firm. A good job but they went bust. Toulon in the fall—we stayed there for nearly three years. It was good, too, but not as good as Orléans.'

Kraus waited. He'd give her all the time she needed to betray herself.

'Then Reims in December of '38 and . . . and Lille in '39, the spring.'

Lille was quite near the Belgian border. Almost imperceptibly Kraus nodded. He didn't look up from the pencil he held by both ends. 'And the boy's father, did he follow you around the country?'

Like a lost dog—was this implied? 'Every once in a while he'd turn up and for the boy's sake, I'd let him stay.'

'But you don't know where he is now?'

'Not since the Blitzkrieg.'

'I think you're lying.'

'I'm not. Please check. Everything I've said is true.'

'We'll see.'

'Look, why not telephone the Hauptmann Scheel at the Kommandantur in Abbeville? He'll tell you who I am, or if you prefer, talk directly to the Oberst Lautenschläger. Both are very pleased with my work and will vouch for my loyalty. I'm simply an honest, hardworking secretary with a son who ought to be able to talk but can't seem to bring himself to do so. Everyone is concerned. They all want Martin to get better.'

Bois Carré fell under Lautenschläger's jurisdiction, a plodding Prussian of the old school who would soon be no longer in control of security because the SS were going to take over. Had she seen plans of the site? Had they been lying around in the colonel's office? Had she told that bastard down the hall about them? Was that why Doumier had taken such an interest in the woods?

'Major, *please*. I beg you. We're going to miss our appointment. If the specialist thinks it necessary, an expert will be called in. A German. Someone from the Wehrmacht. The Oberst Lautenschläger says there are some really good doctors who deal with such things and that it can be arranged. I . . .' She fiddled with her dress and tried to tidy up. 'Ah! I must look a sight. Look, I have to find us a place to stay. We can't wander the streets after curfew. I've promised the boy I'll take him to the Louvre tomorrow. There'll at least be some of the paintings, and I know lots of the sculptures have been returned to the galleries. This business here is all a mistake. We weren't following anyone as their lookout. *Ah, mon Dieu*, Major. Those types, they . . . they wouldn't trust us. A woman with a child is far too vulnerable. If you've children of your own, you'll know all about that.'

'Then why are you so afraid?'

*Sacré nom de nom,* but she mustn't let it get to her. 'Because when a person screams like that, Martin and me, we both know they are about to die. The road, remember? The Blitzkrieg? We were machine-gunned five times by the Messerschmitts, but *grâce à Dieu,* he can only remember the first two times.'

'The Luftwaffe were just doing what was necessary.'

'*Bien sûr,* the roads, they had to be cleared for the advancing tanks and motorized infantry. Even I can understand such a necessity.'

Could she lead them to her contacts? he wondered. Doumier and she would have been missed by now. At the first sign of trouble, their contacts would have gone into hiding.

Getting up, he gathered hers and the boy's papers. Again he said, 'Wait here,' but this time he took the lift. She listened as it went down three floors, then shut her eyes. Suddenly exhausted, she tried to find a reason for their being detained, but of course such things, they could happen at any time. One never knew and seldom was the reason given.

*The parachute,* she said, a silent reminder. *The parachute . . .*

Martin was wandering about the room. Everything he saw, he studied with total concentration. What, really, was going through that head of his? Certainly he wasn't stupid, as the teachers sometimes said, but very bright. He knew his French now—at least she had accomplished this. Night after night they had worked at it. Day after day in those first years she had found him in tears when she had got home from work. Ridiculed by the other children. *Teased* because he had no voice. Laughed at because he was a "bastard" child, pushed, punched, shoved, thrown to the ground and beaten.

Her son. They all thought of him as that. Her heart and his had been broken so many times but they could say nothing of the truth. *Nothing.* She had gone after every child who had ever teased him, had boxed their ears or chased them into the highest branches of the trees in the orchards just like a mother would have done, she to grab an ankle and try to pull the offender down, only to give up when common sense told her she'd best not break an arm or leg. The girls were no better.

'*Chéri*, leave that bathtub alone. Come and sit with me.'

He had climbed into the thing, and when he came over to her, he opened his fist to show her what he'd found caught in the drain.

*Ah merde*, it was a gold wedding band. Long black hairs clung to it. A woman's hairs. Sickened by the thought of what must have happened, she gripped her brow and tried to find a particle of sense in what was happening to them, tried to get a hold on herself. 'I mustn't cry,' she said. 'If I do, he'll think I'm guilty and will then force me to tell him the truth.'

When Kraus came back, the boy was sitting on her lap, the woman calmed perhaps by the closeness of another human being. It would do no good to say, It's all right. I've talked to Abbeville. Instead, he would simply tell her. 'Follow me.'

Desperately Angélique wanted to cry out, Martin, did you erase that little parachute? But of course she couldn't, nor could she look back towards that window.

Kraus had let her go, and she couldn't believe their luck, felt wet and weak and all those things a prisoner must feel when death is at the door and somehow a reprieve has been granted.

As soon as she could, she stopped on the pavement to tidy Martin's hair and shirt. '*Chéri*, you erased it, didn't you?'

Her lips were quivering. Beneath the softness of her tan, the cheeks were pale and tight. Irritably she ran the back of a hand across her brow. 'Well, don't just keep me in suspense, eh? At least let my heart get back to where it belongs and my stomach creep up from my shoes or put my neck on the block for the bread-slicer.'*

He wrinkled his brow. He studied her. He wanted so much to punish her but knew she would only fall to pieces.

'*Please*,' she begged. 'Don't make me go down on my knees, Martin. If they see us standing around like this, they'll think we've got all the time in the world. Try to find a little compassion for the woman who stole your father from your mother—yes, me, I freely admit it—but please remember that I love you dearly and that to make honey, the bee must always

---

* The guillotine, the widow- or widower-maker

find nectar by coming to the flower. It takes two to make love, Martin. Never one.'

When he didn't answer with a nod but gave her that blank look of his, a part of her died. Resolutely, she picked up the suitcases and started out. At five minutes to 4.00, they'd never make it anyway. The clinic was in the Luxembourg, halfway across a city she hadn't lived in since the exodus of June 1940 when it had emptied itself of nearly 1,500,000 souls, and so much for all of the lies she had told Kraus, a worry to be sure, only the more so now. Everything in the city had changed. There were so few cars, there might just as well have been none. In 1939 there had been 350,000 of them; now there were 4,500. *Vélo-taxis* had replaced them. Round and round the Arc de Triomphe they went, these crazy rickshaw contraptions with ancient settees and armchairs behind, other things too. The halves of a bathtub placed side by side, a Renault sedan—a '37, she thought—the motor and front half removed to be replaced between the shafts by a tandem bicycle and its riders.

Young girls, old and middle-aged men, pulled these things, the girls in trousers and sweat-stained blouses that made their seats balloon and their bosoms appear to strain, the men in shabby suit jackets, open-collared shirts, no ties, and trousers that clung to their legs in the heat.

*Ding, ding* . . . German direction signs were everywhere and . . . 'Hey, look where you're going!' Sweat was in the driver's eyes. Four German corporals were guffawing, having the time of their lives with a girl of the streets. Bright-eyed and made-up, the girl laughed, they laughed. Others talked loudly, pointed, waved or sat woodenly in their uniforms as if they, too, could still not believe swastikas were draped beside what had been the eternal flame, lighted every night at 6.30 to burn throughout the darkness, it having had to be extinguished, of course, by the Boches, it having been a symbol of the war they had lost in 1918.

'Martin, don't dawdle. Stay close. Ah, never mind what they've done to our suitcases. They're lighter, *n'est-ce pas*? Always look on the bright side, eh? After the rain, the sunshine.' She tossed her head.

But was it sunshine or had he left that little parachute for them to find?

The SS had taken all of the food and she had thought, too, that her change of underwear would have vanished as well. Underwear was so hard to come by these days. One never hung one's washing out even on the farm unless kept under guard and never overnight. Things simply disappeared and one went without. 'You'll learn,' they had said and she had. Oh yes. She was always learning lessons.

'We've got to find a café or bar,' she said irritably. 'I'll have to telephone. Maybe the doctor will forgive us. He knows we're coming. Delays are inevitable.'

Fat chance. Doctors were a law unto themselves. During the Blitzkrieg they had deserted en masse, leaving their hospitals and patients to fend for themselves. A national disgrace. Not all, of course. One or two had hung on but they were the exception.

The *passage clouté*'s lines of white iron studs were barely visible. Angélique started across, grabbing Martin by the wrist. All but reaching the centre of the thoroughfare that went round and round, she panicked and gasped, '*Ah non,*' and heard the screech of brakes.

German soldiers with rifles and submachine guns poured out of the camouflaged canvas back of the lorry. They ran forward to surround them. She couldn't move, couldn't find her voice, tried to say, Martin, please don't blame yourself.

A sergeant clicked his heels together, bowed in salute and motioned to a corporal to pick up their suitcases. Others guided them to safety, stopping the whole circus of traffic so that everyone else silently cursed them.

Deposited safely on the pavement at the north side of the Champs-Élysées, they were given another bow in salute.

Then the whole thing started up again, the mad round the round, the dervish whose wheels squeaked and clicked but hardly made a sound when one remembered the Paris of before.

Martin gently squeezed her hand and brought it to his cheek, his way of telling her everything was all right, that the soldiers had gone.

'I love you too, *chéri*. If we get through this in one piece, we'll have a celebration. If it still hasn't been dug up, we'll open that bottle of Dom Pérignon we've hidden for when your father comes back. He'll understand why we had to do it. Then I'll pour some over your head in the bath and I'll let you do the same to me. It's terrific. It makes your skin tingle.'

Did he teach you that? wondered Martin. Did he bathe you in champagne?

The *jeton* didn't work in the telephone and she had to go up to the bar again, where the *patron* made her buy another of the little metal discs. It took ages to get through to the clinic, and all the while Martin stood next to her, looking down the length of the café, staring out through the grimy windows. He was trying to get her attention. Every two seconds he'd give her skirt a tug and she wanted to say, Stop it! but couldn't.

'*Allô! Allô!* Is that the *clinique* Albert-Émile Vergès?'

The receptionist wasn't happy. 'Where have you been, mademoiselle? Your appointment was for 4.00.' Et cetera, et cetera.

'Please, we've been detained.'

The receptionist hung up. The line simply went dead. 'Ah no,' she gasped and threw a desperate look towards the *zinc*, said, 'Martin, what is it?'

Two men were looking in the windows. One was shielding his eyes though there was no need since the awnings were out and it was shady where they were standing.

'*Encore un jeton, s'il vous plaît,*' she said harshly to the *patron*. 'Make it two, damn it. I have to get through.'

This time a man answered and when she had explained that the trains had been delayed for hours and hours, he said calmly, 'It's all right. I understand perfectly. Come anyway. I have other patients but will fit you in when you get here. If you're taking the métro, remember that alternate stations have been closed. Vavin is no longer in use so you must get off at Montparnasse-Bienvenue and walk over. It's not far. We're at the southwest corner of the rue d'Assas and the rue Vavin. You can't miss it.'

They were following them, those two men from the avenue Foch. One would go ahead while the other stayed behind.

Down into the métro it was the same. But at the end of the line, they vanished and she had the feeling they had been replaced but didn't know by whom. Even Martin was puzzled. '*Chéri*, did you really erase the parachute? Please, if you didn't, I'll forgive you but only if you tell me the truth. It's important.'

He was just a little boy and she really could forgive him, couldn't she? she asked herself.

Martin found his pencil and paper and wrote, *I'm sorry. I forgot.*

There wasn't an old magazine or newspaper in the waiting room—they would have been stolen to be made into papier-mâché balls, dried hard for the stoves of winter. Everyone had heard about it. News like that travelled far. No coal in Paris, no firewood for that matter. Parisians froze in winter, that is to say, those who didn't have at least one of the Occupier living in their building or had some other connection. There was no milk, no cheese or eggs, and yes, it had been wise of her to have taken the boy to the farm. What else could she have done? And certainly she had had to plead with her life for a place there, a tiny two-room "cottage" of their own and had had to pay the exorbitant rents, which, each quarter now, were being raised to the limit of her salary.

But was it wise to remain there? Could she not see if perhaps a move to the south, to Perpignan or Aix-en-Provence could be in the cards—the boy, his throat, et cetera? Something was going on in Bois Carré and for some reason God had suddenly chosen to connect their lives to it.

God doesn't do things like that, she told herself. Had He opened His arms, then, to welcome the man who had screamed? Had He said, I forgive you your sins?

Probably, but now they were Herr Kraus's only link to whatever information that poor unfortunate had been carrying to Paris, and the SS were certain she was involved. It didn't bear thinking. Martin's future would be an internment camp. He'd be the odd one out just as he was here and at the farm or in the village but without her to watch over him. Without her to care.

She mustn't let it happen.

Nine straight-backed chairs ringed the thin carpet of this waiting room. There were no pictures on the dun-coloured walls, only a wooden crucifix whose nails were too sturdy to be easily pulled.

Five of these chairs were filled with others—three German soldiers, the others civilians, a man and a woman. None of them smiled. All were worried about themselves—why else would they have been here?

Angélique felt sorry for Martin who sat so still beside her, both of them reeking of urine. He'd be crying inside about his throat and worrying about having left his little parachute on that window—he'd know the danger. He was far from stupid, was really immensely intelligent and just like his papa.

He loved her too—he really did. There were times when he would suddenly hold her, times he would just have to touch her or bring her hand to his cheek, but could he ever forgive her for breaking up his home and making others call him a bastard? Could he accept the fact that his father had loved her so much, he had risked his life and had taken his yacht across the Channel in a vain attempt to rescue her before it was too late?

The Blitzkrieg. The invasion.

And could Martin understand that it hadn't mattered, his having hidden in the bow locker of the yacht to stop his father from bringing her to England? His father had become trapped and had had to leave them both on that road, that terrible road.

Abandonment of his mother first, and then of himself— could she confide this to the specialist or to anyone?

Of course not. It would be far too dangerous.

'Martin . . . Martin Bellecour, please?'

'That's us.'

The receptionist and nurse must have gone home for the rest of the day. Dr. Albert-Émile Vergès looked older than his fifty years. He wasn't tall or short but of less than medium height, and the open smock revealed a grey serge waist-coat that was too hot and a white shirt whose collar and tie pinched, though he would steadfastly refuse to loosen them.

Serious dark brown eyes passed over her and the boy, he hesitating but momentarily on herself to say, 'You've had a difficult journey. Come . . . Come this way, please.'

Like a father wanting only to talk to his son, he gathered Martin in but paused to let her go first. She brought the suitcases. He said nothing about them. Theft prevention was simply understood.

'Tell him he's to go into the cubicle and draw the curtain. He's to strip off to his underwear.'

'I thought he was here to have his throat examined?'

Vergès ducked his head in acknowledgement. 'Of course, but we want to see how he is generally. His height, weight, all such things, they give us background.'

She nodded but had always found visits to the doctor's difficult. 'Martin, let me get your clean underwear. I'll pass it through to you. Fold your clothes. Don't leave them lying in a heap. Treat them with respect. They have to last you.'

Vergès closed the door to the waiting room but stood watching her as she opened Martin's suitcase, she to cry out suddenly and to bow her head in despair. 'I'll have to wash things. The butter, Martin. They must have opened the crocks in a hurry.'

'They?' asked Vergès, but she didn't turn, couldn't seem to close the suitcase, was broken by what she'd found.

At last she sighed. 'The SS. We were picked up at the station. We still haven't a clue as to what it was all about.'

If he nodded, she didn't see this, though she sensed with alarm that something subtle had crept into the room.

'It's as I feared,' he said. 'Such things, they're happening all too often these days.'

'Are they?' she demanded, turning to find him looking at her with . . . What was it? she wondered. Suspicion?

He was a grave, pale, serious thing, this doctor of the throat, and she had to ask herself, Is he now afraid?

'Please, I understand,' he said.

'Do you?' she arched.

'Yes.'

He pushed his glasses tightly back on the bridge of a nose that was not arrogant. He stroked the grey-black goatee that gave such dignity, and said, 'Others are waiting. It shouldn't take your son all day to undress.'

'He's worried you're going to operate.'

'Then tell him to forget it. There's a six-month waiting list.'

'He can understand what you say to him.'

'Good.'

'Bring your pencil and paper, Martin,' she called out and then explained, 'It's his way of talking.'

In the surgery, Martin stood on the scales and had himself weighed. He was measured. All his reflexes were tested and every time the specialist had a question, the boy would take up his pencil and write out an answer.

Paper was in such short supply. Would a point come when there was none left for him? she wondered, only to hear Vergès saying, 'That's a fine bit of machinery, Martin. Where did you get a pencil like that?'

'It was my father's.'

But it wasn't. Certainly it was a mechanical pencil with a chromium-plated barrel for extra leads and a clip, but it was *not* his father's. 'Martin . . . ?' she asked. '*Ah, chéri*, did you lose yours?' He'd be so heartbroken.

The boy shook his head. The examination went on but whenever he put the pencil down, her eyes would find it until, at last, she had to say, 'That's monsieur le maire's. I know it is. Martin, what happened?'

He looked at the doctor, then at her and quickly scribbled, *Monsieur le maire gave me his for good luck. We traded for the journey.*

Ah no . . .

Vergès seemed to think nothing of it. Again he continued with the examination. Finally he said, 'There's absolutely no need for an operation. We don't install mechanical talking boxes in anyone. No little wooden doors either. Your problem is all in the mind, Martin. Hypnosis might help. I'm certain of it.'

'*Hypnosis* . . . ? No. No, that's impossible.'

'Please don't be stubborn. It's harmless. It will help him to remember and in doing so, he may overcome the psychosis that prevents him from speaking.'

'I'll have to think about it.'

'Good. Shall we say next week, then, at the same time?'

'Pardon?' Did Vergès not *know* how difficult it was to leave the *zone interdite*?

'Look, I'll write a note to the mayor, explaining the need. If you like, I'll do another for the district Kommandant. Just give me his name.'

'Lautenschläger. The Oberst Oskar. He's a decent man with a difficult job. He rides two horses. The one of the Occupier, the other of compassion.'

Vergès nodded. He felt the breast pocket of his smock, searching for the pencil he had had only a moment ago but must have dropped on the floor. 'Martin, let me borrow yours. You can go and get changed. Perhaps, if she wants to, your mother could give your underwear a quick wash? It'll be wet but in this heat it ought to dry quickly.'

And my own, Doctor? Is this what you're suggesting, you whose fingers tremble as you hold that borrowed pencil?

How cold she felt.

Without a word, she got up and took the boy from the surgery but didn't close the door. Vergès heard the water running in the sink and fought with himself not to close the door, for she had left it open as a challenge, she silently crying out, Did you *salaud*s use us? Is there a message in that pencil?

Turning his back to her, he twisted the barrel open and extracted the slender, rolled-up tube of cigarette paper, pausing only for a moment to grip his forehead and silently say, *Dieu le père*, forgive us. They were innocent.

The bluebottles had found the corpse, and in the stillness of the interrogation room and the heat, the sound of them was irritating. Taking his time, Hans Albrecht Dirksen ran his gaze over the lost opportunity of Henri-Paul Doumier. The flies worried the land surveyor's eyes that were swollen shut and now encrusted. In their hordes, they had entered that gaping mouth. 'You fool,' he seethed. 'Did you *have* to kill him?'

Kraus stood to attention, ramrod stiff and staring straight ahead. 'His heart, Standartenführer. We didn't know it was weak.'

'You didn't know? Come, come, *mein lieber* Sturmbannführer, admit that you were trying to make an impression on the woman and her son.'

This *Hosenscheisser* loved nothing better than to dress him down.'She's hiding something, Colonel. I know she is.'

'*Verdammter Idiot*, would you have hanged her stripped naked and roped to a meat hook, when for all we know, *they* could have been using her and the boy *without* her knowledge? *Patience*, damn it! *Don't* let your lust for power constantly get the better of you.'

'*Jawhol*, Colonel.'

'*Dummkopf*, is it the Russian front you want and the rank of corporal? When I tell you to go carefully, I mean it. Too much is at stake.'

Dirksen went over the report. The imbecile had got nothing out of the surveyor. '*Bitte*, Kraus, interrogation is an art. Try to think of yourself as a painter of still life, not of houses. If you must, imagine the subject naked but apply the brush as though each stroke was your last and the brush sable-tipped. Now tell me where that woman is, or is it that you simply *don't* know?'

'*Ach*, the Oberst Lautenschläger swore we were wrong about the *Schlampe*. He threatened to call the Kommandant von Gross-Paris and make trouble if I didn't . . .'

'Yes, yes, in the wake of the Russian setbacks we're supposed to show "cooperation" with the Wehrmacht so as to get what we want and please the Führer. So?'

It would have to be said. 'She's at the clinic with the boy, her "son".'

'He may well be her son, Kraus. Did you think of that?'

'Yes, Colonel.'

'Well, then, what have we on the doctor? Come, come, damn it, answer me.'

'As far as we know, he's clean. The Wehrmacht use him.'

'*Die Wehrmacht* . . . Since when did that sort of thing *not* make the job of the *Banditen* far easier? Has he any connection with Abbeville and that woods? Have you even *thought* to establish this?'

Dirksen wasn't going to let up. 'None that we know of.'

'You'll keep a watch on him?'

'Yes, of course. And the woman and the boy.'

'Good. Let them feel we've no further interest. If anything comes up, see that you find me. I'll be at the Opéra. *La Bohème.*'

Again there was the usual response from Kraus, but Dirksen didn't leave the room. Instead, he took his time, wanted to be absolutely certain nothing had been missed. But no, the corpse of Doumier was just that, though when he came to the remains of the food the woman and the boy had brought, he had to shake his head in despair. 'Could you not even distinguish between genuine ignorance and deceit?'

Using his pocketknife, he picked over the shredded remains of what must have been a fine ham. The roasted geese had been torn apart. 'The suitcases? You went through them thoroughly?'

'A few clothes and toiletries, nothing else. We examined the linings of the suitcases, but didn't rip them out.'

Well, at least there was that. 'Good. Then she'll only think you've stolen the food.'

Though he hadn't seen her and the boy, he could imagine Kraus's interrogation of them in that other room, the boy not talking because he couldn't, but this one *forcing* the woman to sit across the table from himself while the boy . . . What would he have done? Gone over to the windows to have a look down at the street? Wandered about, lost in his own little world? The bathtub—would he have been puzzled by it? The staves, the smells, the sight of dried blood and fingernail marks?

'Go carefully with this, Kraus. Mess up again and it really will be the last we see of you.'

Out in the corridor, Dirksen came upon the cleaners, two Frenchmen in shabby *bleus de travail* and open-collared shirts, no berets for it was far too hot. No cigarettes either, tobacco being in such short supply, they dared not smoke in a place like this, but they were about to go into the room the woman and the boy had been in. 'Leave it,' he said in French. 'Give me a few moments alone in there. Come back in ten minutes.'

And then, to himself, I have to put my mind into that of a ten-year-old boy and then that of his mother. I have to satisfy myself that they simply didn't know anything of this matter.

Berlin had been adamant about Bois Carré and all other such sites in the *zone interdite*. The SS were to take over their security from the Wehrmacht, who were thought to be incompetent of such a task and would have to be replaced. No word of what was there was to leak out. The sites were well hidden and must remain so on pain of death.

His own and that of Kraus, if not those of others.

# 2

The Jardin du Luxembourg was right across the rue d'Assas from the clinic. It had always offered sanctuary but now it couldn't. Kraus would discover that those pencils must have been switched. First he'd find Martin's little parachute in the dust of that window, and that would lead him to Dr. Vergès. Under torture Vergès would cry out the mayor's name. And then, what then? asked Angélique. Kraus would pull out her fingernails.

The garden threw up the faces of the Occupation, the tired, the old, the middle-aged women in their Depression-era makeovers, the good-looking girls, *les belles gamines* strutting with their current lovers: Wehrmacht, Kriegsmarine, Luftwaffe, SS and Gestapo or simply those on "business" here and from the Reich.

Some of the Boches—and she must be careful about using that term—sailed toy boats on the terrace's octagonal pond where Martin had launched his own, but what was she really to do? Go to Kraus and try to say, Me, I thought I should tell you . . . ?

Hide—where? she asked and cried out silently, *Maudits salauds*, how could you have done this to us? All your reassurances, eh, Monsieur le Maire? All of your protestations of,

'Ah, it's no trouble, mademoiselle. For you we will arrange everything. You and the boy will go to Paris, this I assure you.'

And she had actually *thought* he was being kind!

You're an idiot, she said. You've still got a lot to learn.

Martin was hungry and thirsty, but had forgotten both. Toy sailboats always did that to him. In his imagination, he was right back there in time and crossing the Channel, sailing though to England, not to France, with his father in that one's sailboat.

*Sans moi*, she said ruefully. *Sans son amour*, eh, Martin? But please bring him back to me, don't sail away like that, even if only in your imagination.

She had rented the boat for the half hour. Five francs, it was a lot, but it would take Martin completely away from this city, this country, this *thing* that was happening to them, this little tragedy. And certainly he might remember her years later when a man and might say, I once lived with a Frenchwoman. She used to get me to scrub her back. We didn't have much. It was during the Occupation, so we had to share the bath water. Sometimes I slept with her, sometimes she cried out through clenched teeth, both in joy and despair.

He might even say, I fell in love with her and was jealous of my father. He might, for jealousy was a part of it, but so, too, was anger and rebellion, and even power, for Martin knew he had a terrible hold over her and could use it any time he thought necessary. That little parachute.

Shade grew and the shadows lengthened, the sounds of the people always muted in the garden as in a dream. Lovers kissing, lovers holding hands or doing other things. Water trickling down her cheek and neck to run between her breasts. Cold water, softly whispered words. *Angélique . . . Angélique, I love you. I've come back.*

They kissed. She and that father of his held each other. They couldn't get their clothes off fast enough. Her stockings were getting in the way. Her stockings . . .

Urgently Martin shook her, the sailboat dribbling water. '*Ah, chéri,* I must have fallen asleep. The suitcases . . . ? *Ah non.* Martin, did you see who took them?'

He grinned. He shook his head and nodded towards something.

The suitcases were behind the bench but she wouldn't chase after him like she did at the farm, could only ruffle his hair and force a smile. 'Your father was full of mischief too. Come on, we'd better find a place to eat and spend the night.'

Like his mother would have done, Angélique swept her eyes over him to see if everything was all right, and when she noticed that monsieur le maire's pencil was missing, broke into tears and begged him to tell her what had happened.

Was completely shattered.

*I lost it,* he said, carefully mouthing the words so as to let her read his lips. *It slipped from my shirt pocket and fell into the pond.*

They searched. With suitcases in hand, they walked slowly around the pond, trying sometimes to get between others, always to peer into the depths, but it was so dark down there on the bottom. Dark and murky.

Just when she was thinking, Had it been a blessing, this loss, a man in a light grey business suit removed jacket and fedora, rolled up his sleeves and plunged a tanned and well-knit arm into the water.

'Your boy's pencil,' he said in French so good it rang of the salons of the rue Saint-Honoré. 'Allow me, please, to present it to you.'

He was clean-cut, about thirty or thirty-two, was blue-eyed, blond-haired, sharp-chinned, broad-shouldered, very proper and yes, quite good-looking.

'*Merci.*'

'Hans Albrecht Dirksen at your service, Madame . . . ?'

'Mademoiselle Bellecour.'

There was a white chrysanthemum in the buttonhole of his jacket and when he put the jacket on, he laughed at himself and said, 'I know I shouldn't have picked it but couldn't resist.' And then, 'The pencil, please. We'd better take it apart and dry it thoroughly. You don't want it to rust, do you?' he said to the boy, forcing her to tell him Martin didn't have the use of his voice.

'The Blitzkrieg,' she said.

At once Herr Dirksen was concerned. 'It will come back, Martin,' he said. 'You'll see. All such things happen in their own good time.'

Sitting on the bench beside them now, and using a clean white handkerchief, he took apart the pencil and carefully dried and blew out the barrel, before drying it again. There was only one spare length of lead but it had broken in half and he placed the two pieces carefully on his left knee until ready to fit them back into the barrel. All of this was done under the watchful gaze of the statues that appeared as if gathered about the terrace, the queens of France. Marie de Médicis, Marguerite de Valois, Valentine de Milan, Anne de Beaujeu, Anne de Bretagne—she had known them all by heart once. Calliope, that muse of epic poetry, stood behind their bench, watching the three of them. Sainte Geneviève was over by the bandstand.

'I used to love this park,' she said, trying to find something inconsequential and regretting it immediately, only to recover and add, 'On my rare visits to Paris, I always tried to come here because it was so restful, but I never lived in Paris. I always wished that I could,' she shrugged, 'but it was impossible. Just not in the cards.'

He asked what she did and she told him, knowing even as she did that he would simply ask himself, Weren't secretaries in demand before this conflict the English caused? 'We really must go,' she said. 'It's late and we have to find a place to stay over for the night.'

Martin returned the sailboat to the man who rented them, and she thought, Will I have to pay a little more, but the man saw her with this German and abruptly turned his back on them not out of patriotism, for he willingly rented to these "visitors", these "friends", rather sensing perhaps a Gestapo or SS in mufti. But would that make any difference to her and Martin? Any at all?

'There's an excellent hotel just across the park,' said Dirksen. 'Please allow me to escort you, then perhaps a bite to eat. Yes, yes, that would suit. But a good meal, eh, Martin, not just a sandwich or a bowl of soup.'

It would do no good to say they had other plans, and with

a sinking feeling, she said, 'You're very kind. Martin, the monsieur is to take us to our hotel.'

And then to a dinner she could not afford, the same, too, regarding that "hotel".


At 7.00 p.m. Berlin time as well as here in Paris, ah yes, Dr. Albert-Émile Vergès closed the surgery and locked the door. Pocketing the keys, carrying umbrella and briefcase, and wearing an open, dark grey trench coat and grey fedora, he took the stairs, most of the lifts having been denied their electricity, but on reaching the ground floor, did not leave by the front entrance as was his custom.

Close and in shadow, a *passage* led to a small courtyard behind the building. From there, cutting diagonally among the lindens, the doctor went along the columned walkway on the left. One could hear the heels of his shoes on the granite paving blocks. Now a column, now a glimpse of him. Was he hurrying? That left heel always came down harder than the right.

He paused. He stood stock-still. Was he nervous?

Satisfied, he continued on to open a door into the building behind the courtyard. From there he took the stairs up to the third floor—was it impulse that had driven him to do so? Had he sensed someone was following him, or was this where he was to meet his contact?

It was too close to the surgery and therefore far too dangerous; the terrorists, the *Banditen*, liked to spread themselves out. The limp could, of course, simply have been created by placing wedges of cardboard under that left heel. The thicker the wedges, the more pronounced the limp.

He was standing in the corridor, just waiting and waiting. Fifteen minutes later he came down the stairs to leave by the door that led onto the *impasse* Vavin, a narrow, dead-end street, a slot flanked by towering houses that reeked of mould and urine in the heat and had all but shut out the early evening light.

He was shorter than most and hurried with that limp of his, the umbrella clutched at its middle, the briefcase in the other hand. Though he lived alone with an aged mother who was bedridden, he didn't turn north towards the rue du Tournon and that fine old house that had been made over into flats years ago, but went south. When he got to the *carrefour* Vavin, the intersection of the boulevard Raspail and boulevard du Montparnasse, which was not far, he quickly lost himself in the crowd that flocked to get into the great brasseries of Montparnasse, the Café de la Rotunde, the Select, the Coupole and the Dome . . . Men in uniform milled about, men in suits and fedoras, men with their girls and others looking for a bit of female company. *Vélo-taxis* disgorged, people laughed . . . Where . . . where was he? *Ah merde*, had he vanished behind that *gazogène*\* lorry or behind that open touring car?

Then there he was, sitting well back on the terrace of the Dome, pretending to read his *Paris-Soir*. There were alcohol-free days, but Fridays weren't one of those. There'd be that ersatz stuff that had become so necessary with the shortages, but wine was different. Wine was so of the French it hadn't been cut, no matter which day of the week.

Dr. Albert-Émile Vergès, age fifty. Nose, ear and throat specialist.

Marie-Hélène de Fleury breathed a sigh of relief. It had been good. He had done everything possible to have shaken her off, had been extra careful, but still, he should have left his paper on the table, left his glass of *vin ordinaire* right there and told the waiter he'd be back. Gone to the toilet and for a little look around.

This he now did, pleasing her immensely. And when she was asked by a Wehrmacht lieutenant who was hungry for a woman if she would like a cigarette, she smiled and said, 'Monsieur, *c'est exactement* what I need. *Mon amour*, he hasn't shown up yet and keeps me waiting!'

Refusing all other offers, she found a table inside and next to the far wall where she could see things better. The Dome had thick blue curtains for the blackout, but it was too early yet to have drawn them. Acetylene lamps would give light during the power outages, which had become far more fre-

---

\* A vehicle whose engine uses a gas-producer fired by charcoal or wood, or bottled producer gas

quent. At random, at will or out of just plain necessity, the Germans would switch the electricity off quarter by quarter, *arrondissement par arrondissement*. Sometimes it helped with her work, sometimes it didn't.

The toilets were being watched by others. They weren't her problem. Vergès's table remained empty for about ten minutes, after which the doctor returned and sat down with his back to her.

'*Un café et un pousse-café, s'il vous plaît,*' said Marie-Hélène to the waiter. A coffee with a liqueur on the side. She was due it. 'A brandy, I think.'

Vergès fiddled with his newspaper, glanced at his pocket watch, listened to the ticking of it and waited. Soon the tables on the terrace filled up but still his contact didn't come. Had that one seen her and been forewarned? she wondered. Was the contact a waiter perhaps? In rapid sequence, letting her eyes sift over the crowd, she sorted people instantly into suspects and nonsuspects. Vergès was of the medical fraternity, therefore his contact could well be another doctor. But he also did a little teaching—perhaps a medical student then? It made the adrenaline flow, this constant searching and analysis, this clandestine following of another, and she was good at it, the best—far better than the Gestapo or the SS who were her backup because, *ah oui*, she was a *Parisienne* who could fit right in almost anywhere but also the lover, the mistress of Hans Albrecht Dirksen.

Self-interest always helped, as did dressing in a very subdued, very nondescript way, not unstylish, merely so that it didn't cause one to stand out like a sore thumb.

At 8.16 p.m. the doctor tossed off the last of his wine and went home to his mother. Contact hadn't been made.

Watchful still, Marie-Hélène stood in the gathering darkness beneath a fine old chestnut near the house on the rue de Tournon. The tall wrought-iron gates had gilded fleurs-de-lis atop each bar and, at the centre, an enamelled coat of arms, the Family Vergès. Aristocrats. The last of the line, and lucky too, for they'd managed somehow to have saved those gates from the Occupier's scrap-metal purges.

She waited—it was now her turn to do so—but everything

in her said, It will have to be tomorrow. Tonight was just a dry run. Tomorrow the drop will be made at a place so familiar to our doctor's daily life, no one will suspect a thing.

Tonight he was just testing us. An expert, then? she asked, and thought back over the early evening before answering, They were worried Doumier had given them away and a trap had been set. The doctor must have been coached by someone pretty good, but had still been too nervous. This run will have given him confidence. Yes . . . yes, in a game of nerves only the cold and the calculating survived.

Patience . . . Hans was always urging patience. Even those of the *Résistance* had been forced to use it. In spite of the obvious need to pass the information on quickly, they had shielded themselves by waiting.

That had taken guts. It said something about the leader of this particular *réseau*. It said he was ten times more wary than others and wasn't about to make a mistake. It also said, and this was clear to her, that the doctor didn't know who his contact would be. That implied a safety net which would be very hard to break.

At 8.55 p.m.—6.55 the old time—there was still too much light for comfort in the *place* de l'Odéon. Of medium height, and dressed in a plain beige skirt that came well below the knee, and a soft cream blouse, no hat, no jewelery or makeup, Marie-Hélène threaded her way among the pedestrians just walking normally, not in a hurry so as to blend right in but were they watching her, those *résistants*? Was she now the target, eh? *Ah merde*, she mustn't think like this. No one had seen her. None of the *Résistance* would know she worked for the Occupier. They probably didn't even know that she slept with Hans.

But maybe someday that would be enough, she silently said and hated herself for thinking it. If the Germans packed up and left—if—things wouldn't go well for people like herself. Ah no, they certainly wouldn't.

When Kraus drew the black Peugeot sedan alongside her, Marie-Hélène kept on walking, refusing to notice him.

'Get in.'

'Idiot, do you *want* them to see us?'

He laughed at her distress. Rather than cause a scene, she scrambled into the backseat. '*Salaud*,' she hissed. 'Must you always torment me, always be so careless of my security?'

At the corner of the rue de Médicis and the boulevard Saint-Michel, he turned north and headed straight for the quays, straight to the Île de la Cité, to the *place* du Parvis and the Notre-Dame.

Here there were few people about. The Préfecture de Police was just across the square, the Palais de Justice very close. The light had all but gone. 'Look, I report only to Hans, not to you or to anyone else. That's the arrangement, so why, please, have you brought me here?'

He was enjoying himself. She was quivering.

'I thought it might remind you.'

'Of what? That newborn babies were once abandoned here or that the condemned were forced to make a final confession before being carted off to the *place* de Grève* to be drenched in boiling oil and set alight?'

Sometimes they had used molten lead; at other times, pitch or resin. Five hundred years of such public executions had put their stamp on the square. For examples of utter savagery, the French needed to look no further than themselves and this so-called "centre" of the country. 'The Standartenführer will want me to brief him when he finishes with the Bellecour woman and her son.'

The shrug she gave was dismissive. 'Oh for sure he will, but I'm not presenting you with the gift of my thoughts so that you can claim them for yourself. Vergès didn't make contact. That's all.'

'And?'

'And nothing.'

'Don't be stupid. This is too important.'

'Then take me to Hans. Let him have my analysis of the situation verbatim and from myself.'

The *Schlampe*!

She ducked away, swore, 'Hit me then, eh, my fine SS? Mark my pretty face. *That's* what you really want, isn't it? Well, isn't it?'

---

* A medieval square, and the former name of the *place* de Hôtel-de-Ville

He hated her. He resented the successes, which had been far beyond their wildest dreams. The Mirabeau escape line in the south: Nice and a house on the avenue Mirabeau, then Toulon, Marseille, Nîmes, Montpellier and Perpignan to the Spanish border and freedom, all shut down. Two hundred and thirty-nine *résistants* in the bag, men, women, teenaged boys and girls. All sent to the camps and no one had better deny that those places exist. All of that bunch. All but those who had, of course, been shot or killed in other ways. Ah yes!

The Perrache network in Lyon, right in the heart of Klaus Barbie's territory but unbreakable until her arrival. Innocence in the guise of a lonely but attractive war widow who had also lost her children.

Another sixty-two into the bag and eighteen million in confiscated Louis d'or and uncut diamonds to sweeten things further.

Others, too, and all because of her—Hans Albrecht Dirksen's French mistress. The pride of the SS in France, their little secret weapon. '*Mon cul* is too valuable, Major. You're on borrowed time as it is because you kill too many before the purse of their lips is opened. Hans is watching you very closely, *mon ami*. Now please remove your hand from the front of my blouse, or is it that you would like to tear it from me?'

The waves of dark brown hair, the big brown eyes that were now hard but could appear so innocent, the fine brush of the brows and soft, naturally red lips were those of the wealthy and the pampered who had been thrown onto hard times at the Defeat of 1940 and forced to fend for themselves. First by the use of her ass, and then by that natural suspicion and wiliness of peasant ancestors deeply buried but not quite forgotten.

Kraus fingered the white lace trim of the modest brassiere that had been hidden by the blouse. He hooked his fingers in under the strap of the throat supporter, as the whores, their *maquereaux* and petty gangsters were so fond of calling a brassiere, and he wanted to pull hard but resisted the urge. Naked, she would tremble. Naked, he could make her do *anything* he wanted. 'Don't ever think your kind are indispensable. There are lots more where you came from. All I have to do is drop a certain little dossier into the hands of the *Banditen*. The photos are excellent and they show you in all of those places where you've had your "successes". They connect you, Marie-Hélène de Fleury of the boulevard de Beauséjour and the solitary walks in the Bois de Boulogne when your conscience is troubling you—it does trouble you now and then, yes? Please don't deny it. Cooperate. Learn who your master really is.'

He'd do it too, thought Marie-Hélène.

Kraus let go of her. 'Now start telling me what happened with Vergès. Don't leave anything out, and from now on you report everything to me first. Dirksen needn't know you're doing so. Indeed, if I were you, *mein kleiner Schatz*, I wouldn't tell him of our agreement. I'd just keep it a secret. Sort of like between two lovers who are supposedly happily married to others and don't want to upset their little applecarts.'

Herr Dirksen had a way with him, felt Angélique. He didn't push but gave the impression of one who persevered in his own quiet and quite charming self. And yes, he seemed to want only to satisfy himself about Martin and her, but never asked a question that could even be remotely thought of as threatening. Instead, it was as if he waited only for an opening, a little window through which he could see enough to say to himself, *I was right about them.*

That he knew the city well was evident, and he really had been very kind, this "businessman" from Düsseldorf, this "buyer of cotton, flax and wool", this "manufacturer of bed linens and dress fabrics", and certainly he couldn't possibly have known that in the autumn of 1938, on 18 September, Martin's father had brought her to this same restaurant. It had been so very expensive then, would cost a fortune now, but could he have known of the memories it would evoke? A smile, a look, a lamp being lighted or the way her hand had been touched? The meal, ah such a meal, their glasses constantly refilled, and afterwards the quays under lamplight to pause and embrace until, satiated with that, they had found their little hotel and themselves again and again.

La Vagendende, at *numéro* 142 boulevard Saint-Germain, was of the *belle époque*. Frosted, etched glass gave haunting images of demimondes with swept-up hair, flowing tresses and half-closed eyes. Their plunging necklines revealed the softness of their skin, with lovely little dragonfly clasps in silver or gold to release a halter strap but later . . . later.

On each table there were tall brass lamps with round and frosted glass globes that softly glowed and clear glass chimneys that sometimes smoked. The tablecloths were of damask, the table legs curved and the lines of them flowed continuously to blend in harmony with the rich, dark mahogany panelling, the forests of parlour palms whose leafy fronds were reflected in the mirrors as was the big brass trumpet of the wind-up gramophone.

Wondering what he really wanted of them, Angélique sat with her back to a corner facing the trumpet of that thing that poured out its scratchy rendition of the *Hungarian Rhapsody*. Violins were muted against the constant din, the loud talk, the guffaws, the boisterous bragging of German officers with their French mistresses, German businessmen with theirs, the butter-and-egg boys too, ah yes, the big black marketeers, and the collabos also.

All were well dressed and well fed and now took no more notice of this little threesome, she in a pale blue cotton dress, flowered enamel earrings and . . . and sand-coloured hair that was so drab but now worn to fall loosely over the shoulders. No lipstick or perfume—ah, none of those because to have worn any would have been not to honour the man she loved.

'Martin, please don't wolf your soup.'

'Relax. Let the boy eat. It's only natural he should be hungry.'

She threw Herr Dirksen a look that said, *Oh, and since when, please, were manners not important?*

The purée of potatoes and leeks had been served in blue Sèvres cups that were inset into art nouveau pewter chalices whose chipped ice caused beads of moisture to condense and run down the sides. Martin kept grabbing the chalice's stem and then wiping his hand on his short pants. He ate like a demon, broke bread by ripping it apart like he did at the farm. Then he would dunk it deeply into the soup before cramming it into his mouth. And when done, he finished it all off by wiping the cup clean with more bread and licking the spoon *three* times. First the back, then the front, then the handle and finally back at it all yet again until she finally had to silently say, *Ah, mon Dieu, mon petit*, I know you're worried too. He wants something from us, but what?

Fingers were snapped. '*Garçon . . .*'

'Monsieur?'

'Bring the boy more soup.'

'Certainly. It shall be as you wish.'

'*Merci*,' she managed, the waiter throwing her a look that made her shudder and wonder, Did they all know who Herr Dirksen really was? They must.

'This is perfect,' she said of the soup, with eyes downcast. 'Do you come here often?'

Please be reasonable, he wanted so much to say. Don't let Kraus get hold of you again.

'Pay the others no mind,' he said. 'For myself, I only want a little company, nothing else, I assure you. I simply would like to get to know our French allies better. That's all.'

There were lots of such German businessmen in Paris, felt Angélique, but lots of others too, and yes, there had been some glances at him, some whispers, the eyes turning quickly away from her own, but . . . 'I merely asked if you came here often.'

'Not at all, and then only with those I would like to get to know a little better.'

Had he a mistress? she wondered, only to add, Of course he must! They had taken a *vélo-taxi* from the hotel he had found for them, and Martin, scrubbed and cleaned up as best she could, had been fascinated by Paris at night. A city so different from before the war, one with almost no cars, few lorries and buses—all *gazogènes* those—and tiny, infrequent blue lights that moved or seemed to hover in the dark ether as fireflies do when the moon begins its climb and is soon reflected in the Seine.

Cigarettes, too, had glowed, but no other lights than these and the blue ones, the darkness elsewhere like ink and a hope, a means of escape? To where, please? she asked. It's impossible and you know it. Besides, is he not who he says he is?

Those looks he got, she reminded herself.

Martin's soup came. Startled, his sea-green eyes widened, for somehow Herr Dirksen had played a little joke on him. To grin hesitantly was impossible. It was such a huge plate of soup, her laughter came freely and genuinely so. '*Ah, mon Dieu, chéri*, if you eat all of that, you will eat nothing else and be the size of a giant balloon!'

Earnestly the pencil and paper came out, the answer swift: *I like this soup. It's refreshing.*

Herr Dirksen's chuckle was gentle and honest. 'Eat what you can, Martin, but remember that after the main course, the *salade de homard* here is made a little differently than in other such places and they've a reputation because of it. Big chunks of cooked lobster, lamb's lettuce, *escargots*, too, and tender peas and carrots, all with a dressing of walnut oil and sherry vinegar. The salad is truly magnificent, so save a little room for it.'

With that, they had a Chablis from Burgundy that was gorgeously clean and crisp, the 1933 and a perfect year.'Tell me about yourself,' he said, she to answer, 'There's not much to tell. This'—she indicated the restaurant—'is definitely *not* what we're used to. For us it's the farm and working in the fields, helping out after the regular job is done. Me, I ride my bicycle the twenty kilometres to Abbeville and back, six days a week. Martin, he helps around the farm after school and during the summer holiday. All the children do, their mothers as well. It's accepted, and in another few weeks he'll go back to school.'

Furiously a message was scribbled and thrust at her. *Never! You said I wouldn't have to!*

*Ah merde.* 'Now look, we're not going to disgrace ourselves by arguing, are we? Not in front of all these strangers and as the guest of someone so kind? Be reasonable. Don't sulk.'

*She* was always accusing him of that. *I am being reasonable,* he wrote. *You promised!*

And promises made are those that are kept, but he slammed his fork down and some of the lettuce and lobster had to land in her lap.

Slowly Herr Dirksen shook his head at Martin as if to say,

Now look what you've done to the one person you should love and cherish more than any other, but of course she *wasn't* Martin's mother.

In the *lavabo* she tried to get the stains out but knew that would take ages. The attendant brought a bar of soap, such a rarity these days, it took time for such a simple item as that to register. Furious with Martin, she began to scrub, to demand, Why had he had to do it?

Martin? *Ah non* . . .

She couldn't move, could only see herself in the mirror as condemned. The parachute . . . Is *that* what Herr Dirksen was after?

*She doesn't know anything about it,* wrote Martin. A bit of lobster had caught in his throat. He was going to choke. His face was getting hotter and hotter.

Dirksen handed the boy's glass of wine to him and calmly said, 'I make parachutes myself, Martin, in my firm. Good ones, too, but we're always needing help. Why not tell me what yours was like?'

Everything was going on around them, thought Martin, the waiters like flies about to rush in on the corpse of his salad. *It's special,* he wrote. *It has straps and is made of dark blue silk with . . . with secret markings on it.*

'Yes, yes, that's good. Some of mine are like that too, but how did you come by such a design?'

The monsieur glanced towards the doorway where a curved signboard in coloured glass read TOILETTES-LAVABO, but was he wondering if Angélique would come back too soon? Was he worried that she might?

'Well?' prompted Dirksen. 'Look, we're friends, aren't we? I'm only curious. If you don't want to tell me who told you about such a parachute, we'll forget I ever asked.'

Martin shook his head and diligently wrote, *No one told me about it. There was a field under moonlight. A parachute that is invisible against the sky came slowly down and was quickly gathered in for another time.*

'It was buried?'

*Buried, but why?*

'To keep it safe?'

*Ah! That is so, monsieur, but only the parachutist knows where it is hidden.*

'And yourself, eh?'

Martin frowned deeply at him and thought a while before writing, *It's a really big field, monsieur. The wheat, it has not yet been harvested, you understand, so it is very tall. As tall as this table. Higher maybe.*

They could use metal detectors. There'd be the clips and strap buckles, the chute rings. Lautenschläger could organize a sweep of the field using the guise of searching for old artillery shells from the Great War. That should satisfy the curious.

'Martin, where did the parachutist go after he left the field?'

*Go? Ah! This I don't know, monsieur, for I couldn't see him. The wheat, n'est-ce pas? Me, I'm still not tall enough.*

The basins in the *lavabo* were of the *belle époque* and so sturdy they would withstand the centuries, and yes, the place was spotless. The Boches had made certain of that. Ah! Paris had never had cleaner lavatories. Some of them anyway, especially those the Occupier used, and how was it, please, that such butchers could be so fastidious?

Angélique wiped her eyes but pressed the backs of her fingers to her lips to stop herself from crying and said silently, *Cher Jésus,* help us now, for Martin, he will have been questioned about that little parachute but he'll not tell anyone everything.

She had taken off her dress and was still working on it, couldn't seem to go back in there to face Dirksen, and when the attendant came to collect the bar of soap, she threw it down into the basin, gripped the edge and said, 'Look, who the hell is he, the man we're with?'

Without a grin or smile, and at the age of fifty-six, forty of those years at this job, Léon Balladur said, 'My lips are sealed.'

She tossed her head. 'My purse is at the table.'

Again he ran his eyes over her. 'Then there's nothing we can do about it.'

*Cochon!* she silently cried, but said, 'I . . . I could come back.'

'I'd have to trust you.'

*Salaud!* she wanted so much to say, but held the dress up to examine the stain that was below the left breast like a wound or the weeping of a wet nurse. It would have to do for now. 'Well, monsieur? Ah, me, I appreciated the soap, of course, but the show, it is over, so beat it! *Scram*, as the Americans love to say, and at forty years in just such a place as this, you will of course have remembered them. Maybe they'll come back, eh? Who knows?'

Still he lingered and she couldn't turn her back on him, mustn't, for he'd make a grab for her. She would have to slide her arms into the dress and let him watch.

'You could offer a little something else,' he said.

'I could but am not going to. Now get out. Take your soap. I wouldn't have stolen it. I'm not like that and am sure as hell not from around here.'

There were no silk stockings on this one, no beige seams that had been painted up the backs of her legs to fake it, just light canvas deck shoes from before the war. A sailor, then, of yachts, was she? wondered Balladur. Perhaps that alone might be worth an extra hundred francs from the colonel. 'Enjoy yourself, madame.'

She didn't say, It's mademoiselle, for she knew only too well what he had implied. Martin was a bastard child. Instead, she tried to tidy herself and ended up by washing her face and having to beg another towel. 'Unfortunately, the *patron* allows only the use of one as a courtesy, madame, with the tip, of course.'

'Then give me back the first one.'

'Use the dress. It looks as if nothing can save it.'

'What was that you said?' she shrilled, only to blanch at the thought of its being ripped off her by the SS or Gestapo.

Balladur smiled at her. She'd be quite suitable, this one, he thought. No competition in bed for the Mademoiselle Marie-Hélène de Fleury, the mistress of the Sturmbannführer Dirksen, but pastures perhaps for the Sturmbannführer Kraus. *Ah oui, et bonne chance, mademoiselle,* since you wear no ring and are letting the colonel feed you for the other one to devour.

Turning abruptly away, he began to refold the towels as he had always done, she to hastily cross herself.

But when she returned to the table, it was Herr Dirksen who said, 'Martin is very sleepy. I've kept you up.'

'We had to leave Abbeville at 5.00 a.m., the new time.'

Three the old. 'Forgive me. I should have thought of it.'

'Please don't concern yourself. You can sleep in tomorrow, can't you, Martin? It's his little holiday.'

'And yours?' he asked.

He seemed so sincere. 'Since when do mothers ever have a holiday? We'll go to the Louvre, eh, Martin—at least we'll see what the building used to look like, then we'll take in a few puppet shows in the Jardin du Luxembourg and we'll sail our boats, eh? Two of them, yours and mine and we'll see who wins the race, but there won't be any contest. He's far better than I could ever be and is so like his . . .' *Ah merde,* why had she said it?

'His father?' asked Dirksen.

The life seemed to go out of her. 'Was a designer of yachts but . . .' She tried to shrug. 'That one never did tell me where or with what firm he worked. A moment, that's all it took. Fifteen seconds, I think. Maybe thirty. In love, of course, for without love there is nothing.'

Martin seemed to shrink into himself.

*Liar,* he said to himself. You and my father lived together for nearly *two* years, whenever he was here in France on business, which was a lot, a *whole* lot. You even had a flat here in Paris on the rue des Grands-Augustins overlooking the Seine and the Île de la Cité, *numéro* 37. I found the address on a letter he had forgotten to mail but I soon found myself there, didn't I? The third floor. Five rooms, one of which he used as a drafting room and office when away from home while you were out at your own job. Me, I tore that letter up and *burned* it.

He was picking at his *crème brûlée.*

'The father,' asked Dirksen, 'does he see the boy often?

Fathers are so important, aren't they, Martin? The other half of the equation.'

Their coffee came. 'He's too little to know about the algebra of such things. Up to the Blitzkrieg we used to see his father after long absences, but then . . .' She shrugged. 'He could be dead for all we know.'

'*Martin! Ah non, chéri,* I didn't mean that!'

Martin pelted for the entrance, flew past a waiter, ducked under another's tray and between two tables and shot out into the night.

'*Ah, mon Dieu,* forgive me. I would say such a stupid thing. He misses his father terribly. I do, too, of course, but . . .'

'Come. We'd best find him.'

'Look, I'm sorry. I really am. You've been most kind.'

'Then let me continue to be of service.'

The boulevard Saint-Germain was pitch-dark and apparently all but deserted except for the tiny blue lights of a few waiting *vélo-taxis,* a *calèche* and two chauffeur-driven automobiles, though it couldn't be any more than 11.00 p.m.

Herr Dirksen told her to stay put. He went to speak to the maître d' and the drivers, she to look away and to cry out inwardly, Martin, don't come back. *Hide,* my darling. Find another to care for you then maybe . . . yes, maybe someday your father will come back for you. Me, I know how it is, *petit.* We're no strangers, you and me. Remember Angélique Bellecour in your prayers. It's finished for me, Martin, but please don't be sad. Use your little parachute to find a safe landing.

'*Dead,*' she had said of his father. LIAR! shrieked Martin. HE'S NOT DEAD. HE CAN'T BE.

The street was so dark he felt the hammering in his chest, the panic and swallowed hard as he said, Angélique, please don't leave me here. I don't like it. The Messerschmitts . . .

But there was no sign of them or of her, only this blackness, the air hot and smelling of the sewers. Silence was everywhere. Not a sound. Yet I'm in a city of nearly two million, he reminded himself. Paris, remember?

Cautiously he began to feel his way along the street. There were doorways now and then, and at one, a faint blue light

was all but hidden by the cobwebs in which two moths struggled for their lives. Angélique and himself—yes, yes, that's
what they were like. The spider was attacking one of them.
Which one? he asked and felt its stinger going into his stomach like a cannon shell.

At another doorway, the glow of a cigarette made him
start and hold his breath. Again there was that hammering
in his chest—would his heart explode? *'Explode,'* came a hidden voice from deep inside his head, another voice, a gasp, a
whispered word, a moment he couldn't remember any more
because it was all gone. Destroyed. The Messerschmitts? he
asked and cried out, ANGÉLIQUE, WHERE ARE YOU?

He was in tears.

A man said, 'Let's go.' Hastily Martin wiped his eyes, realizing only then that someone else had been standing in that
doorway. A woman, a girl? He could smell her now. The perfume was cheap and harsh and all those things Angélique had
always said a woman should never wear.

'Try this,' she had said and had put a little dab on his wrist.
'Now wait. Let it mingle with your skin and become one.'

That one had been from Guerlain and very expensive—
'Exquisite,' she had said and had kissed his wrist, had held
that spot to her lips so long the bath towel had slipped from
her shoulders.

He had stolen the bottle of perfume a few days later and
had poured it into the stream that ran across the pasture near
that woods they called Bois Carré that was on its little hill.
He had buried the bottle under a stone up there, she asking,
'Martin . . . Martin, did you take that bottle of perfume your
father had given me?'

He had shaken his head vehemently and she had accepted
this, had worried terribly about the loss and had said sadly,
'Someone must have stolen it.'

In that first year at the farm people had always been taking
things from their house but now there was so little left, they
didn't bother. Her "uncle and aunt" just went in when she
was away and had a look around. They picked over things and
tried to put them back the way they had been, picked through
the letters she still kept hidden in her secret place, she always

thinking she had better burn them but not being able to bring herself to do it.

He's dead. Is that why she couldn't burn them? he asked himself. Is my father really dead, Angélique? Have you been lying to me ever since the Blitzkrieg?

He felt awful. He wanted to die himself.

The street was long but he had no awareness of this as he ran in tears. Ran hard. Ran fast. He tripped . . . fell flat, skinned his knees and hands, felt blood on them and tasted it, saw stars and a blue light—a torch? He screamed. A torch? Ah no . . . 'Mummy, where are you?' he cried out in long-forgotten English. 'Mummy!'

'*Junger Mann*, go home, *ja*? It's too late for you to be out. The curfew has been brought back to eleven this evening. The streets are to be cleared.' All this had been spoken in Deutsch.

Collared by an Unteroffizier, he was yanked to his feet, the blue needle of that torch making him squint as the sergeant said, '*Ach, du lieber Gott, mein junger Freund*, you're going to have sore knees tomorrow!'

Pushed on his way, Martin stumbled and then ran, didn't hear the sergeant call after him, 'Hey, you dropped your pencil. Come back. Well, go if you like. It's all the more for me.'

Later, much later, the tramp of other soldiers came to him and, as he hid in a doorway, he heard a patrol crossing one of the bridges. The Pont Neuf, he thought in panic and, catching a breath, said, Yes . . . yes, that must be it.

The soldiers came on through the darkness. They were marching down the middle of the street, the steel cleats on their boots striking the paving stones so that the sound of them was a solid, *RAMP . . . RAMP . . . RAMP . . .*

The smell was that of sweat and sour cabbage, of saddle soap and stale farts, and they passed by so closely, he could hear them breathing.

After they had gone, someone scurried by. Another ran. There were several with bicycles but without headlamps or taillights.

Then he was alone again and one by one the stars began

to appear from behind the drifting clouds, and one by one he counted them.

Martin hunted for his little parachute with all its silver stars and the moon and clouds. He was certain he could only just see it drifting slowly down into France in secret.

My father's not dead, Angélique. He *can't* be. You never said this before. You always stopped yourself. You *believed* he was alive and that he would come back one day. You really did, didn't you? It wasn't just a lie?

*Numéro* 37 rue des Grands-Augustins, he said and caught a breath, hiccupped and asked, Would my father have gone back there after he left us? Would he still be living there not knowing where we were?

He's British, he said to himself. The Boches would have locked him up unless he had made himself a set of forged papers. He'd do that. Yes, he really would. His French was excellent. He had always spoken it like a Frenchman, knew all of their usual ways, could drop right into those and no one would ever have guessed he was British.

Martin began to search for the address. First he determined that the bridge was indeed that of the Pont Neuf, and yes, the rue des Grands-Augustins and its street of that same name must stretch before him through the darkness.

Feeling for the numbers beside each door, he traced out a 57 and began, by finding each one, to finally come to number 37. But when a car crept slowly past with unblinkered head-lamps, he knew people were looking for him and sank down out of sight.

Then he started banging on the door and crying out, Let me in, though no sound passed from his lips.

The Hôtel Trianon Palace was on the rue de Vaugirard quite close to the *place* de l'Odéon and the Médicis Fountain in the Jardin du Luxembourg. Agitated—worried—Angélique paced the room. She wished she had a cigarette but of course she had had to give that up. Women weren't allowed a tobacco ration, worse still, if one did smoke, it could just as easily bring unwanted attention. Then, too, you couldn't grow it on an unregistered farm either, climate or not, soil or not. The Vichy inspectors of the Ravitaillement* would tear the place apart and arrest everyone. Tobacco was like gold and totally controlled by the state. They even made the damned cigarettes and matches.

Herr Dirksen had said nothing of the terrible bomb damage Hamburg had received 24 July to 2 August from the RAF by night and the USAAF by day, nor that of his home city of Düsseldorf a year ago in September when the RAF had dropped the first of what had been called the "heavy" incendiaries. Had his "factories" gone unscathed?

He had to be of the SS or Gestapo and that could only mean there had to have been a message in that pencil and so much for another appointment, eh, Dr. Vergès? So much for your suggestion of hypnosis and the letters you wrote in support of it to monsieur le maire and the Oberst Lautenschläger.

They would bring Martin back. They could find anybody, these people; how could she have thought otherwise? And they were watching her too. She felt it so strongly but ah! she couldn't go looking for him at this time of night anyway. There were at least three of them. One down the hall, and sitting just out of sight on the main staircase; another by the desk downstairs so as to watch the lift and front entrance, the lift being in service due entirely to there being Germans who would be staying in the hotel.

A third was out the back, in the courtyard, the night warm, so it would be more pleasant there. Constant surveillance. Let her leave if she wishes but don't lose her.

They were waiting to see who she would make contact with and must believe she could lead them to others. Had they arrested Vergès? They must have, but would he tell them she was innocent? Could he really tell them that?

Not likely. To do so would be to betray monsieur le maire and how, please, had that one arranged for Vergès to receive the message in the first place?

There must be others in Paris. Two groups, the one in Abbeville and the other here, but with a link between the two.

---

* Resupplying

Vergès might not even know who his contact was—had they thought of that? And if he couldn't tell them, would they then think that she could?

That gold wedding band Martin had found came to mind with its tangle of long black hairs, it lying wet and cupped in his hand, he saying silently, Look what I found.

*Père éternel*, please don't let it happen. Martin . . . Martin, try to hide. Try not to let them find you. Don't run to the river and the rue des Grands-Augustins. That will only cause them to think you knew where you were going.

At 11.55 p.m. Berlin time, a car drew to a stop on the rue Jacob, its headlamps unblinkered. Unteroffizier Horst Goetze shook the two drunken corporals he had finally located and furiously breathed, 'You stand to attention, *ja*? You let me do the talking. Cars like that are only for people you don't want to know.'

*Verdammt!* They would run into some SS or Gestapo bigwig while on their way back to the *Soldatenheim*. Approaching the right side of the car, thinking that the one in the passenger seat would be the one to talk to, he found a Frenchwoman sitting there. 'He wants to speak to you, not me,' she said in French he couldn't understand.

'*Ach*, sorry, *gutes Fräulein*.' He touched his cap in deference and who was he to question the SS if they liked to haul their women around with them.

'Standartenführer, what can I do for you?'

Dirksen shone the flashlight up over the uniform, noting the thick, bony wrists and burly chest with its campaign badges. Poland, the Blitzkrieg in the west, North Africa, Russia . . . where hadn't this one been? 'A boy of ten years, Sergeant. In tears no doubt and certainly lost. That's his mother and she's beside herself with worry.'

Was it really the mother? wondered Goetze, but *ach*, what else could he do? Reluctantly the pencil was handed over. 'It must have fallen from his pocket when he tripped.'

'At about what time?'

'Nearly 2315 hours, Colonel. On the rue Gué . . . *Ach*, I can't pronounce it. Here, I have a map.'

They played the light over it. The boy must have been heading for the river, thought Dirksen. Martin had run from the restaurant but had quickly left the boulevard Saint-Germain and must have gone up the rue de Seine, only to then take the rue Guénégaud. A shortcut perhaps? Had he been heading for the Pont Neuf, had he known the city that well?

The man on the staircase of the Trianon Palace was smoking a cigarette. He sat with his back to her and Angélique forced herself to study him. He was French, of course. The hair was well pomaded, cut short and parted on the left, the back of the head shaved closely. About forty, she thought. The elbows of the dark brown suit jacket were threadbare, the cuffs also.

Suddenly he cleared his throat. Perhaps he sensed he was being watched from behind, perhaps not. He fidgeted and examined his right shoe whose lace must be knotted in several places, but could she run down there and shove him out of the way? Martin would head for the house on the rue des Grands-Augustins.

Use the lift, she said urgently. An *aspirin*. Claim a headache that won't let you sleep.

*Aspirins*, even with visiting Germans staying in most of the rooms, would be in too short supply. It was rumoured that on the *marché noir* they cost 100 francs apiece, if one could find any.

The stairs to the service entrance were at the back of the hotel and when she caught sight of this one, he was coming up them to check on the other one. A big man, he made no sound, seemed not to even notice the steepness of the stairs, and when he reached the landing at her floor, he didn't look back but only went on through to the corridor, she crouching out of sight and just up the stairs from him.

It was now or never. Grabbing the railing when she could, she pelted down the stairs, saying, Please, God, I have to find Martin before it's too late. I *can't* let him lead them to that house and the flat. I can't!

*Ah merde*, Kraus was standing just inside the door to the courtyard but hadn't turned yet to look up at her, seemed not to have heard, but how could that possibly be?

Sickened, she retreated, and when she came to the corridor on her floor, found it empty, the door to her room closed and exactly as she had left it. Unlocked.

Marie-Hélène de Fleury listened closely to the sound of the river lapping softly against the abutments of the Pont Neuf. They were sitting in the car with the lights off, and the city was so silent she suddenly wanted to be a little girl again, to wipe the slate clean and start over, to stand with her dear *papa* on the bank at their villa near Nogent-sur-Seine. He had asked what she thought she might like to make of her life, and she had said with all innocence, the heavily laden barges plowing past, 'A sea captain.'

He had thought it an admirable vocation for her to aspire to and had said, 'Be the best there is. Strive hard for nothing less. Never allow complacency to enter your mind. Not for a moment.'

And now, Hans and she were listening to the river too.

'It's music, *ma chère*,' her father had said that time. 'Music to soothe the tortured soul.' The pain of having lost his only son, her brother. A drowning accident, a tragedy. Like so many, her father had been in the Great War, and yes, there had been things he would never speak of. But that had been the France he had known, not the present one, and certainly he had been a part of the great debacle, the fall of the Third Republic, and had lost everything.

But would he spit on her now if he knew she had betrayed so many? If still alive, would he have disowned her, a man she had worshipped?

'You're quiet,' said Dirksen. 'Is something bothering you?'

'Hans, please just take me home. You can pick me up later.'

'We have to wait. We've no other choice.'

'But . . . but in the morning I have to follow Vergès. I'll need my wits about me and must be right on top of things, otherwise . . . Well, who knows, eh? Maybe one of them will follow me and I'll not know until it's too late.'

He passed her a cigarette. Wavelets continued to sound as he struck a match and struck it again and again, the wood finally snapping.

Irritably he flung it away and tried to find another, said, '*Ah, mon Dieu*, why can't you people make anything right?'

The French, and yes, the matches, like the cigarettes, were terrible. 'They require patience, Hans. *Patience*.'

'Sorry. I didn't mean that about the French. I really didn't. It's . . . it's just this business. Somehow Berlin received word of it. The Reichsführer Himmler's been after me. He's demanding arrests and claims that perhaps the leader of the Sonderkommando der Vergeltungswaffen Eins* needs another position. The Russian front or in one of the camps!'

She stiffened in alarm. 'How did he learn of this new *réseau* so soon?'

Dirksen flung the matches away. 'Kraus. That bastard must have thought he could climb the ladder more quickly if he leaned it against my back.'

Kraus. 'Hans . . . ?'

'Well, what?'

'This boy, this thing . . . I think it had better be my last assignment.'

'You're not in league with the Reichsführer, are you?'

'Of course not, but is it such a bad idea? It can't go on forever. I don't want to end up in some ditch with my hands behind my back and a bullet through my head or heart.'

He tossed a hand. 'You won't. Not while I'm around.'

'And if you're not, what then?'

Dirksen drew in an exasperated breath. She had been worried about the leader of this particular *réseau*, had said that Vergès must be receiving instructions from someone who not only knew how to go about things but was ruthless enough to sacrifice the doctor *and* the message Martin had been carrying just to keep their security tight. But was there something else? '*Liebchen*, has Kraus been after you?'

'Me? Ah no, of course not. It's just this boy, this woman and her son, what if they're innocent? If so, why I . . . I wouldn't want to hurt them. I couldn't live with that, Hans. Not a ten-year-old boy who has lost his voice.'

---

* The Special Commando for the Retaliatory Weapon Ones, the V-1 flying bombs

Kraus had been after her. 'You've never had cold feet before. Why suddenly now?'

'Because, in listening to the river, I was reminding myself of how I was at the same age. My father was holding me by the hand. We'd had a terrible loss, one that he couldn't forget, neither could I.'

'*Bien sûr, chérie*, but now we don't even know where Martin's father is. We only know there was a parachutist who came down in a field of wheat not far from Bois Carré. As leader of this Sonderkommando, I have to quickly find out what the Wehrmacht have been missing, and you should know and understand the urgency. *Verdammt, mein Schatz*, I need you.'

*My treasure*, but he had never told her anything about those sites, not even what they were for, nor why such secrecy was imperative. Instead he had always avoided it.

'Try to sleep. There's a pillow in the back. Curl up and I'll get it for you.'

'I couldn't. None of it's right, but I'll do what you want because I have to.'

'If Kraus has been threatening you and trying to get you to give him information before myself, I'll have to know of it.'

'He hasn't. Now just let me sit here. I . . . I need to be by myself.'

'Then I'll check again if the boy is still asleep.'

At 5.00 a.m. in pitch-darkness, the curfew ended and the city began to drag itself out of bed, and yes, thought Marie-Hélène, the sound of her wooden heels on the damp paving stones of the rue des Grands-Augustins was overly loud.

'Bijou . . . Bijou, *ma chère*,' she sang out, 'where are you, *petite*? Come to Isabelle. Ah! you naughty thing. You know you're being absolutely repulsive. Staying out all night; defying the curfew. Now listen, you, I really mean it this time. It'll be into the soup pot for you if someone should grab you before I get there . . .

'*Ah, mon Dieu, mon pauvre*,' she said to the boy, to this Martin. 'You've been hurt. Your hands, your knees . . . Are they still very painful? Oh for sure, they must be. It's lucky the Boches didn't come along to find you out here all night in a doorway. Here, let me help you up. Let's see if you can stand okay.'

Martin rubbed sleep from his eyes and tried to moisten his throat as the woman set her torch, with its tiny pinpoint of blue light, down on the stones and felt in her purse for a handkerchief. 'It's clean,' she said, 'so don't worry about picking up any of these strange diseases we've been having due to the lack of vitamins and minerals. And don't mind the perfume. It's as good an antiseptic as anything. Even the hospitals are using it to bathe the wounds, if they're not too big and deep. Saves money too, I guess, so be brave. Steel yourself while I touch you up where it must hurt the most.'

Her light shone on his hands. Gently the woman dabbed at the cuts. Delicate, the scents of bergamot, sweet orange and lavender were there, with touches of cloves and cinnamon. Sandalwood too, probably—all of the very special ingredients Angélique had told him to search for when assessing a woman's taste.

'There,' this one said and smiled so beautifully he felt his heart skip. 'The scrapes aren't as bad as I feared at first. Painful, yes, of course—*ah, mon Dieu*, why wouldn't they be? After all, isn't that the way the body tells us that we've been injured and are in need of help?'

Playfully she touched his shoulder, making him wish with all his heart that he could say, *Merci beaucoup, mademoiselle.* He did try. He really, really did, but it wasn't of any use.

She didn't seem to mind. 'You haven't seen or heard a little dog, have you?' she asked, and he liked the sound of her voice. It had a certain music to it. Gentle and kind but with muted suggestions of laughter at herself for having thought the cuts and scrapes far worse than they were.

'Bijou's a poodle, of course, and very tasty, or so I've been warned. Temperamental, too. Me, I should have known better than to have chosen such, but . . .' She shrugged. 'What is one to do when one is looked at with such sorrowful eyes? I adopted her, but how was I to have known she could be such a wretch? Out all night and causing me to worry and not sleep.'

Again Martin tried desperately to find his voice and felt a fool. Ashamed, he shook his head rapidly, she to nod and say,

'Well, thanks anyway. *Bonne chance*, eh? One needs it these days. Take care of yourself.'

All too soon he was left alone, the pinpoint of her torch growing fainter and fainter, the sound of her heels as well until they stopped suddenly in the darkness, and he heard her coming back, heard the worry in her voice. 'Hey, *mon ami*, are you really okay now? Was the concierge mean? Did she tell you to sit outside and learn a damn good lesson or else, eh? Is that why you weren't allowed in?'

Again he tried to find his voice, as she said, 'Look, why don't you pull the bell and let me give her the tongue lashing of her life? It's not right for her to have done a thing like that. One of the swallows* might have come along and you'd have spent the rest of the night scrubbing the toilets in the district gendarmerie.'

Shaking his head, Martin started out, and when she caught up with him, she said, 'So it's not your house. What difference does it make? Don't cry. I'm a friend, aren't I? Look, why not help me find that wretched dog? If you do, you can share my breakfast. Fair's fair, eh? If not, why you can share it anyway and you can then console me.'

Still he didn't say a thing, and she must really be wondering at such a silence as they went along the street through the darkness, she calling out for Bijou and flicking her light here and there while trying also, she said, to save the damned batteries. 'They're so hard to get now. Two hundred francs apiece on the *marché noir* if you can find one. If.'

A *vélo-taxi* hurried past, the wheels squeaking from the lack of grease, for in Paris they wouldn't even have the pig fat they had on the farm and he'd had to taste since it had been shoved into his mouth on a brush, he lying in the pig shit, having lost the fight.

'Ah! to hell with Bijou. She'll come home when she wants if she's not been slaughtered, gutted, stuffed and ready for the roasting, her hide then to be tanned and made into shoes. Me, I've warned her many times, but she fails to listen.'

Again he tried and tried to speak, she saying, 'I'll bet you're as hungry as I am. Too bad it'll only be the ersatz coffee of

---

* Policemen on bicycles

crushed and roasted acorns with a touch of chicory, no milk of course, for our friends stopped that the day they entered Paris and they still haven't managed to get those trains running even though they're using them for lots and lots of other things. Sending them east, of course. But, I've bread, the national, that grey stuff with the floor sweepings and all the rest like weevils, but you can drown those little buggers in your coffee and chew them up. If you're like me, you'll find them rather tasty and nourishing too. Even the Maréchal* eats them, but he's so dotty now, he wouldn't even notice. He'd just suck on them, having forgotten to put his teeth in. Laval† would have forgotten to tell him that too, since that one does everything for him.'

The boy had been huddled on the doorstep of number 37 and Hans would already have obtained a list of all in that house and on the street too, just in case.

'Is that where your father lives?' she asked and saw Martin desperately shake his head and dart his eyes away from the light. And when the café *patron* let them in, she found a pencil and a scrap of paper in her purse. 'Now tell me who you are, since you must have lost your voice. A cold perhaps, who knows? Write down where you're staying and let me see if I can't help you a little more. My name is Moncontre. Still a mademoiselle, for the man I was to have married is, of course, locked up in the Reich, in a prisoner-of-war camp. But since we've become friends of a sort, why you can call me Isabelle just like he would, and it'll be music to my ears when you recover your voice.'

---

* Pétain
† Pierre Laval, the premier

# 3

The shade was deep, the early morning cool. Water trickled softly over the stone steps of the Médicis Fountain where Acis, the shepherd, made love in white marble to Galatea, and the jealous Cyclops, Polyphemus, knelt in bronze above, peering over the edge of the boulder he would soon push to crush them.

Martin had come back. Angélique knew about the night spent on the doorstep of number 37. It was only a matter of time until things closed right in and they, too, were crushed. She felt so helpless. Utterly frustrated and angry, as if the whole world had suddenly gone mad and all she could do was to stand here and wait for it to happen.

Oh for sure they were being followed all the time and watched. She was certain of it, yet the city went on about its business as usual. The traffic on the rue de Médicis could be seen through the trunks of the plane trees and the tall, black iron fence that surrounded the Jardin du Luxembourg. It was thin. An old priest with a briefcase was passed by two arm-in-arm girls, then a German soldier who was smoking a cigarette, then a bicycle taxi, a lorry with a gas-producer that smoked terribly. Wet and rotten wood probably. Hay too, maybe. But no one would care a damn about what was happening to them. People kept to themselves only all the more so in this Occupation.

Everything in her wanted to cry out, Martin, you *knew* the concierge of that house could identify me! But . . . ah, one couldn't blame him. He was too little, had been far too upset. Had lost monsieur le maire's pencil again and for good, perhaps. One would, of course, have to see. Yes, one would. A little test of her own, for if it *did* come back, she would know right away what Herr Dirksen and Herr Kraus would want of her. Betrayal of everyone. Monsieur le maire and all the others in Abbeville and anyone else she could bring.

'*Chéri*, your father can't have gone back to that house. *Petit*, listen to me. *Don't* switch me off like that! I'm not a wireless whose music you hate. I'm your Angélique, the only friend you have, and you're mine, so friends like that have to stick together, eh, especially when the whole world is against us.'

Had it done any good at all? she wondered. 'Look, I know how much you want to believe he might well have done such a thing, but it's not in the cards. You wouldn't want him to be shot in the street, would you, he trying to escape when they come to tear that house apart and arrest everyone? They will, Martin. They'll rip the floors up and tear the walls apart searching for the clandestine wireless set on which a very different kind of music is played. Secret answers, Martin, to questions asked by the British. They'll look for guns as well, and explosives and you know this. You must. Your father simply won't have been there. He *knew* exactly how valuable he was to the Boches if captured. A designer of racing yachts can design other things. Even in 1938 he was doing classified work for the British Royal Navy. He went home, Martin, during the Blitzkrieg. *Home*, do you hear me? He's alive, yes, yes, but in England. He knew he had a duty far beyond just you and myself, and in the end he had to make a choice that was far greater than the two of us.'

*She* was the one who wouldn't listen. *She* never had, thought Martin. His father would really have gone back to that house. He'd have made himself a good set of false papers and taken another identity, would have lived right in that same flat, right in the very heart of this city.

The Boches wouldn't know who he was. He'd look just like all the other men of his age, even with his dark red hair because . . . why, because he would dye it black. Yes, black! And he could speak Deutsch too, he really could, and the Germans liked and trusted those who could. It was one of the ways of getting right in among them, they not even knowing.

Angélique smiled softly at him and tried to comfort him but he pulled away as he heard her saying, 'Someone else will have taken over my flat. Right after the Defeat, the Germans issued an ordinance that stated that if a person didn't return to their home or place of business, it would be confiscated. Someone else will be using my desk and sleeping in my bed. They'll be eating off that china my aunt Victoria left me in her will even though the dishes were cracked and chipped and would have suffered if auctioned off. She had always hated me as much as she had my father, her own brother, for God's sake. Ah! she knew I wouldn't throw the wretched things out because she had read my character through and through. Whoever has the flat will have found and burned all those photographs and letters I'd been saving and couldn't manage to take on the exodus. They'll have my collection of antique scent bottles too, the ones I used to find in Saint-Ouen.* All such things, Martin. Things that really don't matter anymore, do they, until . . .'

Bursting into tears at the thought of opened trunks and suitcases, of the boxes of things scattered about in the cellars of that house, the mould and mildew on everything now, even on the endless snapshots of her and her lover: Anthony James Thomas, yes! Thomas, Martin, she silently wept, for Kraus would find them and then he'd make her tell him everything.

'*Chéri*, if your father did stay, they will only get him, so please let's pray that all of my things were destroyed or sold off, and that there's no longer any evidence of him or of myself.'

Martin studied the reflections in the fountain's rectangu-

---

* A suburb just to the north of Paris, and location of the largest of the many flea markets

lar pool. Big, empty stone urns stood on pedestals around the pond, just inside the walkway, and he could see their images in the water, that of the ivy too. English ivy.

A matchstick was thrown by one of the men who were pretending not to watch them, and when it hit the water, it sent out its message rings just like one of those secret short-wave transmitters would. *Da, dit, dit, dit . . . Da, dit. Ici Londres . . . Here is London calling.* He often listened in on his crystal set that was illegal and would be confiscated *if* they found it. Sometimes there was too much static, sometimes the Boches were jamming the airwaves. He preferred to listen to the Free French broadcasts from London rather than the BBC's English language program. He found that better, easier to understand. Both, however, would be sure to give the latest news.

Had he forgotten how to say things in English? he wondered. Was he now so fluent in French, he couldn't even speak his own language anymore?

I can't speak anything anyway, he said.

Though her voice would grate, felt Angélique, it would have to be asked. 'Martin, tell me about the Mademoiselle Moncontre, this Isabelle who sent you back to the hotel in a *vélo-taxi*. Tell me everything you can. You said she told you she worked for a big publishing house. Was it Les Presses Universitaires de France? That used to be on the boulevard Saint-Germain and is not far from here. Maybe she can help us.'

It was only logical to thank her. Surely Dirksen and Kraus, since they must be working together on this business, would understand a mother's desire to offer thanks?

*Impossible!* They would simply arrest the woman and then ask their questions later. *Clang, clang* and into the *panier à salade*\* with her. Straight to the Santé or maybe the cells of the Petite Roquette if they were feeling kindly, the Cherche Midi, if not.

'I'd better telephone first. Others will, of course, be listening in, since the Gestapo and their French helpers do this constantly, but sometimes one must take chances.'

Taking out his pencil and paper, Martin scribbled furi-

---

\* The salad shaker, the paddy wagon

ously, *She'll just hang up. She won't say anything. She can't. She's one of us!*

At 8.30 a.m. there was sufficient traffic in the rue de Tournon for a *Parisienne* with a wounded bicycle to pass unnoticed. Marie-Hélène ruefully examined the front tyre and, at last, trying not to break a fingernail, pried the offending drawing pin out. '*Maudit*,' she said to no one in particular, stamping a disgruntled foot. 'Patching kits are impossible to find these days even though ninety-nine percent of the population either runs on two wheels, four if they've a horse and wagon, or else nothing but the feet!'

Just along the street, Dr. Émile Vergès paused to secure the gate, then to look back at the house of his forefathers. Was he wondering if he would ever see it again or merely if his aged mother would understand why he had agreed to become a part of this thing, or was he arguing with himself and saying he need not go through with it?

She couldn't tell at this stage. He searched the street for trouble, looked at her as she leaned over the front tyre—she could feel him studying her closely, said silently, I'm nothing, Doctor. Just a young woman with a little problem. Such minor catastrophes, they happen all the time, *n'est-ce pas?*

At a news kiosk he purchased copies of *Le Matin* and the weekly *Pariser Zeitung*, Germany's own paper in Paris. An eclectic reader, was that it, or were they ID marks to single him out for his contact?

The *Zeitung* faced the world, the *Matin* was hidden. Sweeping her gaze around the square, she searched for others. When he reached the Jardin du Luxembourg, he made straight for the terrace and she hung back. Suddenly he stopped beside the pond and she saw him talking to the Bellecour woman and her son. The boy would recognize her. Others were strolling; others sailing their toy boats. For perhaps five seconds all motion ceased for her, the scene to be recorded starkly in memory. A Wehrmacht lieutenant was over by one of the statues. Nearby there was an elderly Frenchman with his dog, a maid pushing a pram, a solitary Frenchwoman of about thirty-five, in a suit and wearing a large felt sun hat.

The Bellecour woman didn't smile at Vergès but said something so intense the doctor tried vehemently to deny it and, with a dismissive lift of his newspapers, turned his back on them.

Much distressed, Angélique Bellecour watched as he quickly retreated. Then the two went back to their little sailboat, the boy kneeling at the edge of the pond, his mother with hands dejectedly in the pockets of her flowered print dress.

The lieutenant was now no longer by that statue, nor could she see him anywhere. *Ah merde*, said Marie-Hélène to herself, am I, too, being watched? Had she been such a fool? Had whoever was leading this *réseau* set the whole thing up just to trap her?

If I follow Vergès, will I now be followed in turn?

Sickened by the thought, she knew there was only one thing to do. Reluctantly she turned diagonally away from the terrace and headed for the gate that let out onto the boulevard Saint-Michel. She couldn't try to intercept the doctor as he reached the rue Vavin and his surgery. Now suddenly her bicycle was an encumbrance. If she left it against a tree and hurried away, they would know exactly who she was working for. Same, too, if she left it anywhere else but at her apartment.

Try as she did, she couldn't remember what the lieutenant had looked like. Tall, not too thin, not too heavy either and about forty, she felt, the face . . . yes, yes, pleasantly narrow, the chin sharp—was there not something far more familiar. The ears? Ah, that's crazy of me, she said. I've never seen him before, but the thought, it wouldn't go away.

It was in the set of the eyes and the way he stood as if bemused while watching her curiously to see exactly what she would do. Totally relaxed in that grey-green uniform. One of the "green beans" for sure, and yet not relaxed at all.

A Wehrmacht lieutenant with a copy of *Pariser Zeitung*.

'Hans, I'm telling you I had no other choice but to leave it! Vergès may have set me up. Is he being watched by another of that *réseau* he must be connected to? *Watched*, do you understand? Is he being told ahead of time exactly what to do so that they can set up a little *souricière*\* for me?'

'Arrest him,' snorted Kraus. 'Pry the truth from him before it's too late, or is it already that?'

'*Maudit salaud*, how can you blame me for what happened? You weren't there!' she shrilled. 'You didn't have to stick your neck out. You hid here at the avenue Foch behind closed doors!'

'*Verdammte Schlampe*, how dare you?'

'*Ach*, now look, you two, calm down,' said Dirksen from behind his desk. 'Already we know this thing goes far beyond that woman and her son. The Paris section of the *réseau de soie bleue* must be exceedingly well organized. Your beating Doumier to death, Kraus, has cost us dearly. By picking him and the Bellecour woman and her son up at the Gare du Nord, you gave it all away. They must have been onto us right from the first and now the game gets serious.

'Marie-Hélène . . . Look, I know how unsettled you must be, but try to think back over this morning. Do they now suspect you?'

'*Ah, mon Dieu*, how the hell would I really know? Maybe yes, maybe no and not yet, but . . . but we're going to have to be very careful with this. It's not the usual, Hans. The *Résistance* . . . the *Banditen*, yes? The terrorists, if you like, are becoming better and better at it.'

'And you're sure he was wearing a Wehrmacht lieutenant's uniform?' asked Dirksen.

'Why would I *not* have known such a thing? He even looked the part, but . . .'

'*Chérie*, please.' Both she and Kraus were standing before him, the two so at odds, they wouldn't look at each other unless ordered to.

'Hans, I feel I've seen him before but . . . but can't recall where.'

Lyon perhaps, or Marseille, or was it Perpignan? wondered

---

\* A little mousetrap

Kraus, relishing her fears, but saying, 'Berlin are demanding arrests, Colonel. The Reichsführer Himmler . . .'

'And what, please, does he have to say about this?' asked Dirksen.

Kraus paused to swallow, for he knew this *Schlampe* of the colonel's had stiffened and was now looking at him. 'The Führer is also concerned and wishes to reassign the security of the Retaliatory Weapon One sites to the SD[*] and not leave it in the incompetent hands of the Abwehr.[†] I considered it my duty to let the Reichsführer know that things were not being handled as they should if we are to succeed.'

The son of a bitch! 'I see.' sighed Dirksen. 'Then perhaps you should read through the telex I sent him this morning.'

'What telex?'

'Read it, as I've just said, *mein lieber Major*, and might I remind you that is an order.'

Men like Kraus had always to be taught lessons. That was why they rose only so far and were then left behind.

It was dated Saturday 28 August 1943 and given the top secret notation and code name of Blue Silk.

*Enemy agent dropped Bois Carré night Sunday 22 August. Suspect message sent via Abbeville courier to Paris Friday 27 August, suspected courier Mademoiselle Angélique Bellecour, secretary Abbeville Kommandantur, Paris contact Dr. Émile Vergès, specialist and surgeon of the throat and voice, 7 rue de Tournon. Evidence suggests well-organized Banditen network gathering intelligence of V-1 launching sites. If not suppressed, will cause irreparable damage to security. Estimate 10 to 15 days complete suppression, far longer if Sturmbannführer Kraus continues to ignore my orders and do as he did by arresting land surveyor Henri-Paul Doumier, also from Abbeville, and detaining the Bellecour woman and her ten-year-old son. Kraus was ordered to have them all followed and closely watched. Instead, Doumier, under Kraus's reinforced*

---

[*] The Sicherheitsdienst, the security service of the SS and Nazi Party
[†] The intelligence service of the OKW, the Oberkommando der Wehrmacht, the High Command

*interrogation, as per Directive 385770, dated 12.6.42 to all central offices, yielded nothing and died.*

*Request reassignment of Kraus out of Paris before we lose everything.*

*Heil Hitler*

'Kraus, you've been warned and warned, and I have repeatedly covered for you by stating that such interrogations were, after all, authorized by Berlin. But I can't allow this thing to become bigger. The Bellecour woman will give us everything we need. If not the Paris network first, then the one in Abbeville.'

'And if I'm to be reassigned?'

'You know as well as I that it will take time, so let's not bugger about.'

Finding the most significant responses the boy had written for Marie-Hélène over breakfast, Dirksen read it aloud. '"My name is Martin", and beside it, Kraus, look what the boy has drawn, having trusted her so much.'

The parachute was evidence enough and there should have been further arrests, a clean sweep, felt Kraus, but said, 'The woman could easily be convinced to tell us what she's hiding, Colonel. Let me use the boy. Let me show her what will happen to him if she refuses to talk. We're not the Abwehr. This is not a gentleman's game.'

It never had been for the Abwehr, thought Dirksen, but there had been this constant competition between the two intelligence services and Himmler was determined to absorb the one into the SD and expunge it from the history books. So bad had things become, the Paris SS and SD had been forbidden to speak to any of the Paris Abwehr or be seen in their company, and it would only get worse.*

'We can't be soft on these people,' said Kraus.

'And you can't be disobeying my orders and running to Berlin behind my back. Oh, by the way, you haven't threatened to betray Marie-Hélène to the *Banditen*, have you? Photos, that sort of thing, eh?'

---

* Early in February 1944, the SD took over the Abwehr and put an end to this historic and internationally renowned intelligence service.

The bitch! 'Why not ask her? Yes, yes, let's clear the air.'

*Maudit salaud!* 'Hans . . . Hans, I've already told you he hasn't. Why would he, since it might well endanger himself?'

'Then we'll leave it for now. Kraus, what have you found out about the Bellecour woman? Perhaps you should be telling us that.'

And nothing else. 'Only that her story is full of holes. She was born in Tours, and did live in Orléans for two years as a student and single woman but without a son. From there the holes are so many and so big, there isn't a shred of truth.'

And will that information also get to the Reichsführer? wondered Dirksen, sadly knowing that it could very well be likely, that some battles never seemed to end.

Marie-Hélène was looking pale and shaken. Irritably she asked for a cigarette but refused the one Kraus had offered, a bad mistake and one she should have avoided. Something would have to be done to soothe the wounds. 'Kraus, let's play it my way for a few days, eh? If the Bellecour woman shows promise, we'll let her continue. If not, well what can one say but that she asked for it and you can bring her in.'

*Ah, nom de Dieu*, could Hans not see where such softness would lead?

Wisely, the major left the room, and when the door was closed, Hans didn't take her by the shoulders even though she said, 'He's got it in for me and he's dangerous to yourself as well.'

'He threatened you, didn't he, *Liebchen*? He told you he would give the partisans all they needed to pin things on you.'

Everything in her wanted to cry out, Yes! but she was too knowing of the SS and what made them tick, especially men like Kraus. 'Hans, I think I should tell you that in the Jardin du Luxembourg this morning, the Bellecour woman tried to warn Vergès but the doctor vehemently denied any knowledge of things and refused to listen. This can only mean that the leader of the *réseau de soie bleue*—perhaps it was that lieutenant I saw—may well have set the whole thing up, which means of course, that she and her son were simply taken in and are totally innocent.'

Was Marie-Hélène still having pangs of conscience? wondered Dirksen. 'And that is why I used the words "suspected courier" in my telex. If innocent, she goes free. I swear it.'

'Do you?'

There was moisture in her eyes. 'Of course. Now stop worrying so much about Kraus. He's been told to behave and will because he has to.'

Still she lingered. Overnight Hans had turned the office into a command centre. On a map, and on an aerial photograph mosaic of Paris, there were pins marking the house at 37 rue des Grands-Augustins and where the boy had first lost his pencil and then again. The Hôtel Trianon Palace was marked, the clinic of Dr. Vergès, the doctor's house, the brasserie de Dome. Their very route had been traced out. Hans was always so thorough and patient. Even in bed he had that same patience, but did he make love in the same way that he searched for the terrorists—the partisans he'd like to have called them? *Ah oui*, there were similarities, the hesitant, preliminary explorations, the ever-patient pursuit and then the final entrapment, which could, in itself, be so intense, the realization of just what such close a contact could actually bring them when all the senses were alert and striving until at last *le grand frisson** overwhelmed.

Was that why she liked the hunt so much herself?

Mosaics of aerial photographs showed the Bois Carré site and the five others that were near Abbeville. Pins marked the farm and house where the woman and her son were living; lines of thin white string, the approaches and distances from house to woods, and from house to what could well have been wheat fields. Confirmation overflights had been arranged. The Luftwaffe were to repeat photographing the whole area but at low and medium altitudes on days sufficiently clear and apart not to raise suspicion. Maps gave all the roads and villages, the paths and trails even. Already other photos, clandestinely taken here in Paris with a telephoto lens, revealed those closest to the woman and her son here in the city, and when

---

* Great shudder

a technician brought in the latest, Hans placed a fifty-centime piece over that Wehrmacht lieutenant's head and drew a circle around it with a white pen.

'Have this circulated to all sections. If he's really what he seems, then you were mistaken. Now please, *meine Schatz*, I have a report I must finish. Herr Himmler's demanding full details and will have to be satisfied.'

'*Et moi-même?*'

'Go home and get some sleep. You've done well. Don't worry so much. We'll get them. *All* of them. No word is going to leak out about your part in things. Kraus or no Kraus, I'll make sure of it.'

'And what about that flat on the rue des Grand-Augustins? Is that little job for me, Hans?'

She was in the lift when he came after her and rode down to the ground floor. 'La Librairie Hachette. The Bellecour woman has just telephoned to ask if you worked there. Our contact used her head and told the woman you were out seeing the printers about one of the new books the firm is to publish this autumn. The woman is to ring back at noon, so go and do your stuff. It's the very break we need.'

All along the boulevard Saint-Germain, and then on the boul' Saint-Michel, the haze of slowly burning green-wood from *gazogène* lorries and cars that couldn't afford the bottled gas and shortage of charcoal perfumed the air that was washed by the sunlight. And through this gossamer, the plane trees stood on either side, the *vélo* and other traffic between, pedestrians on the pavements, the old, middle-aged and young but with one notable exception. There very few if any young Frenchmen. So harsh was their absence, Angélique stopped on the corner of the rue des Écoles to ask, 'Where have they all gone?'

'The *maquis*,' grunted a passerby. 'The Auvergne, to avoid the Service du Travail Obligatoire.'*

Tattered posters splashed high on the walls to avoid vandalism had been unsuccessful. GIVE YOUR LABOUR IN THE

---

* The STO, the forced labour draft

FIGHT AGAINST BOLSHEVISM, cried one whose Wehrmacht corporal had had his eyes pricked out and his rifle turned into a broom, the flames of which burned at both ends while a little boy, no older than Martin, gazed beatifically up at the soldier while dutifully clasping blonde *maman's* hand. DADDY'S GONE TO GERMANY, read the type. AT LAST THERE IS MONEY IN THE HOUSE FOR FOOD.

The *marché noir*, no doubt, or prison, for that little boy held the match in his hand. And while the mother was cradling baby sister in the crook of her other arm, she was also wearing the Cross of Lorraine at her throat, that symbol of the *Résistance* whose double message was clear enough: If you don't help us, it's the throat for you. But, really, so few could because most were simply trying to eke out a living and were terrified of reprisals, herself also, for the Occupier had a little ordinance for such: the *Nacht und Nebel* decree, namely, get involved and it won't just be yourself, but all others in the family. Notices gave the names of those shot for such, or even for acts of "terrorism" they hadn't even known of. Five, ten, twenty—the numbers had just kept multiplying: the work of a few, stacking up against the numbers of those taken. Even in Abbeville there were such notices. She had to post them. It was part of her job. And yes, she emphasized, now we find ourselves deeply involved and just as unaware as most of those poor hostages. As a result, and it could never be forgotten, that same so-called *Résistance*, fractured into its bits and pieces here and there throughout the country, could be hated by lots, some only with an immediate reason.

Urgently her hand was being tugged at. Martin had to go, but the *pissoir*, it looked so filthy and reeked to high heaven, but he was in such pain even small boys must go in such.

'Be careful,' she said. 'Don't speak to . . . Ah! forgive me. Just don't let anyone touch you. Run if you have to.'

Of two round shells, its outer one hid the customers but for their fedoras and shoulders, some of them. Fleurs-de-lis crowned the frosted glass panels above the rusty, grey-painted sheet iron. The gutter ran. Martin vanished, though she searched desperately for a glimpse of his shoes and ankle socks. *The Val-de-Grâce, head injuries ward,* the note had stated. That was all the receptionist at the Librairie Hachette could give her. The Mademoiselle Isabelle Moncontre hadn't wanted to meet them at her place of work. Oh for sure, that was understandable, but was it too much to hope that she might, in some small way, be connected with others who could help her out of this mess?

In spite of the *Défense d'afficher* warnings, slogans ghosted through that outer shell, in pale white against the grey and the rust: Victory, Laval up against the post, the guillotine for Pétain and all those others. Strong messages, of course, for more and more now felt the end must be in sight. 'Spring,' they called it, taken from a popular song, not necessarily *next* spring yet, but the evidence was there. The Russians were unbeatable, and the RAF and USAAF were bombing the hell out of German cities. Hamburg in particular, and Cologne, and even Munich was getting a plastering, among the many.

Proudly doing up his flies, Martin returned, but chose to show her what he'd found. A piece of chalk. '*Merde*, why must you pick up such a thing? You found it in the trough, did you?'

*Grâce à Dieu*, he shook his head, but he mischievously smiled in that way of his. 'Your parachute?' she asked as if begging, only to feel her heart drop. 'Idiot, we're being followed! You *can't* be doing such a thing. Did you honestly think those *salauds* would need a reminder?'

Swallowed up, they passed by the all-but-empty shops with their long queues for bread, meat, cheese, whatever they used to have before this lousy Occupation had robbed them. But . . . but Martin gently took her by the hand and all too soon, she felt the backs of her fingers against his lips. It's all right, he wanted so much to say, felt Angélique, and pausing to kneel on the pavement, held him.

In the Val-de-Grâce, Marie-Hélène watched as the Bellecour woman and her son received the looks, the smiles, and the empty stares of the Wehrmacht's severely wounded. Uncomfortable, and at a loss at seeing no Frenchmen, the woman stopped one of the doctors, who then told her the truth, namely that except for the most difficult of French cases, the hospital now served only the Reich.

Having asked for the head injuries ward, she and the boy were directed to the staircase and when they appeared, this Isabelle Moncontre called down, 'Martin . . . Ah, Martin, *mon ami*, I should have waited at the front desk, but there was no one there when I got here.'

She hit her forehead with the heel of her right hand. 'I'm so stupid! Forgive me.'

Tentatively Angélique took her in at a glance as they shook hands, the grip firm, not hesitant, the woman solidly reassuring, no makeup, no put-on. Even the dark, wavy brown hair, though lovely, had been simply brushed and pinned, not stylishly coiffed as so many still did, necessary though that might well be for some.

She smiled, too, and it was at once engagingly sincere and honest. A woman, then, of about twenty-eight, perhaps, and very attractive but not deliberately sporting this. Modest to the point of keeping the Occupier at a good distance. The big brown eyes sincere and absolutely enviable.

'You must be wondering why I would think to ask you both here,' she said, 'and for this I must apologize, but you see, I try to do my best whenever possible. Ah! Don't be alarmed. It's because of my brother, André. He's one of the most difficult, and oh for sure he doesn't particularly care for the company he must keep at present, but has no choice. Shrapnel, during the battle for the Ardennes in 1940, spared few and he was one of those who caught too much.'

The shrug she gave at fate was the usual. Most still blamed the generals; others still the boys themselves and the lack of bravery.

'Oh for sure one gets used to it,' continued the woman, 'but he sees so few, just lies there waiting and hoping he'll get better. Martin, I've told him about us meeting like that and our hunting for my Bijou. If you'd like, we could . . . Well, we could look in the door to the ward. You'd see him from there and I could point you out to him and he'd love that. He really would.'

A glance was all it took, the Bellecour woman feeling it

so much, she gave but a duck of her head. Once in the ward, they received the stares, those that were vacant, others with their horrible grins, the half of some of the faces having been torn away, them all just like the thousands and thousands of *grands mutilés* the Great War had given both sides, but maybe far fewer this time around.

'André . . . André, *c'est moi*, here with those friends I've been telling you about. Ah, please don't hide your face. You know what the doctors have said. Behave as though it's an honour and everything is just fine.'

There was no chin, no nose, only holes, the mouth all twisted up, the eyes having lost their lashes, the scar tissue everywhere, the towel around the throat catching the tears.

'Like yourself, Martin, André has lost his voice but the doctors are convinced that sometime soon that will return. A miracle. Isn't that right, André?'

Kissing him on both cheeks, she brushed a hand over the thin blond hair, the scalp so lacerated, the scars were felt.

Out in the corridor she paused to steady herself and then to confide, 'He won't last much longer. There are still pieces of shrapnel they can't dig out, so the infection . . . Ah! forgive me, please. What can I do for you?'

Martin was in tears and terribly upset, and when he demanded to go to the washroom—was there even such a thing?—he drew away and was carried right back to June 1940 and the road south from Paris, and Angélique knew this but didn't, couldn't, wonder why the woman had taken such a chance. She simply wouldn't have known.

But in the toilets Martin would be hearing the Messer-schmitts and seeing the flames, the smashed-up automobiles, and hearing the shrieks, the cries, and afterwards that dread-ful silence before the whole thing started again.

She knew that he'd be wondering if his father would look like that, and when she went to find him, he buried his face against her and she heard herself saying, 'Be brave, *mon petit*. Your Isabelle didn't understand. She simply wanted us to bring a little cheer to her brother.'

And then, she having washed his face and dried his eyes, 'Now listen, you're all I've got. Stay close and keep your eyes open for I need you to watch this one you've met. I'll need your frankest opinion of her. It's important.'

When they returned to the corridor, the Moncontre woman confided that the Germans wouldn't bother them. 'They know me well enough. Please, there's a terrace at the back overlooking the gardens. Some coffee perhaps?' And then, 'It's real but promise you won't tell anyone. Every time I come here I have a taste.'

The flat of Marie-Hélène de Fleury, on the boulevard de Beau-séjour, overlooked the Jardin du Ranelagh. Admirably furnished with leftover pieces from an estate that had been broken up in bankruptcy, and other pieces that had been bought since the Defeat of 1940 and her rise to fortune again, it was quiet in the late afternoon. Sunlight streamed in through the opened French windows. A faint breeze stirred the flimsy lace curtains that had been once fashionable in the villa at Nogent-sur-Seine.

Kraus eased the door shut behind himself, and removing his cap, quietly set it and the key he'd had made on the side table. Pausing to nervously finger his brow, he again told himself that, yes, to invade her very privacy was essential.

There was no need to open the bedroom door. Curled up and deeply asleep, Marie-Hélène, current alias Isabelle Moncontre, lay in sunlight, the thin, lace-trimmed white chemise having crept up above her ass, presenting everything she owned. The right knee all but touched the pillow she had hugged and gripped between her legs until asleep.

The bed—the furniture—he knew was from her childhood. A matching, mirrored armoire gave her reflection and his own. The right breast was exposed and he saw at once that the line of it, and the throat and chin, hips, seat, thighs and even that of the ankles flowed elegantly just like that of the furniture, all being one and she belonging where he didn't and could never have.

The toenails and fingernails weren't painted. Her breath came easily, and when she stirred, he stiffened in alarm and decided that he didn't want this kept woman of the colonel's, this once-pampered child of the *petite noblesse* who could finger so many, to awaken just yet. The eyelids were dusky, the lashes long, but had she been crying? He felt the pillow and thought, yes. Dirksen didn't live with her. He "visited", which wasn't likely now that the hunt had begun in earnest with the Reichsführer's prompting. Too much was at stake.

The Standartenführer had gone to look at the flat at 37 rue des Grands-Augustins, wearing that suit again: the business-man from Düsseldorf, or whatever struck his fancy, but did this one need her loving? Was that why the tears?

Sighing, she turned over—stretched, murmured and hugged the pillows beneath her head, then relaxed, her left hand drifting to rest on that hip, and yes, it was exciting to see her like this, and yes, there would be that exquisite feeling of total mastery over another when, in complete surprise, she awoke.

There was a vial of scent on one of the two bedside tables and beneath a mushroom-shaped lamp by Lalique, the scent from Piver. Unscrewing the cap, he thought it fancy and wondered if she touched herself with it before having sex. He ought to get a camera in here. The *Banditen* would appreciate shots of her like this.

'All right,' he said. 'It's time.'

She sucked in a breath and stiffened. Eyes open now, she waited tensely, was still looking at the windows, not daring to take her gaze from them. 'Hans, is that you?'

Had the *Résistance* come for her so soon? wondered Marie-Hélène, her skin crawling at the thought until she heard herself saying, 'Please answer me.'

Abruptly she flipped over onto her back and saw him, but for several seconds couldn't find her voice. '*Salaud!*' she said and started to get up, started to cover herself only to feel the muzzle of the revolver, to hear him cock it, once on the half, and then on the full. A Lebel *Modèle d'ordonnance* 1873, still used by the French army in 1940 and now virtually untrace-able and one the *Résistance* found common enough. 'Look, I had to sleep, damn you. I was exhausted. I . . .' He let her say it. 'I would have come to you later.'

'But this,' he waved the gun to indicate the flat, 'is far more convenient and private, and far more pleasant.'

'If you kill me, Hans will know it wasn't the terrorists.'

Even under such stress, she was shrewd enough not to have called them *résistants*. 'Get up. Go and sit in that chair. Put on your high heels. The red ones.'

'My *what*?'

Kraus dragged round a chair, a fold-up thing that she had bought in one of the fleas in her darkest days. It had been in front of her dressing table. 'Here,' he said, and when he had found the shoes she liked to wear when out with the colonel dancing and not fingering *Banditen*, she reluctantly leaned over to put them on, her hair spilling forward as the straps of her chemise slid down over her upper arms.

'Now stay like that,' he said, 'until you've told me everything of what went on at that hospital.'

'I need to go to the toilet.'

'That can wait.'

'No, it can't. If you want to watch, please oblige yourself. It'll be a gift from my parted legs!'

She'd pay for that later, but once done, he again made her sit in that chair in exactly the same way, her hands extending to the floor to grasp the back of her right shoe and pull it on, and Marie-Hélène couldn't understand why he wanted this nor what it could mean for her.

'Begin,' he said, and she could feel him looking at her. He frequented several houses—Hans had told her this. They weren't always among those reserved for the SS or the Wehrmacht. Apparently he liked the unusual, the feeling of stark terror he could engender.

'The pencil belongs to the mayor of Abbeville. He and the boy traded for the journey. The mother knew nothing of it. *Nothing*, do you understand?'

'And the parachutist?'

'*Maudit salaud*, are you crazy? One has to use patience. If I'd asked, the Bellecour woman would only have become suspicious. She's not stupid. She's far sharper than she lets on.'

'Then she really is hiding something.'

'Oh, for sure, but me, I don't think it has *anything* to do with Bois Carré and whatever it is you people are hiding from the Allies.'

And enough for a death sentence for herself, were she not still so useful. 'What about the boy's father?'

Resignedly she sighed. 'He may once have lived at that house, but I don't really know. All she said was that he couldn't be living there now but that Martin, being lost like that and in a panic, must have felt he might be.'

'Does the father speak Deutsch?'

'How, please, would I know, eh? Since that is something I simply could not have asked.'

'Touch the floor with both hands.'

Kraus wouldn't hit her, she felt. To mark her up wasn't in the cards since Hans would see that he definitely did get sent to the Russian front. Rape was also not in the equation, not this time, maybe the next, eh? If so, measures would have to be taken and his body disposed of in the river. Lots of corpses had been dumped there over the centuries.

'What about that Wehrmacht lieutenant who was watching them in the Luxembourg?'

'For me, there was something familiar about him but I really don't know what and certainly didn't ask her or Martin, either. Perhaps it was the ears that stuck out, perhaps the eyes, the length of the face, its narrowness—ah, how the hell should I know? But the woman and her son were followed and they both knew this. That's why she tried to warn Vergès.'

'And that was exactly what I wanted her to do.'

'So that you could soften her up through constant terror?'

He'd lay the muzzle of the gun on the back of her neck, thought Kraus.

Marie-Hélène clamped her eyes shut and tearfully blurted, 'She thinks it all must have something to do with that woods and those things that are aligned with London but doesn't know what they're for or what's been going on there.'

Good. It would be the wire and the meat hook for both and this one too, once her usefulness was over. Now he'd finger her neck as Dirksen might and he'd pull her a little closer. 'And Vergès?' he asked. 'What does he think?'

'We didn't talk about the doctor. Had I done so, she would have seen that I knew too much. Hans is right, you know.

Patience is needed. Sometimes it can take weeks before we get what's necessary without having killed them, of course.'

'And time is something we don't have.'

She caught a breath. 'Did you telex the Reichsführer again?'

Kraus let her hold it, then asked, 'What do you think? Your "Hans" left me no choice.'

'Then I must tell you that just because he's well educated and from a good family doesn't mean he won't take the necessary steps to protect himself and all he holds dear, myself included.'

She was waiting for him to hit her, knowing that this little encounter of theirs would begin in earnest, but realizing too, that this was just not the moment. Patience was required. 'You won't be telling him, will you?'

The gun was being pressed harder against the nape of her neck, but now his other hand dug its fingers into her scalp, forcing her to blurt, 'I won't!'

'Good. Now what have you arranged?'

'The Bellecour woman and the boy are to meet my "*Résistance*" contact tonight.'

'Where?'

'I don't know yet. Look, can't I sit up? My arms are aching.'

'Just stay like that. Now *where*?'

It would do no good to argue. 'I have to work out what's best.'

'There's a *maison de passe* at 33 rue Racine, not far from the hotel. Tell her to meet you there and see that she takes a room in the attic.'

One of the cheap hotels that were used by *les filles des rues* and their clients, one of those walk-ins where no papers needed to be left and it was simply in-and-out by day or night, and hour by hour. *Une clandestine*, and no biweekly medical checkups either. For obvious reasons, the *Banditen* had grown rather fond of using them, so it had been a good choice, but what exactly did he now have in mind?

He was pulling her hair. 'All right, it's settled. I'll tell her to try to be there just after the curfew starts.'

Just after midnight. 'And who will you be getting to meet her, my lovely?'

'Me, I'm not your "lovely". Hans may want me to use one of the others.'

'You'll use yourself. Is that understood?'

He'd kill her if he could. 'Yes . . . Yes, of course.' But was it now over, this little encounter?

Trailing that left hand of his lightly over her shoulder, Kraus slid it down to take hold of a breast, she to blurt, 'Please, I won't say anything of your having come here like this. Just go. Leave me to myself. Hans won't hear of it, I promise.'

In answer, he pulled the chemise up until her head was smothered, he to leave her then. Hearing the door softly close, she silently begged Hans to take care of him.

Dirksen left the car next to the *quai* at the bend in the river just downstream of the Pont Neuf. It was cool in the shade of the chestnut trees and the view upriver of the bridge, the Île de la Cité, the jumbled roofs and spires of the Sainte-Chapelle and the Notre-Dame, was one of the finest in this city he had come to know so well. There were still a few barges, though most had been taken long ago for the invasion of England that had never happened, thanks to the RAF over London. No other automobiles were in sight, but here and there couples strolled—German servicemen with their latest, others simply wishing they'd had one of those but reduced to staring at the river or browsing the kiosks of the booksellers.

Beginning to stroll along the rue des Grands-Augustins, he went over things, but did have to ask himself, was it wise to have come alone? He was armed, for things in Paris and elsewhere had changed so much since the battle of Stalingrad had been lost last January, officially announced on 3 Febru-ary with three days of mourning. Now most carried a pistol even when at the Opéra, the Folies Bergère or all other such places, everywhere, of course. But he'd not feel his right jacket pocket. His was a Walther PKK 7.65 mm *Polizeipistole Kriminal*, a favourite of plainclothes detectives and Gestapo agents.

The house at number 37 had been built most probably

in the early eighteenth century and was beside a two-storey*
mansion, but its height and narrowness dwarfed this older
house, its newer storeys shooting up to run cheek by jowl
with the other houses, all facing the river.

Browsing the books of one of the kiosks, he settled on a
copy of Saint-Exupéry's *Night Flight* and counted out the necessary fifty francs not simply because a man carrying a book
appeared less threatening but also because Patagonia intrigued.
Argentina might offer a haven when the time came, for the
Soviets had just smashed through at Taganrog and were now
trying to cut off the Wehrmacht in the Crimea, and the Allies
had just taken Sicily. The Retaliatory Weapon Ones were the
Führer's newest card, but even with those, was it only a matter
of time until they all had to pack up and leave for home, and
what, then, were they to find? Rubble? Argentina looked far
better, but in the interim, there was the job.

He had a list of the present tenants and one of those from
the recent past, the Mademoiselle Angélique Bellecour having
lived at number 37 from 10 February 1936 until the exodus
of June 1940, and so much for the lies. A Leutnant Ernst Wilhelm Thiessen now occupied her flat, but that one had so
far eluded all enquiries. The Abwehr, perhaps, but the OKW's
intelligence and security service was invariably close about its
special agents and, of course, even speaking to any of them
now was *verboten*.

But had Thiessen been the one seen in the Jardin du Luxembourg, the one who had watched the woman and her son
from the other side of the pond while she had tried to tell
Vergès she was being followed?

The entrance to the house had been newly swept, the floor
and stairs polished. When he found the concierge in the cellars, the man was tinkering with the lift mechanism and took
his time to wipe the grease from his hands. 'It's old,' he said,
'so I have to keep an eye on it. Your countrymen are to come
and inspect the hoist, since the Herr Weber and his wife, they
are always complaining. This time, it's the brakes—those, they

---

* Three storeys in North America

say, are slipping and that only engineers from the Todt* will suffice. Herr Weber works for them while that wife of his, she . . .'

Giving that universal gesture of the French, the concierge said, 'Please, let us just go up the stairs and not use it. She listens all the time, so what can a poor man like myself do but agree?'

En route Dirksen said that he had heard a flat was to let, but a hand was tossed at the incredulity of this.

'Then do you have a Leutnant Thiessen?'

Had that been where he had come by the thought of a flat to let? '*C'est occupé* but that one comes and goes. Days, weeks even, we do not see him.'

'And today?'

It would be best to shrug. 'Alas, away again. Marseille, I think, or was it Toulon? Ah'—a hand was raised to stop himself—'it was Caen. Of this I am sure for he has said, you understand, that he would try to bring me a little Calvados. He's always bringing me things. A jar of honey from Saint-Saturnin in the Vaucluse. It was magnificent. Some Pont-l'Évêque from the *pays* d'Auge in Normandy. Superb! Once the *fois gras aux truffes* from Périgueux. None is better. Shrimp, too, from Honfleur.'

A well-travelled man. 'And he's away again?'

Had it needed to be asked? 'Today at noon, the train to Caen, as I have just said.'

And the Forbidden Zone and the Retaliatory One sites, was that it? 'Might I see his flat?'

It was serious. 'Ah, monsieur, that, it would not be possible, of course, and certainly not for such as myself to sanction.'

They had understood each other perfectly, thought Dirksen, as 500 francs in small bills found their way from wallet to pocket: the smaller the bill, the more appreciated, since fewer would take notice when used.

'And another,' said this one in the fine grey business suit

---

* The Todt Organization were building the Atlantic Wall

who spoke French almost as well as the Leutnant Thiessen, thought Hermé Lemoine. To have not understood or expected a little gift would have been but to arouse this one's suspicions further, hence that little extra, but was he of the SS? This he thought most likely, so there would now be further questions.

The flat was on the fourth floor, Lemoine gasping for breath and saying, 'Monsieur, please be sure to touch nothing. Take as long as you wish, of course, but put the lock back on when you leave.'

Herr Thiessen would not be so foolish as to have left anything incriminating, thought Lemoine, but it wasn't good, this one's having come here.

'The former tenant,' said Dirksen, 'was a Mademoiselle Bellecour, I believe.'

*Ah, merde alors.* 'Her . . . her things, they are in storage.'

'Where?'

May God have mercy on him. 'In the attic. Herr Thiessen, he has insisted that it would only be correct to treat her possessions with respect since she didn't return after the exodus. But for all we know, she could well be dead.' Quickly he crossed himself.

'And her son?'

'Her son? Ah! the boy. Now . . . now what was his name . . . ?'

'Martin.'

'Yes, yes, that was it. Mischief. Always running in the corridors and yelling. Certainly children, they must be tolerated, but that one . . . He flew model airplanes down the stairwells and from the windows, greatly disturbing the other tenants. Me, I had to smash several.'

And now are looking decidedly uncomfortable, thought Dirksen, since you've suddenly realized that she could well have been involved in something and is far from being dead. 'Where did she work?'

*Sacré nom de nom*, this one was not going to leave it. 'At a shop on the rue du Faubourg Saint-Honoré. *Le Magasin d'antiquités de Monsieur Georges Avisse et fils*. It's . . . it's near the *place* Vendôme, an excellent location, you understand, but the sons, they are no more. Both were killed in the Great War, the one in the summer of 1915, the other just two days before the Armistice.'

'How is it that you remember it so well?'

Could he *not* have seen this coming? wondered Lemoine. 'The Mademoiselle Bellecour often spoke of it in the past. Before the Defeat, Monsieur Avisse, he was very fond of her. She was like a daughter to him and he most certainly needed someone to fill such a vacuum, he having also lost the mother of those boys.'

'And is he still alive?'

That, too, should have been foreseen. '*Oui, mais certainement.*'

'*Bon.*'

# 4

In the late afternoon, those galleries in the Louvre that had had things put back in place by the Occupier after the Defeat were crowded with servicemen and other such "tourists", but here among the Grecian pottery and Etruscan antiquities there was relative calm. Here there were fewer common soldiers, more officers with their *Parisiennes*, the demeanour subdued, the comparative hush seeming to clash with the din.

Angélique knew Martin and she were still being followed. Even after more than two hours of going from gallery to gallery, they hadn't been able to lose them. Two Frenchmen, the one older, the other younger as before, but was there not also a third man or woman? It was uncanny, but she couldn't shake the feeling of being watched by someone so good at it, they would never discover who it was until too late. But here, even someone like that would tend to stand out, as if transfixed in glass of their own, and she was glad to have held off until now when the crowds had begun to thin.

'I once had a very real passion for these pieces, Martin,' she confessed.

Though she was trying to hide it, he knew she was distressed by the thought of a third follower. The tone of voice would easily give things like that away, but she continued anyway.

'By their very simplicity, *chéri*, such common household items radiate a gentle, uncontrived beauty. Amphorae like these were used to store wine, honey, grain or oil. Every day the people of those ancient times would go to vessels like these before preparing a meal.'

*Hydriae* were for storing water and for carrying it from the wells, and she told him the handles had different uses, the one for holding it securely when on the shoulder, the other two for lifting it. The terra-cotta would keep the water cool.

There had been no sign of Dirksen or Kraus, thought Angélique. Certainly there were SS, but that third follower was different anyway. Faceless, soulless, he or she wouldn't care that she was learning fast how to spot such people.

Always the one would walk on ahead, the other dropping back. There'd be a pause to light a cigarette that was then quickly tossed away. Did they not know that cigarettes were far too valuable, that almost everyone carried a tin for the collected butts, even from the pavement? Tobacco was so scarce, it was the most desirable of currencies. No one threw their butts away except the Occupier and his French friends, *les gestapistes français*, the gangsters and such who'd been let out of jail in the autumn of 1940 and put to work. Others too, of course. Lots of those. Too many.

And oh for sure, they would use the shaded shop windows as mirrors to watch Martin and herself. Instantly they would change direction if Martin and she were to head towards them. La Samaritaine, that largest of the big department stores, had been perfect. Though filled with Boches, like here, there had been lots of chances to pause and pretend to be interested in something, even with the shortages, but there, too, she had the feeling of a third watcher. And if they couldn't shake him or her in broad daylight like now, they'd never do it in the blackout, even after the curfew.

'We play a game, Martin, but every time we make a move, this one has anticipated us, when many times before, the other two haven't.'

Martin knew she wouldn't trust him to search on his own.

Everyone else here was taller. He could dart among them and not be seen. Tugging at her hand to remind her of this, she only shook her head and said again, 'It's too risky. Ah, *chéri*, I know you're good at spotting things, and yes, your running away last night has brought us a new friend, but . . .'

She couldn't bring herself to say she was afraid the *Résistance* were going to demand that she work for them. Coward, he said silently. My father is with those people. He's their leader, Angélique. That's why he didn't go to England!

'Dirksen or Kraus will find my things, Martin. They'll force Monsieur Lemoine to identify me. Oh for sure, he'll deny it at first. He's a good man, but even those can be persuaded in times like this. Then they'll march me to the shop where I used to work and Monsieur Georges, that dear man who would have had tears at the sight of me, will have far more with me in handcuffs.'

But is he even alive? she wondered, suddenly realizing that she didn't even know if the shop was still there. 'I'm a stranger to the city I loved. I've been made to feel an alien who has really done nothing to harm anyone.'

The wine jugs in their glass cases were called *oinochoeae*, and all of them had been decorated. Some of the figures were in black, others in black and brown . . .

'Martin . . . Martin, come and see these. They're my favourites,' she called out. 'These white *lecythi* from Attica are more than twenty-four hundred years old.'

She wasn't even looking at them. She was peering through the glass at the entrance to the gallery and beyond it to the stairwell.

'I first met your father here,' she said, and he knew, from the tone of her voice, that it was a very special place, but couldn't be angry with her for having stolen his father away from his mother.

From case to case they went, she searching for a better view of the entrance to that staircase. 'For hours afterwards,' she continued, 'your father and I talked about these, he sketching them from memory in the café we had gone to. The Tanagra figures, Martin, the white *lecythi* that were used for holding perfume. Me, I kept the sketches but wish I hadn't.'

She was moving swiftly now, and he had to hurry, but when they reached the stairwell, the person she was after had disappeared.

The others, the two French ones, caught up with them, only to stumble back in confusion as she yelled, 'JUST GO AWAY, EH? QUIT FOLLOWING ME!' and threw herself at them.

One collided with a lieutenant who had come to help. There was a scuffle and Martin heard it behind them as they ran, Angélique saying, 'Stay close. Don't let them find us.'

Down and down the stairs they went, knocking into people, being knocked aside until, darting through the turnstiles, they raced for a street, ran up it to turn a corner, then another and another, she finally trying to catch her breath while saying, 'Leave me to watch. Hurry! Wait round the next corner.'

They had lost them. Martin felt certain of it, but when Angélique rejoined him, still catching her breath, she wasn't grinning and didn't shake a fist towards that palace of things, just took him by the hand and held it to her chest to let him feel the racing of her heart. 'I saw the third one, Martin. I'm certain of it. He was wearing the uniform of a Wehrmacht lieutenant, as before, and he . . .'

She turned away to press her forehead against the stones of a building and stamp a foot. 'It can't be,' she swore. 'It can't, Martin.'

People were beginning to take notice and Martin was worried those two Frenchmen would catch up. Tugging at her dress, he wanted to cry out to her, Was it my father?

'His ears stuck out just like yours,' she said and wept. 'He only glanced at me. He knows who I am, Martin. He was looking at you, not at me when I first caught sight of him.'

But if it was, the Germans would shoot him, and in her mind's eye, she saw Anthony with his shirt collar open, no tie, gaunt and unshaven, the hands tied behind his back, the whitewashed post and wall spattered with the blood and brains of others.

'*Mon petit, je t'aime*,' she said, 'but it can't have been him. For three years now I've believed entirely that he was in England, for that is what we had agreed when he left us on that road.'

With the Messerschmitts coming over again. But now you're no longer so positive, are you? said Martin. Didn't I tell you time and again that he was still here in France, but you, you would never listen.

In the heat of the attic, flies buzzed against the grimy, cobwebbed windows. Lost in thought, Dirksen heard them as he had at the avenue Foch when discovering that little parachute. Angélique Bellecour had lied, and the string of her lies had included a son who could not possibly have lived in the flat below. There was absolutely nothing of the boy either down there or up here among the contents of the suitcases and wardrobe trunks he had opened. Not one pair of short pants or even a broken toy or balsawood glider. The concierge had also lied and would have to be thoroughly questioned. Vergès was still free. Marie-Hélène would see to him later, but after their arrests, the mayor of Abbeville and the doctor could perhaps be placed in the same cell or made to confront each other in one of the interrogation rooms. But what of the Leutnant Ernst Wilhelm Thiessen who had occupied the woman's flat since the Defeat of 1940? Was he the one who had been photographed watching her and Vergès in the Jardin du Luxembourg earlier? This could still not be stated with any surety.

The only photograph in the flat had been cracked and frayed at its edges, and clearly it had been carried into battle a good many times. It was of the wife and two children in the Reich. Thiessen's son had looked to be about twelve years old and very like the mother; the girl perhaps four years younger and not at all like her, but had she been like Thiessen?

To not have had any other photos wasn't just curious, since one would normally have had several. This one, too, had been found leaning unframed on the mantelpiece against the left of a pair of exquisite blue-and-white porcelain ginger jars, and it had appeared so out of place, he still had to wonder if it had been deliberately left there to throw them off.

Thiessen, if indeed that was his real name, hadn't just lived quietly when in Paris. He hadn't disturbed one stick of the Bellecour woman's furnishings. He had also, apparently, packed away her personal things with the utmost care. The lingerie had been folded perfectly, the blouses and sweaters too. Each skirt, suit, dress or pair of slacks had been carefully hung in one of the wardrobe trunks, her shoes cleaned and polished—had Thiessen revered her memory? If so, that could only mean they had known each other from before the war.

Such a conclusion could, perhaps, fit with an Abwehr identity, but being one of the special agents now didn't fit with the repeated experience of heavy fighting the photograph indicated. Perhaps he had been transferred to the Abwehr *after* the Blitzkrieg in the west, but if so, where then did that leave his knowing the woman *before* the Defeat? Something wasn't right.

In one corner of the salon downstairs there was a blue-and-white jardinière with a "kentia" palm. The restaurant La Vagengende had had just such palms and the Bellecour woman had noticed them—he was certain of this.

Beside that jardinière there had been a seventeenth-century *bergère* with *tabouret*, both in a plush red velvet. The first had faced into the salon, but from it, Thiessen could not possibly have seen the photograph, yet he seemed to have preferred that chair to all others or the sofa and the settee.

Two lovely sketches by Pierre-Joseph Redouté had hung on the nearby wall. Campion in one, camellias and narcissi in the other.

Here was a woman, then, who claimed to be a secretary and to have a son, but who had lived without the boy and had had a love of old things and passion for collecting. One of comparatively modest means, in the right place at the right time perhaps, hence her having worked for an antiques dealer on the rue du Faubourg Saint-Honoré. Had she travelled as a buyer for Monsieur Georges Avisse? Probably, but why had Thiessen changed nothing? Even the ashtray he had used while sitting in that chair had been taken into the kitchen to be left on the drainboard, spotless and ready for use on return.

At La Vagengende she had let it slip that her son's father

had been a designer of yachts. One room in the flat had been given over to an office, and it was there that he had felt the lieutenant might perhaps have left a little something out of place. The drafting table before the windows had been cleaned, the room too, but there *had* been all the paraphernalia of design— pencils, callipers, protractors and compasses. No sketches, no designs. Just everything else, including mechanical pencils, one of which Thiessen had obviously been examining only to have been called away by something.

It had lain in the centre of the drafting table and when he had picked it up, Dirksen recalled that the barrel hadn't been tightly closed.

Opening it, a single length of extra pencil lead had slid out. There had also been a packet of cigarette papers in the pocket of one of the lieutenant's jackets that had hung in one of the two armoires in the bedroom, the other having been emptied, its contents now up here. But had the woman and her "son" brought a message from Abbeville that had been written on cigarette paper and inserted into that pencil he had recovered for her Martin? Had Thiessen suggested the means?

Only Vergès or the mayor of Abbeville could give the answer. Thiessen's clothes had all borne prewar labels from shops in Cologne and Berlin. Sauer's, a sportswear shop on the Höhestrasse, also Karstadt's in Neukölln and Tietz und Wertheim in the Leipziggerstrasse. His comb-and-brush set had come from a shop in the Hauptverkehrsader Kölns.

If Thiessen was of the enemy, he had gone to great lengths to flesh out his background, even to providing himself with a wife and two children and to burning all of his designs for yachts. Had he killed or found the body of the real Thiessen during the Blitzkrieg and adopted that identity?

Turning back to the wardrobe trunks, Dirksen found her jewellery box and took it over to the window. Many of the pieces were very old, some even from the sixteenth century, he felt. Beautiful things picked up at estate sales in distress. Gold and emeralds, cameos and carnelians, exquisitely wrought earrings of wire gold in tiny baskets that were strung with seed pearls. A rosary of carved garnets, a necklace of topaz. Some diamonds. Rings, pendants, brooches and strands of pearls. Amethysts, aquamarines, jet and amber; a small fortune, undeclared and unregistered.

'She's full of surprises,' he muttered to himself, 'but so, too, is Thiessen. Why else would he not have sold these or at least sent them to his wife, some if not all of the clothing as well?'

Extra care had been taken to protect the three flacons the Bellecour woman had treasured, Thiessen having wrapped each perfume bottle in a slip or chemise and then in a small hand towel and placed them between layers of sweaters. One, in amber-coloured glass, was by Lalique from the turn of the century, and it showed in bas-relief Grecian, neoclassical figures of well-dressed noblewomen, highlighted by a russet patina.

Another was Roman, from the first or second century B.C., he felt. No more than seven centimetres in height, its bulbous little bottle fitted perfectly in the hand, the glass with opaline tones of a bluish-green iridescence over the original greenish amber, the piece extremely light and fragile.

The third was from the eighteenth century of the French nobility, of a deep cobalt-blue that had been enamelled in turquoise and gilt, and it bore the motif of an archer in a forest, a hare above him on the twist stopper.

Packing the flacons away, he then thought there would be little risk of their being missed. Wrapping all of them in but one chemise, he carefully tucked them into a jacket pocket. He would see what this Angélique Bellecour had to say of them, and then he would ask her about the boy's little parachute.

There was still no sign of the two who had been following them, nor of his father, thought Martin. Constantly, but only at the best of times, he had looked behind, while Angélique had taken care of the people ahead and across the street. He knew she was frantic, that she couldn't yet believe that it really *had* been his father. He wanted to say, He'll save us. He'll come only when it's safest, but she really was scared and, if not very careful, would give it all away by throwing herself into his father's arms as soon as they *did* meet.

Between the *place* du Palais-Royal and the *place* Vendôme, the rue du Faubourg Saint-Honoré was crowded. Here common soldiers mingled with generals; here the big boys of the butter-and-eggs business, the BOFs,* and the collabos bought expensive things for their girlfriends.

Distraught, hurrying along, she said, 'It's not safe for him, *chéri.* Our just catching a glimpse of him in that stairwell was enough.'

An open touring car went past, a Daimler full of high-ranking officers. A Rolls-Royce sedan was next, and then a Cadillac, a Ford, two Renaults and a Citroën—those that had been requisitioned or simply left behind in June of 1940, seemed to be here, with all the diesel fuel and gasoline needed, yet all vying with the bicycles and bicycle-taxis, the few *autobus aux gazogènes* and the lorries of the same or the horse-drawn wagons that were making deliveries.

The shop of M. Georges Avisse was up a little street and on the other side. The women were very stylish. Pillbox hats were all the rage, but so far what she had seen in the shop windows said that they weren't handling what they used to. Still, the market was insatiable; business couldn't have been better. And certainly it was one of the ways that money could be sent home, for at an exchange rate of twenty francs to the Reichskassenscheine mark, which had to be spent and couldn't be sent home, there were bargains galore, and to live like God in France had been on every Wehrmacht's lips before the war.

When they came to the corner of the rue d'Alger, they would have to cross over, but was it wise of them? 'I used to love it here,' she said. 'Life was very sophisticated, business very upscale, and maybe God in His infinite wisdom had been trying to tell me I ought never to have aspired to such, but . . .' She shrugged and found the will to faintly smile. 'But I grew with it, Martin. I changed. I discovered I had what so few others have. That sixth sense for what is really the most important thing to look for in a fine antique. Its timelessness. Monsieur Georges, he found this in me and let me travel all over the country for him. Orléans, Aix, Nice, Toulon, Reims, Lille . . . Ah!' she cried and pulled him back. 'I have just given

---

* *Beurre, oeufs et fromage*

you the list of places I told the Sturmbannführer Kraus we had lived in.'

Sickened by the thought, she refused to cross the street. They mingled with the crowd and she again searched for those who might be following. Every once in a while she would stop suddenly to tie a shoelace and glance back at the crowd or go into a shop only to look out its windows at the endless faces.

'It's safe, I think,' she finally said and let a breath escape. 'Come on. Let's get it over with.'

They crossed the street but as they neared the shop, Martin could feel her tensing up. Alarmed, he searched the faces, and when they reached it, she said, 'We can't. We mustn't.'

There was a bronze head in the window, with coiling, fighting snakes instead of hair. Under its gaze was a naked lady in smooth, white stone, and with a long-necked swan caught between her legs. Elsewhere, the painting of a grinning fisherman who had one tooth missing—why would anyone *want* to buy that? wondered Martin. An open jewel case was better, a drummer beating his drum, a vase, a bowl, a goblet . . .

'It's Saint-Louis crystal,' she said of this last, 'and at least one hundred and fifty years old. Do you remember that paperweight I had in my place? The citrine-coloured glass ball with all those strings of tiny bubbles as if rising in it? The one you wanted so much to smash, Martin. *That* was one of the very first paperweights ever made, but at the time, I couldn't understand how you felt, could I? It was thoughtless of me. I should have known.'

Urgently he tugged at her hand and nodded towards a man who then ducked away so that she couldn't see him. Panicking, she said, 'Come on. Hurry!'

They ran. When they reached the rue du Faubourg Saint-Honoré, she clambered into a parked *vélo-taxi*, didn't ask if she could, just dragged him after her and shouted to its driver, '*Allez! Vite, vite! Allez!*'

The man didn't budge. Astride his bike, a dead fag end clinging to his lower lip, he just grinned. '*Salaud!*' she shrilled. 'Why won't you help us?'

He had brought those two from the Louvre. He must have, she felt, but where were they now?

Another taxi pulled alongside, its driver shouting, 'Get in and I'll do what I can.'

The girl was young and brown-haired. Pumping hard, she got them moving and soon they were negotiating the traffic, she just concentrating on going as fast as possible. 'Hurry,' said Angélique. 'Please hurry.'

The two from the Louvre followed, one of them running alongside that taxi and shouting at others to get out of the way.

A truck madly honked, the girl scraping past. At the rue Saint-Roch, she kept right on, the traffic closing in behind with other cars, other trucks, some *gazogènes*, some not and lots of bicycles and bicycle taxis. Not signalling, she turned sharply to the left and cut across and through the oncoming traffic and into a narrow *passage*, but crying out, '*Ah merde!*' and very nearly hitting someone, the others still after them.

'Hang on,' she shouted, and turning left again, went up the rue des Pyramides. 'Are they still with us?'

'Yes!'

'*Ah, mon Dieu*, I knew it wasn't a good idea. Me, I had that feeling. My horoscope said I would be confronted with an "exercise of the conscience", and you're it!'

Making a U-turn in the middle of the avenue de l'Opéra, she took them right back through that *passage*.

'Now lose yourselves. Run, *mes amis*. Vanish!'

There was no time to say thanks, no time to even pay her. Taking Martin by the hand, Angélique ran and only when they reached the river, did they stop to ask, How was it that when most needed, someone had been there to help?

*It has to have been my father*, said Martin, carefully forming the words with his lips so that she could read what was said. *He's pretending to be a lieutenant in the German army. He comes and goes as he pleases and they don't even suspect who he really is*.

Anthony had spoken Deutsch almost as well as he had French. Travelling to the Reich before the war had been necessary to his business, but was he really here in France?

From the attic of the house at number 37, the staircase wrapped itself around the antiquated lift, and the wire cage far below could be seen with its greasy cables rising to the crown-block above.

Dirksen drew back. The concierge, his face pale and grizzled, strained to see up into the attic to discern what was taking the visitor so long. A very worried man, no doubt, but one who absolutely had to be convinced the only course open was to cooperate.

Secretly Lemoine would have realized this by now. He had lied about the boy. He must have known Thiessen would leave nothing incriminating in the flat and couldn't have noticed that pencil.

When he found the concierge in the tiny kitchen of his *loge*, the man's back was to him and Lemoine leapt in fright.

'Potatoes,' he managed of the *potage* he'd been preparing over a gas ring. 'The Frau Weber is most kind.'

'I'm sure she is,' said Dirksen. Most Parisians hadn't seen potatoes since the autumn of 1940. 'Sit, please. Let's talk a little.'

*Dieu le Père*, have mercy. 'Of course, monsieur . . . as you wish.'

Reluctantly he took off the apron, thought to offer a small glass of the Beaujolais the Leutnant Thiessen had given him, then thought better of it. This one across the table from him had to be from the avenue Foch.

'The boy,' began Dirksen. 'You see, I'm puzzled.'

'But . . . but why?' he shrugged and threw out his hands. 'That one was like any other.'

'His name?'

'Martin, as I mentioned earlier before you . . . you went up into the attic.'

For which no such permission had been given, but Lemoine was already sweating, so good, yes good. 'How long had he and his mother lived here?'

To tell the truth was one thing, to lie but another, and to find a compromise, well that would probably not work either. 'Not long. The boy, he came as a visitor. The woman was . . . Ah! she was the mistress of the boy's father. They left three days later to join the exodus and that . . . that is the last I've seen of any of them. I swear it, Captain.'

'Don't presume to address me by rank. You'll only make a mistake.'

A colonel, then, a Standartenführer. 'Monsieur, I'm but a concierge who does not question things he should not question.'

Even though, right after the Defeat they'd all been told to watch and report just such things, and others too. 'Isn't it that these days one is required to question things that don't appear to be correct?'

'*Ah oui, bien sûr,* but you see Herr Thiessen, he is above reproach. Never have I had the slightest concern. Kind, courteous—the epitome of correctness. Like it used to be just after the Defeat, you understand, when all of you people . . . ah, forgive me, please. When *les Allemands* behaved correctly towards us French.'

But now, and for the past two years, we've had the arrests in the middle of the night, the *Avis* notices posted: so and so executed for such and such. Dirksen could see Lemoine thinking this. 'Look, I'll be frank with you. There are a few lines of enquiry my superiors want me to pursue. Men like the lieutenant travel a good deal as you've said, but we're not in the least interested in him, so please don't concern yourself unduly. It's someone whom we have come to feel might be watching him.'

The shrug should be automatic, the gesture open-handed. 'Ah, then, so that's it. Now I begin to understand.'

Reaching for his glass, Lemoine brought it to his lips, only to hesitate and set it aside. 'Can I offer you a little, perhaps?' he asked.

'With pleasure.'

They shared the wine and a packet of cigarettes Dirksen had lain on the table between them. Thiessen lived very quietly. When at home, he would listen to his wireless in the evenings, always the news broadcasts from Berlin and especially the Führer's speeches, then perhaps the symphony. Among the newspapers he regularly read were *Pariser Zeitung*, the German's Paris one, but also the *Völkischer Beobachter*, that of the Nazi Party, then too, *Der Angriff*. *Le Matin* and *Paris-Soir* were the local favourites of his. Invariably he ate at one of two places, so was a creature of habit perhaps. Either Laperouse, which was just up the street and was very good, or a little place on the rue du Cherche-Midi, not far from the boulevard Raspail. *L'Ermitage du père spirituel aveugle-né*, that of the priest who was blind at birth.

'He always says it's very good and quite inexpensive and that it allows him to mingle with the day-to-day so as to listen in and hear what their concerns are.'

Had Lemoine deliberately said this, it being close to the Hôtel Lutétia, the headquarters of Abwehr West, and with the Prison de la Cherche-Midi just down the street of that name?

'La Vagendende, he says, is very restful on a Tuesday when the crowd, it is not so large, and that he wishes he could have taken his wife there at least once. Prunier's for the sea-food, yes? And the Taverne Lyonnaise for its exceptional cuisine. Once, I think, Le Foyot. It's on the rue de Tournon and much frequented still, I understand, by the *grande bourgeoisie* and others, of course. He had an excellent bottle of the Château Lafite there, the 1875, a treasure to be sure.'

It was a restaurant very near to the house of Dr. Albert-Émile Vergès. Marie-Hélène would have to be warned of it, and certainly the concierge had given enough places to rule out Thiessen's being a creature of habit! 'Does anyone ever visit him here?'

Lemoine shook his head a little too rapidly but one must not force things. 'Not even a woman?' asked Dirksen, smiling at the thought.

Again the concierge shook his head. 'Not here. Perhaps elsewhere. This I wouldn't know, of course, because one doesn't ask such things of a tenant, but I have to tell you that he is very much the family man and has spoken often of the wife and children.'

'Back home in . . . ?'

Ah, damn this one! 'In Cologne, I believe, but in the suburbs, I think.'

Which made sense since so much of the heart of that beautiful old city had been destroyed by the RAF incendiary raids of a year ago last May. Hundreds killed, thousands horribly mutilated, tens of thousands made suddenly homeless.

Troubles still in locating loved ones. The glow from the fire-storms had been visible for over two hundred kilometres.

He would ask of the address. 'Perhaps a letter the lieutenant gave you for the post? Perhaps one that had arrived? Surely there must have been something.'

This one was not going to leave it, so a little would have to be offered. 'The Marienburg, I think. Yes, yes, I remember now. He did ask me to post some letters. All three were to an address in that place. One to the wife, one to the son, and the last to the daughter so that each would know he was thinking of them and not feel left out.'

'When?'

'Last week, on Tuesday. Herr Thiessen had just got in from Lyon and had to leave that evening for Berlin.'

'Berlin?'

'Yes, yes, of course. Monsieur, is there some reason Herr Thiessen should not go to Berlin?'

Lemoine having tripped himself, there would be no smile this time. 'Then why wouldn't he have taken the letters with him? It's that simple, isn't it? From here it could take days—weeks even, what with the railways being constantly bombed. From Berlin . . .'

'Ah! of course, that would have been much easier and wiser, monsieur, but you see, the son wanted the postage stamps. Some new ones have just been issued.'

'Oh, and did he now?'

'As did the daughter. The two compete, of course, for the attentions of their father. Most do. Mine certainly did.'

Quickly crossing himself and kissing his fingers, Lemoine said, 'The boy, the Ardennes. He was badly wounded and didn't make it.'

Abruptly he drained the last of the wine into this one's glass who, seemingly satisfied now, lamely asked if there was anything else. And then, 'Such as a place where the lieutenant might perhaps be watched by others yet remain unaware of it?'

This one simply wasn't going to leave it, so one must go carefully, and to each fabrication, the elements of truth to firm up the lie. 'The Bois de Boulogne. He has often said that he liked to go there to take walks, that it reminded him of home.'

'And are you sure of this?'

'Certainly.'

But had Thiessen been watching Marie-Hélène on her walks? wondered Dirksen, alarmed at the thought. 'What about the Jardin du Luxembourg?'

It would be best to shrug and shake the head and say, 'A possibility, for sure, but he hasn't mentioned it. Not to me.'

'Then why was he there when this photograph was taken?'

*Ah, nom de Dieu*, what the hell was this? 'Me, I don't know, monsieur. How could I?'

'Before I went to look at his flat, you said he had left for Caen today.'

'Yes, he did.'

'But when, exactly, was it?'

Nothing but the truth would suffice. 'Early, the one suitcase. The train was at seven,' he said.

Dirksen tossed the photo onto the table and threw up his hands in despair. 'Then how was it possible for that to have been taken in the Luxembourg this morning at about ten?'

A shrug would have to be given, but would it be the post, the little white square and the blindfold?

'You'd best help us,' said Dirksen. 'It's that or the Santé. We know he watched the Bellecour woman and her "son" but didn't make contact with them.'

All along the quai des Orfèvres there were pollarded plane trees and from here, from the Île de la Cité where others strolled, Angélique and Martin could see across the left branch of the Seine to the house at number 37, but it only brought a sadness that was unbearable.

'We can't go near it, *petit*. There are just too many working for the SS and the Gestapo, and even if I really did see your father, how could we possibly prevent him from returning there?'

They hadn't been caught yet but it was only a matter of time until they were picked up and taken back to the hotel Herr Dirksen had found for them, the Trianon Palace. And anyway, they had to go back there so as to be ready for the meeting Isabelle Moncontre was arranging later on.

Across the river, the *bouquinistes*＊ were beginning to take down the strings of artists' prints and old photographs that were tacked to long sticks beside each faded green stall. Now here, now there, last purchases were being made. A German sailor and his girlfriend of the moment were kissing on the lower *quai*. A car drove slowly by the house and Angélique had to wonder about it, as did others, for there were so few cars, but then it was gone and there was only the house.

She thought of her life with Anthony, of coming home from the shop or from a buying trip to find him there. He had had such a gentle smile and manner. Intuitively they had both understood that life without each other would have been impossible, but now was it all to turn against them? And how, please, could that same gentle nature have survived and, yes, turned himself into a *résistant*?

A dark blue Peugeot two-door crept along the *quai* over there, but going in the wrong direction. Did the idiots not care if they were seen by others? Were they *that* confident of their lawlessness?

Two Gestapo plainclothes got out—Hey, let's call them nothing else, she thought. It's simpler just to bulk them under that one label.

Immediately the car drove off, as one of the men went to the left, the other to the right. All too soon, both were hard to find. Only Isabelle Moncontre could help them now. If Anthony really did live in that house under a *nom de guerre*, only that chance meeting of Martin's with the woman could save them. But wasn't it odd that fate should intervene? The cards? she wondered. A hand that the enemy knew nothing of.

They started out. They continued right past the Préfecture de police and when they reached the *passerelle* Saint-Louis, that ugly, narrow footbridge of iron girders that had been thrown up to replace the bridge that had been rammed by a barge in 1939, they crossed over.

---

＊ Secondhand book-sellers

From the Île Saint-Louis, she realizing sadly that they had not even paused for a glimpse of the Notre-Dame or the fine old houses, they went along to the pont de la Tournelle. They could come to that meeting prepared by seeing if Dr. Vergès had been arrested, or they could return to their hotel like good citizens and deny they had done anything wrong, that it had all been a little misunderstanding.

And if he hasn't? she asked. Then those types, they are watching everyone in the hope of catching us all.

Wear nothing distinctive. Try to appear ordinary. Don't avoid the crowds. Look as if you're going where you always have. Pass the eyes swiftly over the quarry. Don't ever let him see you watching him. Remember, it's business. Think of it only as that and always look for others. Those are the ones who most count.

Marie-Hélène de Fleury squeezed the sponge above her head and shut her eyes as the ice water coursed over her. 'Ahh!' she gasped. '*Salaud!*' she cursed Kraus who had left her flat hours ago. Hours of exhaustion and of a sleep so fitful it had been crowded with nightmares. 'Me, I'll see that you pay for your few moments of pleasure,' she seethed.

She would do no such thing, was but a servant of the SS. Even Hans, though he might wish it differently, would see her hanged with piano wire if she killed Kraus.

Shoving the sponge deeply into the bucket she had filled with ice and water, she squeezed it hard over herself and gasped again. 'It's enough,' she said, 'but you'd better, eh?'

And lifting the bucket, stood in the tub forcing herself to watch in the mirror as that sheet of water and broken ice split her hair, she fighting to keep her eyes open and her lips from parting in the scream that must never come.

Water shot over her breasts to drain and tug at the little beard between her legs, the bucket finally coming to rest on the white wicker table she had always kept beside the bath. A table just like we used to have at home, she said to herself. Bath oils, several bars of soap, some in soft shades of blue, yellow or rose, and all scented. The flat of a pumice stone too, and nail clippers, and the file—ah! everything a girl could ever want to make herself presentable, especially when in the buff.

Something would have to be done about Kraus. She couldn't afford to leave it. Hans would have to be forced into doing something other than another light threat before it was too late for the both of them.

At 6.47 p.m. she was outside the southwest gate of the Luxembourg, briefly catching a read from Dumas's *The Count of Monte Cristo* and facing the corner of the rue d'Assas and the rue Vavin. Everyone read such things these days—anything to take one away from the reality of the present and let a person dream of what it once must have been. A Paris and France of heroes, not one of nightmares like she'd had this afternoon.

When Vergès came out of the building, she put the book in her handbag and said to herself, Straighten your skirt. Turn your back to him. Lick a fingertip and rub a mark off your left shoe. Prepare yourself. You're going to get the one he's about to meet. No one else will be in on this today. He's to be left completely free of them, except for yourself because he has to believe that he's alone and safe.

*Ah merde*, it was the Bellecour woman and her son. She mustn't let them see her, must mingle with the crowd, cross the rue d'Assas and stick close to someone, give the image of a happy couple or a group if possible and blend so well, she could just keep going and not be noticed.

Kraus shrieked, 'WHAT DO YOU MEAN, YOU "LOST" THE WOMAN AND HER SON?'

'They got away. They had help.'

'HELP?' he shrieked again, setting the corridors to echoing. Livid, he gave the Frenchman the back of a hand. Once, twice—raking the cheeks with his SS ring.

Blood welled up in long lines down the bastard's cheeks, Kraus smashing him hard in the face and breaking his nose, the man stumbling back against the filing cabinets and knocking things to the floor.

He tried to get up, knew he mustn't protect himself, that to do so would only mean . . .

'Kraus? *Ach du lieber Gott*, calm down! Busting up a good man isn't going to help.' Dirksen had come into the office.

'Good? He lost them!'

'So I gather, but now look what you've done.'

Gently Dirksen took hold of the Frenchman by the chin. 'An ice pack, Victor, and some cognac. At least three glasses. This isn't going to go away for a month or so and we can't have the terrorists fingering you because you're now too easy to recognize. Go and lie down in my office. Don't worry. I'll take care of everything. You'll find the cognac in the cabinet. If you want a cigarette, take some from the box near the sofa. They're American from a downed bomber pilot who didn't want to give them up. Luckys, but a little mild. Here, I'll ring for the doctor. Don't worry, you did what you could and I know that.'

Droplets of blood spattered the floor as Victor Laurent said, 'The . . . the woman did have help, Colonel. There was a girl with a *vélo-taxi*, *Le Plaisir du Roi Soleil*, licence 5365 RP6.' He turned aside to catch a breath and try to wipe his nose with the back of his hand. 'Two old fauteuils in faded wine-red fabric, the bicycle a man's and black, the girl a brunette with shoulder-length hair pinned at the sides with barrettes and curled at the ends. *Ah merde, excusez-moi un moment.*'

He turned aside again to cough blood and spit in his hand, having no handkerchief. 'About twenty years old. Intelligent. Very quick-thinking. Knows the Tuileries well and in particular the area around the *Église de Saint-Roch*. Has good, strong legs, that sense of daring and the courage to go with it. Once committed, that one is very determined.' He shut his eyes and swallowed.

'A university student?' asked Dirksen.

The blood still flowed freely, but Laurent tried to ignore it. '*Peut-être.* A chequered light beige shirt, a man's, a brother's quite possibly.' Again he dabbed at his nose with the back of that hand. 'Brown trousers—those, too, for they were bunched in at the waist by a man's belt. White ankle socks, brown leather pumps. Height 162 centimetres; weight, about

55 kilos; bust medium but not pronounced. Held tightly in, perhaps, so as not to be too noticeable.'

'Eyes?'

Kraus was listening closely, so good, yes good! 'Brown, I think, but can't be positive, of course, since it all happened very fast. The face a medium oval, the eyes deeply set. Ah! there was one other thing, Colonel. There were two bunches of red chrysanthemums sticking out of short lengths of pipe, one on either side of the fauteuils.'

'A Communist?'

Which would have fitted with her being a student, the politics indicating more definitely a *réseau*. 'The red flag, I think, to both torment and thumb her nose at us but she didn't have a Cross of Lorraine at her throat.'

Dirksen nodded and patted the man's shoulder. 'Look, Victor, I'm sorry this little "accident" had to happen. Maybe I can still use you now and then until things have healed. In the interim, can we say twenty thousand francs?' Would that wound Kraus enough, he wondered, or must it be fifty? 'Let's make it five thousand Reichskassencheine. The Sturmbannführer Kraus will understand that it has to be deducted from his pay book.'

One hundred thousand francs and an insult, if ever there was one, to an SS officer. Kraus looked as if ready to draw his gun.

'Standartenführer . . .' began that one, only to clam up as the patient was escorted into the corridor by Dirksen with more kind words. Only when that door had been closed, did Kraus start in with, 'Now I'll never be able to tell that bastard to do anything! Always he and his kind will ridicule me, Standartenführer. Me, your right hand!'

'Not anymore, so let this be a lesson. There will be no beatings, no smashing people up like that one or Doumier. I want us to break the *réseau de soie bleue*, and to do so, Major, we need to take all of them, which reminds me, you've not been putting the squeeze on Marie-Hélène have you? Not after I had already mentioned the possibility. She hasn't called in.'

Kraus knew he would have to empty his eyes of all feeling. 'You've been busy elsewhere, Colonel. Perhaps . . .'

Men like Kraus would never learn. 'Beware of the precipices, Major. Watch for the screes that hang up there as if waiting only for the avalanche to come. Marie-Hélène was to have left word for me when she awakened this afternoon. We had agreed.'

The *Schlampe* had neglected to do so in order to warn this lover of hers but nothing could be said of that. 'Would you like me to send a car around to her flat?'

'Your insolence won't be forgotten, Kraus. You've been telexing Berlin again. All correspondence concerning the Sonderkommando Vergeltungswaffen Eins must be cleared by myself and bear my signature and stamp. Refusal to do so will result in your immediate dismissal.'

Glancing at his wristwatch, Dirksen decided that, since it was now 7.37 p.m., if all had gone well, she should have spotted the Leutnant Thiessen or one of his people making contact with Vergès if, indeed, the lieutenant was the father of Martin Bellecour and a terrorist. But it wasn't like her not to have called in.

'Leave her alone, Kraus. Don't meddle and mess it up, or you'll have to deal with Berlin as well as myself. She's far too valuable and we desperately need her on this one.'

Dr. Albert-Émile Vergès was apparently much better versed in things than before. Soon aware that the Bellecour woman and her son were following but not trying to catch up with him, he had crossed and recrossed the rue d'Assas to be certain there was no one other than them, and then . . . yes, then, had lost them so easily they stood out among the pedestrians, totally mystified as to where he had gone.

Afraid, perhaps, the Bellecour woman swept her eyes urgently across the shop fronts. He had ducked between two *gazogène* lorries. She should be wondering if he had gone into a narrow courtyard and up it or simply remained hidden behind its door. Had he recrossed the street again?

The woman tried a shop, another and another, each time leaving the boy to watch the street until, at last, she had to shrug and give up. Taking the boy by the hand, they were soon lost to sight in the direction of the rue Vavin and, opposite it, that entrance to the Jardin du Luxembourg.

All well and good, and *grâce à Dieu* for small mercies, thought Marie-Hélène. Now it was only the doctor, herself and his contact, but could she be absolutely certain of this? One might never know.

Waiting near the doorway to a bakery, she stood in a queue that was still growing and whose grumbling was constant. Just as she was about to take her turn to enter the shop, Vergès stepped out from the cellar he must have disappeared into, and immediately he began to search the street, of course.

Satisfied that he was now alone, he continued on up the rue d'Assas. He didn't carry his umbrella or wear the grey trench coat and fedora this time. Indeed, he had left his briefcase behind in the surgery, a worry to be sure, for any such difference from habit had to be questioned.

The eyeglasses and the grey-black goatee helped in following him, so too his being of less than medium height, but it was his step she noted most. That left heel no longer came down harder than the right, and she had to ask herself, How could this be? A man with a slight limp, now doesn't have one. A man, who last evening, appeared totally new to the clandestine world is now apparently thoroughly accustomed to it.

He must have removed the wedges of cardboard that had given him the limp. This made her hesitate even as she, too, threaded her way through the browsers, the Germans, the people going home from work, the long and disgruntled queues for this and that, for damned near everything.

When he took a place at the end of the lineup for a *boucherie*, she knew things were about to happen. Everything was utterly ordinary. Perfect for contact, but was he being watched by others, was she herself?

They were very close to the corner of the rue Vaugirard. Vergès seemed not to mind the long lineup. No longer did he bother to look behind or try to use the windows as mirrors. Was he satisfied she was behind him—was that it? she asked and told herself not to think like that. She mustn't ever be afraid.

He waited. Sandwiched between two women behind him, she also waited, and certainly she could touch him if so inclined but . . .

A girl came towards them, smiling, full of the *joie de vivre* so seldom seen these days. A student. A brunette. About nineteen or twenty. No lipstick, no rouge—none of such. Of medium height, too, and with nice shoulders and a very purposeful walk, a bundle of books under an arm and secured by an old leather belt, a briefcase too and large, deep brown eyes that were so clear . . .

'Have you a light?' this student asked of Vergès, he to fumble in a pocket, she finding her only cigarette and thanking him.

There was no way he could have slipped her the message that had been brought from Abbeville by Angélique Bellecour and Martin, not yet, but then this girl said, 'Hey, monsieur, I'll give you fifty francs if you let me take your place. I'm in a hurry.'

The code words? Marie-Hélène felt her heart racing. *Fifty and the message*, was that the way it was to be?

'You can have mine,' said the woman ahead of her, the girl smiling and shaking her head and saying, 'His place is better. Well, monsieur?' she then asked of Vergès. 'Do we have a deal?'

Others . . . are others watching? wondered Marie-Hélène.

Vergès held the girl's books while she found the money. A coin was dropped. Another and another. '*Ah merde*,' cried the student and managed to pick them up, she now drawing in repeatedly on that cigarette, the coins of zinc and with the dead flat ring of the Occupation.

Vergès departed. He didn't even waste a moment to glance along the lineup, was too much in a hurry, so much so, Marie-Hélène was convinced the message must have been handed over, but ah, there was no way of her knowing, short of having them both arrested and the books and everything else torn apart, and *that* was just not possible at the moment.

As the girl smoked the cigarette, the line moved slowly ahead, but again there was the grumbling, the outbursts of bitchiness especially against the line jumpers who could *buy* a place for themselves.

The woman ahead jerked her head that way and said, 'A "student" eh, who has the cash for cigarettes? That one must earn her keep on her back! If that's what they teach them, they should arrest the professors for leading such into the life!'

'Me, I'm studying to be a doctor, madame,' said the girl, 'so that I and the others with me can cut up the corpses of such as yourself. We use them for study.'

'*Putain, friponne, gamine et cobra!* How dare you address me, the mother of ten children, in such a way? Here, you need to see the medals, eh? Medals such as yourself will never have due to *la syphilis!*'

And now the riot, was that it? wondered Marie-Hélène, panicking at the thought of being caught up in the tussle and knifed, yes, *knifed*!

Shoving the woman hard, the girl bolted from the line, leaving her to fall back only to be pushed ahead and into that mother of ten children. 'All right, all right!' she cried. 'Enough. You can have my place too.'

'Bitches,' swore the girl, laughing as she stepped from a shop to catch Marie-Hélène unexpectedly as the woman hurried past. 'The butcher will hang out the flag of emptiness in any case, so what was the use? But me, I'm sorry you felt you had to give up your place.'

Had there been no one else watching them, or was she now to be led into a trap? wondered Marie-Hélène. 'I hate those lineups,' she said.

'Everyone does. Me, too. It's undignified. They make no choices and reduce us to the lowest common denominator.'

Laughing at life as only the young can, she shrugged and, tossing a glance to the rooftops, said ruefully, 'It was my last fifty, but her expression, it was worth it. A whore, am I? A rascal, an urchin, a cobra, no less? She was jealous of my freedom, poor thing. Ten children and only medals from Pétain? Future soldier fodder, but imagine having to feed so many.'

'Are you really a medical student?'

'Me? Of course not. I'm far too squeamish. For me it's

mathematics and chemistry, a little history if it's not too boring, and politics, of course, for you can almost eat that sometimes. I wanted to tell her I could make explosives, but thought I'd better not.'

'And can you?'

The girl threw her a curious look, then said, 'Ah! I'd have to say no, wouldn't I since even the paving stones have ears. Now you must excuse me, mademoiselle . . .'

'Moncontre. Isabelle.'

'I have to go into the bookshop of Monsieur Maurice Patouillard to smile bravely and beg another fifty in exchange for my books, which he will, if fortune finds me, be only too willing to sell back to me—at a small profit, of course.'

'I was headed that way myself. Dumas . . . I've been reading my way through his books, refreshing myself.'

The shop was small, the shelves to the ceiling and crowded, Patouillard gruff, stooped, a giant of sixty with the filthy remains of an uncaringly dead *Gauloise bleue* clinging to the thickness of his lower lip. The glasses had been mended years ago with surgical tape. He grumbled. Disparagingly he thumbed the books, the girl humming and getting more and more restless until . . . 'Thirty. I can go no higher.'

'Fifty. Is it that they have aged so much in a week?' she taunted.

'Twenty. I haven't time to argue. I'm reading Sartre.'

'Thirty. I accept thirty, no less,' *Salaud*, she must have cursed him under her breath, she leaning over the table of secondhand books that separated her from him. A pretty girl with a good figure the other customers, all men and one a priest, had taken note of, thought Marie Hélène.

A flash of innocence was given, a last attempt. 'Please, Monsieur Patouillard, I know you're a good man. My little *chèque d'allocation alimentaire* comes in at the end of the month so that I can eat, isn't that so? But I will bring it straight to you and together we can take it to the Crédit Commercial de France at 103 ave' des Champs-Élysées. No other. My father, he wouldn't change banks even if God directed him to avoid one that was in danger of collapse. He trusts no one but himself on all such matters, the pope only on the subject of abortion and loose women.'

Patouillard blew out his cheeks in exasperation as he looked to others for sympathy and finally said, '"His Holiness", she says, and is he a friend of the family, perhaps?'

'Ah, how could you doubt my word?'

He shrugged. 'It's not possible for one to doubt God's creatures, Mademoiselle Rougement.'

'Yvette, please. You must call me that. It's like we're old friends, isn't that so?'

'Okay. Fifty it is, and with interest. One hundred when your allowance arrives. Don't forget it.'

'My silver, my money, my cash, how could I?'

Names and dates so readily given bespoke an innocence that was reassuring, for no member of a *réseau* would have given them away like that, but when this Yvette Rougement found herself alone and without her new companion, she crossed the rue d'Assas, paused to tie a shoelace that didn't need it, and continued on into the Institut Catholique, the country's most esteemed centre of teaching. Physics, chemistry, biology, et cetera, even including a small museum of antiquities that had been gathered from archaeological digs in the Holy Land. She went along a corridor, her steps heard softly, took a flight of stairs, went along again and came down another to leave the buildings and cross the garden to that lovely old building of the Carmelite seminary. A former prison—yes, yes, in 1790, thought Marie-Hélène. A placard gave the Latin *Hic ceciderunt*[*] marking one of the sites of the September 1792 massacre when 120 priests had been murdered. Reminders . . . but were they those of things to come? Was that girl now leading her on? Were those details and names so readily given in the shop simply to calm her fears and draw her in?

'*Ah merde*, I can't be thinking this.'

Passing through the seminary, acknowledging the stern reproofs of the blessed fathers, Yvette Rougement ducked out a front door and onto the rue de Vaugirard, then she doubled

---

[*] Here they fell.

back twice and crossed over to the Palais du Luxembourg. Screened by passersby, she watched the street until satisfied that she hadn't been followed.

There could be no one else, then, watching her back. *Ah, grâce à Dieu*, thought Marie-Hélène, the girl must have accepted her presence in the bookshop as totally unthreatening.

Dodging through the traffic, the girl ran across the rue de Vaugirard. On the rue Férou she found a house among several that dated from at least the second half of the eighteenth century.

Two sphinxes atop the pillars of the entrance to number 6 gave immutable and uncaring gazes. She had an attic room and one could hear her taking the lift up, which meant there were Germans living here, she to then climb the last of the stairs. But if she really was Vergès's contact, and everything so far had pointed to this, she would be well versed in the routes across the roofs, which was something that would have to be kept in mind. But for now, it was enough. Hans would be very pleased. Being patient with Vergès had paid off handsomely. Unsuspecting, this girl would be no trouble.

# 5

At 10.05 p.m., 8.05 the old, the light was still lovely in the Bois de Boulogne, making the leaves of the acacias greener, the cedars darker, but it gave far too many shadows, creating a fresh uneasiness. Still glinting from the lower lake, it emphasized the wavelets that rocked the little boats at their moorings.

As always, Marie-Hélène had come to wash away the thought of what she had just done, and yes, she hadn't yet told Hans or anyone else the names of those she had discovered. After leaving that student, she had come straight from the Luxembourg, had got off the métro at the Porte Maillot, hadn't even gone home. Had sought the Bois as a child the comfort of its mother's breast. Had had no inkling of any trouble here.

But now? she asked and told herself to keep walking. Now she had to ask, had her earlier fears been correct? Had Vergès been backed up by someone else—the leader of that *réseau*, the lieutenant from the Jardin du Luxembourg? Had he led her along so as to single her out and positively identify her? Had the presence of Angélique Bellecour and her son this afternoon distracted her?

Though scattered and few, there were still others here. Distance could be kept, of course, the tree trunks offering cover, but was she really being watched from behind as instinct had kept telling her? *Nom de Dieu*, why couldn't things be as she had felt so strongly when first getting off the métro? Elation then. Triumph, that warm glow inside, she knowing how good she had been.

She had wanted so much to come here, to sit for even a few moments on the grass beside this little lake, had wanted to catch the last of the sunlight and to hear the nightingales and remember the villa near Nogent-sur-Seine. But would the one who led this *réseau* have really sacrificed that student Yvette Rougement so easily? *And* the book-seller, Patouillard, what of him, if he wasn't an informant for the Boches? And, Vergès, too, included in the sacrifice just to find out who the avenue Foch had been using to uncover such secrets?

Yvette Rougement had felt her okay, but had that lieuten-ant followed her just to be certain?

When Kraus found her, Marie-Hélène was sitting beside the lower and larger of the lakes, arms wrapped about her knees, chin resting on them. She didn't say, You fool, didn't even look up, just said scathingly, 'Idiot, I'm being watched!'

There was a Swiss chalet on the larger of the two islands, it having been brought piece by piece from Berne and reas-sembled during the Second Empire when Napoléon III had given the Ville de Paris all of its green spaces.

'Where is he, then?' asked Kraus, his gaze still on the cha-let where there was a café-restaurant that would now have closed for the day.

'Please just trust my instincts.'

Still she wouldn't look up at him, was playing the pestered *Parisienne* who had no use for the Occupier, and he had to laugh at how instinctively she could drop right into what-ever role was necessary, but there couldn't be anyone watch-ing them. It was simply a case of nerves. Always after a job, she would break apart like this until she had calmed herself. 'You didn't tell me you had agreed to telephone Dirksen this afternoon before you went after Vergès.'

Turning her back on him, she said, 'I didn't say I would.

*There*, does that satisfy you?' This wasn't true—she had agreed
to telephone Hans but . . .

'Then the colonel lied to me, is this what you're saying?'

One SS officer lying to another. Things would go on and
on, and perhaps she *should* tell him everything but couldn't
bring herself to do so. 'Have you still not given a thought
to my security? Continue, Major, and you will get nothing
because me, I'll be dead.'

'Dirksen lied to me so as to find out if I had been putting
the squeeze on you.'

Kraus didn't have a mind for this kind of work. Shrugging
tightly, she said, 'It's still Standartenführer Dirksen, isn't it?
He's still heading up the Sonderkommando, isn't he?'

'But you and I had an agreement.'

It was no use. 'All right, I did tell Hans I'd call before I went
after the doctor and the others, and then afterwards too, but
there simply wasn't time. I had an unexpected and unwel-
come visitor, yourself, and then I overslept. The emotions,
yes? They were completely burned out.'

'And now?' he asked so quietly she stiffened, and he knew
she'd be imagining the little smile he was going to give.

'Now I have to be quiet. I have to think out very carefully
how best to deal with the Bellecour woman tonight. We really
are being watched, so please don't make it any worse. Curse
me, if you like, but walk off abruptly before it's too late.'

'Can you identify Vergès's contact?'

Marie-Hélène felt herself cringe. Wanting to shriek at him,
she said, 'Yes, but the names stay with me until I'm certain
that I know for sure someone really good is watching my
back. I also want a pistol. Since you carry two, and I know
this, kindly leave the smaller on the grass behind me.'

'No one's watching you but myself. The men I brought
with me would have arrested him by now.'

*Espèce de salaud*, how could he do this to her? Those "others" would have all been picked out, maybe even photographed. 'Nervous were you of the Bois, eh? Perhaps then it
would be better if you didn't come here like this, for the one
who has been watching me now also has your number!'

Across the lake, there were two cyclists who had stopped

to enjoy the view. A woman called to her dog. Two girls of about twenty sat nearby. 'Dirksen will . . .' he began, only to be interrupted by her.

'The Standartenführer, I believe. Please don't forget.'

Kraus wanted to grab her by the hair and drag her down into the shallows, to hold her under until she had lost all will to resist, but said, 'Your Hans will be with the Bellecour woman at the hotel he found for her and her son. He'll be convincing her to cooperate. The boy is to return the pencil to the mayor of Abbeville. There's to be no mention of anything that happened here in Paris. Not a word from her or the boy.'

'And she'll take all that in without giving it a thought, eh? Is *this* what you believe?'

'Don't try my patience further. That lover of yours is preparing the way for you to be her contact with the terrorists. You're to be the only one who can offer help. By the time he's finished with her, she'll be so desperate, she'll readily go along and accept you for what you say you are.'

A liar. *Une résistante.* 'Then please don't think to soften her up with anything more. Just try to control yourself. Me, I know exactly how difficult that must be for you, but the success of this little venture depends entirely on our collective patience, even when one is being watched as now.'

'I want the names of Vergès's contacts.'

*'Idiot, Hans is going to hear of this!'*

'The names, damn you!'

*'Never, since we've had such a long conversation!'*

*'Verdammt,* how dare you?'

He'd be quivering with rage, so calmness would only make it all the harder 'Me, I dare because that is all I really have in this world of yours.' Kraus wouldn't give her the gun, would relish the thought of seeing her lying face down in the grass, her hands tied behind her back, her throat slit.

Just when he left her, she wasn't sure, but the light was fast falling, yet without the haze of automobile and truck exhaust, the air over Paris was so very clear, the sunsets were softer and more natural and eloquent. Not flame-red. Not at all.

Feeling gingerly behind, she found the pistol and knew

then that, in spite of all his denials, Kraus must have felt that someone had been watching.

It was a Beretta 7.65 mm, very light in weight and with seven cartridges in the magazine. Pressing it to herself, she lay on the grass, her eyes filled with tears. Hans had never allowed her to carry a gun—it was very much against the rules unless authorized by the higher-ups, and he had always claimed there was no need, but this time things, they were different. This time she was being hunted too.

Alone, a man stood near that café-restaurant. Getting hesitantly to her feet to brush off the grass, she paused to look back at him and say, 'Me, I think I've remembered where I saw you last, monsieur. Certainly you look a little like Martin Bellecour. You've the same ears, that same shape of the head, same brow and eyes, but not the hair—it may have been dyed, *n'est-ce pas*, in Lyon. The *réseau* Parrache. You, *mon ami*, were the only one to have escaped.'

A traveller, a man who could move about the country organizing the *Banditen* but now a hunter because he, too, had remembered.

He wouldn't wave, why would he? He simply stood looking at her from across the water, no uniform now, ah, nothing like that. No subterfuge. Just an open suit jacket, open collar, no tie, hands in the trouser pockets, the feet planted firmly apart as if in judgement.

The chemise was of silk, a pale rose Angélique could still remember feeling next to her skin even though nearly five years had passed since Martin's father had given it to her. The flacon was the Roman one, and the bluish green of its opalescent encrustation highlighted the colour of the silk and the greenish amber of the glass.

The chemise now lay in folds on a table, that little treasure of some Roman woman centuries ago nestled in its silk but fondled by the Standartenführer Dirksen, they in the lounge-bar of the Hôtel Trianon Palace.

Gently he stroked the glass. Had he a great love for such pieces? she wondered, and when he had uncovered the

Lalique, whose bas-reliefs of neoclassical Grecian noble-women had reminded her so much of the Louvre and her first meeting with Martin's father, the colonel stroked that one too. Was he lost in thought and wondering how best to conduct this interrogation?

The deep cobalt blue, turquoise and gold of the eighteenth-century flacon was the last to appear and when lined up, her little collection condemned her and she knew there was no longer any hope, that all was lost.

They were alone. Even the staff had been sent away. Martin was upstairs, guarded by two of the grey mice, the Blitzmädchen who had come from the Reich in their grey uniforms. Telegraphists, secretaries, et cetera. Sturdy Brünnhildes, many of them. Hard bitches when it came to dealing with recalcitrant French. Ah yes.

Dirksen didn't raise his voice. 'Tell me about Martin's father.'

Warily she said, 'There's not much to tell.'

Indicating the perfume bottles, he forced her to demand a little too swiftly, 'How is it, please, that you discovered the address of my flat?'

He mustn't give anything away, he knew, just told her, 'We had located the boy but a woman came along the street looking for a lost dog. Bijou, I think was its name, and before we could close in on him, the woman and Martin went in search of it. What was her name?'

'Ah, that I can't tell you, Colonel, for we never learned of it. Me, I'm grateful to her, of course, and would like to thank her, but we never discovered her name.'

'Surely she must have told Martin what it was.'

'And Martin, please, in the state he was in and after a night of having sat on a strange doorstep? Giselle perhaps, or Juliette. He couldn't be sure, and me I can't imagine why he'd be any more certain.'

*Ach, gut*, she was protecting Marie-Hélène. Again he indicated the perfume bottles. 'In spite of this, we now know that you lived at 37 rue des Grands-Augustins with his father, but that the boy only came to you three days before the exodus of June 1940.'

Concierge Lemoine, if still there, must have told him. 'I . . . He . . . The father and I were lovers.'

Dirksen balanced the Roman bottle upright in his left hand. 'Then the boy isn't your son?'

'Ah! what makes you think such a thing? Of course he is. He was away living with his . . .' It was no use. 'All right, he's not my son. Does *that* make me a criminal for wanting to take care of him? His father went home.'

'To Britain?'

'Yes.'

He set the flacon down in the folds of silk. 'How sure are you of this?'

Anthony couldn't have been living at the flat. He just *couldn't*! 'I'm very sure. You see, I sent Martin's father away before it was too late for him.'

She would offer only so much, felt Angélique, and this one would only demand more, but all he said, and it was a surprise, was, 'Which of these do you love the most?'

He wouldn't break any of them, and she knew this, for Herr Dirksen wasn't like the Sturmbannführer Kraus. 'I love all of them, Colonel, each for itself and equally.'

He even smiled as he said, 'A good answer, spoken truly. I'd have said the same.'

'But I'm the one who's under arrest.'

Holding up a cautionary finger, he said, 'Not under arrest. Under a request for assistance, that's all and a great difference. You convinced the boy's father to leave?'

She tried to look away and finally succeeded. 'The Messerschmitts had come over the *route nationale* south from Paris twice by then. The car had been all shot up, our suitcases, everything. But on the third pass, Martin became separated from us. Anthony started back towards the road but those ME-109s were like angry wasps, dark when looked at into the sun. I . . .'

'Please continue,' said Dirksen gently. 'I know how difficult it must be, but it's necessary.'

How could anyone else really know what those few moments had been like, the anger that had erupted so swiftly between two who had loved each other so thoroughly, the harsh and unkind words? 'I . . . I told him he had to leave and head back to the coast and that yacht of his as fast as possible, but Anthony was terrified he'd lose Martin, that the boy would be killed. He blamed himself, you see? Me, I slapped him hard, trying to put reason into him. Once, twice, three times. We were both terrified but those ME-109s weren't going to leave that road alone and when they started firing at us again, he realized that it was no use his trying to get Martin and me out of France, that alone, he might have a chance. You see, he knew too much they would want from him in Berlin. Hesitating still, he searched the road desperately for a glimpse of Martin. He even cried out that name several times and me, I can still hear the despair that was in him, but . . . Ah, he knew that what I had just said was only too true and that he really had no choice but to leave us.'

'Did he curse you?'

'Is that so bad? He said it was all my fault too, but he didn't mean it. How could he have? In the chaos of those few moments, neither of us were ourselves. Even I had peed myself.'

He'd give her a moment, felt Dirksen. The flacons were beautiful and they did seem to have a calming effect on her. 'You were out in a farmer's field, I gather, but could he have returned to that road?'

'Did he change his mind, is this what you're asking?'

'You know it is.'

'Then I must tell you, Colonel, that he didn't, that for the past three years I have believed absolutely that he had made it and was safe in England. Oh for sure, he'd have taken some with him on that yacht of his, but they'd have got away, since the Messerschmitts, the Stukas and such were busy elsewhere tormenting the defenceless like myself and Martin, but I didn't find him until their fifth pass. By then Martin had run far along the road in terror, poor thing, and was lying face down beneath the man who had tried to shield him and had taken the cannon shells instead.'

'His father . . . Was it his father?'

'His *what*? But why do you ask such a thing? It was just some man whose heart instinctively included a small boy in tears who cried out for his father. In all that distance, I saw no sign of Anthony. None, I tell you. I looked. Believe me, I did, while searching for Martin and cursing myself for what I had done. "Killed" my lover's son.'

'But at La Vagengende last night you said his father might have died?'

'That was a mistake. I . . . I didn't mean to say that. Oh for sure I did think at first that Anthony might have gone back to that road—there, will that help you? But I didn't find him, did I? Martin's just being impossible. He misses his father terribly, and yes, he can't ever bring himself to believe Anthony would have left him, but . . .' She shrugged. 'It's true. He did.'

'Then the boy believed last night that his father had been living in that flat for the past three years, and that is why he went there?'

'It was logical, wasn't it? Martin hadn't been long in Paris. When he ran from us where else was he to have gone if not to that house?'

'The streets were in total darkness.'

'He must have remembered the way. Anthony and he . . . they went for a walk that first day and . . . and must have passed that restaurant.'

And the boy had remembered after a good three years. 'Martin fell and hurt himself last night. A sergeant tried to assist, and the boy lost that pencil again, but fortunately a report was made and we were alerted to the direction he had taken. I've the pencil, too.'

The woman couldn't stop herself from looking at it with loathing. No doubt she was cursing the mayor of Abbeville, the doctor and all the others. Thiessen, too? he wondered, but with that one there was a problem, for in her description of their last moments together on that road, she had indicated a weakness in the boy's father, whereas Thiessen, if he was what they now thought he could well be, had given the impression of nothing but the reverse.

Carefully Dirksen folded the chemise and set it aside with a finality she couldn't help but notice. 'You know what this means, don't you? he asked.

Tears came, her lips parting, she to pause while she thought nothing but the worst, only to blurt, 'Please don't separate us, Colonel. He's only a little boy.'

'But he's British.'

'And you're going to lock *him* up in an internment camp? Not the one at Saint-Denis. That's for adult British men who had been living in France when . . . when it was taken.'

'Poland, I'm afraid. That is what my superiors in Berlin have ordered.'

'One of those camps, those terrible places you people have for Jews, Communists, gypsies and *résistants*?'

Far too many had now heard at least rumours of those, which wasn't good, of course, but . . . 'He knows too much. Look, I'm sorry, Mademoiselle Bellecour, but Berlin are insisting he be taken from you.'

'But . . . but he can't speak. He still has terrible nightmares and even wets the bed at times. Me, I'm all he has, Colonel. Without me . . .'

In despair, she wrung her hands, was sickened by the thought, and said at last, 'Send me with him, then. At least do that. Have a bit of conscience.'

'That's just not possible,' he said, handing the chemise to her so that she could dry her eyes and blow her nose. 'It's the Sturmbannführer Kraus and the avenue Foch for you and a full interrogation. Berlin won't have less. I'd lose my job if I interfered.'

Kraus, ah no.

But was she ready now to cooperate? wondered Dirksen. Things like this were often so delicate. 'It's time, isn't it?'

Apprehensively Angélique waited for him to ask what he now wanted of her.

'What was your lover's name?'

'Anthony James Thomas.' It seemed so strange to be saying it aloud and to the enemy. Quickly he wrote it down in his little black notebook, she staring at the thing he was using to write with. That thing . . .

Dirksen took apart the mayor's pencil, and to show her how simple it had been, tightly rolled up a cigarette paper and slid it into the barrel. 'We know you and the boy were unaware of this, but you did carry a message for the terrorists.

It's my considered understanding that early this evening Dr. Vergès made contact with someone who passed it on to someone else, each of whom will have been followed, and each of whom will be arrested just as soon as their usefulness ends.'

Everyone at the meeting Isabelle Moncontre was arranging for tonight would have to be warned, thought Angélique. She couldn't fail to do so, it was that urgent, but she'd have to bargain with him also, had no other choice. 'What is it you wish of me in exchange for Martin's life and our freedom?'

Had she finally realized he was her only hope? 'Good. That's settled, and I appreciate your frankness. The boy will return the pencil. There'll be no mention of anything here. One week from now you will return to Paris with another message from them.'

There'd be no arrests until then—was this what he was saying? 'And if monsieur le maire should ask us to do a little more?'

'You'll convey this to me, not to the Sturmbannführer Kraus.'

Then the two of them didn't trust each other—was this, too, what he was saying? 'That man who died while we were at the avenue Foch must have been betrayed by someone in Abbeville, Colonel. If I should need to get a message to you in a hurry, would this same one be not only useful but most necessary?'

'That's not possible, but I'll make sure our contact is aware of your new status. At the first sign of trouble, we'll be alerted. If the terrorists move in on you, rest assured someone will come to the rescue.'

How comforting. He'd seen right through her, but was this betrayer in Abbeville's hôtel de ville and Kommandantur? How else could Herr Dirksen get such news so quickly?

Ready to leave, she stood up to extend the hand of agreement, Dirksen noting the squared, proud shoulders, fiercely jutting, deeply clefted chin and those limpid grey eyes that had driven Anthony James Thomas to such a foolishness he would cross the English Channel in the hope of rescuing her. 'Sit down. We're not finished. I asked you to tell me about your former lover. Did he speak or write Deutsch?'

So it was to begin again, was it? 'Fluently? Well enough to pass as one of yourselves—is this what you're asking?'

'You know it is.'

'Then yes. Better than his French, which was very good. Before the war his business interests took him to the Reich many times. He wasn't a spy, so please don't get the wrong idea. He designed yachts for prominent Nazis and his only worry was that they would neglect to pay him. Ah!' She shrugged. 'In that I guess he was absolutely correct.'

'That sort of talk will only cause you harm. Was Cologne ever on his itinerary?'

'Cologne . . . ? But why that city, please? Ah, you won't tell me. Berlin have forbidden it. Kiel, then, and Lübeck and Hamburg *and* Bremerhaven—he had an interest in submarines, yes, of course, but was like a small boy with them. It was nothing. His one passion, apart from myself and Martin, was in designing yachts. Never have I known a man so possessed.'

But he had known far too much, thought Dirksen, and she had admitted that she had tried to warn him to leave the country before it was too late. Smiling inwardly at her mistake, he knew she was full of surprises, and when he was finished with her, genuinely hoped there would be no more of them.

Pulling out the photograph of Thiessen's family, he set it before her. 'Please take your time. Would Martin's father have known this woman and her children?'

Since he had travelled in the Reich so many times. Did this one forget anything she had said to him?

'Well?' he asked.

And don't keep me waiting, oh for sure, but she really was genuinely puzzled and would have to shrug. 'It's possible. Look, I really wouldn't know. How could I? He met a lot of people I never knew. He did tell me about some of the parties, the weekends of sailing, but it was business, wasn't it? And I knew his heart belonged to me and to Martin. What's her name?'

Had jealousy crept in even after three years of separation? 'This we don't yet know but a photo of this snapshot is on its way to the police in Marienburg, a suburb of Cologne. We'll learn soon enough.'

A suburb, but are she and the children dead from the fire-storm, Colonel? Isn't this what you're wondering? Dead and how convenient, the real Theissen dead as well, Anthony having killed him and taken his identity?

Secretly Martin watched the two women who guarded him. The youngest was filing her nails and blowing on them. Her legs were crossed. A lighted cigarette was nearby.

The older one was straightening her stockings. Thinking that he had dozed off, she had hiked her grey skirt to fix a garter.

He had to do it. Somehow he had to warn the Mademoiselle Isabelle that they had been arrested and that she mustn't try to come here or send them a message.

Bolting off the bed, Martin shot out the door. The Blitzmädchen shrieked and stumbled into each other. They were up and after him as he raced past the lift and headed for the main staircase and plummeted down it. Got to get away, he cried out silently. Can't let them arrest her too. Can't . . .

Hitting the second-floor landing, he ducked under an arm, raced past a general and his lady friend, frantically punched the lift button and saw the arrow coming down. . . .

The Blitzes were blocking the corridor. There was no time to wait for the lift. Tossing a glance behind, he tried to decide what to do as they ran at him. He raced away. The corridor soon ended. *Ended!*

Throwing himself at them, Martin fought and bit and managed to get free. The lift had stopped. Its door was closing. . . .

A hand reached out and yanked him in. Kneeling on the floor, the Mademoiselle Isabelle laughed until the tears ran as she kissed and hugged him. 'Ah, *mon Dieu, mon ami*, that was close, eh? *Merde*, I thought you were never going to get away. I've been watching that room of yours for ages.'

Fondly she passed a hand over his head and gave a lit-tle shudder of relief. 'Here,' she said, tucking a note into his pocket. 'Make sure you and your mother memorize the address and the time, then burn it.'

Again she embraced him. He touched her hair, her tears and then . . . then, yes, her lips.

She kissed his cheeks, laughed and said, 'I had to pay the lift operator a hundred francs to lose himself.'

And when they reached the ground floor, Martin was dutifully waiting for his guards who slapped him hard and took him by the ear, she laughing at them and asking, as they crowded into the lift, 'Was he being bad?,' then slipping past them and out. But when they didn't answer and only glared at her, she shrugged and remained watching the gate as it closed and the lift began to rise.

'*Bonne chance, mes souris grises,*' she sang out. 'That one wants to fly, but with hens like you to guard him, I would as well!'

The car was waiting for her in the pitch-darkness of the boulevard Saint-Michel near the hotel, and when Marie-Hélène got into it, she wanted Hans to hold her but he wouldn't.

Still thinking of Martin and what she had just done, she said bitterly, 'I was followed this evening when I went to the Bois.'

'Are you certain?'

'I felt it, and for me that's enough.'

'Then you'd better tell me everything,' he said with a sigh.

Stung by his impatience, she turned from him to stare out into the darkness. 'I think it was the one who got away from us in Lyon. I think he followed me all afternoon and I didn't even notice.'

'That's impossible. Châlus was badly hit. There was a lot of blood in that *traboule* and on the staircase.'

Those were the narrow, filthy, dark passageways that had led from house to house and street to street and she had hated them. 'But he *did* escape, Hans, and none of the others would tell us where he was holed up.'

There had been tears then and now as well, and he had to wonder if she really had been duped into thinking everything had been all right for her this afternoon. Her fists were clenched. She stamped a foot.

'It *was* Châlus, Hans, the leader of the *réseau* Parrache! That bastard had reddish-brown hair and fair, sunburnt skin. He had a narrow chin and big ears that stuck out just like Martin's do. *His son!* And now he's using this whole Bois Carré business to put an end to me.'

What the hell had upset her so much?

'Raymond Châlus,' she went on, and he could hear the anguish in her voice. 'Age forty-two. Tall and loose-limbed exactly like Martin Bellecour will be some day if we don't stop these people. He even has that boy's smile, but he's a coldhearted killer, Hans, and he knows absolutely who was to blame for the loss of all his comrades.'

Lyon, and the capture of sixty-two of that circuit, but that had been eight months ago and Châlus could just as easily have died from his wounds. 'You're worrying too much. Relax. It's the strain. We'll soon have all of them and then we can take a little holiday, you to travel through Switzerland to Berlin, myself direct.'

The RAF were now bombing Berlin during the day as well as at night, and the USAAF, while already hitting lots of other targets, would soon concentrate on it too,* but she'd still have to ask, 'And afterwards?'

For now, he'd have to give her what she wanted. 'We'll plan your retirement.'

And what of Kraus? she wanted so much to ask but couldn't bring herself to. Not yet. 'Everything has been put in place for tonight but me, I just hope it comes off okay, Hans, because if it doesn't, there'll have been trouble.'

'Has Kraus been after you again?'

'No. No, it's nothing like that. Oh for sure, he desperately wants to be the one in charge of looking after the security of those sites, whatever they are, and yes, he believes he's going to get that opportunity, especially if things don't go according to plan tonight.'

---

* First Berlin raid 4 March 1944

Kraus had definitely been after her again. 'He feeds the Reichsführer Himmler telex after telex demanding arrests and will never learn the value of patience. Always the full orchestra has to be in place before the symphony begins.'

And was she to be the contralto?

When she felt his hand slide beneath her hair to cup the back of her neck, his weakness towards the threat of Kraus made her say, 'Please don't touch me. For now I'm alone and must remain so. Besides, if you want the truth, I think my heart has been taken by another.'

A ten-year-old boy who couldn't speak and would sign his name by adding a little parachute. Had the mothering instinct got to her?

'I don't like myself, Hans. Not with this one. Martin's so defenceless, it's cruel of me.'

'"33 rue Racine, at 12.30, an attic room",' said Angélique in a whisper. They were sitting on the bed, facing each other, the grey mice having left some time ago, the note in her hand. '"At just after curfew the *alerte aérienne* will sound". We are to appear as if we have dressed hastily.'

And then? he asked, indicating the note the Mademoiselle Moncontre had given him.

'We are to join the hotel's other guests and leave by the main entrance, but when we get to the street, we are to quickly turn to the right so as to slip away.'

She held her breath. Martin knew her heart was racing at the thought, but that together they would do it, he just knew they would, and thinking it would help, gently reached out to brush her tears away.

Kissing his hand, holding it tightly to her lips, she tried to smile. Martin must never know what Herr Dirksen had asked of them, not if she could prevent it. 'At the corner of the rue Monsieur-le-Prince we are to go left and continue to the first intersection, cross over and take the left again. The rue Racine.'

*Count two houses and then the third,* said Martin, shutting his eyes and moving his lips so that she could see that he had memorized the note. *A small blue light marks the door. Others will be returning from the shelters in the* place de l'Odéon, *a false alert.*

'And then?' she asked so softly he felt her lips pressed gently against his brow. They were warm and moist and she was trembling a little, and the smell of her was different from that of the Mademoiselle Isabelle. Not sweeter. Not anything like that. Just different.

*We are to ask for a room in the attic,* he said, letting her read his lips. *We are not to listen to the* patron. *We are to demand a night's rest and present him with the tip of five hundred francs.*

'It's a *maison de passe,*' she said. 'No names are necessary in such places. It's not like a regular hotel where everyone has to show their papers when they register. It's a house, Martin, where *les filles des rues* take their clients for their little moment.'

Mystified, he said, *Oh,* and dropping his gaze, settled it on the base of her throat. 'You are to pay no attention to what's going on there, do you hear me?' she said. 'We're doing this for your father's sake.'

*And because he has asked it of you. He's their leader, Angélique, and is the one who told the Mademoiselle Isabelle what to do.*

'That's impossible and you know it. He's in England, Martin. He got safely away. I swear he did, so let's not argue.'

Again she read the note and then again before letting him destroy it while she remained sitting there studying him. 'You're only ten years old,' she said at last, 'and certainly your childhood is nothing like it would have been had you stayed in England with your mother.'

Reaching out to her, she felt him touch her hair and then her lips but couldn't know that he had done this with the Mademoiselle Isabelle.

'War's not pleasant, Martin. We've only to think of what happened to Mademoiselle Moncontre's brother.'

*That's why she's a* résistante, he said, mouthing the words. *That's why she and my father are helping us.*

The leather cord, a dark brown bootlace, had come from that room in the avenue Foch where Martin had left his little parachute in the window dust and had found some woman's wedding ring. It was bloodstained and dry, but he looked up at her with . . . Ah, what was it? wondered Angélique. Apology?

A plea for understanding, or for forgiveness for having taken it too, and not told her?

'No matter,' she said, and taking it from him, securely tied his left wrist to her right one. 'Now hold my hand. That way people won't question things or see the lace. We can't become separated. You couldn't cry out to me if we were.'

So *there*, no argument! He could see her thinking this. Her hand was sweaty. Her fingers had shaken so much, she had had trouble tying the lace and, impatiently refusing his help, had used her teeth to pull the knot tight. A thing she had hated doing and had spat several times afterwards because of the dried blood.

Ready, they waited inside the door of their room. At just after midnight, the air-raid alert was taken up by the hotel's alarm system, but still they didn't leave.

'Others must go first,' she said.

The corridor next to the main staircase and the lift were soon filled with Germans. All stood two by two in order, waiting for their turn. Most were in various states of uniform, but some wore suits. There was no panic, no appearance of concern. Now a step, now a wait. There was lots of room on the other side for people to come up the stairs but who would want to?

In spite of this emptiness, the guests all stuck to the down side, causing Angélique to wonder, what if a bomb were to strike?

Down, and down again, thought Martin, but slowly this time.

When they reached the darkness of the rue de Vaugirard, the sound of the sirens swelled and hurt the ears, but apart from the Germans in the hotel, few Parisians seem to pay any attention, enjoying perhaps the chance to just be outdoors.

Together they turned away to the right and soon, on the rue Monsieur-le-Prince, there were fewer sounds other than those of the sirens. No one hurried by. Indeed, she felt they were alone. Unlike Berlin and so many other cities and towns on the Continent and in Britain, Paris had been declared an open city and hadn't suffered more than an occasional stray hit. Oh for sure, the Renault Works, in the suburbs at

Boulogne-Billancourt, had been targeted in March of last year, and misplaced bombs had killed an estimated five hundred, but the city itself had remained virtually unscathed. A downed aircraft might cause a building to catch fire or consternation if bits of it were found the next day on the Champs-Élysées. A crater at Longchamp had interrupted the races on 5 April of this year,* moving those elsewhere to one of the suburbs. But generally, as a result, Parisians tended to ignore the shelters and go back to sleep. Maybe later—next year perhaps—that would change.

Counting the seconds between each wailing, Martin would squeeze her hand as if his heart was beating through his fingers to her own, but finally the air-raid sirens stopped.

They went along the street through the pitch-darkness. There were no tiny blue lights from the *vélo-taxis* and other bikes, their red taillights too—all had been cleared from the streets at midnight, the curfew. There weren't even the pin-points of light from the cigarettes of passersby, nor occasionally those who shielded blue-blinkered flashlights. Paris had never been quieter. The hush, when they stopped to listen, that of at least 2,000,000 and all others, those of the "visitors", perhaps 100,000, who really knew? More, of course, along the Atlantic Wall and not just in the cities and towns or villages.

Two cats cried out from the middle of the street as they picked a fight. 'Come on,' she whispered to Martin, 'by now they'll have begun to search for us.'

Somewhere a car started up and they heard the screech of its tyres. Another and another did the same, and soon there were the headlamps as the cars raced down the street, a spot-light showing up the shops and the steel shutters that had been rolled down and padlocked for the night.

Their backs to a wall, they huddled in an entrance and pulled their knees up tightly but it was no use. The spotlight struck the shop and filled the top of the doorway. Now it was being lowered . . .

The beam flicked away to focus on the other side of the

---

* A deliberate RAF raid to stir things up. Though several were killed or wounded, the races that day had continued.

street and dance over the doorways, but when they didn't find anyone, the car didn't turn the corner onto the rue Racine. Instead, the engine was switched off, the headlamps, too, and the spotlight.

A car door opened and Marin felt Angélique pressing the back of his hand to her lips.

'He has to be nearby,' swore one of the men in Deutsch. 'We'll go along to the rue de Vaugirard and start all over.'

When the beam hit her, it was blinding. '*Aufstehen,*' he said.

*Get up.* 'Please, we . . . we became separated from the others during the alert.'

Kraus kept the light on her. He didn't say anything more, and when she and Martin stood, Angélique thought he was going to hit her.

'Go back to the hotel. It's just down the street and around the corner. Hurry.'

They were looking for someone else. It began to rain, and soon they were drenched, but by going past the hotel and around the block the other way, they finally found the *maison de passe* where the meeting was to be held. Jammed into the corridor, and still on the narrow staircase, they stood with German soldiers and their prostitutes, and oh for sure, these guys should have been in their *Soldatenheim* beds.

The house stank of urine, cheap perfume, sour cabbage, pickled pork hocks, grease for the boots, mould and disinfectant, namely the *eau de Javel* that was made in Paris and was used to wash all the railways station windows and skylights blue for the blackout.

The *patron*, a grizzled, moon-faced, uncaring individual, puffed on a cigarette that was falling apart but took his time getting the rooms straight and making sure everyone had paid. Additionally, there was much jostling, lots of laughter, the "girls" all over the age of forty. Mascara had been ruined by the rain, false eyelashes were either gone or askew, the lipstick on some smudged, on others all but worn away. Bleached or dyed, the hair had been plastered down by the rain, their drenched blouses too tight and too open. All were girls who could no longer find work in any of the 140 licenced brothels and had been reduced to using places like this.

'Oh he's so little,' they said of Martin. 'Is it your first time, sweetie? Ah! she robs the cradle to tease herself.'

Peeling, the wallpaper had once had a border of spring flowers, the paint of the doors and trim flaking, and when she said, 'We need a room for the rest of the night where we can sleep. The attic, please,' the *patron* was perplexed.

Sucking in on that cigarette, he coughed and exploded. 'But . . . but that is impossible. The hotel, it is full.'

'You shameful slut,' hissed one of the women. 'You should know better.'

'It's illegal, isn't it?' said another.

'Tender. That one will be tender and tasty,' chimed in yet another.

'He's my *son*, damn you!' she cried. 'We were caught out after curfew and warned to get indoors. The *flic* who brought us here said that the attic would be best, that it wasn't used for . . . for well you must know what!

'Martin, plug your ears!'

A tigress, was that it? wondered Odilon Grégoire, and giving her the shrug she probably deserved, shoved two tags into hands that squeezed past her own to grab them. 'Please,' she begged.

A German corporal, a fair-haired, pimply-faced boy with a broken tooth, took the tag he'd been handed and grinned at her, and when she became even more flustered, grabbed her arm and hoisted it for everyone to see.

'Ah!' said Grégoire, 'and why is it, please, madame, that you have lashed the boy to yourself if he is your son?'

It took all types—Angélique could see them thinking this, the prostitutes intrigued, she stammering, 'It's . . . it's not what you think. He . . . he can't speak. He's lost his voice and I . . . I was afraid I might lose him.'

'Out!' insisted Grégoire. 'Get on the street where you belong. It's against the law.'

How pious of him! 'And isn't what you're allowing here also against the law? Don't the Germans have forty brothels in Paris reserved especially for their common soldiers, and aren't they forbidden to visit any others, since in places like this there are no medical checks?'

'Venereal diseases notwithstanding, madame, who am I to question the pleasures of a chance meeting in the darkness? Me, I only offer a little light now and then, since it helps to make the *chapeau anglais* used as it should be and not blown up like a balloon!'

The hypocrite. Business had never been better, baksheesh simply having been paid to the bloodsuckers among the Paris gendarmerie and the German military police, the Felgendarme. 'Please, I don't mean to cause any trouble. We simply want to go to sleep. We're not from Paris, we're from the country, from near Abbeville, and are here in Paris for a doctor's appointment. A specialist.'

'Ah, let them have a room,' said one of the women, all heart now. 'If the boy pees the bed, make her pay a little extra.'

'Five thousand,' said Grégoire.

'Pardon?' she shrilled.

'Five hundred,' said the same one. 'Twenty-five of that is for the room and two hand towels, the rest for his little retirement, but if he tries anything with you, just call out. Every week he has one of us for nothing. It's his little privilege. Two sometimes, and both for comfort.'

The room was up five flights of stairs. It was hot and dirty and there were bedbugs. 'Now we must wait,' she said to Martin. 'Hey, we'll be all right. You'll see, she won't forget us.'

Hands in her coat pockets, Marie-Hélène fingered the Beretta. There were four cars lined up in the darkness on the rue de Vaugirard, and the sound of the rain hammering on them was so different from that of its striking the paving stones, it had put her even more on edge. Kraus must be up to something of his own with that *maison de passe*. She would have to call things off. Hans would have to be told.

The rain came steadily. It found the upturned collar of her coat and trickled between her shoulder blades. It struck her face and seeped into her shoes but still she waited. They were having a little conference in the lead car and as she cautiously approached it, tobacco smoke trailed through a tiny gap where a window had been rolled down.

Someone got out. She stepped back. Caught in the middle of the street, she couldn't run as from car to car he hurried, and at each said, 'The Gare de l'Ouest.* Stay together.'

Things must be okay then, but still there was hesitation in her and for several minutes she remained where she was, listening intently to the dwindling sound of the cars as they raced away.

Hurrying now along the rue Racine, her crepe soles making little sucking noises, she found the door to the house unlocked and quickly stepped inside, into darkness and silence.

'Please, I will not lock it, yes?' whispered Grégoire from so close, she jumped. 'The attic,' he said. 'Room seven.'

Finding his groping fingers, she pressed the tight roll of five thousand francs into them, he to then hear her cautiously making her way to the staircase and up it as he hurriedly crossed himself, for one had to do what one had to. One could not object, not these days.

Leaving the lock off, as ordered, he retreated to his cage and tried to settle down, but it was no use. Working for *les Allemands* made him nervous. A raid? he wondered and didn't want to think about such a thing, for they could well smash the place to pieces and not even this one's five thousand would compensate for the damages and loss of business, but what was a poor man to do?

There weren't just German soldiers spending the night with their girls of the moment. There were others who slept with theirs—Frenchmen, yes, and others too, who slept alone. Ah yes, two from Marseille perhaps, or Lyon. Young men, little more than boys of eighteen or twenty and ripe for the STO if caught, but boys he hadn't told the Sturmbannführer Kraus about, a sudden and unforgivable lapse of memory. *Résistants?* he had to wonder, not liking the thought, but again, as with the SS, the Gestapo and *gestapistes français*, one could not object.

Trapped in the middle, one simply had to tough it out.

---

* Also known as the Gare de Montparnasse

One of those young men would be on the third floor, at the back, the other . . . now where would that one have stationed himself, considering that only one room had been requested?

Each had carried the shabby, cardboard suitcases the Occupation had granted. Their coats had been buttoned up even in this heat, the rain perhaps, except, of course, that they had arrived before it.

One could only sweat and listen.

When she reached the second floor, Marie-Hélène went cautiously along between the staircase and the rooms until a probing foot came up against a wire. It was stretched at ankle height, taut across the corridor between a baluster and the electrical wires, which were fastened to the skirting board. *Kraus,* she wanted to cry out, but this . . . this couldn't have been left by him. He must have thought the house safe, the fool!

Sickened, she looked questioningly up into the pitch-darkness of the stairwell and then back down the way she had come. Lyon? she wanted to cry out. Châlus? Is it Châlus in a German uniform? Had he used the Bellecour woman and his son to trap her?

The sounds of snoring came, and then . . . then from up on the next floor, the rhythmic squeaking of bedsprings and a muted, '*Couchez-moi, mon brav.* That's it. A little higher, yes. Get it right up in there.'

If she could reach the boy and his mother, felt Marie-Hélène, she could use them as hostages. If Châlus was the boy's father, he wouldn't want to see them killed.

Stepping over the wire, she went on and up the stairs, each foot pressed down so gradually, the board or step beneath the tattered runner squeaked but softly.

There were no more trip wires, but on the third floor, the door to a room at the very back was not quite closed. Waiting, she wondered what to do. Retreating, she decided to creep by it on hands and knees, and when on the fourth floor, undid the belt of her coat and tied it tightly across the corridor at ankle height at the top of the stairs, using a baluster and those same electrical wires on the skirting board.

Up in the attic, she took time to find the skylight to the roof, only to discover that the ladder was already in place and the window unhooked. Everything, then, was ready for her assassination and their escape. Châlus planned to get the Bellecour woman and his son away.

The toilet below was Turkish and cramped. Just a hole in the floor with a flat metal dish, a foot pedal and a pull chain, and water all over the place when used. Niagaras of it, the stench terrible, a constant drip from the skylight.

Gingerly she climbed down the ladder and went along the corridor until she came to number seven. It was all too risky; she'd have to choose another place, another time, but would Châlus not tell them the truth about her?

She would have to kill him. She had no other choice.

Up on the roof, the rain struck her and when she reached the first chimney to hug it tightly, the Beretta slipped away and she heard it clatter on the copper sheathing before it dropped into emptiness.

'Martin . . . ? *Ah, chéri*, don't take it so hard. Something must have come up. These things, they're never certain.'

*She's been arrested*, he cried. *Now they are yanking out her fingernails!*

'*Petit*, please. She'll come when it's safe. We have to believe this, otherwise everything is lost.'

He buried his face against her chest and wept as she tried to comfort him. *Salauds*, he cried at the Boches. *Cochons! Killers!*

'*Courage*, Martin. *Courage*. Your father would have wanted you to be brave.' But would he really have? she wondered. Anthony had been the gentlest of souls. He had detested the very thought of war and had lost his own father in the previous conflict. This *Résistance* leader Herr Dirksen thought had lived in her flat would have had to become the exact opposite of Anthony. Hard, shrewd, a ruthless killer who was always one step ahead of the Germans and their friends.

Try as she did, Angélique couldn't reconcile herself to such a change. Martin's father *had* escaped and was in England where he had been for the past three years. Doing design work for the Royal Navy, yes, of course, but not killing people, not directly.

'Come on, Martin, let's lie down for a bit. So what if there are bedbugs, let's make hotels of ourselves. We're both exhausted. We'll leave this place well before the curfew ends. We'll return to the Hôtel Trianon Palace. Those who are watching for us will be far too sleepy to notice.'

He had found his thumb, poor thing, and when she kissed his cheek, it was still hot but a little cooler. 'Sleep, that's it, *mon petit parachute*. Sleep.'

She dozed, fought to stay awake, mustn't drift off. Martin depended on her. 'Martin,' she murmured.

The rain was constant, but here belowdecks in the cabin of the *Alcyone*, she felt it warm and dry, and they lay naked, Anthony kissing her hair, her eyelids, cheeks and throat, she feeling the soft brush of his lips until their bodies were as one.

Boots sounded, racing up the stairs from floor to floor. A shriek was given. A door flew open, splintering. Another and another. Someone tripped and fell headlong down the stairs. '*SALAUDS, YOU HAVE DECEIVED US!*' cried out someone in French.

'*UNE RAFLE!*'\* cried another.

But then the Deutsch came: '*DUMMKÖPFE*, GET BACK TO YOUR *SOLDATENHEIMS* AT ONCE!'

'ALL RIGHT, ALL RIGHT! HEY, WE'RE GOING AREN'T WE?'

Clubs swung, couples were being torn from their beds and flung into the corridors, some to yell as they fell down the stairs. There was more pounding, more cursing, more shrieking. A gun went off. A man cried out. A burst from a machine pistol tore plaster apart. Suddenly everyone was shrieking, crying, screaming.

*Pound, pound, crash, crash!* 'OUT! OUT!' *Smash, smash.* Boots racing up those stairs, chasing someone. '*ARRÊTEZ!*' Another burst of firing, the return of pistol fire, the pop, pop of it heard against the terrible racket of machine pistols.

'*LES TOITS, MES AMIS. LE SALAUD, HE IS GOING OVER THE ROOFS!*'

The door flew in. A machine pistol opened up. Angé-

---

\* A police roundup

lique shrieked and tried to shield her head. Martin screamed, 'FATHER! FATHER!'

Over and over again he screamed for that father of his, but hands were now on her shoulders, her arms, face and hair as she cried out, 'MARTIN! MARTIN!'

Slammed against a wall, she lost consciousness momentarily, was dragged up, hit twice across the face, punched, kicked, she trying to speak, trying to defend herself.

A hand grabbed her by the throat. She couldn't breathe . . . Must breathe . . . Martin . . . Martin . . .

'FATHER! FATHER!' he shrieked. 'FATHER, PLEASE SPEAK TO ME. IT'S MARTIN. MARTIN!'

'WHERE IS HE, DAMN YOU?' shrieked a voice in French.

She tried to answer. There was more firing, more sounds of running, more shrieks. Lights found her. Lights blinded her. There were men but they weren't in uniform. They were *gestapistes français* who pushed her repeatedly against the wall and shrieked, 'WHERE IS HE?'

The sound of fabric ripping came. Now a seam, now another until at last she realized it was her dress.

The strap of her brassiere broke. Naked, cowering before them, Angélique tried to cover herself. 'I DON'T KNOW WHO YOU MEAN! I DON'T!'

They shone their lights over her. They didn't believe her and grabbed her by the arms, yanking her from the wall.

But someone must have said something to them, for they left as suddenly as they had come. Now they were up on the roof.

Left in semidarkness, aching all over and with only the light from the corridor, she couldn't find the will to move. Martin must be somewhere. Martin? she asked herself. I must find him.

And then, uncertainly exploring each breast, each shoulder and gripping the stomach they had punched and kicked, she realized that Martin had cried out for his father, that in the midst of the gunfire he had found his voice but had used English.

'Martin . . . ?' she said hesitantly. 'Martin, are you all right? Speak to me, please. I know you can, my darling. I heard you calling out.'

The road was littered with wreckage. A baby's brains were all mixed up with its blood and skin and those of its mother. A man sat slumped against the car that was turned onto its side. A dog whimpered. Flames rose from the windows of the car. A front wheel kept turning and turning.

'Please, sir, can you tell me where my father is?'

Grey and slippery with blood, the red-netted, stringy, blue-lined tubes kept bulging out of the man's stomach to glisten in the midday sun. Both hands tried to stop them. The man couldn't understand what had happened. Bewildered, he looked up.

Bulge, bulge, they kept on slipping through the blood-soaked, clasping fingers. '*Mon papa, monsieur*? Have you seen him?' Seen . . . What was that word in French? wondered Martin. '*Un Anglais, oui? Un homme*? Tall . . . with reddish-brown hair like mine and sea-green eyes. His ears stick out too.'

The man didn't understand English. He just stared up at him with that same stupid, uncomprehending expression. Then he toppled over, just like that, and the rest of his guts rushed out in snaking coils until they, too, lay still and the blowflies began to swarm in.

Farther along the road, a seven-year-old girl lay sprawled on her back beside a wicker pram. Blood trickled from her nose and lips. She had wet herself and emptied the rest.

This baby in the pram had been smashed to pieces too, just like the other one, but then the Messerschmitts came back and it began to rain, and the rain of cannon shells and bullets changed into a rain of water, which would wash the blood away, he supposed.

Martin blinked to clear his eyes. Down from him, two roofs over and beyond other chimneys, men with torches and guns had finally captured the one they'd been chasing. A boy of maybe eighteen had been badly wounded, his shirt drenched; he was trying to say something. Perhaps it was, Why did you have to shoot me? Perhaps it was, We'll get you in the end.

But then it came clearly in French, 'Why was the other sky-light locked?'

They paid no attention. Helped to his feet, the boy thought they were going to take him back into that house, and for a moment it looked like this would happen as they negotiated a narrow ridge.

They'd question him. They'd torture him, thought Martin. But what if he were to call out to them in English from here— yes, yes. No one would expect him to do that. Distracted, the boy, a *résistant*, might have a chance.

He began to step forward but a hand on his shoulder stopped him. 'Don't. You mustn't, Martin. They'll kill me if you do.'

It was the Mademoiselle Isabelle and she had been hiding behind one of the chimneys on this other and higher roof.

'Martin, I have to get away. Everything depends on it.'

The rain came steadily. The torch beams of those guys, those *gestapistes français*, were searching the roof down there for a better place to stand.

Gripped tightly, Martin felt her cheek against his. Some of her hair now clung to his brow. Beneath the damp smell of the rain, there was the faint smell of her and of a fear that made him tremble. 'Shut your eyes,' she said, and there was a hardness to her voice he couldn't understand. 'You must,' she grated. 'This won't be pleasant.'

It began to rain very hard and the sound of it drowned out anything more the young man might have said as he struggled weakly to get free from those who held him. They laughed. They had pistols and machine pistols and they hunted for *résistants* and evaders of the forced labour, the STO—the Service du Travail Obligatoire—but he hadn't been guilty of any of those. He couldn't have been, for he had *asked* why that skylight had been locked.

Laughing, they threw the young man from the roof. He didn't even scream. Then one of them said, 'That's it, eh, *mes amis*. He flies to meet the angels.'

'*Salauds*,' breathed Isabelle Moncontre, pressing her cheek so hard against Martin's the salt of her tears was mingled with the rain. 'They'll pay for this, won't they, my little parachute? Your father will help us kill them all.'

Hidden on the rue de Vaugirard, the cars started up and soon there was only the sound of the rain.

The flat on the rue de Beauséjour was in darkness and Hans left it that way because she wanted him to, Marie-Hélène following him through to the salon to open the French windows to the balcony and listen to the rain.

'I can't go on with this,' she said. 'I'm finished.'

'You're going to have to. We have no choice.'

He was refusing to understand. 'Those two terrorists were waiting for me, Hans. They *knew* I would be using that *maison de passe.*'

She was really worried and would have to be calmed. 'Look, you know that can't be true. The wire across the corridor was simply a safety precaution for themselves.'

Ah, damn him! 'And their door being ajar? Yes, I suppose that, too, could have been a precaution, but what about the one who waited on the floor above, eh? Who the hell was *he* waiting for, if not myself?'

A third man? 'Thiessen, Châlus, or whatever Anthony James Thomas is now calling himself, couldn't have known you would be meeting the Bellecour woman and the boy there. In any case, Kraus covered your back. Without the men he sent, where would you now be?'

Dead, was this what he really believed? 'So am I to be indebted to your second-in-command? That's perfect, isn't it, and exactly what he wants you to believe. Myself also, no doubt.'

She would have to be warned. 'Berlin have been after me again. Kraus is essential. They're telling me to listen to him or else.'

'Then ask yourself, please, if he knew enough to cover my back and to bolt and wire those skylights, why did he not warn me? He *knew* about those two who were killed, Hans. He must have. He's out to get us and you know it!'

She wouldn't understand how serious things were nor why he had to take Kraus's part. 'He felt the Bellecour woman might need convincing, so he organized things. Now the woman will accept you totally.'

So that was it, that was why the raid? Was this what he was saying? She couldn't believe it of him. 'I could easily have fallen from the roof, then where would you be?'

'You were *supposed* to have been in the room with the woman and the boy. *Everything* depended on their acceptance of you.'

'And were my clothes to be torn from me too, Hans? Was I also to have been smashed up against a wall?'

He didn't answer but was he still so blind, he wouldn't question what had happened? 'Then why, please, did those *gestapistes français* of his not take that wounded boy from the roof and into custody? Why didn't Kraus think it necessary to have questioned him, especially since he could well have led us to Châlus?'

His back was still to her. 'The idiots got carried away, that's all. They were to have taken them to the avenue Foch. Those were their orders.'

'*Ah, mon Dieu*, I'm not hearing this.'

Furious with him, for he wasn't listening, she went out onto the balcony to lift her face to the rain and shut her eyes. Martin would be no problem, but what of Angélique Belle-cour? That would have to be seen. And Abbeville? she asked, dreading the thought of what was to come. 'He's out there, Hans. Raymond Châlus, that unfinished business from Lyon and the *réseau* Parrache. Theissen—James Anthony Thomas—are they really one and the same? Please don't tell me you're still working on it.'

'Thiessen's wife and children are alive and well and at the address in the suburb of Marienburg. Apparently the couple separated just before the Blitzkrieg in the east and the fall of Poland. Certainly divorce is not currently allowed in the Reich, not without very special permission and she continues to try to get this, just as he continues to write to her and the children as if nothing had happened between them.'

Nothing. 'That's not what I asked you.'

'Abwehr-Paris still refuse to answer my queries about him being one of their special agents, so I have made an urgent appeal to the Reichsführer Himmler. As soon as Berlin have something, they'll telex it.'

But wasn't the Abwehr on the downslope and Himmler about to absorb it into the Sicherhietsdienst, so much so that here in Paris each side had been forbidden to speak to or associate with the other? 'Châlus could have taken up writing those letters, Hans. Châlus.'

Pulling off her things, she let the rain hammer her as it would the bodies of those two who had died. 'Were those *"résistants"* Kraus's men, Hans? Were they duped into doing what they did? Please, this I have to know because before they threw that boy from the roof, he demanded to know why the skylight he was supposed to have used had been locked?'

There was no answer, and when his car started up, she listened to it until, again, there was only the sound of the rain.

# 6

The third-class carriage was old and of a style Angélique hadn't seen in years. One of several, it had been pressed into use due to the removal of better rolling stock to the Reich. Each compartment was no more than a box that would seat four people. A small, square window had been placed too high for viewing the countryside when seated. Martin had to stand on his tiptoes until she, stiff and sore and sweating in this airless coffin, had taken down their suitcases and piled them on the floor for him.

Now the rhythm of the wheels, never fast, kept sounding until she thought she would go mad. Martin wasn't "speaking" to her. She was certain he had seen one of the *résistants* die last night, but had yet to tell her anything.

He had cried out in English for his father. For one brief instant, he had found his voice but had he also remembered what had happened to Anthony on that road south from Paris? Had he?

Have I lied to him? she asked. Have I been wrong in believing that Anthony was safe in England? Did he die on that road and is that not why Martin lost his voice, and is this why he doesn't want to have anything to do with me now?

Those gangsters of the *gestapistes français* hadn't raped

her but had left that feeling of total panic and terror. She was bruised and battered, her right breast badly discoloured and still hurting, the left shoulder and other places too. Lots of them. If they could have beaten her to death, they would have. Chance alone had intervened.

Those guys must have found Isabelle Moncontre on the roofs but had taken her down through one of the skylights in the adjacent houses. She's been arrested, hasn't she, Martin? she said to herself, dreading the thought. Me, I've been a fool, haven't I? And getting to her feet, went over to the window to wrap her arms around him.

He shook her off, would have smacked her if she had let him. 'Your father's in England, Martin. He *can't* help us. He left us on that road because I made him leave. He knew too much and . . . and lacked the courage needed to . . . to have kept silent when arrested.'

There, she had said it at last. The proof positive, but was everything finished between her and Martin now? A coward . . . Was she calling his dear papa that? She knew he would be thinking this and that he would hate her for it.

'*Chéri*, these times, they're so very different. Who's to say how any of us would react when faced with what those people would do?'

It was no use. Martin really had shut off his inner wireless set and had taken its aerial down, but as she watched him, he stretched, and in the top right corner of that little window, drew his signature parachute in the soot.

Below it he found room to put a dot and a dash, followed by a little gap, and then a dash-dot and another dash-dot, and, after a second gap, a single dash.

'Martin, please erase all of that immediately. *Ah, mon Dieu*, what is it with you? You know what they'll do to me if they find that.'

She was quivering with anger and he knew this as he drew a heart and then added the dot and a dash and then the dash followed by another and two dots.

A. J. T. loved A. B.—Anthony James Thomas loved Angélique Bellecour—but who will save us now? he asked and wrote two dots, followed by two dashes. I. M., Isabelle Moncontre.

'You know I can't read Morse. You know how dangerous it is for you to do that. Must you crucify the "mother" who loves you?'

Your own didn't, she wanted so much to say but couldn't bring herself to hurt him like that, had never said it to him.

Still he kept his back to her and she had to wonder what the hell had happened on that roof? 'Martin . . . *chéri*, did you remember the road south from Paris?'

*YOU'LL SEE*, he wrote in French and then, at the sound of the brakes, erased everything.

'What the hell's the matter with you?' she demanded when he sat down opposite her. '*Grâce à Dieu*, it's good we have this box to ourselves, though me, I would *wish* for better company!'

He said nothing. He just sat there like a peasant, not crying, not even shedding a single tear. Just looking at her as if at a dumb animal he was about to slaughter. A rabbit perhaps.

Slapping his face hard, she burst into tears, he to silently say, *Cry! That's what you should do.*

'I can't understand,' she blurted. 'What's happened to turn you so against me?'

He didn't answer. He got up and left her alone to weep and nurse her bruises, but once in the corridor, said aloud and softly to himself, 'Yes! I really have remembered that road and the Messerschmitts that machine-gunned us. Me, I know what really happened to my father. The sound of that gunfire last night made me.'

The train had stopped, and in the heavy stillness of this Sunday afternoon nothing stirred but a few chickens, a worn-out dog, one old stationmaster who was too tired to care, and a handful of flies.

Martin despaired. Picquigny was little different from all the other places along the railway line from Amiens to Abbeville, but here the land did come down through the trees from the plateau above the valley. An old castle had been smashed to pieces so long ago that smashing hadn't been necessary in this war or in the one before it and the one before that one. Some of the cellar walls still remained, and the stone staircase to what must have been the dungeons. Maybe *résistants* were hiding in those dungeons? Maybe.

Fighting . . . there had always been fighting along the Somme, but she wasn't coming. The Mademoiselle Moncontre must have been arrested, though she *had* said last night that she would try to meet them today. She really had.

Angélique didn't know a meeting had been promised. She didn't know *anything* anymore.

He wasn't going to tell her he had remembered or that he could speak. He wasn't going to tell anyone, not even the Mademoiselle Moncontre, if she hadn't been arrested. He was going to keep it all a secret. He had to. Otherwise monsieur le maire *and* the Germans would know he didn't need to carry a pencil anymore. 'Besides, that way I can help her, too, because the Boches, they'll not expect me to be able to talk and will think me stupid just like everyone does at the farm.'

There was an old church and an *abbaye* in the village, and he could see these while standing on the platform next to the steps that were off the rear of the third-class carriage and between it and the general-goods wagon. Upriver a little, one of the canal wardens was listening to two German corporals whose Mauser rifles were slung over their shoulders. They were sharing a cigarette, all three of them, and beyond them, a long line of poplars followed the towpath. All the lower branches had been removed and only the tops had leaves, which stirred and shone a dusty grey against the pale grey-blue of the sky.

The bark of the poplars was a grey green but much lighter, much nicer than that of the German uniforms. There were sooty black spots too, and as he watched the poplars, some starlings that had gathered in a newly plowed field suddenly took wing, black and noisy but faintly so in the heat.

Distant from them, he heard a bell ringing with great urgency. A bicycle with a carrier basket came into view, the bike being pedalled like the blazes along the towpath towards them, and he saw at once that it was the Mademoiselle Moncontre. 'Hurry,' he whispered aloud. 'Please hurry.'

She came on swiftly, but the path was bumpy and he thought she might fall if not careful. At one place she hit a half-buried boulder and the big handbag she had in her carrier basket leapt so high, she had to risk her life to push it down.

The corporals turned to watch, as did the canal warden, the stationmaster and the dog. A worn, plain brown leather suitcase was roped to the carrier rack behind her and she pedalled right up to the station to breathlessly ask if she was too late, and to lean her bike against the wall while she went in to get her tickets.

Martin knew he mustn't wave or acknowledge her in any way. He must keep his eyes on the soldiers, but also search the road beyond them for others.

The corporals were supposed to examine her papers and they began to walk towards her, she checking the bicycle over but not removing the suitcase. 'Must you charge me extra for it?' she complained to the stationmaster. 'Hey, I can leave it on the bike, can't I? It'll be okay like that?'

She was charged the extra, and with the bike once more in hand, walked it right past, and as she stood waiting, Martin watched as it was lifted up and taken into the baggage wagon. 'Tie the bike to something. Make sure there's no damage,' she said to that one.

Catching up with her, the corporals thought that maybe they could have a little fun, but she found her papers and handed them over, didn't say anything, and when they grinned at her, she looked down at their uniforms and frowned so deeply, they began to think that something must be wrong. Were there stains, their flies open?

Embarrassed, they had to look for themselves, but she didn't give them a moment, was really defiant and very pretty, and yes, she did have lovely brown eyes and soft dark brown hair that was brushed back today and pinned at the sides with bow-shaped barrettes. The plain white blouse was nice, the beige skirt too, even the white ankle socks and the scruffy brown leather shoes. No lipstick. Maybe not even any perfume. A bathing towel hung part way out of the woven straw handbag she carried instead of a purse.

'*Excusez-moi, s'il vous plaît,*' she said to him, and stepping past, went up into the carriage.

So far so good, thought Martin. Now he must remain on the lookout so as to give warning if necessary.

The compartment was stifling, the Bellecour woman distraught.

'What are they doing in Bois Carré?' asked Angélique bitterly. 'What's so important they would kill people to protect it?'

A cigarette would help, felt Marie-Hélène. She would light and share it, would have to be straight with this one but mustn't mention those aerial photos of the site that she had seen in Hans's office. 'We don't know. That's what I have to find out.'

'Didn't that message we brought to Paris tell you anything?'

Had it all been but a waste? Having been put through such a difficult time, the Bellecour woman should still have been able to calm herself a little by now. 'What's happened? If you'll forgive me for saying so, you don't look well.'

'How could I? But never mind, I simply want an answer.'

Taking the cigarette from her, she would snuff it out to emphasize things, thought Marie-Hélène. 'The message only told us that the Boches were building something in the woods and that Bois Carré isn't the only site. Apparently there are five others near Abbeville and all are hidden by woods, so it's something really big.'

'And?'

A tough one. 'A simple sketch gave the layout. A square house of some sort, a long, narrow clearing through the woods. Stranger still, there were two long things that looked like skis that had been lain on their sides. I'm going to have to get in there, but right now, don't know how I'll do it.'

'When we were at the avenue Foch, the SS beat a man to death. You do know of this, don't you?'

'Yes, of course, also that he wasn't the only one to die.'

The two last night. 'Someone in Abbeville, or in the surrounding countryside, betrayed that man, but if you ask me, Mademoiselle Moncontre, how is it, please, that if monsieur le maire and his friends felt so strongly there might be one in their midst, they didn't send the message with that man but used a boy who couldn't even cry out his name?'

'That's another matter I have to clear up, but they may not have felt betrayal possible. They might simply have been cautious, and that's why they chose to switch pencils with Martin.'

'Who is keeping a watch in the corridor for you, isn't he?'

This one was questioning far too much for her own good. 'It's necessary. Look, I'm sorry it's not pleasant, but . . .'

'Even children have to help? Is this what you're telling me?'

Must she be so difficult? 'Oh for sure, I don't like it any more than you do.'

'Then tell me, please, what happened on that roof to change him so much. Now he hates me. He won't even "talk" to me or write a word.'

Relighting the cigarette, she passed it to Angélique. 'I'll speak to him. It's the shock of having seen one of our people thrown from that roof. We were trapped. Not only had all the skylights of the nearby roofs been wired shut, those bastards had installed iron grilles inside them so that even if the glass was broken, it would do no good. I thought they would take me too, but then Martin found me and . . . and together we waited it out.'

So that was it, shared moments of danger. 'He's in love with you, and what he felt for me has been handed to you on the platter of his innocence. Treat it tenderly, mademoiselle. The bankroll of his trust is never secure.'

Had jealousy intruded? wondered Marie-Hélène.

In tears, Angélique turned quickly away, but said, 'Two young men, no more than boys were killed. It's hard to imagine such hatred could exist. Frenchmen against Frenchmen.'

The sadness and disbelief that such a thing could happen were very real, therefore the answer must come softly and earnestly. 'That's the way it is.'

'Then please tell me why those two were even in that house?'

'*Ah, mon Dieu*, you ask too many questions! You should

know that's not wise. They were my backup and I'm glad they were there. Otherwise it would have been you, me and Martin, and we would . . .' She shrugged. 'Well, who's to say what would have happened?'

The cigarette helped a little, just talking to someone, a little more, and when Isabelle Moncontre took a bottle of cognac from her bag, that too, helped.

'Martin's father . . . Is he the one who leads your *réseau?*' asked Angélique. 'Look, I know I shouldn't have asked, but Martin now believes it entirely.'

'And yourself?'

She shook her head. 'To me, Anthony is in England and I've always felt this.'

'Do you still love him so much?'

'As from the day I first met him in the Louvre. We had our differences on that road south from Paris during the exodus, but I could never hold any of that against him. He knew he had to leave, that what I had said was true. He simply didn't want to leave Martin behind. Everything in those few tragic moments came down to his son. Anthony, he . . . he blamed me for our having left Paris with all the others, and then for having stopped him from going after Martin when everything had been shot up like that and those ME-109s were coming back for yet another run, but it was the only thing I could possibly have done. For him to have stayed in France would have been far too dangerous. You see . . .' Was it safe to tell her, to tell anyone? 'He had done things for the British while in the Reich on business. Gathering military intelligence—ah, I knew this. At least I suspected it, and when I found some sketches he had made from memory, I knew it but didn't tell him this until . . . until those last few moments together. He . . . he then accused me of having spied on him.'

Isabelle Moncontre looked at her with . . . ah, what was it? wondered Angélique. Suspicion? Fear? A deep interest, most certainly, for the woman now drew on that cigarette and held the smoke in for as long as possible to give herself time to think, but what, please, were those thoughts?

The leader of the *réseau de soie bleue* had to be Anthony James Thomas, felt Marie-Hélène. Alias the Hauptmann Thiessen, alias Raymond Châlus. Unable to take the brittleness from her voice, she said abruptly, 'I can't tell you who leads us. It's far too dangerous. Look, I'm sorry, but far too many others depend on him.'

'He's good, isn't he?'

'The best. Exceedingly careful. Always one step ahead of the SS and their friends. In Lyon eight months ago it was a disaster for us, but he has learned from that and now takes no chances. He hunts for the SS and those who help them, and just as hard as they hunt for him and the rest of us.'

'Yet if he takes such care, how is it, please, that those *gestapistes français* and the Germans knew you were to meet us in that house?'

A shrug would be best. 'Perhaps there was a foul-up, but this we really don't know. Those types, they often raid the *maisons de passe*, searching for evaders of the STO and for Jews on the run. It could simply have been that.'

Again the Bellecour woman listened to the wheels of the train until at last she said, 'What were the names of those two boys they killed?'

'Are names so important to you?'

'It's often all that is left to remind us of a life, and then but briefly.'

'I can't tell you. The Germans will print something but even then no one will claim the bodies. Fear will prevent this. Also they carried false papers.'

'How can you do this sort of thing?'

Was it acceptance of her at last? wondered Marie-Hélène. 'Because we must. Because if we don't, we'll have those people on top of us forever.'

'Have you a gun, a pistol?'

'I lost it last night.'

'And yet you can still . . . ? The SS, Herr Dirksen . . .'

'The Standartenführer, a colonel.'

Reluctantly Angélique told her what was expected of Martin and herself. Isabelle Moncontre listened gravely and nodded. Lost in thought, she again took her time to consider things.

And now, at last, wondered Marie-Hélène, is it to be a

moment of understanding between us? 'Then you must do as he asks, but we will intercept the next message and will substitute another. That way the Germans will think we know far less than we do.'

'And yourself?' asked Angélique.

'If you see me, we must pass in the street as total strangers. Me, I'll contact you if necessary.'

'Am I to warn monsieur le maire?'

'No, I'll do that. You must play your part or everything is lost. Remember, please, that this Dirksen will have his own people in the area. They'll be watching you all the time.'

'And Martin?'

'Martin, too. The very fact that they've not arrested Émile Vergès indicates how serious it is. They want to take all of us and our only hope is to play along with them for a little.'

'And then?'

'Escape lines are being arranged. Safe houses—farmers we know we can trust absolutely. Then you and Martin to Switzerland, I think. Myself . . .' She shrugged. 'Into the south again, the Vaucluse this time perhaps. It's too early to say, but I can assure you we'll be one step ahead of them all the time.'

Her gaze is so sincere, thought Angélique. She's very aware of the risks and is incredibly brave. 'It's Martin's father who leads you, isn't it?' she asked. 'Somehow Anthony stayed behind and hid himself so well, he could live in my flat and no one knew until . . . until I had to be so foolish as to insist on a specialist for his son.'

'Does Martin look like him?'

'You've seen it too. Martin's like his father in so many ways. Anthony speaks Deutsch like a Prussian and can imitate almost anyone. He has that knack of dissolving himself completely into another character. While at Cambridge, he took part in every amateur theatrical he could and planned to become an actor. Martin has some of that gift. Had the war not come along, he might well have become what his father had wanted most for himself.'

An actor. A Wehrmacht lieutenant, an Abwehr agent, Raymond Châlus.

Isabelle Moncontre's hand came to rest on her own, the

concern in her lovely eyes deep. 'You and Martin will escape, as will your Anthony. Always you must believe this.'

To try to smile was difficult. 'Me, I don't really know what to believe anymore. Anthony was always very good at fixing things. Engines, clocks, wireless sets, all those sorts of things. Designing yachts came as naturally to him as it did for Martin to build his own crystal set and learn how to read and use Morse. And *that* was all before I ever met Martin.'

*Merde*, what was this? 'Please, he's *not* your son?'

Did it matter so much? 'He's Anthony's. Martin . . . Martin, he hid in the *Alcyone*'s bow locker when his father came to take me from France before it was too late.'

'The *Alcyone*?'

'Yes. A seven-metre yacht. Anthony had as great a love of the early Greeks as myself. Alcyone was the daughter of Aeolus, keeper of the winds. When she married Ceyx of Trachis, son of the Morning-star, they were so well suited and happy in their love and lovemaking, she foolishly referred to him as Zeus, herself as Hera, thus angering the gods. When he was killed in a terrible storm, Alcyone threw herself from the rocks and into the sea.'

A typical Greek tragedy—was this what Isabelle Moncontre was now thinking? wondered Angélique, but the woman remained so lost in thought, something else would have to be said. 'Anthony always had a streak of fatalism, that's why he gave the yacht a name like that. He did it on a dare to himself, I suppose. His marriage was splitting up and he had found another great love. His father had been killed on the Somme in the Great War and now, in a final irony, I find myself taking the grandson of that one back down the Somme to a final battle.'

'Did he tell you where he had left the yacht?'

'But . . . but why would you want to know such a thing?'

A faint smile should be given. 'Because it may provide us with an escape I hadn't thought of.'

'But . . . but surely it will have been destroyed in the bombing or taken by someone.'

'Perhaps, but if needed, is it not worth locating?'

There would be coastal patrol boats, Messerchmitts and

other aircraft to contend with, submarines that would surface . . . 'How is it, please, that you have such connections? Deauville is in the *zone interdite*.'

'As is Abbeville, yet we come and go, don't we?'

Anthony couldn't have told his *réseau* about the yacht and must have had his reasons, but, 'I . . . I could never sail her alone.'

'Nor would you be expected to.'

The rhythmic sound of the wheels came. The cigarette butt had been tucked away long ago.

'Tell me about Martin's mother.'

'Evelyn . . . ? She was the daughter of an Anglican bishop. It was a good marriage, everyone said, and Anthony . . . I know he must have believed it, because he doesn't do anything without a lot of thought, and he loved her—he really did, but . . . Ah, how should I put it so as not to cheapen myself?'

'She was repressed. Unable to give herself totally.'

This one must know the ropes, but had she been sleeping with Anthony? wondered Angélique, alarmed at the thought. 'Martin loved his mother very much, but if you ask me, Mademoiselle Moncontre, I think he saw himself as her protector, and when his parents had a terrible row just before Anthony left to get me, Martin had to stop it from happening. And now . . . now again he has come to hate me, but this time I don't know why. I really don't. I love him as my own. You see, he's all I've got. I know it's selfish of me, especially when I've stolen him from his mother.'

'Does he "talk" of her a lot?'

'Not at all. Not since the Blitzkrieg and that road south from Paris. Me, I don't think she ever loved him in return. I think she must have looked on him, remembering only what she had had to go through to get him. He was to have gone to a boarding school that autumn. At least the war, it has saved him from such a fate, and perhaps living with me has broadened his experience a little.'

'Will he ever use his voice again?'

There was no time to answer. Martin was at the door and the alarm in his tear-filled eyes told them it was all over.

'Keep calm,' said Marie-Hélène. 'We're at the control for the *zone interdite*. Let me leave ahead of you both and remember, please, that we aren't to know one another. We're total strangers.'

The line moved slowly, the sun beat down to bake the siding onto which the train had been shunted. Soldiers were everywhere, the dogs held back by thick leather leashes. There were Gestapo, too, some even wearing the black uniforms, though such had gone out of fashion in 1940 to be replaced by the grey of the SS to which, of course, they were associated.

The one who sat at the table between the barricades wore the black one with the red armband and black swastika on a white circle. The Gestapo Munk was about fifty. Officious, he took his time to question everyone, while Kraus stood back and aloof, enjoying the spectacle.

A *panier à salade*, one of those infamous grilled, cubicle-chambered, black iron salad baskets the *flics* of Paris, Lyon and other large cities and towns used to cart people off to the cells, sat idle on the road, which here ran alongside the railway tracks. Kraus's car was parked in front of it. Two armed SS stood guard, waiting for him. There were camouflaged lorries as well.

Across the river, the broad, flat floor of the valley held verdant marshes, large open stretches of shallow water, islands, some of which were treed, and then the Somme canal against the far bank.

Nearly three kilometres long, a *chaussée** to the other side offered no hope of escape, for its bridge had been dynamited in the centre and at three other places, as had all but one of the many crossings. The May-June Blitzkrieg of 1940 had been bitter and, during the French retreat and then the rout, Rommel and his Seventh Tank Division had crossed just upstream from here on the only remaining railway bridge.

The little village of Long, perhaps of four hundred souls in all, clung to the hillside over there, and at the foot of it, on the other side of the entrance to the *chaussée* and beside the water,

---

* A causeway

there were the red brick, with white stone walls, and the slate mansard roofs of an eighteenth-century château.

It all looked so peaceful. Ducks and swans cruised the nearby ponds, blackbirds sang and the harshness of their repetitious calling was set against the muted, intermittent shuffling of the line.

Angélique took a step. Martin was just in front of her, Isabelle Moncontre seven places in front of him.

At a nod from Kraus, two corporals led their dogs along the line, one on either side, and when they reached her, Angélique felt them pause. The dogs sniffed at the suitcases, at the smears of rancid butter that hadn't been completely cleaned away, and at the taint of the meat Kraus and the others at the avenue Foch had taken.

The moist snout of a German shepherd touched her bare left leg and went up it until she cried out in silence, Mustn't move. *Can't* tell it to go away. *Can't* ask him to pull it back.

'Heini, *komm mal her*,' said the guard, yanking the animal away.

'*Merci*,' she managed, but the other dog was at the suitcases.

'*Öffnen, bitte.*'

'But . . . but there's nothing. Just a few clothes that need to be washed. A dress that's been ripped.'

'*Schnell, ja?*'

Hurry. She crouched. The dogs began to get her scent again. Saliva wet her cheeks, her ears, her hair as she undid the straps and opened both suitcases.

Everyone watched. The line had completely stopped. 'There's . . . there's nothing,' she managed, fighting back the panic. A torn slip fell, a brassiere . . . He grunted and the dogs were pulled away to worry someone else.

Martin didn't even help her to close the suitcases. He just stood looking at her with that same dumb-ox gaze.

'When we get home, I'm going to have this out with you!' she hissed. 'Beware the woman shunned, Martin. Watch out for her talons!'

*Then look, you stupid thing*, he said silently, those lips of his forming the words. *See who's in the line.* Use *the opportunity to find the ones they're after.*

'Ah no,' she gasped, and turning as she crouched, ran her gaze back along the line. Had the Germans deliberately made the third-class passengers get off first so as to cause panic among the others?

There was a priest who carried a prayer book. Tall and thin, he had brown hair. Two sisters were in front of him and it was obvious all three were together, she telling herself one must look as if going about one's daily business. One must blend in with the others.

The priest was in his forties, and the steel-rimmed specs he wore did little for him besides helping the vision. His ears stuck out, the chin was pointed, the skin fair and looking as if it didn't take well to the sun.

As she looked at him, he blankly returned her gaze for what seemed the longest time, but it couldn't have been any more than a couple of seconds.

One of the sisters, a novice, was the girl who had rescued them with the *vélo-taxi*. Angélique was certain of it.

Quickly she turned away only to meet Martin's gaze. *Are you so blind?* he mouthed, tormenting her until she begged, 'Why are you doing this to me?'

Isabelle Moncontre had reached the barricade and from there the question asked came so clearly, 'Where is your baggage?'

'My bicycle's on the train.'

There were two tickets. The Gestapo Munk looked up at her and said, 'I asked of your baggage, a suitcase perhaps?'

'I'm going to my sister's in Abbeville. Our mother is very ill. I . . . I have everything I need there.'

But she also has a suitcase, thought Martin. It's brown and old and roped to the rear carrier of that bike.

Her papers were examined and held up to the sun. 'The stamp of the Commissariat de Police de Paris and that of the Kommandant von Gross-Paris are smudged. Please step aside.'

'There's nothing wrong with those!'

'STEP ASIDE!'

The shriek he'd given caused the dogs to leap and bark. Marie-Hélène couldn't understand why there should have been *any* problem. Hans, she cried out inwardly. Hans, what the hell is this? And only then realized that she now had an excellent opportunity to view the others in the line and to look back at each of them, they at her.

That priest, she said to herself. Those sisters . . . That younger one, doesn't she look a lot like that *résistante* Yvette Rougement, that priest like Raymond Châlus?

A sickness came. The other nun seemed quite genuine. Well up in her seventies, she wore glasses. Sweat moistened the pale brow and made the blue eyes blink as she gazed back at her not with sympathy but with a hardness that was cruel.

'*Bitte, Fräulein. Euere Papiere.*'

'*Pardon?*' She leapt.

A Scharführer nudged her hand several times, she finally understanding and saying, '*Merci.*'

Alone and feeling Châlus's gaze and that of the two sisters, Marie-Hélène walked between the barricades to stand and wait until everyone else who would be allowed to continue had passed through.

Kraus wasn't grinning. He was still watching the line, but would he pluck that priest and those nuns?

The one seemed so at ease. He spoke quietly to the elder sister. Perhaps he said, It won't be long now; perhaps he said, That one is our angel of death.

Abbeville had been the site of fierce resistance during the Blitzkrieg, and for days afterwards, one lone man had killed a German soldier a day and they had never caught him. But would Châlus, if this really was him in the guise of a priest, not plan to link up with this other one?

Marie-Hélène searched the line for the two who were to watch her back. Both were wearing faded *bleus de travail*, boots and berets. One was to have carried a carpenter's tools, the other, the frayed canvas satchel of a bricklayer. Their papers would state that they were en route to jobs with the Todt Organization, which was building the sites at Bois Carré and other places near Abbeville.

Both would be in their late thirties. Experienced men and tougher than they looked.

They weren't there, and with a sinking feeling, she realized she was to be completely on her own, that Kraus had prevented them from coming.

The two sisters were being let through the barricades with hardly a glance, the priest as well.

They met in Abbeville, in a goods' shed along the tracks where, unlike other passengers with bikes, she had been forced to collect hers. Kraus was waiting among bales of produce that were destined for the Reich. 'Idiot!' she said, so near to tears she was flushed with anger. 'What the hell did you think you were doing by singling me out for others to notice? You should have detained that priest and those nuns.'

Worried, she started for the bike, only to feel him grip her by the arm. 'A moment,' he said.

He had given her that thin-lipped smile of his. 'Well, what is it?'

Kraus felt he could smell the fear, but had that priest really been Châlus? 'Had I detained them, the mayor and the others would have been alerted. This way, they'll suspect nothing.'

Was he really such an idiot? 'And for how long? An hour? Two hours? How could you do this to me?'

She would always doubt him. 'The same way I saved your life last night.'

'*Maudit salaud*, then why, please, did those *gestapistes fran-çais* of yours not take that one from the roof into custody?'

Dirksen would have told her it had been a mistake, but apparently the colonel hadn't been convincing enough. 'The fools disobeyed my orders. They got carried away.'

'Ah no, monsieur. Those boys you killed weren't *résistants*. They were among that gang of yours. Hans might believe you, but not me.'

And you have just signed your death warrant, thought Kraus, but he would leave it for now. 'That priest and those sisters are booked through to Noyelles-sur-Mer. Apparently the elder of the sisters must make a pilgrimage to the Chinois

Military Cemetery. Her brother's grave. We'll check it out, of course.'

'And the younger one?'

'Is with her as a companion.'

'Then what of the priest, damn you?'

'Companion to both.'

Tossing her hands in despair, she said, 'Hey, I'm not hearing this? From Noyelles-sur-Mer and that cemetery, which is just to its east, what's to prevent them from vanishing up the road and into the Forêt de Crécy?'

'They'll be watched every step of the way.'

Did he really believe that possible? '*Bonne chance,* Major. *Bonne chance.* That one, that Châlus, he does the unexpected. From that forest it will be quite easy for him to find his way to Bois Carré without your knowing. It's near the tiny village of Yvrench, is it not? He'll fit right in, wearing those things and with that prayer book, but when needed, he'll lose that garb faster than you can breathe.'

She really was determined to prove him an idiot. 'But that'll take time and keep him from contacting the mayor here until after you've done so.'

She would dismiss such idiocy with a toss of her head! 'Again, me, I'm not hearing this. Is it, Major, that you've learned nothing of their methods? That priest will have already tipped off the mayor who'll be waiting for me.'

'Perhaps, but that's a chance we have to take.'

Was it possible that he already knew the mayor had been alerted? 'Look, it's all off. Tell Hans his little pigeon has been compromised.' She tossed a hand. 'Hey, monsieur, you ride the bike. Me, I give you the benefit of the British wireless set in that suitcase. Perhaps you can radio Berlin for help. Perhaps, if the terrorists catch up with you, its transceiver will be the one thing above all others that convinces them you're genuine.'

Unpliable, she would never agree to work with him, felt Kraus. Always she would run to Dirksen. 'I want Châlus, and you're going to give him to me.'

So that was it. Kraus would be the one responsible for clearing up that little bit of unfinished business. Raymond Châlus.

Gestapo Berlin and Himmler would be grateful. 'I didn't get a close enough look at that priest to say for certain it really was Châlus.'

'But you were the only one to see him up close in Lyon, and your description of Thiessen, this "Father Boulanger", matches exactly what you said back then. That is why I had you stand aside at the control. You were to have confirmed it.'

'And me, I'm telling you I have my doubts and can't yet be positive.'

She was holding back so as to let Dirksen know of it first, but he would have to go carefully. 'Tell me what passed between you and the Bellecour woman.'

It would do no good to hide that from him. 'They'll go along with what has been asked of them. The boy believes firmly that his father is in France and heads up the *réseau de soie bleue*, the woman, she . . . she now believes it also, even to thinking that her former lover might well have been sleeping with me.'

'Perhaps she has gauged your character correctly.'

The pig! 'Where is Hans? Why isn't he here?'

She wasn't going to like it, but it did feel good having to tell her. 'Berlin. The pressures of work. Report after report, always it's that way, so he felt he had to stay at the helm.'

The avenue Foch, but was her usefulness now all but over? wondered Marie-Hélène. Had Hans felt he had better sever himself from all contact with her, or was it perhaps that he was trying to warn her that her safety depended on keeping things to herself until he could deal with Kraus? 'Look, I'll need another gun. I lost the other one.'

Which had been found in the street below. 'That was very thoughtless of you, since it could well be used to kill one of us or our friends.'

In Paris. 'The loss couldn't be helped. I was on that bloody roof!'

And doubtless had slipped. 'I've nothing that can be spared at the moment, but will see what can be done.'

Was it that he *wanted* her dead? 'And Châlus, Major? If he gets me, you won't get him, but if I get him, you can claim the credit.'

Which would, of course, be safest for her since the *Banditen* would be only too interested in the truth, but her begging hadn't been convincing. 'Perhaps you would pass along such a credit, perhaps not. How could I be sure?'

'Because I'm telling you now. Hey, me, I'm the one who has to risk her life, aren't I ? To go in there without a gun, is to go in there naked.'

As she watched, Kraus fingered his brow and passed a smoothing hand over that closely trimmed dark brown hair that was parted exactly like the Führer's. Always he would give himself away with such little signs of nervousness when he felt he had won something.

'You'll say nothing more of the one who was thrown from the roof. You'll report everything to me, before giving anything to the Standartenführer. All arrests are to be made by me, not him. I want a clean sweep. All the filth is to be removed both from here and from Paris. The *réseau de soie bleue* is to vanish from the face of the earth at the execution posts. This I have promised the Reichsführer and Reichsminister Himmler. Don't be among them.'

He'd see to it too, if he felt it useful. The wireless set would be evidence enough for her to be swept up in the net and Berlin none the wiser, even though Gestapo Paris's Listeners had provided it *and* would expect it back. 'What's to happen to Hans if we're not successful?'

How good of her to have asked, but he'd leave it unanswered, felt Kraus. 'I'll see that you get a gun after you've convinced the mayor you're on his side. For now that is all we have to say. *Auf Wiedersehen*, Fräulein Marie-Hélène de Fleury, or would you prefer Fräulein Isabelle Moncontre? But remember, please, that I have a copy of your dossier the *Banditen* would appreciate. Don't make me use it.'

For a long time after he had left her, she was unable to function. Then slowly, as if she still couldn't face what was to come, she wheeled the bike through the ruins of the town until she came to two of its remaining buildings: the red brick hôtel de ville and Kommandantur, with its bomb-damaged white stone belfry, and the much older, much taller two Gothic towers of the Church of Saint-Vulfran, whose roof had collapsed in places. Nearly everything else in the centre of Abbeville had been reduced to rubble by the Stuka attacks of 20 May 1940 and the ensuing firestorm. Built mainly in the sixteenth century, over two thousand houses had simply been turned into an inferno out of whose ashes had risen, she was certain, a hatred of the Occupier that could only have festered during the past three years.

Seen from the ruins, the bicycle with its suitcase was leaning against the wall and had been left unlocked, thought Angélique, but as Isabelle Moncontre went up the steps of the Kommandantur and hôtel de ville, this *résistante* must have remembered that theft could happen even on a Sunday and in a place such as this, and that though there were two Wehrmacht sentries on duty, even they could not be entirely trusted.

Returning to put the lock on, she paused to look uncertainly across the barren wasteland of what had once been the heart of a fine old town. Then she, too, like all others who had got off that train, went in to register or to report her return, for this was indeed the Forbidden Zone but with that little added emphasis of the top-secret things that were going on in Bois Carré.

The suitcase had remained behind.

'Martin. Martin, listen to me, *please*,' said Angélique. 'Before we meet monsieur le maire, who will have come in from his Sunday off, as will all of the others, I have to have your answer or can't continue.'

He didn't say a thing, just kept watching that suitcase, and when she insisted on an answer, he picked up a flat chunk of plaster and sent it whistling among the ruins. '*Martin!*' she snapped. '*Ah, mon Dieu, idiot*, that novice we saw was the girl who rescued us, but was that priest really your father?'

Silently he let that dumb-ox gaze of his settle on her until, furious with him, she again wanted to slap his face. 'Please,' she begged, restraining herself.

Her clothes were a mess, her hair too. A ruined wall was behind her. There was a window above her and, yes, a charred timber that could fall at any moment. *You slept with my father so many times*, he said, letting her read his lips. *You lay naked in his arms and yet you can't even say it was him?*

'Must you torment me like this?'

There were tears, and she said that if that priest really had been his father, then things had changed him terribly. 'When he looked at me, Martin, there was no longer any love or even recognition.'

*Then there, you have your answer*, he said, letting her read his lips. *Maybe it's that you are no longer the temptation you once were.*

'Listen you, if it was your father, we must tell the mayor the truth.'

*You'll be shot.*

'That's a sacrifice I'll have to make.'

Now tears filled *his* eyes and he wanted to hit her, to kick and punch and yell at the top of his lungs—yes, yes, just to show her he could really speak!

*But . . . but what about the Mademoiselle Isabelle?* he silently asked, nodding towards the bike. *What about the orders she gave us? Are they not* his *orders?*

'Then it was him, wasn't it?' she said. 'And me, I can only hope you're right.'

The smell of the ruins came to them, that of plaster dust, cordite and ashes that seemed never to dry but in the heat of a summer's afternoon gave up their dampness to sting the nostrils.

Stooping to pick up the suitcases, she found that he had got to them first. '*Merci*,' she said. 'That's better. Now come on, let's get it over with. Me, I don't like lying to anyone. Lies always have a way of coming back to haunt a person.'

*Even lies to the SS?* he asked and knew she was thinking of the Major Kraus and the Colonel Dirksen.

Canals had serviced the docks, the dye-works, textile mills and warehouses that were now no more but for the accusing fingers of their red brick, often half-ruined chimneys. Still choked with rubble and flooded by the gates downstream that held back the water, the canals stank of sewage and rotting vegetation.

*Hortillonnages*—market gardens—formed hectares of lush

green, rectangular islands both upstream and downstream and these had been put back into use that first summer. Among the open stretches of water there were wooden landings and walkways, and the tarred, flat-bottomed boats the farmers used. But of the quaint old houses and narrow streets with names like that of the He-Mules or the Bridge-for-the-Wheelbarrows, there were no more.

'Martin . . . Martin, why did your father not give us some sign? A smile, a lift of his hand—a signal just to let us know he loved us?'

He's not in love with you anymore, he wanted so much to say but would have to touch her hand since that would calm her a little.

Kissing him on the cheek, she brushed a hand over his hair and said, 'You're forgiven, I think. It's not been easy, has it, this trip?'

The bicycle with its suitcase was gone and when they went into the hôtel de ville, monsieur le maire was not waiting for them. The little room the Germans had given him for an office was empty.

Angélique collapsed against a wall and for a moment, the sickness rose in her throat and she shut her eyes, tried to stop herself from thinking, He's been arrested. *Arrested!* But everything was going round and round. The Kommandantur, the long counter with its brown linoleum top, its signs and notices in French and in German. *For the acts of terrorism on 13 August 1943, the following* . . . Ten this time in Amiens and where must it all end?

Martin was tugging urgently at her hand. There was still no sign of the mayor—why wasn't he here to meet them?

The counter, indicated Martin. Madame Dussart and Frau Hössler were waiting.

'Ah, forgive me,' she managed, her voice sounding overly loud in the near-emptiness of the place. 'The stomach upset. The food in Paris, it . . . it was not so good as everyone says. At least, not for us, of course.'

Finding their papers, she spread them on the counter before Véronique Dussart, a coworker she knew well yet who didn't even smile now or let any warmth enter those lovely blue eyes that could, in reflective moments, become so sad but were now far too wary. There was no recognition whatsoever from Frau Hössler who stood stiffly and unyieldingly to the left. Both of them were blondes, but here the similarities ended except for this . . . this new coldness.

'Véronique, what's happened? Monsieur le maire, has he been . . . ?'

In her midthirties, and with a husband languishing in a prisoner-of-war camp in Germany and all her petitions for his return rejected, Véronique Dussart had much to be bitter about. Three children and living with her in-laws in two crowded rooms. Work six and seven days a week and no one to share her loneliness at night.

Of medium height, she had always held herself well and had been proud and defiant, never underhand, but now? wondered Angélique. Now . . . ?

There was lipstick and a little rouge to accent the clear skin that would still be the envy of others when she was much older. The face was thin, the hair in curls and waves, the forehead high, the nose a little too sharp perhaps, but the eyebrows long and beautifully curved, the eyes moist.

Quickly using the cancellation stamp on the *laissez-passers*, she stamped the *sauf-conduits* too, ticked off the identity cards, nervously flipped through the ration books, wrote down their names, the date and time, and passed everything along the counter to Frau Beate Hössler, but said nothing. Absolutely nothing. 'Aren't you even curious about how we got along?'

Still there was no answer, only an increased moistening of the eyes and the nervousness of fingers that flew away as her back was turned.

'Someone did their duty,' grunted Frau Hössler. 'The terrorist Doumier was apprehended in Paris and killed. She suspects yourself of telling the authorities, as do others. The trip to Paris was perhaps your reward.'

Ah no. 'My reward? And do you think this too?'

The woman didn't even shrug. In her thickly atrocious French, she simply said, 'I, too, must do my duty.'

Greying rapidly, the woman had bleached her black hair and then had dyed it blond, but the colour these days wasn't so dependable, the shade could change from week to week, and always the roots showed through. A war widow who had lost her husband on the Somme in 1940, she had shaved off her eyebrows to catch another man perhaps, but had used pencil to replace them without much success. Powder and rouge might have helped, were it not for the lipstick she wore, and perhaps she really had been loved by that husband. Who was to say? She had followed in his footsteps to tend his grave and do her part to oversee those responsible for his death, the French. A Blitzmädel, one of the rank and file. From Upper Swabia. Sweat stains surrounded the armpits of the field-grey tunic that bulged.

'Doumier . . . ?' managed Angélique as the woman scrutinized their papers. 'I don't even know who you mean.'

'Of course. It's what the Oberst Lautenschläger has said.'

*Ah, grâce à Dieu* for that one, but what had happened to the mayor?

'Your ration tickets,' said the woman. 'There are too many.'

'We skipped a lot of meals, Frau Hössler. There was so little food in Paris, it . . . well, it seemed the only thing to do. Are they now out of date?'

Brusquely the head was shaken. The slablike cheeks moved and the big, blocky face with its overripe lips and flaring nostrils became grim with determination. 'I will remove four meat tickets, six each for the bread and the same for the butter and cheese.'

And damn the woman. 'There was no butter, nor was there any cheese.'

'That is impossible. Paris has everything.'

Not even bread or milk. 'Look, we didn't eat in any of the black-market restaurants so as to avoid using those.'

'The black market? What, please, is this to which you are referring?'

The pudgy fingers gripped the ration tickets as if to tear them apart.

'You took food to Paris. This I know,' said Beate. 'It was illegal. That, too, was a privilege you were given, but it is one that I must question.'

And had others thought it a privilege?

The big lips moved again. 'Just because you are employed here does not mean you can disobey the rules.'

'We didn't! Martin . . . Martin, did we break any rules?' Had the mayor been arrested?

The emptiness of the boy's gaze was far from good, felt Beate, but he did look thinner and paler than usual. *Ein Kind der Liebe,*˙ and unhealthy like so many French children.

She clucked her tongue and pursed her lips. 'Very well, for Martin's sake, I allow the return of the unused tickets this time.'

'That's really very kind of you.' But the booklets were still being withheld.

'Well, what did the specialist say?' asked the woman.

'That we must return in a week. He . . . he thinks hypnosis might help.'

Then the disease was a matter of the mind. 'It's nothing. You needn't be so worried. One is just put to sleep and then awakens at the snap of the fingers.'

'Yes . . . Yes, I guess that's how it will be if . . . if we're allowed to return. That's why I have to see the mayor, Frau Hössler. Where is he?'

Véronique, with her back to them, was standing so still it was evident a breath was being held.

'He is with the Oberst Lautenschläger at the château,' said Frau Hössler. 'The Hautpmann Scheel and the Sturmbannführer Kraus will take you there.'

Kraus, ah no.

In splodges, daubs and full, bold strokes whose white paint had run, the huge letters cried out, *NOUS LES AURONS! MORT AUX BOCHES! LES CORBEAUX AU POTEAU!*

We'll get them! Death to Germans. The crows, the writers of poisoned-pen letters and the informants, up against the post!

And then, along a little farther on that same ruined wall of that same brick warehouse, *RAPPELEZ-VOUS DOUMIER.* Remember Doumier.

---

˙ A child of love

Perhaps two hundred carefully tied bunches of red chry-santhemums lay below the surveyor's name. A dozen work-men in faded *bleus de travail* were trying to remove the let-ters but hadn't stepped on any of the flowers. Their work was slow, and when questioned angrily by Kraus who had the car stopped, they said the paint had seeped into the pores of the bricks.

'THE FOOLS!' he shrieked in Deutsch. Livid at such inso-lence, he smashed the foreman in the face and sent him fly-ing.

Stunned and bleeding, the man tried to get up but knew he shouldn't, and when the jackboot came at him, the sound of breaking ribs could be heard.

Blood bubbled from his lips. His eyes rolled up.

'You've punctured a lung,' said the Hautpmann Scheel. 'You had no right to injure him.'

'I HAVE EVERY RIGHT!' shrieked Kraus. One didn't need an interpreter to understand. 'This district is to be placed under SS jurisdiction.'

'Not yet, Sturmbannführer. I still have my orders. My com-manding officer must be consulted.'

'Consult if you wish, but have that one taken to the cells.'

'To the hospital, I think, and quickly.'

'How dare you countermand me in front of them? There's a crisis in Abbeville. This . . . this . . .'—Kraus indicated the slogans on the wall—'is evidence enough. An armed insurrec-tion is imminent.'

'No it isn't. Oberst Lautenschläger has . . .'

'Arrested that mayor?'

The Hauptmann Scheel saw no further sense in continu-ing the argument in front of listeners, all of whom would soon repeat what had been said, and any of whom could well belong to the *Banditen*.

Scheel was young, perhaps twenty-eight, but battle hard-ened. Calmly he slid the car into gear but paused to nod at the cluster of men. They were to take the foreman to the hospital. The car, and the camouflaged lorry full of armed soldiers of the Waffen-SS that followed, came to a turning, Martin look-ing back, Angélique too.

Already a two-wheeled cart had been found and the man lain in it. But had the mayor been arrested? she wondered, silently crossing herself, for if the Waffen-SS were to take over security, Kraus would pull out her fingernails, have her half beaten to death, and then use the bathtub.

Panicking at the thought, she gripped Martin's hand and held it tightly against the leather of the seat.

She was fighting for control, he realized, and moving closer, pushed himself right up against her. *I'm sorry*, he said, mouthing the words, though she couldn't see his lips to read them.

Among the trees and underbrush there was a stillness that made her listen, felt Marie-Hélène. Pausing with the bike she was pushing, she let the wooded scarp come down to her from the plateau above. A spring issued from the base of the scarp. Like so many along the valley of the Somme, its waters fed a river that hardly moved, but here the spring was anxious, and in the near-silence of the day she could hear its faint trickling.

The woman had been right. A narrow path led to a rock-laid basin, a mere cup in the hillside. To meet at any time was dangerous—yes, of course, and she didn't like the thought of it, but Kraus had forced the issue. Châlus as well, if it really had been him. There had been no sign of the mayor and there should have been. The Bellecour woman and the boy had had to go into the Kommandantur to sign in, and they would have been expecting the mayor to have been there to meet them, but he hadn't and the two at the counter hadn't looked happy either. Indeed, when the Blitzmädel had left them momentarily alone, the other one had all but burst into tears when spoken to.

So, there, she said as if wanting to reassure herself. It has to be this way. I have to find out everything I can about that *réseau de soie bleue* and quickly.

Laying the bike down in the underbrush, she took off her blouse and brassiere and, using the face cloth she had brought, took the opportunity to wash, the water ice cold. Kneeling on the mossy stones, she bathed her face first and, in a moment of what seemed pure luxury or abandon, ducked her head beneath the cut-stone lip from which the spring issued.

The water had the faint taste of sulphur but she let it fill her mouth and swallowed, said at last, and as if again, 'I have no other choice, nor does she.'

When a timid Véronique Dussart looked up from the path below, her blue eyes didn't rest for more than a moment on those of the one she had come to meet. Embarrassed perhaps, that gaze fled from the bared breasts and shoulders to duck away to the purse in her own hands and then, in futility, to the towel, which had just been dropped.

A corner of the towel had fallen into the water. 'What do you want of me?' she said at last. 'I . . . I only did it to . . . to bring my husband home.'

More than a million-and-half Frenchmen still languished in POW camps in the Reich. Letters, infrequent at best and ruthlessly censored, helped but little or not at all, and then had to be written on the back and returned. Otherwise, it was only the postcards, those, too, blacked out as if at will, but . . . 'You betrayed the surveyor, didn't you?'

'Must you ask it of me? Must you hear my confession?'

'It's necessary.'

Their eyes met at last and it was all the Dussart woman could do to say, 'Then yes. I overheard them talking.'

One must be firm but gentle. 'Who?'

Quivering, she said, 'Didn't Monsieur Doumier tell you that when tortured?'

The woman looked so weak and desperate, felt Marie-Hélène. The pale yellow dress was really nothing much and the straps of the prewar leather sandals had been broken two or three times. 'Please just answer.'

'Monsieur Doumier and Father Nicolas. I had gone into the ruins of the church. Though the roofs of the nave and chancel collapsed during the bombing of 1940, there were still places where one could sit quietly and pray. I was asking for God's help in . . . in bringing my André home. No one else was around. I know there wasn't. Just those two and they . . . they hadn't noticed me, nor did they.'

'But have you returned to pray there since?'

'Yes, of course. Each day, I . . .' But why was this one from Paris looking at her like that?

'Would Father Nicolas have realized who the betrayer of Doumier was?'

'NO! How is it that you can think such a thing? I have three children. My husband . . .'

'Calm down. It's safe here. We're alone. I've checked. You weren't being followed. Stop worrying so much.'

'Me, I can't help but worry. I hate myself for what I've done. If anyone finds out, they'll . . .'

Burying her face in her hands, she swiftly turned away to sob, 'This war, it is crucifying me! No one will understand. How can they?'

Hands took her by the shoulders. Véronique tried to avoid them but they pulled her round and made her bury her face against a shoulder to cry until a breath was caught and held, and she could finally nod and say, 'Please, it's all right. I just have no one I can talk to about it.'

The Gestapo Munk had made her a deal. Marie-Hélène let her gaze sift over the woman. Véronique Dussart didn't look the type to betray anyone and this might have caused the terrorists to be less suspicious but not now, not after Doumier had been arrested and the mayor . . . 'What has happened to monsieur le maire?'

'I don't know! Can't you see that's a part of what's troubling me? They simply came and took him away.'

The Gestapo, wondered Marie-Hélène, or had it been Kraus? 'Would you like a cigarette?' she asked, only to see the woman shake her head and hear her saying, 'No . . . No, I don't want to accept anything more from you people. It's hard enough for me to have told you Father Nicolas is also involved.'

'Then you must tell me if any of them suspect you.'

'They won't. They all think it was Angélique Bellecour.' There, that too, had been said, thought Véronique bitterly.

'You told people she was the one,' sighed Marie-Hélène, but it was a complication that couldn't be allowed to interfere.

'Must you accuse me so with your eyes?'

'Just answer me. My life is in danger too, so we're in this together.'

'Then, yes! Even though she is my friend and has helped me lots with my children, with food she brings in from where she lives.'

'But will she now try to determine the source of this accusation?'

'No! How could she? I'm not a risk to you. I won't tell anyone we've met. Why would I?'

A cigarette was necessary if only to calm the woman and when she had lit one, Marie-Hélène picked up her blouse and brassiere and laid them on the nearby bushes. 'Does the sight of my breasts bother you?' she asked and saw the woman shake her head and look away.

Inhaling deeply, she handed the cigarette to her. 'There, that's better, isn't it? Why not come and sit down? Ah! let's bathe our feet. It's so peaceful here. Perfect. You chose wisely.'

Their shoulders touched. Their feet touched and their thighs, their ankles too. Their skirts were hiked.

'I've lived in Abbeville all of my life. My brothers were always exploring the countryside and often took me with them.'

'Good. I may need their help. They're not involved, are they?'

'The . . . the one died in the Ardennes in May-June 1940. The other, he . . . he has lost both legs and wouldn't be of any use to the *Résistance*. For him, as well as for myself, life it is finished.'

The cigarette was taken back, the lungs filled. 'That's not fair, is it? What did he do in the war?'

The one that's still going on, was this what she implied? 'He was a wireless operator. Signals. The artillery shell that chose him could just as easily have chosen another.'

*Ah, mon Dieu* . . . 'Do these people have a transceiver?'

So *that* had been what she'd been after. 'It isn't Henri who helps them. He only advises on the electrics.'

Henri. Her maiden name would be easy enough to obtain. 'And the set?' asked Marie-Hélène.

'They don't have one yet. All right, they're trying to build one so as to make contact with London, but Henri . . . Oh for sure, he works at it, he talks, he plans, but spare parts, they're not so easy to get.'

When the cigarette was finished, Marie-Hélène found her bag and carefully tucked the butt away in her tin. 'Rinse out your mouth and wash your hands. We wouldn't want anyone smelling tobacco on you. Use a little of the moss. That'll help.'

And then, as the woman was bending over the spring to cup a hand, 'Who else is involved?'

Letting the water drain from her hand, the woman warily asked, 'When am I to hear that my husband is coming home?'

As with the Gestapo Munk, so with herself. 'Soon. I'll look after it. Don't worry. A week, ten days at the most. Count them off. As soon as I hear he's on the train, I'll let you know.'

'I wish I hadn't done it. He'll hate me if he ever finds out.'

'Three years without your man can be an agony, can't it?'

'How would you know?'

'You're right, I wouldn't. I'm sorry. Now here, use my towel to dry your face but first wash it again. No tears. Hey, try to smile, eh? Everything's going to be okay. You'll see.'

Véronique took the towel from her as she knelt over the water to bathe her face again. This business, it should never have happened. Never! The *Résistance*, the Father Nicolas and Doumier . . . Why had God put her in the church at that precise moment and made her feel so desperate?

Things would be all right. This woman from Paris knew what she was doing. She would never have removed her blouse and brassiere like that if there had been any danger. She hadn't asked about the Gestapo Munk or if she had gone directly to him with the information she had sold for so much.

The towel was pulled and wrapped around her head. Blindfolded—suffocating—Véronique panicked, and as she fell forward, she tried to scream, tried to get a breath.

Straddling her tightly, Marie-Hélène brought the boulder down one more time, then bowed her head in exhaustion and gasped, 'There . . . there, it's done, madame, and forgive me but it had to be.'

Pulling the woman over onto her back, she removed the towel and threw it into the spring to soak. She washed her hands and arms, her breasts, throat and face, then ripped the yellow dress open, yanked at the brassiere until it was around the woman's throat, and removed the white underpants to leave them caught on an ankle.

One sandal was tossed onto the path so that it would appear as if lost while trying to escape. After rinsing the towel, she used a corner of it to soak up some of the blood, which she then smeared on the woman's inner thighs and pubes. It would have to do. The thought of a little violence might help them to conclude what was needed, but from her bag she took a pair of scissors. Pausing for a moment, since it was a terrible thing to do, she hacked off the woman's hair and let the dampened moss and bloodied earth accept it.

'I'm sorry,' she said again. 'I really am, but I couldn't let you tell them we had talked. Besides, we couldn't have them thinking the Bellecour woman had betrayed them. Sadly it has to have been yourself.'

Taking the scissors well into the surrounding brush and trees, she buried them as deeply as she could, was glad she had thought to bring them. Using the woman's lipstick, she printed *For Doumier* on the flat white stomach that had so many stretch marks, then made the Cross of Lorraine below, added *corbeau* for good measure and left the lipstick there as finished business for others to find.

Bathed and dressed. She wheeled the bike with its suitcase down to the road and was soon heading back into Abbeville. She would have to find the place she was to stay overnight, but first must try to discover what had happened to the mayor.

# 7

An Aubusson carpet covered the floor of the Château de Bagatelle's winter salon. It was soft and spread its delicately hued floral patterns to panelled, sculpted, mirror-hung walls that were highlighted in blue enamel and gilt but did nothing to still the panic that was in her. Angélique stood with Martin in the centre of the salon. They were alone. The Hauptmann Scheel, having told the Sturmbannführer Kraus to wait in the entrance hall, had shown them in here.

High above them, exquisitely delicate porcelain flowers from the Royal Vincennes factory gave the chandelier the glow of welcome even in the fading light, which crept in through French windows. She still didn't know if the mayor had been arrested and wondered if he was in there with them, for a shrieking had started up, Kraus lashing out at the Hauptmann Scheel in front of the colonel and others. The harangue was in Deutsch, and though she had picked up some from working at the Kommandantur, she couldn't catch everything. The mayor's name came up. That of Father Nicolas. Others too.

A crisis. An insurrection. Terrorists—*Banditen*—crawling all over the place. Himmler demanding an example be made of Abbeville.

Martin felt her leave him. He saw her cross the room to one of the windows and knew she was feeling terrible. He wanted so much to tell her everything, that she had been wrong about it all, that though she had lied to him about his father ever since that terrible day, he forgave her. He had found his voice.

She felt him take her by the hand. 'Forgive me, Martin. Dear Jesus, why us, eh? Why your father?'

Why the mayor, why Father Nicolas, why that young girl who had helped them with the bicycle taxi in Paris? Why, please, Dr. Vergès or Isabelle Moncontre?

Because they care.

Caring isn't enough, she said inwardly. Life is what this is all about.

The shrieking of Kraus and the loud and angry voice of Oberst Lautenschläger came to her. They were in the summer salon at the back of the château, but had they arrested monsieur le maire and Father Nicolas?

The château was just to the southeast of Abbeville, just off the Paris road, and it overlooked the Valley of the Somme and the wooded scarp, which here came down in gullies and hills.

It was lovely. It had survived all the wars since construction had begun in 1752 and had taken over forty years to complete. Of the pinkish-red brick and white stone of Picardy, it had a first floor with bull's-eye windows above the French ones of the ground floor. A grey slate, mansard roof with attic dormers rose above spacious lawns.

But now? she asked. Now beauty and terror sat side by side. The Sturmbannführer Kraus insisted the district was under SS control. Angered, the Oberst Lautenschläger told him he would take his orders only from the OKW, the High Command, and not from the SS. He called Kraus a lout and told him to sit down.

Abruptly, silence descended. The château, of thirty rooms at least, became so quiet Angélique swore she could hear the stirring of the swastika flag above the entrance.

The Hauptmann Scheel had deliberately parked the car as far as possible from the château. It was at the head of a row of six others and two camouflaged lorries whose soldiers of the Waffen-SS sat about on the grass with their weapons and waited too.

A killing campaign. A hunt for *résistants*, was this what was about to take place? The parachutist . . . Martin's parachutist. Were they going to be blamed for something that didn't even exist?

'Your father, Martin. Do the Germans know he's in the district?'

And the Mademoiselle Isabelle? he wanted so much to ask but couldn't bring himself to use his voice. Not yet.

A servant, one of the former owner's staff perhaps, came to scatter grain and cracked maize on the lawn through which the driveway passed and against which the vehicles were parked. As if having timepieces of their own, ducks, geese and white swans came in from the marshes to feed, but two male peacocks rushed to defend their territory. The soldiers got up to watch.

Now the peacocks made war and the sound of them was sharp and furious as they chased the others in defiance of all that was sane.

Martin indicated the cars and gradually some sense returned and she saw what he wanted her to tell him.

'The Gestapo Munk is here,' she said, defeated.

Munk's jurisdiction was not only Abbeville and the control into the *zone interdite* but also encompassed the surrounding countryside in the *pays de* Ponthieu, to the east of the Somme, and Vimeu to the west. Tolerated but barely by Oberst Lautenschläger, he was, as he had demonstrated at the control, suspicious, arrogant and cruel. A bad combination. Every time he had come into the Kommandantur, she had felt he would discover the truth about her and Martin.

Rumour had it that Herr Munk suffered terribly from hepatitis and that this had been why Gestapo Berlin had sent him here. Rumour had it, too, that he had caught the disease in a brothel and that it still threatened others in such places.

He didn't like women, and certainly he didn't like or trust the French.

'Monsieur le maire doesn't have a car anymore, Martin. He had one in 1940 and '41 but that privilege was taken when he was caught transporting grain to feed the pigs he kept illegally at one of the farms, and now he walks or rides his bicycle like almost everyone else. Therefore, he must have come in Herr Munk's car,' she said emptily. 'Therefore, he has been arrested.'

Martin insisted she should look closer and she said, 'That little blue Renault is the car of the sous-préfet Allard. He's in charge of Abbeville and the districts of Ponthieu and Vimeu so has to contend with the Gestapo Munk. That other Renault, the big black one, is préfet Pallière's. He's based in Amiens, so the meeting here, it must be critical. But those two top police-men, they have no love for each other and if you ask me, I think M. Allard is more inclined to look the other way and let the *Résistance* work. He's more than an acquaintance of the mayor. They grew up together, both fell in love with and mar-ried sisters from the same family, both went to war together, fought in the trenches, buried their comrades and . . .'

They were no longer alone. The shrieking and the angry retorts had ceased.

Steps sounded in the corridor. One by one the visitors, each putting on his fedora or military cap, left the château to cause the ducks and geese to fly a little, the swans to move away.

The peacocks were satisfied but to this display, the visitors remained impervious.

From behind her and Martin, the Oberst Lautenschläger cleared his throat. A big man, a giant with all-but-shaven dark grey hair and a massive brow, he had faded blue and often rheumy eyes. There were paunches under them, more so now, she thought but wondered if it wasn't the fading light that caused her to notice such a thing. The sagging jowls also.

'*Ma chére* Mademoiselle Bellecour,' he said, and she could see that though he tried not to show it, he was still deeply upset and embarrassed by the ruckus. 'You must forgive me,' he continued in his thickly accented French. 'Berlin are not thinking clearly. They're so far from us, they panic. This busi-ness of Doumier, it's unfortunate.'

A soldier all his life, he had, she surmised, just been told in no uncertain terms that he wouldn't be one for much longer.

'Well, Martin, how did you get along with the specialist?'

Martin gave him the broadest grin he could. He nodded, shrugged—went into such a pantomime of relief. No cutting open of the throat and installing a little wooden door. No voice machine.

'The head, the brain, the hypnotism?' said the colonel. 'Yes, yes, I understand.' He looked at herself. 'You must, I gather, return to Paris in a week at which time the doctor will attempt to remove the blockage of the mind that has caused the loss of the voice. Please, it will be arranged. There'll be no problem. If this was all I had to contend with, my days would be welcome.'

Kraus must have told him, but the colonel could know nothing of Vergès and what really had happened in Paris. Nothing! 'You're very kind, Herr Oberst,' she said and fought to smile and to lie, yes lie! 'Paris was lovely as always but a little different.'

'Good. Yes, that's good. My dear, please come and sit down. There is something I must warn you of. Martin, do you think you could find Frau Oster in the kitchens? Write her one of your little notes. A glass of lemonade—the real thing—and a slice of her *Bremer Klaben*. It's a type of cake—sugary and with sugar dust—or perhaps you would prefer some of the ginger-bread, the *Pfefferkuchen* she made with honey from my family's estates near Lüneburg.'

They waited for Martin to leave the room, he to look back at her once in uncertainty and then again.

'Your son has your well-being at heart, mademoiselle. I like to see that in a boy. Now listen, please. Though it is hateful, and I despise such things, there is a rumour about that it was yourself who betrayed this surveyor to Herr Munk. Apparently the Paris trip I authorized was your reward.'

'But . . . but I still don't even know who Doumier was. He can't have come to the Kommandantur. I'd have remembered the name.'

'Yes, yes, I told that imbecile Kraus as much but you have to bang those types on the head ten times, not just once or twice like soldiers. They've never been under fire. Herr Munk didn't deny the rumour and should have.'

'Then . . . then you know who gave him the surveyor's name?'

Lautenschläger's eyes moistened. 'That is not for me to say. Herr Munk implies that it was received in one of the anonymous letters but I feel that one struck a bargain with a poor woman whose despair could no longer be contained.'

'Not Véronique . . . Please, you must tell me it wasn't her.'

He ducked his head to one side. Even seated, he was so much taller than herself. 'This I can't say until the matter is settled, but the terrorists, the *Résistance*, you do understand, may come for you. What I can do is detail men to watch over you.'

'No . . . No, that wouldn't be right, Colonel. Then everyone who suspects I might have done such a thing would believe it.'

How wise of her, how brave, but the *Banditen* mightn't listen. 'Then what, please, do you propose?'

'That I face my accusers day by day and deny it.' But *had* Véronique done such a thing?

Mademoiselle Bellecour would never have turned Doumier or anyone else in, felt Lautenschläger. Though she didn't wear her patriotism on her sleeve, he knew it was there and that he had to respect her for it. 'A parachutist,' he said, looking away as though lost in thought. 'Sturmbannführer Kraus says a British agent was dropped into our area a few days before your trip to Paris. He seems to think Martin knows something of this.'

'Martin? Ah no, Colonel. Herr Kraus, he is mistaken.'

'He's insisting I allow him to turn the countryside upside down and shake it until this parachutist and all who help him are arrested.'

'Was Monsieur Doumier not the one to have told him of this parachutist?'

Was she trying to protect the boy by asking? he wondered. 'Doumier may have told Kraus many things,' he said cautiously, 'or, yes, absolutely nothing. But if Martin knows anything of this matter, please convince the boy to tell me before it's too late. He may have some misguided sense of loyalty—yes, yes, I can appreciate this—but with Herr Munk and the Sturmbannführer it can only lead to tragedy. I warn you because this rumour of yourself isn't right. Now please, there are things I must arrange. My adjutant will drive you to the farm.'

He stood and held out a hand. As he gave her a curt bow, he said, '*Au revoir*, then, until tomorrow but come an hour or two later than usual. You'll be tired after such a journey.'

And monsieur le maire, she wondered, what of him?

The road was far from straight but followed the southeastern edge of the old tidal estuary of a tributary, which had joined the Somme in distant years. Canals, flooded reaches and *hortillonnages* were now in dusk, while the uppermost leaves of the poplar trees caught the last of the light.

Angélique sat with Martin in the backseat of the car, their suitcases between them. Gradually the road climbed out of the valley. There were more trees—everything was such a contrast to what was to come.

At Saint-Riquier, some ten kilometres from Abbeville, the land gave up and became the battlefield of sticky, flint-encrusted clay it had been in so many wars and through so many generations of backbreaking toil. The fields could be almost endless, the hedges dividing them pulled down in the late 1920s and again in the late 1930s as the horses had been sold off and mechanization had crept in. Conversely the fields could be small, like postage stamps, for the soil, it wasn't good, and now of course the hedges were creeping back, for the tractors had been taken even during the Blitzkrieg and then in the autumn of 1940.

Sugar beets and other root crops were grown—potatoes, yes, and rutabagas, the former for shipment to the Reich, the latter to Paris to replace the potatoes that had gone the other way. Maize, barley and wheat were on the higher ground where the drainage was better—in places she could see the marching of their stooks. Copses lay in gullies; woods on modest rises. Oak, beech and hornbeam—Angélique could smell the scent of their rotting leaves and remember the hard, dry paper of them, the wet ones too, ah yes.

The acorns were roasted with chicory or barley or whatever else and ground to make "coffee". No sugar, even though there were factories that processed the sugar beets.

Now flat and straight and desolate, yes, for she was afraid and depressed—ah, there was no hope, how could there be?—the road continued out across the *pays de* Ponthieu past tiny clusters of farm buildings and one isolated little village, past a few cows, chickens, goats—all that sort of thing, even a struggling orchard of the small, hard green apples that, as in Vimeu and in Normandy, would be pressed into cider.

The mayor? she asked herself. Father Nicolas? What had happened to them? They had been 'taken away,' Véronique had said—Véronique. Had that poor soul really accused her of betraying Doumier to save herself?

The farm was not big and it was some distance off a side road that just waited for the next rain to make her life a misery. The buildings, like most other farms in the *pays*, were long and low and had no windows facing west because that was the direction the wind and rain mostly came from. Here they didn't whitewash their walls whose plaster had been daubed onto sticks. Here, like elsewhere in Picardy, they did tar the base of each wall against the dampness of rain and seeping manure and cattle piss, but God forgive you if you asked for whitewash to pretty the walls or attempted to grow flowers.

They had no time for such things. Not when work began before dawn and one went to bed long before the curfew ever thought of starting.

The roofs were of faded, S-shaped, reddish-brown Flemish tile that funnelled the rain, and these tiles caught the bleakness of the setting sun.

The dogs didn't even bark—they seldom showed any inclination to friendliness but were kept solely as beasts of burden and for other chores.

The youngest children, streaked with dirt, sucked their thumbs or stood in their rumpled dresses or whipcord breeches with leather knees and seats, falling kneesocks or none, and wooden sabots or bare feet, as if staring at visitors from the moon.

Had the older ones, the boys especially, armed themselves with flints to throw?

All her furniture—every last stick of their meagre possessions—was heaped haphazardly in the dung- and straw-littered yard within the broken quadrangle around which both house and barns and her little two-room "cottage" huddled under one continuous roof.

'*Ah, mon Dieu*, what the hell is this?' she exclaimed, bolting from the car. 'Marieka, you Flemish cow! Felix, you bastard Walloon! You go too far. This, it is the limit!'

They had accepted the rumour and had thrown her and Martin out. No warning. Just like that. *Fini*.

Her appeal to their respective ancestries landed on deaf ears. The grizzled moon face, with its big eyes and flat, wart-encrusted nose, was impassive and Angélique saw at once where Martin had acquired that dumb-ox gaze. Now in her eighth month and proud of it, Marieka folded her arms over her bulging apron and spat, '*Corbeau! Putain! Parisienne chatte!* How could you have deceived us?'

The car started up, the Hauptmann Scheel considering it prudent to leave.

Two old, black bicycles with worn tyres and the promise of patching kits taped to the frames in front of their rusty, unpadded seats, leaned against the wall of the "cottage". Cattle bawled, chickens rooted about, the pigs were noisy in their sties next door and all the things she had put up with and had conquered and come to, yes, appreciate if nothing else, rushed at her.

'The mayor,' hissed Marieka, giving a toss of a head that looked as if hewn from frost-tinged plaster and festooned with a tired mop of blond wool, 'and the *curé*, so please don't keep the people's voice waiting, nor that of the Lord.'

'How pious of you!' shrilled Angélique. 'I know my rights, you two. Me, I'm going to court over this—yes, yes! Even if it's the last thing I do.'

'We'll see, then, shall we?' taunted Marieka. 'But remember, my fine mademoiselle from Paris, the corpses of *les corbeaux* are never plucked for the pot in these parts as they are now in that city. Here they are always left hanging upside down from the skeins of barbed wire to warn away others. Yours will no doubt create quite a stench!'

The bitch! 'I nursed you when you were ill with that terrible flu last winter. I fed your brats and that . . . that husband of yours. A bad marriage, your father always said and shook his head in despair and to think that I took your part and preached patience and understanding to that kindest of men. "Love", I said. *Ah, mon Dieu*, how foolish of me!'

Martin tugged at her hand. *Monsieur le curé*, he mouthed the reminder. *Monsieur le maire*.

They were inside the cottage, sitting in the straight-backed chairs they had rescued from the heap.

'What's this, then?' she said scathingly. 'A court of its own? One of enquiry, eh? And here I thought you both had been arrested. *Me*, I grieved. I distressed myself with thoughts of you both in prison and up before the post! But now . . . *Ah, Sainte Mère*, what the hell is going on?'

If a performance, it had been a good one, felt Father Nicolas, looking her over and only then saying out of compassion perhaps, 'Please sit down. Here, you may take my chair.'

'It's mine, I think.'

'Please don't be so bitter, Mademoiselle Bellecour. These things, they are necessary,' grumbled Honoré Ledieu.

'*Necessary?*' she shrilled. 'We didn't even know who that man they tortured was. Ask the colonel. He'll tell you it was Véronique who gave Doumier away.'

'Véronique?' gasped Ledieu, throwing a look of utter despair at the *curé*, the ramifications of such a revelation tumbling through both. 'Father, what is this she's saying?'

'That the eviction was as winter's first storm. Premature.'

Honoré Ledieu hunkered forward to take up the pipe he had let grow cold. Father Nicolas stood to offer her the chair again.

They had been using an overturned nail keg as a table, and on this there was a lighted stub of a candle. One of her own, no doubt. Stolen by the children or by their mother or their father, only to be requisitioned by these two.

'Look, I can't be certain it was Véronique and I hope and pray it wasn't, but as I stand before you both, I swear we had nothing to do with betraying that poor man.'

Father Nicolas irritably ran a hand over his crinkly, iron-grey hair. 'Martin,' he said, not looking at him, 'please go out-side. We have things to discuss with your mother.'

'Martin, you stay right by me. They would only beat him terribly, Father, and I can't have that. Besides, he has some-thing for monsieur le maire. Martin, please return the pencil to him. And here . . . here,' she reached into her handbag, 'is the doctor's note requesting that Martin be allowed to return to Paris in a week.'

The Sturmbannführer Kraus would kill her if she told them she had been forced into working for the SS. This way she had a few days, a week at most, to decide how best to warn them. Anything could happen in that time. *Anything* and, yes, Isabelle Moncontre had said they were to do exactly as they had been told. The return message from these two would be intercepted on its way to Paris and another put in its place.

The pencil and the scribble from Vergès for returning to Paris next week were held only for a moment then abruptly set next to the candle, the mayor's deep brown eyes searching her own for the slightest hint of trouble. Tall, broad shouldered—a bull of a man in his youth—Honoré Ledieu was all nose. That thing through which he breathed was cleaved forward like the blade of an axe, while the rest of his face, the thick and dark brown moustache, the bushy greying eyebrows . . . even the ears, all were as if pinned back and he perpetually facing into a gale.

At the age of sixty-two, he had suffered many defeats, including the loss to the Stuka dive bombers of the fine old house that had been in his family for over two hundred years.

He knew men. He owned and ran two of the largest brewer-ies in Abbeville, a roaring business these days, ah yes, and *yes*, he had been arrested for the affair of the illegal piglet-rearing but that had really been a cooperative effort, his turn at the time of the arrest and seizure of his automobile. Father Nico-las had been just as guilty, as had the sous-préfet, the dentist, et cetera, et cetera. Seven of them in all but only one arrest.

They were old friends.

'Tell us what really happened in Paris,' he said, and she noted that Father Nicolas had moved to block the door and was now leaning against it.

Half lies would be best. 'It's true we were picked up and questioned.'

'By the Sturmbannführer Kraus?'

'Yes, but . . . but he let us go.'

'Now did he?' asked Father Nicolas. Well educated, well read far beyond the needs of the church and parish, he was of medium height. Piercing dark eyes sought saint and sinner alike. Badly wounded in the trenches of that other war, he had lost the top half of his left ear, the tip of his nose, the eyelashes, which still struggled to grow in, and four fingers of his left hand. A grenade he had scooped up and had thrown back while attempting to grant absolution to one of the enemy.

He had a wry sense of humour, a liking for children, creamed turbot and smoked eel, a firm belief in God and in being fair, especially when listening closely to the condemned.

'Kraus got nothing from us,' she said, her voice distant. 'We did hear them torturing someone—this Doumier, I think it must have been—but we never saw the man and I don't think he gave them anything useful. I'm certain of this but'— she shrugged as she recalled things—'but I can't really say why I feel this way.'

'And the parachutist the Germans claim has landed?' asked Ledieu suspiciously.

It would be wrong to smile, no matter how strong the temptation. 'Martin drew it in the dust on one of the windows. His little signature, yes? I . . . I didn't realize this until after we had been released. Martin, he . . . he told me then.'

'Mademoiselle, what is this you're saying? That it's all a mistake?' demanded Ledieu, throwing Father Nicolas a startled glance.

'Oui. Look, I'm sorry but that's the way it was.'

She was lying again, thought Martin. She had known all about the parachute up in that torture room. The lies, they would pile up until the house of their cards would have to tumble.

Should they trust her? wondered Ledieu, again looking past her to Father Nicolas who shrugged this time and shook his head, both casting agreement and doubt, as was his custom. Always, then, he was right, either way.

Angélique Bellecour had never raised more than a first whisper of concern, and in the past three years they had found no cause to doubt her loyalties. 'Was there any trouble with the pencil?' demanded Ledieu. 'Please don't lie to us, mademoiselle. We are only too aware of what our German friends might do.'

She shook her head a little too hastily, he thought. If she was working for the avenue Foch, all was lost.

'My child . . .' began Father Nicolas from behind her by the door.

'I'm not a child, Father. Please don't patronize me.'

'Forgive me, but if you have anything to add, you had best confess. Too many lives are at stake—Martin, your silence is absolutely necessary. Don't write notes to anyone about it. If you do, you'll burn in hell for all eternity and I won't be around to grab the extinguisher.'

The Mademoiselle Isabelle would be making contact with them soon. Martin wanted so much to tell them this, but had already been sworn to secrecy.

It was the mayor who said, 'The Germans are to "sweep" Abbeville and the *pays de* Vimeu and Ponthieu clean in their search for this "parachutist". Were things not so desperate, I would enjoy laughing at Kraus and the Gestapo Munk for the fools they are about to make of themselves.'

'Every farm will be searched,' warned Father Nicolas grimly, but why did he still look at her as if she *had* betrayed them? wondered Angélique. 'They'll come here too,' he added.

'But will find our things out there,' she said. '*Ah, mon Dieu,* Father, if you really do love God, as everyone says, please ask Him what the hell am I to do.'

'Ah! of course. I'll see that your things are put back.'

'And for now you will trust me, Father? Is this what you're saying?'

She was tough and no doubt could be brave, but would that tongue of hers not get in the way? 'Until the matter is settled, yes.'

'Then tell them, please, to stop hiking the rent. Me, I'm not paying another sou. Tell them also to give back every-thing they've stolen in the past three years and if they read my private letters again, be sure to say I'll torch their barns and houses in the dark of night!'

'Ah!' He leapt, tossing a hand. 'I'm glad I never married!'

The priest left them and when the door had closed behind his comrade and friend, Ledieu told her what she ought to know. 'That couple, your landlords, are not related to you in any way. Long ago Father Nicolas and myself did what had to be done to protect you and your "son".'

The registry . . . the residence cards that had been given without question, she thinking she had fooled everyone! The ration tickets . . . all such things.

'Johannes Vanderlinden is known to us as well as to yourself, mademoiselle. We learned of the letter of introduction he gave you for that daughter of his.'

'Marieka's really quite happy with her Félix.'

'Yes, yes, but you chose Ponthieu in the early days of the Defeat. Perhaps it is that you remembered how isolated these little farms could be?'

'In June of 1940, Monsieur Vanderlinden helped Martin and me get back through Paris and away. He was an associate of my employer. That is how he knew me. He advised me to stay at the farm and lie low, and it was he who wrote we were related to his daughter, Marieka.'

Good, she was telling the truth. 'Now, please, the rest of what happened in Paris. Did Vergès receive the pencil before or after Kraus had examined it?'

Something would have to be said. 'The Sturmbannführer didn't examine it. He shrieked at Martin to give him his name and when Martin couldn't, he . . . he released us.'

More lies, thought Martin, fingering the gold wedding band in his pocket.

'Was Vergès compromised?' asked Ledieu.

'No! I . . . How could he have been?'

'Perhaps. Perhaps not. This we will have to determine.'

The ride home in darkness was long, and it wasn't until they had reached the house on the outskirts of Abbeville that Ledieu and Father Nicolas examined the pencil.

When unrolled and warmed at a low heat, the cigarette

paper that had been inside it yielded: *You will be contacted.* It was enough. The request to see the boy in a week only confirmed things.

'Martin, did you remove the cigarette paper Herr Dirksen put in monsieur le maire's pencil? He was showing me how it had been used. Ah! So much has happened since, I forgot to tell the mayor and Father Nicolas.'

Alarmed, he rapidly shook his head. She frowned and then said, 'It was just one from the packet he had in his pocket. It couldn't have had anything written on it.'

Tenderly she brushed a hand over his hair. Leaning closely, she kissed his brow and the kiss was warm, the bed was warm, the pillows soft and caring, and he could feel her breasts pushing against the rough cotton nightgown she wore.

'You're so like your father,' she said and smiled softly. 'What will I do when I meet him, eh? Go crazy, I think. Drink him in and love him so hard, he will have to forgive me for shouting at him like that and saying those things.'

Her eyes closed, and in that moment, he thought she *was* beautiful. Her breath came slowly, evenly now and she was at peace, she must be. Noting the curve of her chin and neck, that of a partly hidden shoulder as well, he thought she could be quite alluring. He had seen her naked lots of times—necessity did make such a thing possible, had even scrubbed her back and she his own, but she had lied to him about his father. A big lie, a huge one. Repeatedly she had said, 'Your father's in England. You *have* to believe this, *chéri.* Now don't cry anymore. Please don't.'

The nightmare had come, the sounds of the cannon shells so real as when they had rained hard along that road to the screams and cries and the killing of people, the spattering of brains and guts and blood. Then the ME-109s had left and a silence like no other had come, but after it the shrieks of despair and much weeping, yes, yes, and the stench of cordite, burning rubber and death.

'Martin . . . Martin, what were you thinking?'

She had opened her eyes and was looking intently at him.

*Nothing*, he let his lips tell her, and turning away, hid his eyes from her.

'*Ah, mon Dieu*, don't take it so hard. Everything has to get better now. Your father and his friends will come. I know they will. Maybe they'll take us to the Haute-Savoie, maybe to Perpignan and we'll cross over into Spain. We'll be out of here, *chéri*. We'll be able to sleep in peace and have anything we want to eat. We'll never have to worry about men like Kraus or Dirksen again, Gestapo Munk too.'

Lies and more lies. She hadn't yet said a word about Isabelle Moncontre, and none whatsoever about Bois Carré.

Reaching under the pillows, he found the wedding ring and brought it to his lips, a woman that they knew nothing about, only that the SS of the avenue Foch must have drowned her.

Sometime later Angélique heard it fall onto the carpet and roll until it reached the stone floor to topple over. 'Martin . . .' she began, only to realize that he was fast asleep.

The wind began to rise, and in the stillness of the night, it picked up the dust among the ruins, causing Marie-Hélène de Fleury to blink and duck her head as the hammering of hobnailed boots passed by.

The mayor and his friends had gone on before the patrol. They were now in among the ruins of the warehouses that here stretched alongside the canals in Abbeville's former industrial heartland.

She waited. The wind tended to hide the sound of things she needed to know. Among the ruins, it caused sudden noises. A brick or chunk of mortar falling, the banging of sheet-metal roofing, the rolling back and forth of an empty oil drum.

She started out again. Walking with the bike was difficult, for there was rubble scattered everywhere. She had to confront them, had to convince them—Kraus had left her no other choice, so, too, had that "priest" Châlus and his novice and that elderly nun. The sooner she got this over, the better.

They would worry about her having followed them—she'd have to say she had only followed the mayor and the *curé* from the mayor's house on the outskirts of town. She'd have to convince them that she had thought they had been arrested and that she had taken one hell of a chance in staking out that house of his and waiting.

Why didn't you speak to us then?—she knew they would ask her.

I was afraid someone might have seen me. I didn't want to endanger anyone.

Your papers—*Bitte, Fräulein, euere Papiere*—would they try that one? Speaking in Deutsch to catch her out?

My name is Isabelle Moncontre and I come to you from Paris at the request of Raymond Châlus who is the leader of the *réseau* to which myself and Dr. Vergès belong.

Convincing them wasn't going to be easy. She wished she had a gun, but would having one not also cause suspicion? Guns were still so rare, women in the *Résistance* seldom if ever carried them.

Would they have her searched?

In her mind she quickly went over her clothes. The shoes had been inexpensive and were from the Trois Quartiers, from before the Occupation; the skirt was from the Galeries Lafayette, another of the giant department stores, also purchased before the war. The blouse and sweater were from Le Printemps, in the boulevard Haussmann—prewar also and, yes, from another of the department stores. She had had so little money then. The woven straw bag? she asked. Ah! it was like so many others. Spanish, yes, but she was certain it had no name-tag.

Hans had bought it for her in Perpignan after they had shut down the Mirabeau escape line, all 239 of them arrested.

Her step-ins were from the Bon Marché department store, the brassiere and half-slip from La Samaritaine. All prewar also and not in the best of condition now. Lots of mending, so okay there as well.

Me, I'm fine, but oh for sure, messieurs, I come as a scythe because that is the way it has to be. *Moi-même contre vous.*

When she found them, she found their bicycles first in an adjoining shed. Unguarded—were they such fools, such innocents as not to have posted a lookout?

Everything that was in her handbag was mentally ticked off and only then did she realize that she had left the towel with the body of Véronique Dussart.

Pulling out the face cloth, she hurriedly dug as deep a hole as possible in the rubble at her feet and buried it. Then she straightened up, felt the knots, the ropes that tied the suitcase to her bike and, leaving it and the bike behind with the others, picked her way through the darkness and rubble and went in to interrupt their little gathering.

No guns, no lookout here either. *Sacré nom de nom*, how could grown men be such fools?

The muffled voices of four came from behind the coal-fired boiler of the steam plant that had once powered this mill. Light from a kerosene lantern shone on the dusty, cob-webbed ceiling and walls. There were no windows.

'I'm telling you it was Véronique.'

'*Non. C'est impossible. Ma nièce*—you're crazy, Monsieur le Maire. Me, I deny it to your face!'

'Now calm down. If it was her, a tribunal will be held to deal with the matter in the usual way.' One of the other two had said this. The voice was deeper, but it, too, had the ring of being accustomed to authority.

'We'll arrange the trial for the day after tomorrow,' said the mayor. 'Father, you and sous-préfet Allard can be the ones, and you, yourself, Eugène. Let us have you as the third voice. That is only fair.'

'*Bon*. I accept with pleasure for I know the good name of my family will be cleared.'

A stuffed shirt, was he, that one? she wondered.

'Now let us pass on to Bois Carré and the parachutist the Germans believe has landed.'

What they said next she didn't hear, for the muzzle of a gun had been jammed into the small of her back. For perhaps ten seconds all sense was lost. She caught a breath and fought for sanity, dragged in another breath and felt the man's lips against an ear. Châlus . . . was it Châlus? she silently cried, seeing herself lying face down in the woods dead!

He didn't say anything, this one behind her. He simply let her feel his breath against her ear.

Blindfolded, for someone else tied a wet towel over her eyes—yes, a wet towel, but was it hers? she cried. She was taken by the arms and forced to walk the last few steps silently crying out, Hans . . . Hans, I told you it was Châlus.

Someone forced her into a chair. Someone else dumped her straw bag onto a table. At last a young man's voice broke through. 'Your name?'

Somehow she found her voice—he was too young to have been Châlus. 'It's on my *carte d'identité* and the visitors residence permit.'

A tough one, was she? wondered Honoré Ledieu, looking her over. She was young, about twenty-eight, and plainly dressed, though this last could mean nothing. Her dark brown hair was thick and worn in waves that were pinned back by inexpensive barrettes. Of medium height, she sat straight up but no longer gripped the edges of the chair.

'Isabelle Moncontre,' said someone—she couldn't tell who and assumed it was the one who had blindfolded her. Was that one Châlus? she wondered. The voice was older, more mature than the one with the gun, but younger, she thought, than those of the mayor and the sous-préfet.

The identity card must have been passed to someone else, for a different voice said, 'Born 18 September 1915, in Toulon.'

'Yes, my father was a ship's captain.'

'You don't have the Toulon accent,' said someone else, the *curé* she felt.

'Of course I don't. When I was two, he died in the Far East, off Mindanao, in a typhoon. Mother took my sister and me to live in Paris with her father. I grew up in Saint-Ouen. *Grand-papa* had a stall in the Marché aux Puces, on the *impasse* Simon, the Paul-Bert stalls—secondhand things. His specialty.'

She had what seemed the right accent for Montmartre, thought Father Nicolas but where, please, was the patois, the slang? A pretty girl could so often be far more dangerous than a plain-looking one.

He wished she had been plain.

'Present address?' asked another of the older men.

'*Numéro cinq, troisième étage, l'appartement sept.* Three flights of stairs. I live alone with my mother. *Téléphone 56:42:13.* Why not ask her, if you are foolish enough to telephone? The concierge, Madame Aumont, will bitch about having to go up those stairs but she'll do it if you prevail on her enough.'

There was a pause, and perhaps they looked questioningly at one another, but then one of them said dryly, 'When we need a lecture, mademoiselle, we'll hire a hall for you and invite your friends.'

'*Bien sûr*, monsieur, please do. They're not the Boches.'

'We didn't say they were.'

She had been talking to the sous-préfet Allard. She was certain of it.

Someone spun the cylinder of a revolver and when it had stopped, everyone waited for the trigger to be pulled. 'Don't do that, idiot!' cried the one named Eugéne. Was he the nervous one? The weakest link? The stuffed shirt.

'Look, messieurs, we don't have much time. I'm just a courier. Wouldn't it be best if you were to examine the little present my people in Paris asked me to bring you? At considerable risk, I might add. Yes, it was considerable.'

She waited. She didn't turn her head so as to attempt to fathom their individual reactions. Finally someone said, 'What present?'

That had been the young one with the gun, the spinner of revolver cylinders. A tough guy—was this what he thought of himself? And what of the one who had blindfolded her? What of Châlus? Could that one still be him? 'It . . . it's tied to the carrier of my bike.'

Someone, the mayor perhaps or the sous-préfet, must have indicated that the little gift should be fetched, for tough guy left the revolver on the table. She was certain of this and *that* really *had* been a mistake for she could have been followed. Others could be waiting out there. Others.

Châlus would never have been so careless. The two who had caught her must have come upon her unexpectedly.

The suitcase was set on the table and the catches sprung. The smell of cigarette smoke and kerosene mingled with that of the bricks—all such bombed-out places had that taint, this one of coal dust too.

'*Ah, grâce à Dieu, mon Père*, it's a gift from heaven,' exclaimed the mayor.

'A British Mark One transceiver,' said Allard with more caution. 'You're full of surprises, mademoiselle.'

It was the mayor who brushed this aside. 'Jean-Pierre, please remove the blindfold. She has passed the test with flying colours, eh, *mes amis*? The answer to all our prayers.'

The candle had gone out. The wind had picked up. Wide awake, her heart racing, Angélique lay in bed listening to the night, straining to hear what had awakened her. Only then did it dawn on her that Martin had gone outside. The call of nature. Bravery was needed at any time but in winter, real courage.

The toilet, the dump, the cave—King Louis's chair—was jammed between cowshed and piggery so that the stench became unbearable in summer, and in the heat, the flies and mosquitoes a torture, the wasps also.

When he didn't return, she crawled out of bed, grabbed a shawl, did *not* put on her shoes, and went after him.

He wasn't in the toilet, nor at the pump where in winter one had to break the ice to freeze with the shock of the douche.

In summer, the mud was always there.

Crossing the yard, she went out into the surrounding fields, newly ploughed and furrowed in ruts so deep, Marieka in her state must have heaved at the harness.

'Martin . . .' She tried to keep her voice low. 'Martin . . .' she called.

Nothing. Only the sound of the wind. A sigh. 'Ooo . . . Ooo . . .' and then two short, sharp barks. Not those of a dog, she thought. A fox was out there in the darkness, hunting for voles and mice. 'Martin,' she called more strongly.

The barking ceased. 'Martin, come back to bed. I can't have you tired out. Not when I need your wits about me.'

She was really worried. He could see the dark silhouette of her standing against the star-filled sky.

'Martin, please don't try to spy on that poor vixen. Let her hunt in peace. She has enough worries of her own.'

A loner, a creature of the wild sometimes, he had become accustomed to stealing away for hours, causing much dispute about lost labour and, yes, much concern.

When he joined her, he wrapped his arms about her waist and hugged her dearly, knowing he would be forgiven.

*I am of my father, aren't I?* he said, looking up at her and holding her by the hands, knowing too, that she couldn't read his lips. *You heard me, Angélique. That was* me *who was making the sound of that vixen.*

Hiking her nightgown, she squatted to pee and he listened to the blessing she gave the dark and heavy clods of clay. As always she excused herself by saying, 'The earth needs it more than I do.'

They went back but just before the entrance to the yard, they both turned as if at some mutual signal and looked off towards the northwest, towards Bois Carré which was on a distant rise. 'Félix will be harvesting the maize soon,' she said. Nothing else but that. The maize.

Hand in hand they went in, each to wash and dry the feet before bed.

In the morning Martin was gone. This time a note had been left, but with only one thing on it, his little parachute. He had taken command. He had been dropped into France from the belly of a British Halifax bomber. He was, in his imagination, the enemy agent the Germans were looking for.

# 8

There was fog still in the valley, dew on the leaves, and this made the ground a cushion so that their steps, as they climbed to the body of Véronique Dussart, were muffled. Sous-préfet Allard was in the lead, Father Nicolas behind him, and then the mayor, Honoré Ledieu. Back at the road they had left the one who had found her and the two men Allard had delegated to keep the scandalmongers at bay.

Without a word, they continued uphill, the sound of the spring seeming to fill the air, until at last . . .

'Well,' breathed Allard, grimly, 'whoever did this left no doubt about her.'

'Exactly *who* did it?' asked Father Nicolas in a whisper.

'Yes, who?' said Ledieu bleakly. ' The Committee . . .'

'We *are* the "Committee",' said Allard impatiently.

'We didn't authorize this,' went on the mayor, crossing himself and muttering the Our Father only to be interrupted by the touch of Father Nicolas's hand.

Allard was of medium height, and when he dragged off his fedora, one saw at once that he was all but bald. The big, flat nose, wide-set, large brown eyes, massively furrowed brow and down-turned lips were all a part of the world's greatest doubter, Ledieu told himself, but cautioned that this was good and had saved them many times.

The nostrils were flared, the face broad, the big, thick ears not always those of a listener.

That double chin was favoured in thought. The scar, the fold, the cleft that ran from beneath the lower lip well back and to the right and up the line of Théodore's jaw, had been the work of trench warfare, and ever since then his razor had attempted to harvest the seam, but unsuccessfully.

'Rigor has set in,' he said. 'Let's give it four hours to begin and add to those, the hours of the night plus two.'

'Then she was killed just after work and before returning home,' said Ledieu.

'But by whom?' insisted Father Nicolas, reaching down to pick up the towel, only to hear Théodore saying, 'Don't touch a thing.'

The towel was in the water. Ah! there was blood all over it.

'A rock,' grunted Allard, nodding to indicate the boulder.

'Violation before or after death?' asked Ledieu.

'Honoré, control yourself!' scolded Father Nicolas. 'Please try to remember the dead, they have some rights.'

Allard threw the priest a sharp look. 'Rights? You talk of rights? Did Doumier have any?'

'Honoré, please tell the good father, first that she was not a virgin, but with three children, and secondly that such things as a violent rape could well happen after death, as well as before it. He's not to be so pious about her rights, either,' went on Allard. 'We shall let Coroner Chastel decide the issue. Now listen, you two. She is to remain exactly as she is, the eyes open, the hands flung back, the legs spread.'

'Her hair . . . She had such lovely hair,' said Ledieu. 'She worked for me. I recommended her to the colonel.'

'Her children, Honoré. Put them foremost in your mind. We will have to find homes for them elsewhere and as far from Abbeville as possible, unfortunately for all concerned, especially their poor papa.'

'Yes. Yes, of course, Father,' said Ledieu. 'They mustn't be allowed to suffer for her crime.'

Allard bent over her. Though not a detective—he had been a mill owner before the Great Depression of the 1930s had taken that from him—he had seen enough murders to know one had to look beyond nearly everything one saw. 'Her hair must have been cut off with scissors.'

This was logical enough but . . . 'But what man carries scissors?' managed Ledieu.

'Perhaps he had shaved and was about to give himself a trim when she came along the path?' offered Father Nicolas.

'You innocent! Then why, please, is her sandal lying on the path?' demanded Allard.

'Ah! she was chased from the road, of course. Forgive me, and forgive my "innocence", Théodore. It's a pity I've not seen as much of life as yourself.'

'Now look, you two, we must remain resolute!' said Father Nicolas.

'Then tell him, please, that the towel was wrapped around her head before the boulder was used, and that the towel, it is from La Samaritaine in Paris. *Paris, mes amis.*'

Must Théodore be so suspicious of everything? wondered Ledieu. 'That could well mean my own household or yours, *mon vieux*. Towels like that are not difficult to find, especially since so many of us lost everything in 1940 and had to accept the generosity of others. In any case, everyone who passes through here has to register. I will go through the lists and have a little look.'

'Then you also don't think it was one of ours who did this, or one of the Boches,' breathed Allard.

Ledieu shook his head. 'Not the Boches, and not our own. How could it have been?'

'*Corbeau,*' muttered Father Nicolas, staring at her stomach. 'It's the Cross of Lorraine all right.'

Taken aback by what they had had to confront, they were unsettled, for they couldn't know the ramifications. To the Germans she was an informant and her death could only mean that there really was a *Résistance* in the district and that it was well organized, thought Ledieu. 'The hair . . .' he said, letting the tragedy of it get to him.

'But she wasn't sleeping with one of the Boches, was she,

yet that's what the haircut indicates,' grunted Allard. 'She was betraying Doumier.'

'It's all the same, is it not? It's only fornication of a different sort,' countered Ledieu. 'Maybe I would have cut off her hair myself, had I killed her.'

'*Ah, mon Dieu,* you two are such a pair! Start thinking,' insisted Allard, furiously indicating this and that and her hair. 'If the scissors were to hand, then why the towel and the rock?'

He had a point. 'Perhaps they were an afterthought?' hazarded Father Nicolas.

'Precisely! Now we're getting somewhere. We receive an unexpected visitor, a courier from Paris . . .'

'You're forgetting the message we received saying that just such a one would arrive.'

'All right, this I acknowledge. Also that she brings us what we most desire, but what happens next, eh? We get another little bonus! Women . . .'

'Are *what*, please?' asked Ledieu. Clearly Théodore didn't like the trend of his own thoughts.

The sous-préfet tossed a hand. 'Women are more inclined to have scissors, that's all I meant.'

And the towel. He was still thinking of it and of Paris. 'Then that includes the more than sixty-seven percent of the adult citizens the war has left us,' cautioned Ledieu. 'No doubt any woman who suspected what Véronique was up to might have wished to use the scissors only to realize that such implements, they are so scarce they're worth a life sometimes, and would afterwards constantly remind one of the deed they had done.'

Irritably Allard ran a hand over the dome of his head. '*Bon*! I needed to be told that. Perhaps our courier didn't come alone then, as she has said. If one stands in her shoes, such a thing as company would best be kept quiet, at least for a little until she has grown accustomed to us. They may have done us a favour here, but if so then that implies that the *réseau* she belongs to in Paris knows far more about our affairs than we do.'

He had a point there, too, the others gravely acknowledged. All three of them stood around as if uncertain of what to do. Cigarettes were offered and gratefully accepted. 'The colonel's,' said Ledieu. 'Lautenschläger left the packet on my desk the other day, saying that the French could do much better.'

They were *Gauloises bleues* and made in Paris by the state-owned tobacco company.

'It's terrible, isn't it,' said Ledieu. 'Carrot tops, oak leaves and sweepings from a sawpit!'

'From a barn floor, I think,' said Father Nicolas, looking curiously at the smouldering end of his cigarette. Anything was possible these days.

They would have to be told of the other matter, thought Allard. 'The Mademoiselle Moncontre said that the Germans might try to infiltrate us. A priest, she thought, and a novice.'

'Infiltrate?' bleated Ledieu. 'Why did you not warn us of this last night?'

'Because I didn't hear of it until after you had all left. When we were alone, she told me.'

'They'll have to be killed. There'll be reprisals,' said Ledieu. 'Ah, damn the SS and the Gestapo! The Oberst Lautenschläger will have no other choice.'

As mayor, Honoré was always the one to have to deal with such things and therefore a worrier. 'Not necessarily,' cautioned Father Nicolas. 'The Germans won't publically admit those two in such a disguise were working for them.'

'In any case, we have to find out who they are and see that they are conducted out of the district without the Boches immediately learning of it,' said Allard firmly.

A trip on the water, then, a voyage out to sea with iron weights.

'Infiltrators will be known to the Gestapo Munk and to his visitor, the Sturmbannführer Kraus,' cautioned Father Nicolas, 'but not likely to the colonel.'

'The control's list of names will give me who was on that train and where they were going,' muttered Ledieu, irritably flicking cigarette ash onto the corpse only to stop himself and throw the others a look of apology.

Again they looked at what had once been a living, breathing human being they had all known. Each noted the sagging breasts that had been greedily suckled by every one of her children. Three, ah, damn it!

'For now we must concentrate on this,' said Allard. 'A woman would have thought of using the scissors, the lipstick too,' he added stubbornly. 'A man would simply have left her in haste or pinned a note of warning to her dress. Chastel will have a better look than ourselves, due to your presence among us, Father, so we will leave the evidence up to him.'

'Must you? I'm not so innocent! Besides, let me remind you, if I may be so bold, she wanted only happiness for herself and those children. We should keep that in mind and condemn ourselves for not having paid far greater attention to what was happening to her. We all knew how empty she felt. Myself, I admit, more than others, so God forgive me.'

'Yes, yes,' said Allard gruffly. 'Her brother, Henri, will have to be told. Will you do it, Father?'

'Of course.'

'Then let us hope he doesn't successfully hang himself this time. We need our electrics man now more than ever. That wireless set . . .' said Ledieu.

Honoré was right. 'It has to be fixed. Those tubes . . . the railway workers. Why the hell can't those bastard Bolsheviks be more careful?'

'All of our *cheminot*s are not Communists,' said Father Nicolas, picking a shred of "tobacco" from his lower lip but deciding not to save it.

'Perhaps you are right, Father, but that still doesn't help us. We have to find replacements or that set of hers is absolutely useless,' said Allard.

'Must you be so suspicious of the Mademoiselle Moncontre?' sighed Ledieu. 'The risks she took, the danger—have you forgotten this? She couldn't have known the tubes would be broken. Henri has said the Mark One is notoriously delicate. She's a woman, too, not an expert in electrics or wireless sets, and she comes to us in good faith. Please let's not think otherwise.'

One had best step into it, thought Father Nicolas, or these two would be at each other and shouting over the corpse. 'The glass from the tubes was still in the set, the tubes themselves still plugged into their circuit board.'

'Then you both believe she really is okay?' asked Allard.

Must he still have doubts? wondered Ledieu. 'Isn't it a little late for us to be questioning such?'

'It's never too late and you know it!' But had Véronique come here to meet someone? 'Just what the hell was this one doing here, eh? This spring isn't on her route home. She had the children to attend to, the urgency of their evening meal, all such things.'

'What about the funeral?' asked Father Nicolas—it had to be asked.

'There won't be one,' said Allard firmly. 'I want the casket closed, Nicolas, and don't give me any talk of absolution. Let the people imagine what she looks like, and let her be buried in an unmarked grave and outside the cemetery.'

'You really mean that, don't you?'

'As your God is my witness. She must be an example to others—can you not see that? It's a tragedy, yes, yes, of course, but let's not have any more of them.'

'He's right, Nicolas. That's how it has to be,' said Ledieu. 'Into the ground, yourself beside the open grave, no one else. They can all watch from a distance, should any wish to.'

'Even her children?'

Nicolas had baptized her, and then later, her children, and he had conducted the marriage service as well before those had come along. 'Even them. Please,' said Ledieu, taking him by the arm, 'this is the way it has to be. Oh for sure, we would all wish it otherwise, but it would be foolish of us to grant her anything more.'

'Then the Boches, they will take note of it and condemn you both.'

'Ah, they can think what they want, as they will most certainly in any case, but if I have to, I'll tell them I received a threat in the night. Nothing on paper. Simply words given after the pebble at the window had awakened me; words from the "*Banditen*".'

And with that, thought Father Nicolas sadly, you confirm the seriousness of our existence in their midst.

The wind came sharply on the Monts de Caubert and when Marie-Hélène set aside her alias of Isabelle Moncontre as she looked up at the Christ on that heavily timbered cross, the wind stung her eyes and made her lips part.

Buffeted, her dark brown hair was blown across her face. She tried to brush it aside but it was no use. Crouching, she forced the stems of the tight bouquets of red chrysanthemums into the holders, then stood back with hands together in prayer, head bowed.

Afterwards, after this single minute or two, she stood rigidly to attention and gave the solemn salute of a *résistante*.

There, she told herself, it's enough. But was it? she wondered. No one else was about, or was there? No one watched her every move to judge and condemn, or did someone?

Through some whim of sensibility, the Oberst Lautenschläger had had the antiaircraft batteries emplaced on the heights well to the north of the Calvary. She knew she couldn't even see those 88 mm cannon from where she stood, so was safe from others suspecting she had gone there to meet someone among the enemy.

The note from Hans had been brief. She still couldn't believe he had come all the way from Paris to meet her in secret. She was anxious to see him, to hold him and be held, but had she been followed from Abbeville?

Nerves . . . Was it just nerves and the excitement she felt at the prospect of seeing him again and so unexpectedly?

Far across the flat floor of the Somme Valley, where the sinuosity of the river and the straightness of its canals melded with the verdant hectares of trees and farms, the seemingly endless plain of Ponthieu stretched away and into the east.

Raymond Châlus is over there, she reminded herself. He can't have doubled back and come here to find me, not yet. He can't have, she repeated, trying to reassure herself. And searching the distant landscape, let her hair blow forward to cowl her face while sunlight shone on swaths of ripening maize, wheat and barley, a patchwork quilt of them and of newly plowed fields. There were woods and copses too, and the tiny, huddled clusters of farm dwellings and villages.

Blinking to clear her eyes, she took a breath and dropped them to the cards she had fastened to the stems so that each bouquet held the same message: *Doumier. Remember Henri-Paul. Keep him always in your thoughts.*

After receiving the note that had been left at the *pension* where she was staying, she had bought the flowers and with them in her carrier basket had ridden out of Abbeville and up the road that had climbed so steeply to the heights. Caesar had built an encampment here in 57 B.C. Fully fourteen legions—from forty-two thousand to eighty-four thousand men—had been bivouacked here, surrounded by earthen ramparts and entrenchments. Now all that remained was the agger, the mound and upon this, the Christ on the cross had been raised.

What would he think of her, this Christ of her childhood? Would he condemn her to eternal damnation for having killed Véronique Dussart? Caesar would have praised all such things as noble acts of war.

Abbeville, when seen from the heights, lay even more dramatically in ruins, the heart of it all but completely destroyed. De Gaulle, *la grande asperge*\* some were now fondly calling him, had pulled his forces back to here in late May 1940. They had tried to readvance across the Somme, had tried to push Rommel and his panzers out but it had been of no use.

In the end, his men like so many of the others, had fallen into retreat and, yes, she said, into what had quickly become a disgraceful rout.

It had said something about the French, then, the Defeat. It had divided the nation into two groups. Those who welcomed the Occupier with open arms and legs, yes, and those who were forced to solemnly go along with things if only to survive.

But now? she asked, looking again across the valley to Ponthieu but searching for a far distant little woods, that of Bois Carré. Raymond Châlus, a priest travelling with a novice

---

\* The big asparagus

but no longer as those. Châlus had been a man of many talents. An actor and a good one, that rarity of rarities, a man who through the accident of war had become his true self.

She had so little time. A day, two days—perhaps less. The backup Kraus had deliberately turned away might have come with Hans, but she doubted this.

Still afraid she had been followed, she walked the bicycle along the path that ran from the Calvary southward at the top of the escarpment. There were no springs up here. They would be far below her among the trees at the base of the escarpment but still the path became so similar to the one Véronique Dussart had timidly climbed, it made her heart race and as the path went downslope a little among the trees and underbrush, it narrowed until, at last, in a cul-de-sac of grey, lichened rocks, there was a place to leave the bicycle.

A stone bench gave perfect views across the valley, though a constant reminder of Ponthieu stretched away. Sounds tended to come up the escarpment but were far distant. She took the time to look closely around and back up the path, even to retracing her steps about a hundred metres.

From a point just off the path, she waited among the trees and underbrush . . . waited for whoever it was to come along but either they were far better at it than herself, or not here at all.

Uncertain still, she returned to the bench and from there, climbed nimbly to the ruins of a stone hut.

It was empty. The scattered refuse of the soldiers who had used it in May of 1940 lay about. A French helmet with a bullet-dented rim met her eye, a tattered, bloodstained gaiter, a boot whose lace had been cut to free it from a shattered leg, a cross that had been whittled out of softwood, empty sardine cans and broken wine bottles. Shell casings were everywhere.

The much-thumbed photograph of a naked girl who offered herself from the coverlet of a rumpled bed lay impaled on a wall nail.

The smell of old sheep's dung, urine, stale sweat and mouldy straw came to Marie-Hélène, that of sulphur dioxide too, baked from the rocks in the walls by the heat of the sun. The sound of the wind was here, in the cracks of the roof through which she could, in her silence now, see the sky quite clearly.

I have no gun, no weapon of any kind, she said to herself. Ah, damn, I *wanted* Hans so badly, I believed totally in the note that had been left for me. I didn't question it and should have.

There *was* someone outside, and that person was taking their time.

Crouching, she picked up the broken neck of a wine bottle and, by unrolling the right sleeve of her shirt-blouse, managed to hide the thing in her hand.

Come then, she said. Come in and let us meet face to face, me with my back to the wall.

Far out on the plain of Ponthieu, Angélique caught a breath. Slowly, as if in a nightmare, she stopped pedalling and stood with the bicycle between her legs.

Kraus, she gasped inwardly, her heart racing. They were all alone on the road. There was no one in sight, just that cursed car of his, its driver behind the wheel and one other sitting in the front while the Sturmbannführer paused as he got out of the back to grin and then to laugh at her.

Perhaps thirty metres separated them. He crooked a forefinger, motioning her to come to him. She swallowed tightly.

With what seemed to take ages, she walked the bike towards him. The wind tugged at her dress and made it flap. It bared her bare legs, revealed her knees, was cold and hot and everything in between.

'*Bonjour,*' she managed.

Kraus had come forward of the car so that now they faced each other alone.

'What are you doing out here?' he demanded.

Involuntarily she shivered. 'Nothing. I . . . I'm on my way to work, Sturmbannführer. I'm late enough as it is.'

With the wind, the flowered print dress clung to every cleft. The simple, pale grey-blue knitted cardigan was open. Buttons ran down the front, buttons as on the dress of Véronique Dussart.

'You're lucky,' he snorted, coming so close he blocked the

wind but forced her to look him in the face. 'You've friends. Your sentence of death has been lifted by another.'

Was he going to hit her, grab her by the hair and force her to come with him in that car? 'I . . . I don't know what you mean. A sentence of death?'

*Lies . . . This one would always lie,* thought Kraus. The sand-coloured hair was tied severely back. The wide-set, grey eyes were furtive. The chest rose as she sucked in a breath and prepared herself for the fist. *So gut. Ja, gut!*

Quickly he told her about the body that had been found. Instantly she crossed herself and bowing her head, turned away in tears and then thought better of it and turned back. Shutting her eyes, she squeezed tears and he watched as they ran down those softly tanned cheeks, the wind flattening them so that they didn't touch her lips.

'Has the terrorist Ledieu received the pencil?'

She tried not to cry but it was hopeless. Martin was out there among the fields, creeping up on Bois Carré. Martin . . . 'Yes. Yes, my son returned it to him.'

Her "son". Kraus pulled the bicycle from her, she releasing her hold on it.

Thrown onto the verge, its front wheel turned and Angélique saw the spokes amid the swaying wildflowers. They were like a late summer's day of freedom, a beautiful tableau, and she wished with all her heart that she was but gathering them, but he stood behind her. Now she could only see that big, black ugly car whose driver, and the one other, were watching.

'Make sure Ledieu suspects nothing.'

When she didn't answer, he shrieked at her, she leaping to cry out, 'Yes, damn you! Yes,' and weep.

They drove off. Long after the sound of their car was gone, the sound of it stayed with her until she cried out in anguish, 'VÉRONIQUE!' and then, 'MARTIN, PLEASE DON'T DO IT!'

But Martin couldn't hear her. Martin was lying among the tall, waving maize whose ears were golden and bursting at their pods, so much so, the dry under-leaves were a rough parchment that rattled whenever touched by himself or the wind.

Three soldiers were just upslope of him at the edge of the

forest and they were bored with their job of guarding Bois Carré. They lounged about and constantly smoked cigarettes. Though he couldn't understand their muted, often broken bits of conversation, he thought it was of girls, of whores they had fornicated with, and of home.

Bread and women, he said to himself. Beer and salt, and turning over onto his back, lay between the furrows looking up through the stalks to the cloud-drifted sky above.

The parachute was of dark blue, almost black silk. There were silver clouds on it and silver stars and shooting stars and, yes, a big yellow moon, and as he had come slowly down from above at night, he had guided it by pulling in on the straps or letting others out until, with a touch and a quick roll, he had landed in the darkness.

No one could ever have seen him because the parachute was invisible against the night sky. It was special. But now the Germans would begin to look for it and now there was but little time.

Pulling himself forward, he squirmed away towards the north so as to get around the sentry post. His father would have wanted him to do this for the Mademoiselle Isabelle who was so pretty and risked her life constantly.

The faint scent of her perfume came to him in memory, of jasmine, yes, and sandalwood, of other things too. She was everything Angélique wasn't and he knew he was in love with her and that he would gladly die for her.

The ruined hut on the Monts de Caubert was close, and when a leaf stirred outside, Marie-Hélène stiffened and gingerly felt the razor-sharp edges of the broken bottleneck in her hand. The *réseau de soie bleue* had come for her. They would accuse and condemn and cry out harshly, 'Marie-Hélène de Fleury, alias Isabelle Moncontre, alias Nadine Delaunay, alias Geneviève Vicomte, alias Martine Ecquevilly, you are hereby charged with . . .'

Those were the names, the lives she had lived. Châlus would tell them everything he knew of her. They would be only too aware of what she had done. He really hadn't been in the *pays de* Ponthieu, heading for Bois Carré. He had come back to Abbeville to warn them and to trap her.

Would they beat her, force her to reveal how much Kraus really knew, how much she had withheld?

The sous-préfet Allard would be the first to enter the hut. They'd all have to duck to avoid the lintel. The others would crowd in behind. The one with the revolver would stand behind Ledieu, the mayor, and a little to his right. He would notice the photograph that was beside her on the wall, but would it distract him?

She must dart beneath Allard's arm and fight her way between and past the other two, slashing the gun hand deeply, slashing the face, the wrist, the jugular until, colliding with Châlus, she had . . .

Was it really him out there? she wondered. Had he really not been in Ponthieu as she had thought?

Châlus was the only witness to what had happened in Lyon, the only survivor. Would he say to her, You were going to betray a ten-year-old boy who has lost his voice? Would he have her thrown against the wall to demand, How could any woman do such a thing?

Would she spit at him and try to smile in contempt? Would she cry out, Because I have to! Because I agreed to do what I did for love?

Ah no, not love, she confessed. Born into wealth and privilege, you craved it.

The door was broken, its weathered, unpainted boards splintered. Nudged, it swung in on its leather hinges as she silently prepared herself and said, Please God . . .

'Marie-Hélène?'

'Hans . . . ?'

The neck of the bottle smashed against the wall, she tossing the thing aside and taking two half steps. As he ducked to enter, she threw herself at him and fought to kiss him hard and bury his head against her breasts, to hug and hold him and cry out, 'Hans . . . Hans, is it really you?'

Laughing, crying, she found his lips again, found his neck and, wrapping arms tightly about it, pulled herself hard against him. 'In,' she cried. 'In, Hans. *Please!* I have to have you in me.'

She tried to drag him to the floor. She lay in the rubbish, pulling at the buttons of her shirt-blouse, opening it, tugging at her brassiere until it was above her breasts and he was looking down at her and saying, '*Liebchen*, easy, eh? We haven't much time.'

'It doesn't take much!'

He laughed, he grinned and yes, it was good to hear him do so but . . .

'We're not peasants,' he said.

She was breathing hard and as he watched, her hands moved down to hike her skirt, but he shook his head and told her not to be so silly—*silly!*—that there would be plenty of time for such. 'Weeks, months, you'll see.'

Something must have happened. Beneath that veneer of his, there were deep shadows and she knew then that in spite of the laughter and the smiles, he was afraid.

'Berlin,' she said, pulling down her brassiere. 'It's Berlin, isn't it?'

How quick she was to read his mind and see the truth.

Dirksen helped her up and brushed her off as she buttoned her shirt-blouse and tucked it into the waistband of her skirt.

'Kraus doesn't just want my assignment,' he said. 'Abbeville is to be made an example of. Oberst Lautenschläger's incompetence—his weakness towards the French—is to be exposed. He's to be seen as a slacker at a time when the Reich can't have any, and Kraus is here to do the necessary for the Reichsführer.'

She tidied her skirt—couldn't look at him now, needed time to adjust as he said, 'All aspects of the Retaliatory One security are to be placed under SS command. Bois Carré and the parachutist are to be the excuse, Kraus the instrument, and Lautenschläger the Wehrmacht's guilty party, to be retired in disgrace and oblivion. Kraus will then take over command completely.'

'And you?' she asked, hesitating.

He picked bits of straw from her. 'Am to be recalled.'

'When?'

How alarmed she was, how lost and frantic. 'Three days. That's all we have in which to wrap things up.'

'But . . . but you just said we would have weeks, months together?'

He had such a soft and gentle smile, sad, too, as he touched her cheek and brushed the backs of his fingers down it.

She was desperate. 'If we do it successfully, what then?' she demanded.

He would have to tell her. Only then would she do what had to be done. 'Kraus still takes over. Berlin have something else in mind for me. I'm to be watched and toughened up. I've been too weak, too easy on the terrorists. Like Lautenschläger, I've failed.'

'Yet we caught so many. Does that not mean anything?'

A little impatience would suit. 'Everything is subordinate to the security of those sites. The Americans will be devastated by what we do to London. Nearly a hundred sites are to be aimed at it on the first day. A *hundred*, Marie-Hélène, each firing twenty or thirty bombs in that day alone and every one of those of about a thousand kilos of high explosive. It's so big the British will never recover and will sue for a peace the Americans will have to go along with.'

Flying bombs . . . He really believed it too, and when Hans took out a cigarette and lit it, she saw how desperate he was. He didn't like the tough approach, had always left that to others and had felt he was above such things.

'You should have joined the Abwehr,' she said. 'Though they've done an awful lot of things just as terrible as the SS and its SD, it's still far more of a gentleman's service.'

'The Abwehr,' he said and grinned and tried to laugh at things but failed. 'They're still refusing to give me details of Thiessen or even acknowledging that one's existence. They realize that the Führer and the Reichsführer Himmler have it in for them and that they're fast losing out to the SS and our Sicherheitsdienst. By the end of the year, they'll no longer exist. Sucked in by Himmler, dissolved, absorbed, whatever, even banished from the history books.'

Moving closer, she put her hands on his chest. 'Thiessen has to be Martin Bellecour's father. Everything fits. The boy is convinced of it. Now, too, the Bellecour woman.'

He drew away from her. 'Even the yacht fits.'

'The *Alcyone*,' she said. 'And where, please, did you find it—you did, didn't you?'

She had always wanted to know if the information she had gathered had been correct. 'It was exactly where she said it would be. In Deauville.'

Sighing, she said, 'Then Anthony James Thomas really did remain in France and the boy is absolutely correct in thinking this.'

'But is he really Raymond Châlus?' asked Dirksen, stepping nearer to place the half-finished cigarette between her lips.

Inhaling deeply, she quickly nodded. 'The same. He has to be.'

So Thiessen of the rue des Grands-Augustins was Châlus of the Lyon Perrache network and the boy's father, but did it go deeper still? he wondered. Did it go right back to Perpignan and the Mirabeau escape line?

Caressing the softness of her throat, he kissed her on the lips and said, 'Stop worrying. We'll get them.'

'And then?' she asked.

They were so close now, she was trembling. 'Spain. Madrid or Barcelona. You can take your pick.'

Lightly Hans kissed her again. 'And you?' she asked, a whisper.

The time had come. 'It all depends on Kraus. He's been putting the squeeze on you, hasn't he?'

In despair, she pressed her forehead against his chest and wished he would hold her tightly, but all he did was to ask again and she had to look up at him and answer, 'Yes.'

'He'll never learn, will he?'

She would give him no answer but would search his eyes, knowing now what he wanted of her—yes, of her!—but forcing him to say it.

'What you tell him must trap him, *Liebchen*. Berlin must be convinced of it, and then made to see that with Kraus out of the way, I'll have to remain in command.'

One could only toss a dismissive hand at such idiocy. 'They'll simply bring in someone else,' she said, furious with him.

He was ready for her and, dismayed, she realized he'd been waiting for this very moment, that all along he'd been planning for it.

'Not if I get tough with those we take. Not if Berlin hear of it, and they will.'

He would do it too, and she could see this now and felt, yes, a sadness that could only deepen. 'The loss of self, it's not good, Hans. Come to Spain. Let's leave all this before it's too late for both of us.'

'My brothers in the SS would only come after me and you know it. They wouldn't give us a moment's peace until they had hounded us down and killed us.'

Giving her a moment to consider this, he asked, 'What have you managed to find out so far?'

Was it to be nothing between them now but business? 'The *réseau de soie bleue* has as its committee, the mayor, the priest, Father Nicolas, and the sous-préfet Allard.' Hans took out the small, black leather-bound notebook he had always used for such details and began to write down the death sentences she would give him. 'The dentist Eugène Lefèvre, the foreman of one of Mayor Ledieu's breweries, a Joseph Marchand, and an evader of the STO, a Jean-Pierre Gaudeau who hides out among the *hortillonnages* of his uncle. Also the legless brother of Véronique Dussart. That one may be able to fix the wireless set, but we shall see.'

She had done amazingly well. 'You deserve a medal,' he quipped and grinned but knew she would only be upset with him for suggesting it. There were no medals for such as her. Besides, to publicly award her anything would be far too dangerous for her.

'Allard is the tough one,' she said coldly. 'The constant doubter. The mayor tends to accept the obvious, though he questions things too. In a pinch, he and the sous-préfet will be formidable—they're both former soldiers, as is Father Nicolas. Also Marchand, the foreman. In all the time I was with them last night, that one said nothing. He simply sized me up.'

Methodically she finished the cigarette and was careful not to leave the butt lying around, even to brushing away the ashes from the wall where she had stubbed it out.

'The STO evader Gaudeau has one of the old Lebel *Modèle d'ordonnace.*'

'The eleven millimetre or the eight millimetre?'

'The black powder, most likely.'

He nodded to indicate that the former were still effective enough, though they could misfire due to that ammunition having been stored by the French since 1873. 'Anything else?'

'Châlus-Thiessen is travelling in disguise as a priest and with a novice who is really the *résistante* Yvette Rougement, that girl in Paris who helped the Bellecour woman. Châlus and Yvette went on to Noyelles-sur-Mer ostensibly to visit the graves of the war dead and will, I think, now be in position for a close look at Bois Carré. Kraus didn't have them arrested. It's not like him to leave such an opportunity.'

Though hard and unyielding now, she was still terrified of Châlus and justifiably so but would have to be told the truth. 'He's letting you nail all of them and then lead him to Châlus. He knows Châlus is in the area, not just to find out what's been going on in Bois Carré but also to put an end to you.'

She turned away to prevent herself from breaking down, waited for Hans to comfort her, and when he didn't, placed both hands against the wall and leaned on them to steady herself. 'So I'm to be sacrificed, eh? Kraus sent my backup away, Hans. He did!'

'What have you told him?'

Emptily she answered, 'He only knows about the mayor, I think, not of the others yet. The Gestapo Munk would have arrested them before we arrived had that one known of them.'

'Then keep their names to yourself. Keep our Sturmbann-führer guessing.'

Did he really think it would be so easy? 'And what if Kraus comes for me; what then, Hans?' she asked, facing him now.

Another cigarette was dragged out and lighted to hide the truth, was that it? she wondered.

'Tell him things are delicate, that you're so close to being accepted, nothing must intrude.'

Was Hans really so desperate? she wondered, and placing her back against the wall, folded her arms across her chest. 'He'll only see that I no longer have the wireless set—had you not thought of that?'

Irritably he flicked ash away. 'Tell him you left it in your room at the *pension*—tell him anything, damn it. Just stall that bastard for a little.'

This wasn't the Hans she had known. 'And what if he's aware I'm lying? What then?'

He couldn't look at her. 'Deal with it. Kill him yourself. I'll swear it wasn't you.'

He left her then, left her feeling so alone and leaning back against a ruined wall wondering what the hell to do to stop it all from happening, and when he returned, he had the ruck-sack he had taken into the mountains as a boy.

'There's a stripped-down Schmeisser in an oilcloth, two hundred rounds, and a Luger with fifty. See that this mayor of yours receives the Schmeisser, then single Kraus out and lead him into a trap. Make certain he's killed.'

He was serious. 'Why don't you do it yourself? A lonely road—there are lots of those. A walk through the ruins—ah! there are plenty of those too.' Why her?

'Because I can't. Because if I did, my death wouldn't be so pleasant and you know it.'

Ah yes, an SS man must never kill one of his fellows. They used piano wire to garrotte them but first would castrate and then torture. 'The mayor won't want any killing that can't be hidden or attributed to natural causes. There'd be reprisals. Hostages.'

He tossed a hand. 'For every omelette there are casualties. Tell him that.'

How French Hans had become. 'And Châlus?' she asked, still watching him so closely it made him feel uncomfortable.

'I *don't* know! I wish I did, but we'll get him this time because we have to. Use his son against him. *Ach, verdammt*, let the boy lead both Kraus and him into a trap. Do some-thing! You have no other choice.'

An order, was it, or else? 'Me, I've risked my life for you many times. Already I've told the sous-préfet Allard that this "priest" and "novice" might try to infiltrate. At the very most this can only delay Châlus a day or two, no more, I assure you, and in the end, if he's not stopped, he'll confirm that I'm that very infiltrator, but I'll never know how things are until the end.'

Pinching out the cigarette, he crumbled it to dust. 'Look, I wish I could be here to help but I'm not even supposed to have left Paris. If Berlin find out I disobeyed, they'll . . .'

He glanced at the rucksack and, swearing at himself for having used it, said, 'Destroy it. Don't let Kraus find it. He would only trace it back to me.'

And what of us? she wanted so much to ask, but softly said, 'You leave me many things to do but nothing for myself.'

'You have the Luger. Use it.'

'Hans, how can you say this to me? To *me*?'

'Everything is waiting for you at your flat in Paris. Your new *carte d'identité*, new passport, travel permits, *sauf-conduit* for the *zone interdite* along the Spanish border—everything to get you across the frontier and into Spain without question. Also one hundred thousand Reichskassenschein and a letter of introduction to our consular general in Madrid.'

Two million of the Occupation francs. It was little enough when all was considered. 'So, it's good-bye, is it?' she asked and saw him shake his head.

'Not at all and you know it. As soon as Kraus is out of the way, I'll take over again. Do this for me and you can have anything you want. *Anything*, Marie-Hélène. We'll destroy London and win the war. We'll turn back the Allies. Even the Russians will be afraid of what we have.'

Bois Carré was but one of many such sites and yes, the destruction of that city alone could well cause the Allies to rethink their position but didn't such a prospect of mass destruction also seduce the minds of those who would use it?

Wanting so much to say, I pity you, she shrugged and said, 'For me, I only hope you're right.'

Noyelles-sur-Mer was at the head of the Somme Estuary and from this little seaside village, the rippled sands and channelled muds at low tide formed a huge and glistening apron. The wind was from the west, and it would bring much rain. Allard could smell it, but would it cause problems? he wondered, thinking of what had to be done.

Seagulls and terns fought for scraps among the floating refuse—German scraps, he told himself—but the sound made him think of the Marquenterre. There were thousands of such birds in that place but also migrating ducks and geese and sandpipers and they offered perfect shooting now only for Germans. Grey-blue herons too, and swans and spoonbills.

He could taste them. Not the herons—ah, not one of those from the spit of an open fire, but merely for the sport and to say one had shot one on the wing. Slow . . . *mon Dieu* but those things had been so slow. Like Dorniers, Blenheims or Wellingtons.

'Do you remember the dunes, Nicolas?' he asked. The two of them had come the fourteen kilometres from Abbeville, north down the Somme Valley in the tiny Peugeot the Germans had allowed him.

'It's not a day for boyhood memories, Théodore. It's a day for us to find this infiltrator priest and his novice.'

'I was only asking so as to remind myself of the things I value most.'

'The camping trips.'

Life! but there was little sense in saying this. 'Those girls we used to meet, Father, and the things they urged us to do with them while under moonlight among the dunes.'

'If I remember it, we played cards and sang songs. They wore bathing suits, towels and kerchiefs and there were far more of them than there were of us.'

'You have no imagination. Constant prayer must kill it!'

The Marquenterre was just to the east of the estuary, where the tidal flat was at its broadest. Reclaimed after the Middle Ages, the land had been found so wanting, the area had been left as a wasteland that had quickly been taken over by sand dunes, salt flats, scrubby patches of woods and isolated, marshy ponds.

'One could hide there, perhaps,' offered Father Nicolas

with the shrug Allard knew so well he didn't need to look at his friend to see it.

'They would use the dogs and spotter aircraft to find us,' he grumbled. 'Besides, there are coastal batteries, pillboxes and minefields.'

'We may not have to hide. Not yet,' said Nicolas.

'At Mers-les-Bains there might be a lugger or a trawler. It's just a thought.'

'You would never leave your wife and family to face things alone, myself my parish.'

'Then let's get this over with.'

The Auberge of the Annoyingly Fertile Cat wasn't much. Norman-looking in its entire, with half-timbered walls, low ceilings, shutters and leaded windows, it had somehow avoided the ravages of 1940, but the staircases were hell and begged for a damned good shelling. Far too steep, too narrow for the cautious approach and too noisy. Impossible to do anything but look up and into a pistol perhaps.

When shown the room, they saw right away that the priestly cassock and novice robes had been left behind but were neatly folded on the bed. From the room, the roofs stepped down to freedom.

'One night, that is all they have spent,' lamented the *patron*. 'I have wondered at them sharing such a small bed, Monsieur le Sous-préfet, but,' he shrugged, 'with God there are always mysteries and to each such life, the secrets.'

Where had he come from, this idiot? wondered Allard, snorting inwardly but grunting dispassionately, 'The sister? The older one?'

The head was tossed. 'Ah! she didn't share this room. She's among the graves, searching as she does each year for the stone of her long-dead brother. Though she has seen it many times, the memory is, alas, in other places, the mind also.'

Allard sucked on a tooth. Father Nicolas fingered the cassock. 'And the others—these two?' he asked, indicating the cloth.

The *patron*, a man of sixty who must have spent his life

digging for clams and mussels and eating them, shrugged and threw out the hands of desperation. 'Gone to heaven perhaps, as angels.'

'Idiot! this is serious,' swore Allard.

He had meant it too. 'Gone east, well beyond the war graves here. On foot. Me, I have seen the two of them as they waved good-bye to the elderly sister.'

'Who will, no doubt,' offered Father Nicolas, 'return these garments to whom they rightfully belong.'

'Is the church mixed up in something?' asked the *patron* dodgedly.

Allard drew himself up and frowned as a police administrator should.

When they found the elderly sister, she was indeed lost among the graves and of absolutely no use to them. A note was securely pinned to her habit: *I am Sister Juliette from the Carmelites of the rue d'Assas in Paris. As you think of God, please return me to them and so direct my path.*

It was Father Nicolas who wished her well. Allard simply looked to the east along the empty road, which here found its lonely way across the plain of Ponthieu towards the Forêt de Crécy.

'They must be heading for Bois Carré or to one of the other sites,' he said. 'But if infiltrators, as I've been told by the Mademoiselle Moncontre, then why would they begin their task at the source of our interest?'

'Because only by searching for what we desire to know better can they prove to us they are genuine.'

'Was it one of them who killed Véronique?'

'You know that's impossible. The distance, the train times . . .'

'Yes, yes. I'm only asking because I already have the answer, Nicolas. If not the priest and his novice, then who?'

'Our Mademoiselle Moncontre?'

'There's something about her that still tugs at me. Why, please, did she wait to warn of the infiltrators until she was alone with me?'

'She wasn't sure. She only thought they might be.'

'And now, is it that we find they are, or is it that like the good sister, we must be told by another which path to follow?'

It was quiet along the Transit Canal amid the ruins on the outskirts of Abbeville and when she thought it safe, Marie-Hélène took the rucksack from her carrier basket and gently lowered it into the water. The stones would weight it down.

As it sank from sight, bubbles of marsh gas rose until, at last, there were no more.

Hans had asked her to kill for him but when the *réseau de soie bleue* ceased to exist, she had the feeling there would be nothing left between them. Her usefulness would be finished. She would be, and now was, too well known.

The Schmeisser and its two hundred rounds were hidden in the hut near the Monts de Caubert—she had found a good place for them along with thirty rounds for the Luger. All else was in the woven straw handbag.

Kraus wouldn't cooperate any more than would the mayor. Both would have to be forced into meeting face to face and alone, but to that, Kraus would never agree. At best, he would come with a few others. There would be an exchange of fire—he could die in that, but far too much depended on pure luck.

Pushing the bike, with her bag in the front carrier basket and half open for easy access to the Luger, she started out again. She would ride to the northeast to have a look at Bois Carré from a distance. Only then would she decide what to do.

Between the villages of Caours and Neufmoulin, two camouflaged lorries full of Waffen-SS roared past, the wind taking their dust and chasing them. No smiles. No whistles. Just the brutal stares of the impassive.

Then a Wehrmacht one came along with a few laughing boys in the back who, on seeing her, eagerly signalled to their sergeant to stop and give her a lift. This was often done for pretty girls, but they had the SS's German shepherds with them and these constantly took interest, so much so, that when they got to Saint-Riquier, she said that she had to get out, that she was home.

Grinning, they left her in the village, left her with a final sight of those dogs, all five of them with heads out over the tailgate, watching her.

'Dogs . . . ? *Ah, mon Dieu,*' she managed. 'The search for the parachutist.'

Suddenly the telex had stopped and the phone lines were silent. In the stillness of the Kommandantur, Angélique heard Frau Hössler roll the lozenge around so that it clacked against the back of the woman's teeth.

When excited, when nervous, she constantly popped these ersatz things into her mouth. Papers were being brusquely stacked, pencils tidied. Dogs . . . Were they to use dogs? Martin was in those fields next to Bois Carré. Martin wouldn't know about the dogs until it was too late.

The Kommandantur and hôtel de ville had been a mad-house. Furious with Sturmbannführer Kraus for having called in a detachment of Waffen-SS without proper authority, Oberst Lautenachläger had brought down the mailed fist of a Prussian general. All hotels, inns and *pensions* were to be searched, all farms, villages and towns within a radius of fifty kilometres. Train schedules, bus schedules—even flights into and out of the nearby Lutfwaffe bases—were to be checked. All wireless traffic for the past ten days was to be thoroughly scanned for clandestine signals that might have been missed. *Banditen* from Paris were in on this Doumier affair. They were to get those people—GET THEM!

A priest, a novice and an aging nun . . . Would the dogs tear them apart? Would Anthony escape? Could he? And what of Martin?

Frau Hössler pried open the tin and offered a lozenge. 'They are *gut, ja*? Menthol, eucalyptus *und der Pfefferminze.* Very suitable for the throat.'

Angélique shook her head and gave a whispered, '*Merci,* you're very kind. Later perhaps.'

The woman was adamant the dogs would soon root out the parachutist while keeping at bay those who had hidden him. 'You will see,' she said and sucked on that thing. 'Nothing will get past the Waffen-SS. Those boys, they know their duty.'

*Dieu mon Père,* please! begged Angélique silently.

'Those dogs have been specially trained. They're very vicious. Myself, I have seen such things. *Ach*, but I have. One caught the escapee by the throat, another rushed for the genitals—it is the same with wolves. They tore him to pieces in less than a minute and had to be dragged away lest they feed and get a taste for its sweetness.'

I'm going to vomit, said Angélique silently but somehow managed, 'I'll just take these papers into the mayor's office. Then shall I make you a cup of coffee?'

'Coffee, yes. You don't look well. You have had a shock. Frau Dussart was your friend—this I have seen. But how is it that you French find it so easy to betray one another?'

'Véronique was beside herself with despair. The Gestapo Munk must have forced her to . . .' Ah, why had she said it? 'I'm sorry, Frau Hössler. I *am* upset. Please forgive me.'

Was the Sturmbannführer Kraus using this one? wondered Beate Hössler. From the counter she could see the Bellecour woman standing with her back to her before the mayor's desk, but of course Ledieu was not here. He was at one of his breweries. He wasn't a paid mayor. Voted in before the war, he had simply been allowed to continue.

Calmed a little, the Bellecour woman went round the desk to place the papers beside some others, only to hesitate again.

The Oberst Lautenschläger's telephone began to ring. Muttering under her breath, Frau Hössler went to answer it and found the Riechsführer Himmler shrieking and demanding reasons—yes, *reasons!*—why the colonel hadn't answered the phone himself.

The list on monsieur le maire's desk contained the names of all those who had gone through yesterday's control at the entrance to the *zone interdite*. Angélique saw hers and Martin's. Faint pencil marks encircled those of a Father Boulanger and a Sister Jacqueline Chevalier, the novice.

She reached for the eraser and began to remove the marks.

'What are you doing, please?'

Frau Hössler filled the doorway. 'I . . . You . . . you know how fussy the Gestapo Munk is. There were some accidental pencil marks. I . . .' It was no use. 'I erased them.'

'Show me.'

'Yes, of course.' Angélique saw the mechanical pencil Martin had taken to Paris. Quickly she used it to encircle her own and Martin's names. 'The mayor was just glad to see we were home, that's all. You know how concerned he's been about my son.'

'Please hand me the mayor's magnifying glass. It is in the top drawer, at the left.'

'All right, you win. Give me back the list.'

The woman did so. Rapidly Angélique encircled every name she could, but faint lines were discovered and were matched with the names of Father Boulanger and Sister Jacqueline.

'The Sturmbannführer Kraus will be notified of this, Mademoiselle Bellecour. For now I tell the Unteroffizier to mount a guard over you. Perhaps it is that the Sturmbannführer will accept your answer, perhaps he will wish to question you further.'

'And monsieur le maire?' she asked.

'Will be questioned also. It is not right he should have encircled those names and you should then have tried to hide this from me.'

Being mayor was not easy; hunting for answers one hoped not to find, the most difficult task.

Ledieu pushed the bike out of sight behind the shed and hurried along the path. The *Pension des trois soeurs* was on the northern edge of Abbeville and just off the road down which Véronique Dussart had gone to her death. Théodore Allard had insisted he have a look while Father Nicolas and himself were searching for the "priest" and his "novice". It was a modest house and had never been suspect, so it troubled him to have to ask to see the Mademoiselle Moncontre's room, but he had no choice. The committee had voted: two to one.

Most of the guests were not German—indeed, at present there were none of those. The other guests were getting on and chose to live quietly: two widows from the previous conflict, and three veterans, all of whom had been badly wounded in that same conflict and were on meagre pensions, a national disgrace. And oh for sure, the widows would, no doubt, often

join forces to accuse the pensioners of cowardice in the face
of battle. So many had died in the Great War of 1914–18, it
was only natural for others to blame those who had survived.
Over a billion and a half artillery shells alone had been fired
across the plains of northeastern France and Belgium. This
legacy of old shells was constantly killing or maiming farmers, construction workers and the curious, especially boys.
While the fighting had been to the south and east, at Amiens,
Le Cateau, Verdun and so many other places, Ponthieu had
experienced the British Expeditionary Force with its bivouacs
and training grounds, and as a result, such buried surprises
cropped up from time to time.

The *patronne* was blond, blue-eyed and very fair skinned.
She reminded him of Véronique and this worried his conscience, for he didn't want to compound the betrayal of the
one with that now of another.

'Madame VanKleist, you have a lodger from Paris, a Mademoiselle Moncontre.'

'She's not here. She's gone out.'

'Ah! of course. It's but a small matter, but would it be possible to leave a note in her room?'

'Notes . . . Is that one using the *pension* as a PTT?"

'The room?' grimaced Ledieu, fighting for composure and
fiddling with his fedora.

The woman gave the shrug of, Don't expect me to answer
things I'm not supposed to know.

Ah, damn this war, thought Ledieu. Damn the lies, the
fear, the little things that so often tripped one up.

The room was as if barely used—Isabelle Moncontre had
had little luggage but the wireless set. A modest nightdress was
neatly folded over the back of a worn fauteuil whose brown
upholstery and yellowed antimacassars brought little cheer.

The window overlooked the road. A plain pair of step-ins
had been washed in the hand basin and left flattened on a
hand towel, spread in hopes of their drying.

There was little else.

'I thought you wished to leave a note?' asked the *patronne*.

---

* *Poste, Télégraphe et Téléphone*

'The note . . . ah yes. Permit me to write it in privacy, please.'

'As you wish. Who am I to say?'

Left alone, he didn't know where to begin. Théodore was just being his doubting self. Nicolas was leaving the matter in the balance as always so as to be credited with being right.

Madame VanKleist would be listening from the corridor. Though he eased each of the bureau drawers open, they were not quiet and yielded nothing.

The mademoiselle travels light out of necessity, he silently cautioned himself. 'Look for the little things,' Théodore had insisted. 'In this clandestine war we are fighting, it is those that are often the most important.'

There was little enough. A worn toothbrush in the water glass, no toothpaste or tooth powder—ah! such items were so hard to obtain even on the *marché noir* and costing a fortune. Five hundred francs for a two-hundred-milligram canister.

The toothbrush was from before the Defeat. 'The face cloth,' Théodore had said. 'Look for it. Remember La Samaritaine.'

'Our sous-préfet can dwell on things as our dentist does a sore tooth with no anaesthetic!' he muttered to himself.

There wasn't a sign of the face cloth, which would, no doubt, be white as had the towel that had been used in the killing. The hand towel here was obviously that of the *pension*. The step-ins were of plain white cotton, the faded label revealing that they had been purchased in Paris at the Galeries Lafayette. Before the Defeat also.

This is ridiculous, he scolded himself. She's from the *Résistance* in Paris, has been sent especially to us at great risk to herself and everyone else there, has brought us a wireless set and has *warned* us of possible infiltrators.

There was one thing, but he thought little of it, only a boyish pleasure, for the book beside the bed was *The Count of Monte Cristo*.

'Dumas was always a favourite,' he murmured.

The binding was of a dark blue leather with gold leaf on the spine. One of a treasured set, no doubt, but the inscription was not made out to herself, but to a Jean-Baptiste Bernard de Fleury.

It had been dated 3 March 1914, de Fleury's tenth birthday at Nugent-sur-Seine, upriver of Paris.

'By then I was in uniform,' he said sadly, 'and soon to hear the Kaiser's shells bursting overhead.'

Martin Bellecour had been an avid reader, and as Ledieu left the room, he idly wondered if the boy had discovered Dumas.

'The note?' asked the *patronne*.

'Ah! I've forgotten. It's of no consequence, Madame VanKleist. I shall no doubt meet the mademoiselle in the street and can tell her.'

Halfway up the road, he wondered if his not bothering to leave a note was not another of those little things. 'Must loyalties always be questioned?' he asked, reminding himself that the house had never been suspected of harbouring anything other than its regular tenants and an occasional visitor.

'The PTT . . . ? Then who *had* left her a note? Who knows she's here but ourselves?'

Théodore had suggested she might not have come alone. That must be it. The note had been left for her by one of them.

But if they had killed Véronique, how was it, please, that a *réseau* in Paris knew more of what was going on here than they did themselves?

No one would question his making yet another survey of the docks and ruined warehouses. When he reached the meeting place of last night, Ledieu put the bike out of sight. Coming here would be of no use, but he had to force himself to remember every detail. How had she known where to find them? Had she followed him? She had come in and had leaned her bike against the others.

Right here, he said, letting the broken slats throw their shadows over him. Rubble littered the floor—bits of broken plaster, lath and concrete. Her footprints were in the dust.

Hurriedly he began to brush them away. The Nazis . . . the Gestapo Munk and Sturmbannführer Kraus would notice them if they came here, if . . .

'Ah! what's this?' he asked. The rubble had been pushed up into a little mound.

When he uncovered the face cloth, he found he couldn't move but stood with that thing dangling from his fingers. What did it mean? he begged. Why had she thought it necessary to hide it before coming in to them, *to them*?

Had she killed Véronique? She must have.

Doumier had been betrayed but until the body of Véronique had been found this morning, they hadn't known who the betrayer had been.

But this one had. 'Infiltrators,' she had warned them. 'Infiltrators, ah no . . .'

# 9

Hidden in Bois Carré, the building was very long. It had no windows but, having darted inside it, Martin was forced to continue for fear of being discovered near its entrance. Increasingly the darkness grew. The walls were higher than he could reach, and he wished he was taller so that he could count all the rows of blocks the construction workers had used. The floor was of concrete, the width no more than two bicycle lengths. A strange sort of building—a tunnel, really, but lying above ground. Perhaps the walls were as much in height as the width.

When he looked back, he could no longer see any light because the tunnel took a bend before quickly reaching its open end where sliding doors would be fitted.

The tunnel was completely empty but for himself, of course. He felt the wall at its far end and panicked at the thought of darkness closing in but slapped himself hard and said to himself, Behave. You are a man now. This isn't the only tunnel. They are building five of them in and near the woods and all are exactly the same, so what, please, are they to be used for?

This was a puzzle. Two of the tunnels were just outside the woods, for Bois Carré was not so very big. Perhaps six or eight hectares, he thought. A little woods, then, and one the Germans had completely taken over.

Roads led to each tunnel but also from each entrance to a square building that was quite small and perhaps only twice the width of the tunnels but placed next to a set of narrow rails that ran through the trees and rose up from among them at one end.

'A launching ramp,' he softly said.

The soldiers had as much as confirmed this. Overhearing them had not been as difficult as avoiding them. Time and again the words *Vergeltungswaffen Eins* had been heard. *Bomben die fliegende.* Flying bombs. London . . . the City of London, England.

The tunnels must be houses for the bombs but if so, then what did they do with the wings? Take them off? It must be so.

Knowing that he had to, he began to count the blocks in one of the rows along its length. Soon there were a hundred, then two hundred and fifty and only then was there light coming in from the entrance.

'It's at least three hundred blocks long,' he whispered and swallowed tightly at the thought of leaving the tunnel. Should he wait until nightfall? Should he take a chance now—there wasn't anyone working near here. Beyond the tunnel, the road from the entrance went away and through the woods to the square house and the launching ramp, but there was still lots of cover. He could hide under the ramp if he had to.

With his back to the innermost part of the bend, he crept along and into the light, but when he heard voices approaching, he retreated. A torch was switched on. He ran. He cowered in a far corner at the back against that final wall and with no hope of escape.

Steps echoed. Voices boomed. The beam of the torch was flung across the walls and roof—he could see it so clearly because the men, they were in the straight part of the tunnel and now well inside the bend. Their shadows were huge.

Vibrations from hobnailed boots rang out. '*Ist fern genug,*' said one of them. '*Nun zeigen Sie mir was Sie haben, ja?*'

A bag was set on the floor between the two men. Bottles

clinked. A rucksack followed it. *'C'est de l'eau-de-vie de poire et du calvados. Il y en a cinq, vous comprenez? Cinq.'*

A hand was held up. Five fingers.

*'Ich gebe Ihnen zin des Schinkens.'*

*'Schinken, was ist das, s'il vous plaît?'*

*'Geräuchertes Schweinefleisch*—oink, oink. *Schenkel Hauch der Rauch.'*

*'Jambon. Ah! C'est très bien. Trois boîtes.'* Three fingers were held up.

They settled on two tins of ham and some rubber things the Unteroffizier stretched and snapped to show how good they were and laughed as he did so.

They shared a cigarette. Then the Unteroffizier said, *'Dies Spurhünde kommen sie hier in den Wald, ja? Es ist besser dass wir fortgehen.'*

*'Le parachutiste ne peut pas être ici. C'est impossible.'*

*'Sie haben ein Witterung. Ein Parfüm.'*

The Unteroffizier made the sounds and motions of a dog getting a scent. It was enough. They were going to bring the dogs into the woods.

Cloud shadows fled across the ripening fields to darken the maize where only the helmets and sometimes the shoulders of the Waffen-SS could be seen.

Elsewhere, long, thin lines of soldiers waded through waist-high wheat and barley or broke the clods of newly ploughed fields under jackboots into whose tops had been stuffed stick grenades.

Marie-Hélène could see it all quite clearly from a copse some three kilometres to the west and downslope of them. Kraus, the Oberst Lautenschläger and others were standing in a cluster surrounded by bare earth. The colonel was insisting the sweep be continued westwards; Kraus wanted the woods to be searched at once.

The dogs would settle it and they did. When released from their leashes, their handlers running uphill after them, they raced for the woods.

The Sturmbannführer started after them. He tossed an

insult over his shoulder. Oberst Lautenschläger clenched a fist perhaps, but didn't shake it at him.

As they converged on the woods, she tried to see a way of isolating Kraus and having him killed by others but the only way to be certain was to do it herself. When he asked for the names, she must reach into her handbag for the list she would say she had made for him. There wouldn't be much time. The Luger would have to be ready, no safety on, and a cartridge in the chamber.

But where to do it? In her room at the *pension*—would he be so thoughtless as to blow her cover by coming there?

In the ruins of that hut? Yes . . . yes, she would tell him to meet her there. She'd say she thought the terrorists must have hidden things there and that she was going to take a look at it.

That would be best. Kraus would then think there would only be the two of them. He'd like the thought of being alone with her.

Gradually everyone entered the woods and soon the fields were empty of them but now there was shouting, now there was insane barking, now the instantly rapid and decisive firing of a Schmeisser.

And then . . . then as the dogs must have been grabbed and put back on the leash, silence. Even the rooks winged their ways in flight without a sound.

She searched the line of the woods and fields. Had they killed Châlus? she wondered. Would they drag him out by the heels or stand around looking down at him?

The novice too.

So silent were things, Marie-Hélène found it uncomfortable and had to turn to leave, but when she reached the road, the sous-préfet Allard and Father Nicolas were waiting for her.

There were binoculars in Allard's hand, tears in the *curé*'s eyes but were they those of gladness or grief?

'It's not safe,' she said and heard her voice as if given by a stranger. 'The countryside is crawling with them.'

They looked at her, these two. Allard's nostrils flared in doubt, Father Nicolas just stood there saying nothing. At last Allard found his voice. 'Your priest, mademoiselle, and the novice are no longer visiting the graves of others.'

Then it had been Châlus in the woods—were the *curé's* tears those of gladness? she wondered.

'How is it, please, that you knew of them?' he asked.

'One soon learns what to look for,' she said, not avoiding that doubter's gaze of his. 'Look, I only suspected them of working for the Gestapo. But I have to tell you, messieurs, I'm glad they were in the woods today.'

'Yes, yes, the gunfire has given a suitable warning,' acknowledged Father Nicolas, 'but why would they choose to go there if working for the Nazis?'

So that was it. 'Because there are construction workers among whom there are most likely sympathizers if not those who are already involved in the *Résistance*. Contact must have been attempted so that infiltration could begin.'

'Then why risk taking a woman with him?'

'He probably didn't. They would have split up. Châlus to enter the . . .' Ah no . . .

'Châlus?' asked Allard.

'Yes. The name he's using is Raymond Châlus. Her alias is Yvette Rougement. They followed me from Paris but when they continued on, I . . . why I felt I should at least warn you of their presence.'

'Yet you *knew* who they were,' mused Father Nicolas. 'You could have as much as led them to us.'

'I had a wireless set with me, didn't I? What, please, was I to have done with such a thing? Lugged it around for days?'

The wind tugged at her wavy dark brown hair and at the collar of her shirt-blouse. A not unattractive young woman. Tough, oh yes, thought Allard. 'What had you in mind by coming here?' he asked.

'What do you think?' she countered. 'Everything we need to know for the British is in that woods.'

'Yes, but there are also five other such sites in the country-side around Abbeville.'*

'I haven't got to any of those yet, but maybe if we worked together, we could visit all of them and find the one with the weakest security.'

---

* And many more right to the Pas de Calais and into Belgium

'She has a point, Théodore,' said Father Nicolas. 'Standing out here on this road will only bring company we don't want.'

'Then let's tie her bike to the back and give her a lift into town.'

Were they planning a little something for her? 'Look, we shouldn't be seen together.'

She was good, thought Father Nicolas. If one had wanted a quick answer, what better to have given?

'Later, then,' said Allard. 'The same place as last night, the same time. We'll map out a strategy then and decide how to divide up the work.'

She tried to smile—it was a brave attempt but he had to ask himself, What is it about her that, like the clouds above, casts doubt upon her? The toughness, her aloneness, the way she defiantly looks at us as if, yes, she is calculating what we'll do.

Only then did he notice that she had moved her right hand to her bag and that it was now all but in it.

'Until tonight,' he said and nodded curtly at her. 'Come on, Nicolas, we had better get back to town.'

They left but she didn't look away towards Bois Carré, to what must be going on there. She followed them with her eyes until, at last, the car was hidden from her.

'They're up to something,' she said and was torn between running to Kraus for help or continuing alone.

No one had yet left the woods. It was still far too quiet and she had to wonder what was going on in there, had to ask, What have they really found?

The dogs were slavering. Held back by their leashes, they repeatedly lunged towards the boy who could just be seen among the shells, beneath the low roof of corrugated iron that covered them.

'GET HIM OUT OF THERE AT ONCE!' shouted Kraus, setting the dogs to leaping harder. 'SHOOT HIM IF HE REFUSES. HERE, GIVE ME THAT, *DUMMKOPF*. THE RIFLE AT ONCE! I'LL SHOW HIM.'

'*Ach du leiber Gott*, Sturmbannführer. Not unless you wish to kill us all and who knows how many others.'

Lautenschläger yanked the rifle from him and thrust it back into the hands of the one who had given it up. 'Don't ever do that again,' he said to the corporal. 'I'm still your commanding officer. A soldier without his weapon is no soldier.'

*Verdammt*, what the hell were they to do? he wondered. There were warning signs posted all around the dump, which had been deliberately placed out of the way near the edge of the woods. Barbed wire surrounded it, but this alone wouldn't have held back the dogs. By some stroke of bureaucratic bungling, the Wehrmacht's bomb-disposal unit had put off moving the shells until they had received word on how and where to destroy them, for they weren't ordinary shells and the boy had gone to ground in the one place the dogs would refuse to venture.

Corrosion—verdigris—its whitish-green encrustations were everywhere among the artillery shells from that other war of 1914–18. Buried in a hasty, shallow grave and discovered during the early stages of construction, there had been no choice but for them to have been exhumed.

Now the shells, all six hundred and eighty-two of them and all for the 10.5 cm Leichte Feldhaubitze, lay five and six deep in rows, and the dark warren of their maze held the boy.

Blood streamed from the damage the barbed wire had inflicted to Martin's forehead, ears and hands. Tears mingled with it. His nose was abruptly wiped with the back of a hand. Terrified, cornered, he stared out at them.

'He'll soon want to vomit,' said Lautenschläger. 'Who, please, has allowed the loss of a grenade from his boot-top?'

They were gathered round, perhaps one hundred and fifty battle-hardened men, both Wehrmacht and Waffen-SS. The wind was in the branches of the trees above and when no answer came, the colonel calmly said, 'I'll know the reason for such a loss, gentlemen, and then I will ask you all to leave. Please be sure to walk upwind of us and seek the highest ground.'

A Gefreiter stepped forward and to attention.

'So another of my own men is at fault,' breathed Lautenschläger sadly. 'And what have you to say?'

'He grabbed the grenade as he darted past me, Herr Oberst.'

'Excellent. I commend the partisan valour that must run in his veins. You are now an Oberschutze.* Your sergeant fills your former rank. Both of you will suffer the loss of a month's pay and be confined to barracks when not on duty.'

'*Jawhol*, Herr Oberst.'

'Now where were we?' he continued and, indicating that Kraus should accompany him, walked to the downwind side of the dump. 'The visibility is better here. You see, Sturmbann-führer,' he said, indicating Martin. 'The boy understands fully the fundamentals of our stick grenades. He has unscrewed the cap at the base of the handle and has drawn out the pull-cord so as to hook a finger through its ring in readiness.'

'I'LL DO IT, HERR OBERST! I'M WARNING YOU!'

'Yes, yes, Martin. I'm very glad that you have found your voice. Allow me, please, to instruct the Sturmbannführer, then we'll talk.'

'TELL HIM TO LEAVE ANGÉLIQUE ALONE! TELL HIM THERE ISN'T ANY PARACHUTIST. THERE NEVER WAS.'

'NO PARACHUTIST? HE'S LYING!' shrieked Kraus.

'*Ach, ein Moment, bitte*,' urged Lautenschläger. 'First, had you shot the boy, the force of the bullet would have carried him back and most assuredly it would have propelled the grenade from his hand, thus priming it.'

'*The Reichsführer und Reichsminister Himmler will hear of this!*'

How tiresome. 'Let us hope he doesn't. The detonation would no doubt fail to carry that far but would, I am certain, leave a magnificent crater, ruined walls and foundations, and a cloud of mustard gas you would, if still alive, have trouble explaining.'

'The boy is lying. He's one of them. I knew it from the moment I set eyes on him and that supposed mother of his.'

'No parachutist, Martin?'

The colonel had crouched so as to peer in at him through the coils of barbed wire and the signs. 'No, Herr Oberst. It's my little parachute. I drew it in the dust of a window at the avenue Foch and he must have seen it and thought I meant a

---

* A lance corporal

real one. It was all a game, a way of telling myself how I came to be here in France.'

A game . . . 'I'm a bachelor, Martin. I've been one all my life, so have never had children, but I think I'm beginning to understand. Sturmbannführer Kraus has made a mistake and . . .'

'A BIG MISTAKE!'

'*He's lying. Can't you see that,*' hissed Kraus. '*The boy's father is a known terrorist!*'

A *résistant.*

Martin withdrew from them in tears. They were bringing it all back. They were making him think things he didn't want to. He huddled among the shells so that they couldn't see him anymore. There was the smell of crushed geranium leaves and broken stems right next the ground and it did make his chest tighten and his head buzz, it did upset his stomach and increased the stinging in his eyes.

'Martin, is this true?' asked the colonel.

Was it true about his father . . . ? Angélique thought so. Angélique had always insisted his father was in England and safe, whereas he himself had recently come to believe that wasn't so and that his father was alive and in France and with the *Résistance*, but then . . . then she had changed her mind and had agreed. His father had been living in the flat on the rue des Grands-Augustins ever since the Defeat and the road south from Paris, ever since the Messerschmitts. He had been using false papers and the identity of a German officer, a Leutnant Theissen. He had followed them from Paris dressed as a priest. The Mademoiselle Moncontre was one of his *réseau*. So was the girl with the *vélo-taxi*, the novice.

Martin stretched the pull-cord out until it was taut. Under his breath he said scathingly, 'Angélique shouldn't have lied to me like that. I forgive her, yes of course, but can't allow the Sturmbannführer Kraus to torture me for fear I should cry out the name of another, that of the Mademoiselle Isabelle.'

Had the boy been speaking to himself? wondered Lautenschläger. 'Martin . . . Martin, listen to me, please. I'm going to send the Hauptmann Scheel to fetch your mother. Let's hold off doing anything until she arrives, but if you feel sick, crawl out from there. No one will shoot you. I give you my word. Stand beside the shells if you wish but do so upwind of them. It's not good for you to breathe that stuff. It will burn your lungs and blister your skin. Even though it's years since I was gassed, I still get blisters. It can make you blind.'

The boy threw up. Bent double, he retched several times. Lautenschläger held his breath and counted to three and then to five, but the grenade didn't go off, and when Martin crawled out with it still in hand, the boy found he couldn't stand up. When he spoke, his throat was suddenly torn and he panicked at the thought of losing his voice again.

Tears streamed from him. 'I have to talk to Angélique,' he croaked. 'There is something really, really bad that I have to tell her.'

The minute hand of the clock in the Kommandantur hardly moved. The hour hand was impossible. Angélique was desperate. Martin had gone to Bois Carré hours ago and still she didn't know what had happened to him. An "accident"? she wondered. A "tragedy"?

At first she had felt it a blessing that he couldn't talk. Everyone would have known he was British. The Germans would have sent him to the internment camp at Besançon that was for British women and children who had such passports,* but now . . . now he wouldn't even be able to cry out, to tell them to pull the dogs away.

No one had told her a thing, but all who had entered the Kommandantur, the Germans especially, had avoided looking at her. Word travelled so fast in the countryside. Whispers went right round the place, and well before the object of them was notified, everyone else knew about it. The death of a close relative or friend, an accident, a suicide, an arrest, it was all the same. One was left guessing, worrying, tearing one's heart out while everyone else knew all about it and didn't say a thing.

Frau Hössler attended to matters at the counter. The guard,

---

* Later this camp was moved to Vittel, American women then joining them there in the autumn of 1942.

a doughy-faced boy of seventeen, hesitated to let his prisoner see him stealing glances at her. Angélique would avert her eyes and he would chance a glimpse, but did he ask himself if he could kill her if an attempted escape was made? He sat so stiffly in a straight-backed chair beneath the clock and with his rifle awkwardly across his knees. She sat opposite him and, between them, along the adjacent wall from one French window to another, there was a long row of filing cabinets.

Those windows weren't locked, not that she could see, but could she yank one of the drawers fully open and bolt outside? Could she run very far before the bullet hit her?

Monsieur le maire had blustered his way around Frau Hössler. It had been really magnificent the show that poor, desperate man had put on. He had threatened the woman with disciplinary action—the encircling of the names on that list had been the Gestapo Munk's doing, not his own. How could she have thought otherwise? Et cetera, et cetera.

The least the woman could expect would be a reprimand from the colonel; the worst, a stiff letter of dismissal.

But he hadn't given the prisoner a glance—he hadn't dared.

At 2.05 p.m. Father Nicolas entered to ask of him. 'He is at one of his breweries,' grumbled Frau Hössler. 'The one, I believe, that is along the Transit Canal.'

'What's she done, then?' he asked, giving a nod towards the prisoner.

'She is waiting, that is all.'

'Then why the guard?'

'Because it is necessary.'

'I was only tidying that list, Frau Hössler. You upset me and that is why I encircled as many names as I could. You didn't *trust* me!'

'Silence! You are not to speak unless spoken to.'

Father Nicolas grinned at the exchange and muttered, 'Good. That's as it should be. Women are best when silent. It saves the ears.'

'I want to go to the toilet, Frau Hössler. I demand to go. Father, she is refusing to allow the most normal of requests.'

'A pity. My dear Frau Hössler, let your prisoner at least visit the office of necessity.'

Blustering, the woman found the key and thrust it at him. 'Then you are responsible, *ja*, and will escort her.'

They were outside and into the car before the guard realized what had happened. Helplessly the boy watched as they raced away among the ruins.

'The sous-préfet Allard was driving,' said the boy.

'Oberst Lautenschläger and Sturmbannführer Kraus will hear of this,' stormed Beate. 'There is something going on that is not right.'

The brewery was beyond the ruins. They drove straight into the drying shed. The closeness of sacks of barley, hops and beet sugar gave a warm and pleasant smell to which was added the ever-present odour of fermenting wort. Monsieur le maire was at the rear of the building. He was rubbing a few kernels in a palm but tossed them away, a thing he would not normally have done. 'Now, mademoiselle, we want the truth. I'm grateful, yes of course, for your attempt to hide my encircling of those names but who, please, are this priest and novice?'

They had surrounded her. The car was parked just inside the doors, which the sous-préfet had closed and bolted. 'The priest is Martin's father, a leader in the *Résistance*; the novice is his assistant.'

Doubt, alarm—so many things passed between them but not a word.

'Together they have followed us to Abbeville but for what reason,' she said, 'I simply don't know. Perhaps it's that his father will try to reach the farm to get Martin and myself safely away, perhaps they have other things to do.'

Things like Bois Carré and finding out what was going on there.

It was Father Nicolas who asked of the pencil and she knew then that monsieur le maire and the sous-préfet had agreed beforehand that the priest should be the one to confront her.

As quickly as she could she told them everything that had happened in Paris. They were sickened by it.

'And the note, the message I found?' asked Ledieu in despair.

'Herr Dirksen used it to show me how messages would be sent but it was only a cigarette paper. There wasn't anything written on it, was there?'

'Herr Dirksen . . . ?' he asked.

'Yes. The Standartenführer.'

'*Ah, mon Dieu*, Nicolas . . . Théodore, what is this she's saying?'

It had happened. The bottom had fallen out of everything. 'That we face an almost certain death,' said Allard. 'The others must be warned at once.'

'*Wait!* Tell us, please, of the Mademoiselle Moncontre,' said Ledieu.

Sadly she told him. 'Martin is in love with her. He'll do anything for her, even to trying to find out what is going on in Bois Carré. He's there now. I'm certain he is, but . . . but I don't know what has happened to him.'

They ignored her concern for Martin. They didn't have time for it.

'Did you know she had brought us a wireless transmitter?'

'The suitcase . . .'

'Yes. Did you know she had warned us that your priest and his novice might be infiltrators?' demanded Ledieu sharply.

'But . . . but why would she do that? She's with them. They're all from the same *réseau*. They must be.'

It was the sous-préfet who said, 'She knew of Véronique, mademoiselle, and we now realize she was responsible for that one's death.'

This was crazy. It was insane. 'But how could she have known of Véronique? That's just not possible.'

'Impossible, yes,' said Allard grimly, 'unless she had been forewarned by the SS, and Véronique posed a risk she could not live with.'

Angélique blanched. 'A risk . . . ? I'm not hearing this, messieurs. Martin believes in her absolutely.'

'But do you?' asked Father Nicolas.

'*Yes!* She proved it on two occasions in Paris. Ah! you're

very wrong. She was almost caught and had to hide on the roofs nearby.'

Again they looked from one to another. The need for haste tugged at them. 'Please tell us about these "occasions",' said Ledieu. 'Go carefully. Give the smallest details.'

'Honoré, we haven't time!' said Allard, clenching a fist.

'What has she done, please?' asked Angélique.

'Done?' he answered. 'She has betrayed us all.'

'Then why haven't you been arrested?'

'That is what we wish to know. Perhaps it is that she hasn't yet given Kraus and the others our names; perhaps it is that they are simply waiting until she can point the finger at all of us.'

'A Judas,' swore Ledieu. 'I trusted her. I vouched for her.'

'We all did,' cautioned Father Nicolas. 'The shame of it is on each of our heads.'

'If only that wireless set of hers would work,' said Allard sadly. 'If only those tubes hadn't been deliberately broken.'

'Henri is working on it,' muttered Ledieu absently, his mind torn by other matters. 'Henri will do the best he can on such short notice.'

Henri Vallin was the legless brother of Véronique Dussart. His shop, if such was what one could call it, was in a converted garage he shared with his parents. He had the front half of the building, the living quarters were at the back and above in the loft, and Marie-Hélène could see through to the makeshift kitchen where the mother was sitting alone and weeping.

A sawdust burner, one of those converted oil-drum stoves, sat in a corner gathering dust until the cold weather. The clutter was everywhere. He dabbled in fixing small appliances—a hair drier for some *salon de beauté*, toasters, waffle irons, electric light fixtures. There were coils of scavenged copper wire, small bins of different-size fuses, porcelain wall-sockets, clamps, rolls of electrical tape—a second industry in used bits and pieces the Occupier had let his friends accumulate for him.

Wireless sets too, a few of those: console models and desktop ones. People were desperate for news. Though most didn't possess such things, all wanted to listen—but watch out if you did to anything other than Radio-Paris, Radio-Vichy or Radio-Berlin. To do otherwise was to invite arrest.

Swich off, sure, but they'd check the position of the dial, and if it was where it shouldn't have been, that was enough.

The fierce and dark blue eyes beneath the hank of jet black hair that hung over his brow were puffy with rage, tears and bitterness. The face was thin, the shoulders also, the arms long—a wasted man, a shell of his former self. Unshaven, pale and shaking ever so slightly, he glared at her.

The work shirt was open at the collar and stained.

'No one should come here because of my sister but now, suddenly, a visitor.'

He was dangerous, she told herself. One look at him had convinced her. 'They brought you the Mark One I gave them. I only wanted to ask, How bad is it?'

So this was the courier who had come from Paris, this was the girl who had arrived on the very day Véronique had been assassinated. Just how the hell had she found the shop?

'Those tubes are very fragile. You shouldn't have been so careless. The crystals were also shattered. Without them and the tubes . . .' He shrugged. He tried to find a cigarette and when he did so, she found the box of matches only to hear the acid of, 'I'm *not* an invalid! Give me that. Lousy matches. Pétain's state-run monopolies only lead to incompetence!'

The wood was too brittle, the heads snapped off so easily. Five times out of seven, the wretched matches wouldn't strike a light.

The box was flung away. Retrieving it for him, he tried again and finally drew in on the cigarette as a man desperate for relief. 'The tobacco is shit as well, but it's the crystals I want to ask you about.'

'The crystals . . .' she managed. 'What, please, are those?'

'Thin slices cut from hexagonal crystals of the mineral quartz. Very delicate. Each thickness lets in or out only a very narrow band of short-wave signals. That Mark One of yours was equipped with three of them. One crystal for daytime transmissions at perhaps frequencies from 6,735 to

6,765 kilocycles per second, another for nighttime, perhaps at from 3,220 to 3,250 kilocycles, and a third for emergency use only.'

Why was she deliberately keeping her distance—afraid of him, was she? he wondered. 'Here, let me show you.'

He removed a piece of veneer from the underside of the steel-topped bench and, reaching in and under, found what he was after. A matchbox.

Shaking the flat, clear, glasslike fragments out into a palm, he indicated she should come closer and when she held his hand to steady it, he looked at her defiantly and shrugged. 'No morphia. No cognac, Calvados or *eau-de-vie*—there are too many alcohol-free days, eh? Therefore constant pain. The tobacco is so lousy and so scarce, one tries always but it is of little use.'

Up close, she was handsome, not beautiful but good looking, a *Parisienne, ah oui*, but was such plainness of dress really her nature?

Taking a pair of tweezers from his shirt pocket, Vallin arranged the fragments into two small squares, each the size of a one-franc, twenty-centime postage stamp. 'That one is for daytime use, the other for night.'

'And the one for emergency use?' she asked and felt his hand momentarily stiffen and then begin to tremble again.

She had such beautiful eyes. Very clear and of that deep, brown shade so often termed "bedroom".

The fine brush of her eyebrows was noted, the texture of her complexion. No makeup, no lipstick, no earrings even. Ah, thought Marie-Hélène, he tries to note everything.

'The emergency crystal, yes. That's the one I want to ask you about,' he said. 'You see, *ma chére* Mademoiselle Moncontre—yes, I have your name. Jean-Pierre, he gave it to me when he and Father Nicolas brought the set last night to what is now this house of grief.'

She waited. He watched as her chest rose and fell—was he looking for hesitation there? she wondered. Had the sous-préfet Allard and Father Nicolas got to him today? Had they told him to watch out, that they had met her near Bois Carré and had had a little chat?

'The emergency crystal, yes.' Again he reached under the workbench with his right hand; she still holding the left one with its fragments.

He opened the matchbox using only the fingers of his free hand. 'You see, it's not broken, is it?' he said of the crystal.

He let her look at that thing nestled in cotton wool in that little box. 'Not broken?' she heard herself asking.

'Why, please, should the emergency crystal survive and the others be smashed?'

No one in Gestapo Paris-Central had told her a thing about any of this. No one, the idiots! 'I . . . I don't know. How could I? They just told me to deliver the set to you people, that's all.'

But was it? he wondered. Moisture had gathered in those lovely eyes of hers. Her chest rose and fell a little too quickly.

'The frequency is for daytime use only. 5,965 to 5,995 kilocycles per second. I measured it. You have to use something in the 6,000 range in the north for daytime transmissions, more if you're in the south near Toulon, say, or Marseille. At least 8,000 kcs there, but that's okay except that one would have thought nighttime best and something around 3,000.'

'Look, I don't know what you're trying to say. I've done nothing but risk my life!'

Anger made the colour come into her cheeks. He would try to smile so as to calm her. Yes, that would be best.

Removing his hand from hers, he put everything safely away, then looked up at her for the longest time and finally said, 'Do you find it disquieting to have to face a cripple?'

'Of course not! The Germans will suspect you less. It's perfect. Why should I?'

Perfect, was it, not to have any legs?

He nodded and held up a hand to stop her. 'So okay, I'll tell you. There wasn't a code book with the set. If we should be able to get it working, we would have to send it clear and at a frequency predetermined by that emergency crystal. Does that not strike you as exceedingly foolish, given that for all we know, the Gestapo could well be listening in for that particular range of wavelength?'

She shrugged, and that gesture encompassed all of her, but then she glanced past him to the open doorway into the kitchen.

'*Maman*, her heart is broken,' he said, still watching her closely. 'One son dead, another like this, and the daughter she always favoured and praised, dead also but in disgrace.'

'I know nothing of this. Please, I'm so very sorry to hear such things. I came only to see if there wasn't something my people in Paris could do to help get that set in working order.'

'Then tell me, please, how these "people" of yours came by it in the first place?'

He suspected the truth—that was clear enough. 'I only do as my chief commands. The set was recovered from a field near Le Mans and sent on to us because its parachutist operator had broken his neck on landing, but as we already had our own, this one could be spared. There's a great urgency about what is going on in Bois Carré. Everything we can do must be done, so it's been given the green light. Top priority.'

He thought about this and then asked, 'Would you care for coffee? It's not the real stuff but one gets used to it as one does all else.'

Was he stalling in hopes of company? she wondered. '*Un café . . .* ? Yes. Yes, of course. We have to drink that wretched stuff in Paris. There's nothing else, is there?'

He called out to the mother who, without a word, got up to do as bidden.

I have to kill him, thought Marie-Hélène. I can't have him asking such questions, not when sous-préfet Allard and Father Nicolas are also questioning things. But are those two about to descend on us—was that it—or the one who had delivered the wireless to him, Jean-Pierre?

'Could I go and help her?' she asked and heard him say, 'Suit yourself. She'll only give you a flood of remorse.'

'She needs comforting. It's not good to be left alone at such a time.'

'My father has gone to pick a quarrel with Father Nicolas about the burial. They should be here soon.'

Had he said it as insurance? Pressure to the vagus nerve would cause instant death. The mother was old, distracted, confused in her grief and unsuspecting, but it was no use. She'd have to come back.

Kraus, she said to herself. Go to him and give him the names. Hans isn't here. You're completely on your own, but if she did, Kraus would win and take command of everything, herself included.

Flames leapt from the hay rooks and granaries at the farm where Angélique Bellecour and the boy had been living. Cattle bawled. The woman, Marieka, looking swollen and bigger than a house, gnashed her teeth and tore her hair. Begging God to intervene, she set up a constant blubbering so guttural it was impossible to understand.

'THE PARACHUTIST, YOU *HURE*!' demanded Kraus.

The littlest of the brats milled about the woman's bare feet and puffy ankles, which were mired in dung and mud. They cried. They begged her to comfort them—several tried repeatedly to climb into her arms and clawed at her dress and swollen breasts. One of the older boys broke free and dashed in to save his mother only to have an arm and shoulder broken.

'*I will ask you once more,*' seethed Kraus. 'WHERE HAVE YOU HIDDEN THE BRITISH PARACHUTIST?'

She didn't comprehend. The boy tried to tell him there wasn't one and for this, he received the butt of a rifle.

'Stupid cow,' swore Kraus and, cocking his pistol, placed its muzzle against her brow.

She fell to her knees among the brats, her big, rough hands clasped in prayer and when he fired, she gave a blank look and rocked back a little before falling face down in the muck.

The children shook. The littlest ones tried to speak. Noses ran, mouths gaped. An ice-cold rain began to fall.

'Fire the house and barns. Let this be a lesson to them.'

Half the paltry belongings were strewn about in the yard. The husband had been in the fields with two of the oldest boys. All had dropped their scythes and tried to make a run for it. Beaten, they had given but the same answer. No parachutist. 'Lies . . . they were all lying!'

Dragged back to the farmyard, they had been beaten sense-less and now lay near death.

Kraus went from one to another to finish things. 'Now the next farm,' he said, 'and we don't stop until we have him.'

The rain was constant. It beat upon the roof of the car and struck the windscreen, flooding over the struggling wiper-blade. It formed puddles in the fields and on the road and washed the blood away.

Angélique sat in the backseat. Ahead of them perhaps sixty heavily armed Waffen-SS trudged along the road oblivi-ous to the rain. Mud clung to their boots. Some of the sol-diers had taken things from the farms they had raided and had bulging pillowcases thrown over a shoulder. One had a collection of six or so women's black leather handbags, another a chicken under each arm, another a rucksack, another a suitcase. Food and money, what little there was of this last unless the Louis d'or had been tucked away for years in some secret hide. Jewellery, too, and family heirlooms. Anything that could be snatched. A pair of candlesticks but without the candles.

The Hauptmann Scheel had come to the drying shed in search of her. There hadn't been any sense in not going out to him. The mayor and the others needed time and this she had given. But now? she wondered. Now would they all be arrested and shot?

She turned away to search the fields for some sign, bit her lower lip so hard, the taste of blood filled her mouth as she cried out inwardly, Martin . . . Martin, do you see where it has all led?

A little parachute, a piece of make-believe he had dreamed up to shield himself from the reality of what had happened to him. The absence of his father, the living in France—certainly she had told him straightaway on that road south from Paris three years ago that his father was alive and had had to leave them. The times she had lain awake cradling him in her arms. The constant nightmares. The terror of that road. Her finding him lying beneath the man who had shielded him.

Blood and brains . . . How had she found the courage to

wipe them off, she desperately crying out . . . 'Martin . . . Martin, have you seen your father?'

The nights, the dreams, the whispered reassurances, 'He's safely in England, *mon petit*. He did get away and is thinking of us all the time, and when this war is over, he'll return to take us from this place.'

The farm, the pig shit, the overripe stenches, the petty thefts, the constant bickering, the enforced drudgery of hard labour in the fields after a day's work at the Kommandantur and the long bike ride home.

The constant hikes in the rent. The loss of all privacy.

There were no prisoners with the soldiers and when she forced herself to ask, the Hauptmann Scheel said, 'None are apparently being taken.'

The rain filled the furrows to overflowing. The clay tended to soak it up yet also keep it out, as it had during the Blitzkrieg, but would Anthony and that girl Yvette Rougement have even the remotest chance of escaping across those fields?

Not with the dogs after them. The dogs.

When the road that turned off towards Bois Carré was reached, she asked the Hauptmann to take her to the farm first but he shook his head. 'It's not possible.'

'The woods are forbidden,' she said, but he didn't respond.

The rain blotted out the landscape. She tried to see the farm but it really wasn't visible from this road at the best of times. Would there be fire there too? she wondered. Would Anthony and Yvette have been trapped—caught waiting for her and Martin to return?

Would they have already been killed?

Anthony would have known Isabelle Moncontre was an infiltrator. He would have planned how to deal with her. How could the woman have done the things she must have? And Martin? she asked as the car entered the woods, passing by an odd-shaped concrete-block structure, a railway tunnel perhaps, but above ground.

Martin would be heartbroken. Perhaps he didn't need to be told yet about his Isabelle. Perhaps there wouldn't be time in any case.

The Oberst Lautenschläger was waiting. 'Please tell your son he mustn't do this, mademoiselle.'

'Do what, please?'

'Come. Come and see for yourself.'

The "coffee" wasn't bitter as it should have been nor had it been sweetened with saccharin. At least two heaping tea-spoons of real sugar had been used.

Alarmed, Marie-Hélène glanced past the legless veteran in his wheelchair to the mother who had refused all help but now stood silently watching from the doorway to her kitchen.

The taste of the sugar lingered. The rain came hard on the corrugated iron. Dampness brought an intruding chill.

'Is the coffee not to your liking?' asked Vallin.

Someone must have come to the back door. Father Nicolas perhaps—no arguments about the daughter's burial. Just word of an infiltrator. Herself. 'It's only that I'm not used to sugar,' she said apologetically. Vallin had tasted his and had known right away that all his doubts about her had been true.

He set his coffee aside and pushed that hank of black hair from his brow. 'Véronique gave *maman* half of the nearly two kilos she received from the Gestapo Munk as her immediate reward for betraying Doumier. Oh for sure, mademoiselle, my little sister lied to us about how she had come by it. That's nearly twenty-five hundred francs worth on the *marché noir*. She said one of the German sergeants had taken so much off the back of the butter-and-eggs lorry and in such a hurry, he had dropped a sack. Her good fortune. We even laughed with her and celebrated.'

'Ah!' she softly exclaimed, tossing her head a little. 'Then why, please, has your mother chosen to use it?'

She set her cup and saucer down amid the workbench's clutter. Vallin told her to finish it. 'Her heart is broken. Please don't smash the fragments into smaller pieces.'

'I can't. I'd best be going.'

How wary she was. 'It's raining. You'll only be drenched. Wait a little. The rain will soon pass.'

His dark blue eyes never left her for a moment. Her bag

was on the workbench and nearer to her. The mother hadn't moved. Sentinel to their little confrontation, the woman lingered. There was still no sign of Father Nicolas or of the husband. Were they waiting too, in the kitchen, waiting for someone else to enter the shop through the front door? Châlus . . . Was it Raymond Châlus?

'Look, I have to leave,' she said and started for her bag. He shot forward in that chair of his. He ran it right into her and tried to grab her. The mother let out an insane cry and dashed into the shop wielding a meat cleaver . . .

Knocked to the floor, Marie-Hélène tried to get a fix on them. The son was coming at her again with that chair, the mother was now right behind him. . . .

The woman gave the chair a brutal shove. Marie-Hélène rolled out of the way and scrambled to her feet. *'Don't!'* she shouted and lunged for her bag. The cleaver hit the metal-topped bench. The woman swung it hard. She ducked. The bitch swung it again. *'Maman!'* cried the son, but it was too late. The Luger leapt, the woman collapsed, the cleaver skidded across the concrete floor and went in under the bench.

Breathlessly clutching her bag and pistol, Marie-Hélène backed away towards the front door. Again the rain hammered on the corrugated iron.

Father Nicolas had still not appeared, nor had the husband.

Châlus . . . is it to be Raymond Châlus? she wondered.

*'Kill me too!'* cried Vallin, but by then she had reached the door.

Bolting it, she began to walk towards him, he to back away. There were tears. The loss of his mother, the bitterness he felt at the unfairness of life, the hatred he had for people like herself. 'Châlus,' she said. 'It's him, isn't it?'

She seemed so sad—afraid and desperate and not unlike a lover who has lost out and must now suffer.

When he refused to answer, she told him Châlus was Martin Bellecour's father. 'For three years now he has operated out of Paris, living and moving about freely as a German officer, a Leutnant Thiessen, but building escape lines and organizing *réseaux*. When he discovered I was back in business and following his people in Paris, he set about finding me.'

Still there was no answer. The wheels of the chair had come full stop against the body of the mother. 'Châlus was the only one to get away from us in Lyon,' she said and tried to smile but it was no use.

Vallin wet his lips in uncertainty. 'Châlus?' he managed.

'*Yes!* He's the best of them. Far cleverer than the Sturmbann-führer Kraus who wants him desperately, cleverer also than my lover, the Standartenführer Dirksen.'

Did she have a need to tell him this? wondered Vallin uneasily. Just why the hell hadn't Father Nicolas or one of the others intervened?

'He's travelling with a student, a girl named Yvette Rougement of the rue Férou in Paris. I followed her into the bookshop of M. Patouillard, and of course, I followed Dr. Vergès to whom you people had sent your message with the boy. That was clever of you, but not nearly clever enough.'

Though he wanted to sting her with cries of traitor, Vallin knew it would do no good. 'Châlus will get you. He's with us, mademoiselle. He and the girl Yvette are out there in the lane. They're waiting for you now. You'll never get away from them. *Never!* Do you understand? Not when you know so much about us and can give our names to those who would hunt us down. Hey, *ma petite Parisienne*, what does it feel like to see *résistant*s caught in your web? Do you experience a little rush of pleasure, eh, *le grand frisson, peut-être?*'

She was very close to him now. If he tried, he might just take the pistol from her, thought Vallin. Could he manage it?

The sound of a car came to them through the din of the rain and she held her breath, wondering if it was the sous-préfet. Vallin wanted the gun in her hand. He wet his lips again, knew he ought to try, but imperceptibly she moved a little closer. 'Go ahead,' she said. 'Show me you have the balls to give a girl such an orgasm.'

His hand shook. Furtively he glanced at the Luger, then lifted his eyes to meet hers. 'Châlus,' he wept but was blinded by the blood on his hand.

There was no one in the kitchen, nor in either of the two small rooms that served so many purposes, and when at last she had gone out into the rain to find her bicycle, she found its tyres flattened. There was no other sign of Châlus, nor of Father Nicolas, only punctures she couldn't repair.

The lane was long. There were puddles. All too soon she was drenched but couldn't turn back, must never do that.

Down by the Transit Canal, the ruins of a textile mill offered temporary shelter but once inside it, rubble fell and she cried out in alarm, 'CHÂLUS?'

More rubble fell. Rainwater gave a herculean flood to the broken lip of the floor above. As the water cascaded onto the concrete floor at her feet, sticks of lathe, boards and all sorts of rubbish were carried down.

'CHÂLUS,' she cried out. 'I KNOW YOU'RE MARTIN'S FATHER.'

The rain didn't stop. The sound of its waterfall was joined by that of others.

Once under the ceiling and behind the waterfall, she looked up in uncertainty. 'Châlus,' she murmured. The boy must be her hostage. The father would come to the son, and to the woman, to Angélique Bellecour.

The walk through Bois Carré in the rain was an agony of doubts and conflicting memories. The road south from Paris in June of 1940 came to her so clearly, Angélique heard the Messerschmitts and saw the people scatter. She heard Martin screaming for his father, felt Anthony push her away, heard his, 'Damn you for stopping me.'

Saw him running towards that road, towards Martin. Heard herself crying out, 'Anthony, you have to leave us!' felt him fighting her as she held him. Tasted his tears, the fear, the rage at himself and at her. The bitter words.

Saw Martin as she got him off the road and to safety. 'Martin, your father had to leave us!'

But had he really? *Had he?* She had wanted it so much, she had searched for him and for Martin again and again, and finding only Martin, had believed it.

The Oberst Lautenschläger was ahead of her, the Hauptmann Scheel behind. They passed through ferns and under-growth that was so heavily laden with moisture, the fronds and branches all but touched the ground, and everywhere with the rain had come the smell of rusting iron, of mildew-laden cloth, corroding copper and bronze, and lead that had grown white from that other war.

She heard the Messerschmitts pass down over that road again and again and again, walked dazed and in shock amid the aftermath of each attack and saw the dead, the wounded, the horribly smashed-up families, the cars and wagons on fire, the heaps of burning mattresses, a boy beneath a heavyset man who had shielded him.

'Martin . . . Martin, *chéri*, please put that thing down.'

'NO!'

They had come to the edge of a clearing and were not far from a long ramp that lifted gracefully up through the trees in a gentle curve.

Shells . . . old shells . . . She read the warning notice beneath its skull and crossbones and sucked in a breath. There were rows and rows of them behind him. 'Martin, it's no use. We've lost. The Sturmbannführer Kraus and those with him are searching for your father. They're burning the houses and barns.'

Still she hadn't realized he had found his voice. She was still trying to lie to him. 'He's *dead*, Angélique.'

'Dead . . . ?' She turned away as if struck. 'Martin, what is this you're saying?'

'He died on that road, Angélique. He was hit by the can-non shells. His back was all smashed to pieces and when I found him underneath a car, he stared at me but . . . but I couldn't wake him up.'

Ah no . . . 'Anthony? But . . . but that's just not possible, Martin. We saw him get off the train at the control yesterday. We saw him in Paris, in the Jardin du Luxembourg.'

'We *didn't*! It was only someone who looked like him.'

'Then he didn't live in my flat?'

'HOW COULD HE HAVE?'

'Mademoiselle,' interjected Lautenschläger. 'The grenade. Please get him to put it down.'

She moved past the colonel, and when she reached the barbed wire, knew she could go no farther.

Martin was so pale and frightened—cold too, and wet right through. He was her son now—he had to be.

The handle of the stick grenade was clutched tightly in his right fist, the ring of the pull-cord hooked around the index finger of his left hand.

'You lied to me,' he said.

Rain washed the tears and plastered the reddish-brown hair to a brow that was so like Anthony's. It made the ears that stuck out so awkwardly look bigger still. 'I lied to myself,' she said. 'I had to believe your father got safely away.'

'DON'T COME ANY CLOSER!' he shrilled and, startled, she saw that the colonel and the Hauptmann Scheel had found a plank to place over the barbed wire.

'*Chéri*, let them put it down. I want to hold you, Martin. I need to talk to you. We belong together, you and me.'

'They can do it, but mustn't come any closer than yourself.'

'I stopped Kraus from shooting him,' said Lautenschläger, 'but the next time I won't be so lucky.'

She thanked him and said that he had always been very kind to her and Martin.

The hem of her dress caught on the wire and she had to stop to free it. The board was narrow, and once she slipped and nearly fell.

Crouching, she looked at Martin and he at her. 'Shall we die together?' she asked, and when he didn't answer, said, 'Maybe we should vote on it, eh? If your father is really dead, then who has been living in my flat and keeping my things for me?'

'The Lieutenant Thiessen.'

'And doesn't he look like your father?'

'A little.'

'And isn't he the *Résistance* leader we saw at the control dressed as a priest?'

'Perhaps.'

'Then your father didn't die on that road, Martin. You were mistaken.'

'I wasn't.'

She felt the backs of his fingers touch her cheek to try to still her trembling lips. She said, '*Chéri*, are you certain?'

'Positive. I took the pencil from his pocket, Angélique. I knew he would have wanted me to have it.'

'The grenade,' said Lautenschläger and saw her gingerly take it from the boy to stand with it in her hand.

'Please leave us,' she said. 'Martin, make sure they do, then come back. I'll wait for you.'

Anthony had died on that road. Anthony was gone from her.

Not even the constant rain could detract from the place. The farm of Alphonse Diard and family was well to the north of Bois Carré, much closer to the Forêt de Crécy and far better, far richer than most. It possessed a fine, turreted house of red brick that had been all but untouched by the Blitzkrieg of 1940 and was more like a small château. Had it not been for one of the other farmers confessing to having seen the parachutist being hidden here, they would not have come so far.

'I want him,' seethed Kraus. 'I want the two *Banditen* who came from Paris to spy on the installations at Bois Carré and the other sites, and then to take the parachutist into safe hiding.'

This was outrageous. '*Ah, mon Dieu*, Major, we wouldn't hide such people,' said Diard firmly. 'The Oberst Lautenschläger considers myself and my wife and family loyal subjects and, yes, friends. Please consult him. He will vouch for us.'

'There isn't time.'

'We supply the barracks in Abbeville and Saint-Valéry-sur-Somme with many things.'

'There still isn't time.'

'The colonel drinks my Calvados and *eau-de-vie de poire*.'

'He'll soon be on his way home so if I were you, I wouldn't count on him.'

The barns and other buildings were some distance from the house and downwind of it. This one's guard dogs had set up a racket at the intrusion of others and had had to be shot.

'Our dogs found a kerchief in the loft under that mountain of hay you've been keeping up there,' said Kraus.

'I know nothing of that!'

They were all alike, the French. They lied to save themselves. 'Then how is it a girl's kerchief was found in the largest of your barns?'

'One of my daughters must have misplaced it.'

'Under the hay?'

The thing was of a soft beige. Had they planted it themselves? wondered Diard. 'No such people have entered that barn or any of the others without our hearing of it! The dogs, *n'est-ce pas*? The ones you had killed. They used to make such a racket if even a stray cat came by. One they didn't know, that is.'

Turning away to confront the wife, the daughters and the son, a boy of fourteen, Kraus knew what he had to do. All were being held by the arms by men of the Waffen-SS. The farm help had been herded against one of the turret walls and now huddled in terror, drenched to the skin.

The dogs were waiting.

'*Ach*, we know the parachutist was dropped near Bois Carré last week,' he said, deliberately looking off towards the woods, which were far to the south and not visible in the rain or at any other time, so good, yes, good. An excellent place to lie up. 'We know the evaders, the terrorists you harboured and fed—yes, fed!—must have gone that way.'

He threw out an arm to stiffly point towards Bois Carré, then turned back. 'Now it's simple. Either you confess and tell us what you're hiding, or we'll persuade you.'

The garden in front of the house was being ruined by uncaring jackboots. 'Please, I beg you, Sturmbannführer, this is all a mistake. As God is my witness, we know nothing of this. My dogs would have given fair warning and I would immediately have sent word to the colonel after first having apprehended the villains with pitchforks.'

Then why the tears if such a loyal citizen, why the stench of fear and panic? 'Start with the youngest daughter,' said Kraus, tossing his head her way. 'Strip her, then let's hear what he has to say.'

'NO! I BEG YOU, MONSIEUR.'

It was the son who, pale and shaken and in tears, blurted, 'Papa, forgive me. I hushed the dogs and let those two stay in our barn. I did it for France.'

'ANTOINE!'

They all began to shriek. Forced to his knees, the son cried out, 'THEY WERE EXHAUSTED FROM RUNNING AND HAD COME A LONG WAY TODAY. THE GIRL HAD TWISTED HER ANKLE. THEY SAID THEY WOULD LEAVE AS SOON AS THEY HAD RESTED UP A LITTLE AND THEY DID!'

The boy's cheeks were fair but flushed with alarm, the eyes those of the mother. 'When did they leave and which way were they headed?' asked Kraus.

The boy swallowed and shook his head but confessed when the clothes of the younger sister were torn from her and she cowered among the men.

'At . . . at about two o'clock this afternoon and . . . and heading towards Bois Carré, I think.'

The kerchief had been used to bind the injured ankle. There was blood on it and scraps of skin and rust—a piece of metal had done this, an accident, but not a sprain. A girl from Paris, a student in the guise of a novice, and now . . . 'What was she wearing?'

Perhaps the boy didn't hear or comprehend. When repeated, the question came as a shriek that made him jump, and through the blubbering came, 'Trousers of . . . of a dark brown corduroy, a . . . a blouse of dark brown and . . . and a cardigan, brown also.'

Châlus . . . She had been with Raymond Châlus. 'And the parachutist?' asked Kraus, straightening.

When no answer came and only the sound of the rain intruded, he grabbed the sister by the hair and pulled her over to her brother. Forcing her to her knees, he said, 'Answer or I will give her to the men.'

'They . . . they didn't say anything of a parachutist, monsieur.'

'Nothing?'

'ME, I DON'T THINK THEY WERE AWARE OF ONE!'

Crumpling the kerchief into a ball, Kraus furiously jammed it into the boy's mouth and threw the sister from himself.

'Let him listen to her screams, then kill them all and burn the place. I want Châlus. I will have Châlus and the parachutist and the student, the others too, all of them.'

The *réseau de soie bleue* would be finished—stamped out. Erased from the face of the earth.

The smell of broken geranium stems rose from the ground with the rain but the Oberst Lautenschläger had refused to leave. And when he told Angélique Bois Carré had been cleared of all others but Martin, the Hauptmann Scheel and themselves, she again asked him to leave and this time to take Martin with him. 'Get him well away from here.'

She was determined and very upset, had suffered a great loss, but still didn't comprehend the magnitude of what she intended. 'I can't,' he said. 'There are enough shells in that dump to kill or maim for life all who are downwind of us for ten or even twenty kilometres—I really don't know how far. That gas will drift into the hollows, Mademoiselle Bellecour. Every living thing in its path will experience terrible blisters, the agony of burning eyes and lungs, blindness and choking, the coughing up of blood. What you intend will put this site completely out of bounds for months. It lingers.'

'The Führer will have you arrested,' she said. 'He'll hold you responsible, won't he?'

There was much sadness and genuine regret in her voice.

When he didn't say anything but stood at the other end of the plank that lay across the barbed wire, she asked, 'What is it you are building here?'

'That doesn't concern you.'

He looked old and grey in the rain, a big man, a giant stooped and, yes, still uncertain of her. 'I'm afraid it very much does, Colonel, since we are on opposite sides of this war.'

*Lieber Gott*, she was going to do it!

'Please see that Martin is looked after and not sent to any internment camp. Please leave me to myself. The Sturmbannführer Kraus may be downwind of us with those men of his. I hope so, Colonel. I really do hope so.'

*Verdammt!* was there nothing he could do? 'Please,' he begged. 'Have a thought for others.'

'And you, Colonel? Do you have such a thought here? What is that ramp for?'

'Flying bombs,' said an intruding voice in very good French.

Lautenschläger swiftly turned towards it, Angélique gasped and heard herself saying, 'The priest . . . The girl of the *vélo-taxi*.'

They stood among the waist-high ferns and underbrush and yes, they looked exhausted, the girl in severe pain. And yes, the man with her had a revolver.

'Châlus,' he said of himself and then, 'This is my comrade in arms, Yvette.'

He *did* look like Anthony. He was of about the same age but a little older perhaps. He even had the same big, awkward ears that stuck out and made of him an overgrown elf, the same high, narrow brow, pointed chin, long nose and curious way of always seeking the most minute of details even when firmly decided.

Thin . . . Anthony had been thin, she told herself and said, 'Anthony, is it really you?'

# 10

It was getting dark now and in the ruins of the textile mill Marie-Hélène hesitated. She knew one of them was watching her but where was he?

Rainwater still dripped and pooled and ran everywhere. The growing dusk made deeper still the shadows of canted iron beams and splintered timbers, mangled gearboxes and looms whose frames were horribly twisted. And all was seen against the shreds of clothing and cloth that were caught and hanging as if on laundry lines like rags.

And everywhere there was the smell of wet wool, old and broken bricks and concrete dust. Father Nicolas and the others were hunting for her, she trying now only to escape, to reach Kraus and tell him everything. She had come down a staircase so littered and heaped with rubble, the sudden avalanche of it had constantly threatened. She had sought a way out on the floor above but had been turned back by the tangle of wreckage.

Châlus . . . was it Châlus who was watching her? If so, he would be remembering Lyon and the *réseau* Perrache, would know she had followed first one and then another and another of his people and had accumulated name after name because she had been good at it, the best.

He would know that even after all but himself had been arrested, many had been horribly tortured in the search for his whereabouts and maybe this would weigh on his conscience and maybe it wouldn't. The cellars of the Hôtel Terminus, eh, Châlus? she taunted silently. The one who had her toenails ripped out only to have the torture stopped as Hans had come into the room to quietly talk to her over a cigarette and a cup of coffee—*coffee!*—how could Hans have thought of such a thing? The woman had been stark naked, so terrified and in such shock and pain she hadn't comprehended a thing he had said to her and hadn't even realized her fists had been clenched so hard, the fingernails had driven themselves deeply into her palms.

Others had been strung up by the wrists or ankles and savagely beaten. Others had been dragged screaming to a bathtub full of ice-cold water only to have their screams, their futile struggles stilled until, gasping for air and vomiting—panicking—they had been shrieked at again and again: 'WHERE IS CHÂLUS?' and nearly drowned once more. Kicking, thrashing, their naked buttocks upended—men, women, young boys and girls, what had it really mattered if in the end he had been caught?

Oh yes, Châlus would understand that for the *réseau de soie bleue* and for his son and Angélique Bellecour, only one person stood between them and death.

She chanced a step and when she saw Father Nicolas, she saw the iron bar in his hands.

'That's far enough,' he said. 'You can't escape us this time.'

She sensed that, yes, someone was behind her. Châlus . . . Was it Châlus?

She turned and fired. Father Nicolas gave a shriek of rage and rushed at her. The bar hit something metal and bounced, knocking the Luger from her hand. Ah no . . . NO! *'Let go of me!'* she shrieked and bit and kicked. He dragged her down. Her head hit something sharp. He was too strong for her. He was pinning her arms to the rubble . . . 'HONORÉ!' he yelled. 'HONORÉ!'

The mayor would come running, the others too. Bucking—arching her back—Marie-Hélène tried to throw him off.

'Ah no you don't, my pretty!' he cried and slammed her head back.

Dazed and bleeding, she tried to fight him off, tried to get away. Must kill him . . . kill him. A priest, a priest!

Momentarily a wrist was freed. He was trying to grab that iron bar. He was going to kill her.

Groping in the rubble, she found a chunk of concrete and tried to hit him with it.

'BITCH!' he shrieked. 'HONORÉ, WHERE ARE YOU?'

'I'M COMING, NICOLAS. HOLD HER!'

'THÉODORE . . . WHERE IS THÉODORE?'

'DON'T TELL ME SHE HAS KILLED HIM?'

She gave a gasp, a ragged sigh. Now only the sound of the rain came clearly. Always the rain and the constant dripping of water. Everywhere, water.

Ledieu tried to catch a stifled breath. 'Nicolas,' he hazarded. 'Are you all right?'

He was certain he had found the right place but when, in all but total darkness he cautiously made a circuit of the area, he couldn't find them.

Against the constant dripping of the water, he heard a resonance that was repeated over and over, the sound both a sigh and a warning. He had no light. They had come unprepared. 'THÉODORE!' he cried. 'NICOLAS!'

When he found, quite by accident, the Luger, he felt certain God had given them the edge and that now at last, they could put an end to this infiltrator from Paris, this traitor, this servant of the Nazis.

A voice came hesitantly from the floor below perhaps, or from the one below that. 'Honoré, are you making that noise?'

It was Théodore and soon he quietly said, 'Jean-Pierre and Eugène are watching the canal in case she escapes and tries to reach the Kommandantur.'

'Have you a light?' managed Ledieu.

The sounds were muted. The constant dripping could and did often hit every note in the keyboard of such, but then there was also this gentle sighing, this resonance, as if it questioned the success of their little hunt.

The beam of the sous-préfet's torch pierced the darkness to

throw the shadow of Father Nicolas onto the broken walls and heaps of tangled wreckage.

Caught in the skeins of wire, and with some of it wrapped around his neck, Nicolas bounced slowly up and down from the gaping edge of the floor above.

Marie-Hélène waited. Ledieu would have to go to the assistance of his friend. They couldn't allow the corpse to continue hanging. The head would soon be severed. Ledieu would have to kneel on all fours, would have to find something with which to cut that wire.

A shadow to her, she saw the Luger in his hand almost at the same instant as he fired. Châlus . . . where was Châlus? Not here . . . not here . . .

The corpse plummeted to the floor below. The head hit the broken concrete. *'Idiot!'* hissed Allard. *'Why couldn't you have been more careful?'*

More careful . . . more careful . . .

Bois Carré was no refuge. Down across the fields, in the dusk and rain, the helmeted soldiers in their capes and gas masks, and with their guns at the ready, fanned out and soon the dogs were hungering up the slope through the maize, the barley too, and soon it would be all over.

Angélique pulled Martin to her. Apart from a harsh, 'Mademoiselle, we do *not* know each other,' Châlus—Anthony, yes—had given no hint of memory, of love or caring, only a bitter hardness, a cruelty and swift decisiveness, an impatience that didn't become him even in such a moment of crisis.

He would detonate the mustard gas. He would envelop them all in a blinding, choking fog that would burn the skin and the lungs. He had no thought for her or Martin or even for Yvette Rougement. Having taken the grenade from herself, he had ruthlessly jammed it among the shells and had soon found construction cord enough to run this from the primer ring to himself so as to detonate it at any time.

He had taken the colonel and the Hauptmann Scheel hostage even though the Sturmbannführer Kraus might welcome such a thing.

Stubborn still, he hadn't wanted to listen to the colonel or herself. And yes, he had changed drastically. No soft and half-hidden smile for Martin. Only an outright denial, a rejection and a fierce determination to accomplish what he had come to do.

'Sabotage,' said Martin softly. 'He'll kill the Mademoiselle Moncontre too, if possible.'

'*Chéri*, don't let her make you feel so betrayed. Women lie all the time, isn't that so?'

'And men?' asked Martin bitterly. 'Men like my father.'

'They're liars too. Why else would so many women like myself or your mother find temptation their ruin?'

'I think I love you, Angélique.'

'And you're not lying to me?'

She felt his hand in hers, felt him put an arm about her and press his cheek against her. Fondly she caressed the back of his head. 'I could sleep and sleep, Martin, but in a warm and comfortable bed like we so often shared, and with you to bring me coffee as you used to when I awakened on a Sunday.'

The dogs were still held back by leashes, thought Martin. One could run from them. One could climb into the branches of the highest trees only to be dragged down by the soldiers and torn to pieces even as the mustard gas rushed to fill the lungs and . . .

'He was on that road and lying under a car, Angélique. He was all shot to pieces and dead, I tell you. *Really dead!*'

'*Ah, mon Dieu, chéri*, you were mistaken. It's understandable. In the confusion, you saw many who had been hit by cannon shells. One bloodied face and shattered brain became another.'

She wasn't going to believe him. 'I took his pencil. Me, I closed his eyes. Was I mistaken by those?'

'Then your father was terrified, just like us. Perhaps he'd been hit, who's to say? And when you closed his eyes, he must have let you do this in his terror, for he couldn't move himself, but it helped him to get back his sanity.'

'Then he forgot all about us. Is that how it is, Angélique?'

No memory of them. 'Come on, *mon cher*. Let's find Mademoiselle Yvette so as to be with her when the dogs come.'

'Don't run into any of the tunnels. Don't try to hide in

them. There's no escape from those. They're all blocked up at one end and have no windows.'

The ankle that had been badly sprained had been deeply cut, and earlier, when Angélique had bathed it, she had seen the girl wince and had heard her say, 'It's no use. You must leave me.'

But now? wondered Angélique as they waded through the rain-soaked ferns to where the girl sat on the ground, leaning against an oak and with the colonel's pistol in her lap.

She looked exhausted, not the picture of determination she had been in Paris with that *vélo-taxi*, nor was she so sure of herself. 'Pray for me,' she said. A girl of nineteen or twenty who would call up her horoscope and claim their rescue an exercise of conscience.

One could not lie to her. 'The dogs,' said Angélique and saw her throw a worried glance towards that side of the woods.

'The dogs,' she whispered and crossed herself. 'The shells . . . ? Is he going to detonate them?'

'Come on, Martin and I will take you with us.'

'No! You must go yourselves. Run! Try to get away from here before Raymond, he . . .'

They got her up but she really had had it. Repeatedly, since leaving the auberge at Noyelles-sur-Mer early this morning, Anthony had forced her to run on that ankle and now the girl had nothing left to give.

The dogs would race through the ferns. They would leap at each of them and knock them to the ground. Shrieking, rolling over and over and trying to cover their faces, their heads, each would feel the dogs biting deeply until . . . until the shells exploded and a heavy rush of stinging yellow fog swept over them. A last, choking, blinding memory.

The tunnel was near and though Martin had warned her not to hide in one of them, that is where they went. They had no other choice.

Against the edge of the woods where the barley stubble ended, three figures had emerged and at a word from Kraus, the men ceased moving forward and stood still.

The dogs were calmed. Perhaps fifteen or twenty minutes

of dusk remained. There was no letup in the driving rain, which still came from the west.

'Go on,' said Châlus not looking at the Hauptmann Scheel but using Deutsch as good as any of them. 'Go and tell him I want to talk.'

A foolish attempt. Perhaps sixty metres of stubble separated them from the SS. 'That one, *mein Herr*, will not listen,' said Lautenschläger, gruffly nodding to indicate the Sturmbannführer. 'There's blood on his hands. Like the dogs, he has its scent and finds he enjoys it.'

'The wood is surrounded,' interjected Scheel. 'You have no choice but to surrender.'

'You know I can't.'

'And he can't let you escape, can he?' countered Lautenschläger, still looking down across those sixty metres. 'Herr Himmler would be most displeased should that happen.'

'The men will be entering the wood behind you,' hazarded Scheel. 'You can't assume those who are on the other side of it will also have been given the order to halt. In no time they'll cut that cord of yours and pick you off.'

Snipers . . . were there snipers?

'Give up,' said Lautenschläger. 'Let me use what influence I have to see that you're put into Abwehr hands and are not left to that one.'

There were lorries but these were under guard and solidly blocking the road to the woods. To break out and cross the fields in this rain was impossible even under cover of darkness.

Grimly Châlus ran his gaze along the line of men. Again he worried about snipers. '*Verdammt!* Get Kraus up here now,' he shouted. 'Go on!' He shoved Scheel and all but jerked the cord taut.

*Lieber Gott,* sweated Lautenschläger. 'What about your son? Does he mean so little to you?'

'He's not my son, but even if he was, it wouldn't matter.'

'Is the death of that woman the SS have been using so important?'

'For me, yes, and for France.'

He had meant it too. Even in the rain and the falling light

and against such odds, thought Lautenschläger, this one gave no sign of wavering. 'To be resolute is admirable but I greatly fear you will have to go to him. Kraus just won't have the courage to come to you.'

Slowly Châlus let the spool he held on a short stick unwind the cord. He didn't say anything but indicated with his revolver that they were to do as suggested.

Schmeissers were trained on the terrorist. Snipers? wondered Lautenschläger. Each footfall sank deeply into the soil. Mud clung to his jackboots.

'Call off the dogs and tell your men to bugger off,' said Châlus to Kraus when they had all but reached him. 'If you don't, I'll detonate the ammunition dump. It's just up there behind us among the trees.'

So this was Châlus, thought Kraus scornfully looking him over and wanting to shriek, *I CAN HAVE YOU KILLED WITH THE FLICK OF A FINGER!* This was the one who had got away in Lyon and had then clandestinely hunted down and followed Dirksen's little pigeon. This was the one who knew where the parachutist was hidden. 'The SS don't parley with *Banditen.* You of all people should know that.'

'Where is Marie-Hélène de Fleury?'

He even knew her real name but would he give up that of the parachutist so easily? 'Busy fingering the members of the *réseau de soie bleue.*'

'Get her here and I'll leave the dump alone.'

A man of limited purpose. It would soon be dark. 'That could perhaps be arranged.'

So much, then, for Kraus's refusal to parley.

'Clear the road of the lorries and bring the de Fleury woman to Bagatelle Château,' interjected Lautenschläger firmly. 'Until then, Hauptmann Scheel and myself will remain as hostages.'

How soft of him and he a colonel, thought Kraus. 'The infiltrator may be difficult to locate.'

'*Don't be a fool, Sturmbannführer. Listen to what I've said!*'

'*Get her!*' hissed Châlus.

By now those on the other side of the wood would have entered it, thought Kraus. A first priority would be to secure the munitions dump. 'There's no need to be offensive,' he said offhandedly. 'Such arrangements must always be conducted in a civilized manner. Is that not so, Herr Oberst?'

He was up to something—the terrorist saw it too and gathered in the cord. 'Wait!' breathed Lautenschläger. 'Call off your men, Sturmbannführer. If you don't, this site will have to be abandoned for a considerable time.'

The dogs had made no sound, nor had Yvette cried out in alarm or the others, that boy and his mother, and that could only mean one thing, felt Châlus, letting his gaze move swiftly over Kraus and the colonel and Hauptmann Scheel. The memory of Marie-Hélène de Fleury was all too clear. He saw her as the soft light of evening had descended on her in the Bois de Boulogne, saw her returning to her flat on the boulevard de Beauséjour, and in Lyon talking to another and another of his people. Dressed plainly as always so as to blend right in, and clever, far too clever.

'*Salaud!*' he cried out and savagely yanked on the cord.

The telephone to Paris was impossible. The woman who ran the PTT in a far corner of a makeshift *tabac* and *bar-café* was adamant. 'It's forbidden. There are no lines. The switchboard operator in Amiens will simply tell you this. No calls are allowed from the *zone interdite* to anywhere in the *zone occupée*, or from here to there. Just for the Germans who have their own lines.'

Marie-Hélène was frantic. She had run from the ruins of the textile mill, had managed to find this one lonely blue light in a town of ruins and empty spaces that had been plunged into the blackout. 'Look, I know this but I have to call Paris. It's not just urgent, it's vital.'

She threw a glance over a shoulder at the heavily curtained doorway, saw the patrons in their worn clothes all staring at her and turned back to the woman who, with the eyes of a dumb ox, took her in and devoured her state.

Fresh blood trickled down a forearm where the blouse had been torn. Marie-Hélène plucked at the fabric and, suddenly self-conscious, tried to pull the blouse away a little from her front. 'My hands,' she said. They were badly scraped and bled at the fingers and thumbs. 'My knees . . .'

Madame Monnier pursed her lips. 'Is it not the hospital you wish?'

'No! It's Paris, damn you!'

Had German soldiers raped her or had she been violated among the ruins by others for having offered herself to those very Boches? wondered Aurore Monnier.

Clucking her tongue, she said, 'Wait here. We're not without heart,' and when she came back through from the bar, she put a glass of *eau-de-vie* into the telephone-wisher's hands. 'Drink it. All of it. Down the hatch, as the British say.'

The *marc* was rough. Gasping, ducking her head to clear her throat and eyes, Marie-Hélène managed a feeble, '*Merci*,' and then anxiously said, 'Look, they're still after me. If they come here, please tell them you haven't seen me.'

A gang rape, *ah merde*, what next in these troubled times? 'How many?'

'Five, or four. I . . . I can't be sure. All of them drunk, the youngest maybe eighteen and . . . and from Lübeck or was it Bremen?'

Again the woman left her but when she returned from the bar, she slid a short, lead-weighted club through the counter slot of the cashier's cage. 'I would give you a knife but those are illegal to carry. Why not just stay here?'

'I really do have to call Paris.'

The words had been given almost in a whisper. The boy-friend would need to be told, thought Aurore. The shame of what had happened—yes, yes! One should get it over with so that life could go on. 'Then you must put what happened to those in charge of the Kommandantur. Look for the belfries of the Church of Saint-Vulfran and then that of the Komman-dantur and hôtel de ville. These you will see distinctly against the night sky but only if the rain, it has stopped.'

An older man came through, a relative of the *patronne* perhaps, in a faded denim jacket and shabby beret, which he hurriedly dragged off. 'Allow me, please, to guide you. It's the least we can do, mademoiselle, so that you will understand in your heart that all men are not like those who have defiled you.'

Somehow she found the strength to smile faintly and to find that former graciousness that had stood her in such good stead. 'Very well, I accept. *Merci.*'

She took no time at all to push the curtain briefly aside to reach the door. Once in the rain, she searched the darkness—listened hard and said, when he, wearing his rain cape, had joined her, 'They're out there. I can feel them.'

'Come. It's not far but we'll take a different route than the usual. Here, give me the *baton.* I was once a sailor. Not even the five of them will stop us.'

In the darkness and the rain it was so hard for her to tell which way they were heading. She thought things were all right. They seemed to leave the ruins, to walk out across an open space—the square in the centre of town and near the Kommandantur and hôtel de ville—but all too soon there were walls on either side of them and doorways. She was certain of it and asked how long had he been sitting in that *bar-café,* and he said, 'Not long. The *apértif, n'est-ce pas?*'

A former sailor . . .

The street became a walkway that climbed low stairs. 'It's just up here a little,' he said, but of course most of Abbeville was flat, so what the hell were the stairs for?

He didn't knock. The rain beat down and when she heard him grunt, she knew the door must be very heavy or stuck.

It slammed behind them and in the pitch-darkness, the smell of rubble came to her. That, too, of incense and beeswax.

A match was struck again and again until the sound of it flared outwards at her as it glowed. They were in the undamaged part of the Church of Saint-Vulfran. They were right next to the Kommandantur . . .

'Mademoiselle Moncontre, I believe,' said Ledieu. 'At last we meet again and these,' he indicated the others, 'you already know.'

She felt her back stiffen, her shoulders become squared. The proud de Fleury chin her father had prided himself so much in would be jutting defiantly.

When her voice came, she heard its calmness and knew *Papa* would have been proud of that too. 'Where is Châlus?'

'The "priest",' said Allard. 'Not with us, mademoiselle. Gone overland, I think, to Bois Carré, to the slaughter of so many by the Sturmbannführer Kraus.'

Word of what must have been going on had reached them. They would kill her. The one called Jean-Pierre had given his revolver to the sous-préfet Allard. Ledieu, the mayor, still held the Luger Hans had brought her. 'Might I have a few moments before the cross?' she asked, sensing they wouldn't kill her here in the church and that they would probably first want to question her.

Someone had lighted a candle. She couldn't see his face for he held the little taper well before himself and didn't lift his head to hers.

It was Ledieu who said, 'There is, alas, no time for prayers, but did you give Father Nicolas any, or Véronique, or her brother or mother?'

'Honoré, be quiet,' said Allard. 'Let her confess before her God. The longer the confession, the longer she remains alive. Everything you know about this Châlus, mademoiselle. Everything.'

Was Châlus their only hope? wondered Marie-Hélène. 'And the Sturmbannführer Kraus?' she asked. 'Shall I tell you about him?'

'Of course.'

The tunnel was long and very dark, and when they entered it, the dogs made little sound but came on swiftly. The girl, Yvette, fired the pistol once, then twice. Stabs of flame caused the eyes to blink, but still the dogs came on, the whisper of their paws picking up where the echo of the shots left off.

Angélique pulled Martin more tightly against herself. The girl cried out in anguish and fired twice more, this time pointing the gun at the floor in front of them so that the bullets ricocheted. A dog was hit and yelped—whined terribly and set up a racket the others ignored as they raced on through the darkness.

She fired repeatedly at the floor, the bullets pinging off the walls and careering along the tunnel. There was a sharp yelp, another and another, she emptying the gun and giving a cry that was torn from her.

Over and over she rolled, shrieking—filling the tunnel with the sounds of her. Angélique pushed Martin to the floor and tried to cover him. 'MY HANDS!' she shrieked. 'MY FACE, MY NECK!' Skin was torn. Blood rushed out. Infuriated, the dogs raced in, biting, tearing, tugging until . . .

They backed off. Growling from deep inside, they waited, panting as torchlight filled the tunnel and the sound of hob-nailed boots came to rest.

'*Ach, mein Gott,* will you look at that,' swore one of the men. '*Heini, komm mal her, ja? Guter Hund.* Let go of her now.'

The dog released the girl who gave a sigh.

Terrified—cradling her left hand and panicking at thoughts of a torn face, a missing ear, a scalp that had lost its hair—Angélique obeyed and didn't resist when told to sit up.

'Ahh . . .' She gasped and found herself worrying about Martin. Martin mustn't look.

'It's all right,' he managed, but it wasn't. Yvette Rouge-ment's throat had been ripped open. Her face, neck, hair and hands—her arms, breasts and thighs were covered in blood that glistened under torchlight even as it ran.

With a grunt, one of the men grabbed the girl by a wrist and dragged her back along the tunnel and finally into the rain to leave her lying faceup in the mud. Her clothes had been torn to shreds, blood draining rapidly to mingle with the water. 'Yvette . . . Yvette,' sobbed Angélique. 'We didn't even know your real name.'

'*RUHE!*' shrieked one of the men.

Slammed hard in the centre of her back with the butt of a rifle, startled by the blow, Angélique panicked as she pitched forward to hit the ground hard. Martin tried to save her. Mar-tin shrieked as he kicked and swung at them, and when he fell on top of her, his body was limp and she felt his saliva draining down her cheek, hot against the coolness of the rain.

'Châlus . . . Raymond Châlus,' swore Kraus, sucking in a breath through clenched teeth as he stood over the terrorist. 'How does it feel now to have had one of those old Lebels pointed at an SS officer but with a bullet that fails to fire?'

The cord had been cut and, when yanked, it had come freely. No explosion. No mustard gas.

Châlus had then jammed the gun against the back of Kraus's head and had pulled the trigger. 'He can't answer you,' said Lautenschläger, breathing in deeply. 'You've broken his teeth and his jaw, his nose also. He doesn't look well, Sturmbannführer. I doubt very much if you will ever get anything from him.'

'*These people do it all the time. He's only faking. AUFSTEHEN!*' he shrieked at Châlus.

The swollen eyes tried to look up into the torchlight and the rain. The battered lips fought to move. Savagely Kraus kicked the bastard in the ribs and then in the groin. Doubled up in pain, Châlus choked and vomited blood.

'Shoot him. Here, let me do it if you won't,' said Lautenschläger.

'He's fine. He's only faking. GET UP!' shrieked Kraus.

Châlus rolled over and grabbed him round the ankles. Taken by surprise, Kraus toppled backwards. The terrorist scrambled on top of him and sank his teeth into an ear. Kraus shrieked and fought back.

Rolling over and over in the mud, the two were finally pulled apart. Kraus gripped his ear and when he took his hand away, it was covered with blood. 'BASTARD!' he screamed.

They held Châlus. The Sturmbannführer beat him with a rifle and when finally released, the terrorist collapsed. '*There*, Colonel. Now do you believe me?'

Kraus was breathing heavily. Blood streamed down the left side of his neck from an ear that had been savagely torn. He clamped a handkerchief to the ear but removed this several times to see if the wound had been staunched. 'Châlus will pay for this!'

The others came down from the woods, dragging the boy and his mother. Kraus found his pistol. Lautenschläger cautioned patience. 'Some photographs perhaps,' he said. 'For Berlin.'

'Very well. Some photographs. And when we have the others and the parachutist, they will all be left hanging by the neck from the belfry of the Kommandantur.'

One of the men mentioned the dead girl. Kraus insisted she be thrown into one of the lorries. 'We will leave her outside the Kommandantur and punish anyone who attempts to cover or remove her body. Bloated, her corpse will be a constant reminder to them.'

As it will be to ourselves, thought Lautenschläger ruefully and asked himself, Why is it that men like Kraus always seem to succeed?

He pitied Châlus and the Bellecour woman. He wondered what would happen to the boy and if it would be possible to save him.

Martin can't be blamed for this, he told himself. It really isn't his war. But it was, of course, and therefore he could not be saved.


Water was pooled on the floor of the ruined Church of Saint-Vulfran. Marie-Hélène listened to the pitter-patter of droplets through the pitch-darkness that, with the seven of them, was all around her.

They were going to kill her. They were each, in his own way, violently hostile towards her. Some, like Jean-Pierre, wanted to play with her emotions, then to beat her, to punish her harshly before killing her.

Others like Honoré Ledieu, even as they despised her, despised themselves for having to do this in a church. They would have preferred the privacy of the ruins along one of the canals, but that had not been possible. Not now, and so they felt very uncomfortable. Also they were ex-soldiers and to them the killing of a defenceless woman, even if an infiltrator, struck hard at the conscience.

All were afraid but knew for sure only that she could not yet have given their names to Kraus who knew only that the mayor was involved.

She hadn't told them about Hans having their names, had kept that little secret from them, though the sous-préfet Allard suspected she was hiding something. And, yes, Hans would take care of them but had he been sent to Berlin? Had he been stopped on the road home to Paris and simply taken to the aerodrome? He would have had to give his notebook to someone else or it would have been taken from him.

In any case, these men were doomed but did not yet know it fully. But were they thinking Châlus might offer escape for Ledieu and his family? Were they thinking, as they shared their cigarettes, giving none to herself, that perhaps the others could safely lie low and go about their daily lives once she had been dealt with? The fools.

Rubble had been cleared so that a narrow passage led through to the nave and under where the vault of its roof had collapsed. Ledieu went first; Allard followed closely behind her so that there would be no chance of escape. The rain struck her hard and she bowed her head but when they reached what must be the transept, the rain suddenly ceased.

There would be less rubble here, for the roof above must still be intact. Perhaps a path had been cleared to the south and north doors, the pews ending well before the steps up into the chancel.

Once out in the square, she could make a dash for the Kommandantur. It was very close and there was *nothing* between it and the church but emptiness.

Allard felt her hesitate and stabbed the muzzle of his revolver between her shoulders. 'Go on, then. Make a run for it. Give me the excuse to finish you off before we have to listen to your prayers.'

'Théodore, that's enough!' hissed Ledieu nervously. 'Switch on the torch. It will be better.'

No torch came on. Uncertainly she felt for the first of the steps only to stumble, to cry out and grab for the mayor.

The rain was cold and she was drenched to the skin, and as she lay there in the torchlight looking up at them in terror, they all looked down on her. Did they want to kick her, to break her ribs, to hear her cry for mercy?

The beam of that blue, cloth-shuttered thing in the sous-préfet's fist went out. *Salaud*, she wanted to scream at him.

'Kneel,' said Ledieu. 'Prepare yourself.'

Ah no . . . 'But . . . but we haven't yet reached the altar?'

'For you, a little distance is necessary,' he sighed and she knew then that there must be both a sacristy and a chapel near the altar and that the doors from each of them would offer escape if only she could reach one of them. If only . . .

The blue of the torchlight found her again. As she knelt and hastily made the sign of the cross, she began to cry. The dark brown hair whose plainness had fooled so many, clung to her cheeks and brow and neck. The left arm of her shirt-blouse was torn. Three buttons were now missing from its front but either she had no time for modesty or was unconscious of her state. Or perhaps she had deliberately ripped the blouse open.

There were bruises, cuts and scrapes, and yes, thought Ledieu sadly, she did look very afraid and vulnerable. A pretty girl who, like so many others, had willingly given herself to the enemy.

But unlike those others, this one had done far more than the unforgivable.

Her voice came faintly as she said the Lord's Prayer in Latin but soon choked on her words and vomited and they had to hold her head down.

'*Adveniat regnum tuum*,' prompted someone—had it been the dentist, their weakest link? she wondered. Was he to her left?—yes, yes, he was. And from there, the aisle to the altar would be clear.

Prodded by Allard's revolver, she blurted, '*Fiat voluntas tua, sicut in . . . in caelo, et in terra.*'

'That's enough,' said one of the others—the silent one, the foreman from the brewery. He was standing next to the sous-préfet and all but behind her but where were the others? Was there still so much rubble on the floor they couldn't get closer?

'They've gone to guard the exits,' breathed Allard. 'Try any of them if you wish.'

The confessions began. Quickly she told them why Raymond Châlus had come to Abbeville to put an end to her. 'Châlus will try to save his son and Angélique Bellecour,' she grated, displaying a little of her former toughness. 'The Sturmbannführer Kraus is well aware of this and will attempt to use them to trap him, so you must first get rid of Kraus if you are to survive.'

This one was really something, felt Allard, but had she the means with which to do just such a thing?

'Berlin are promoting Kraus,' she offered, her hands still tightly clasped in prayer, her back straight, head bowed, every muscle in her ready to spring. 'He's to take over security for all of the Retaliatory Weapon One sites.'

You tease, sighed Allard. You're so deceitful, it's really quite a marvel, but me, I am now wondering exactly what you are contemplating.

'Please tell us about those sites,' said Ledieu. He was between her and the wall on which there was a statue of the Virgin. He still had the Luger Hans had given her. The pale blue light from the sous-préfet's torch left the mayor largely in darkness but gave to the plaster Virgin an opalescent hue.

'The Nazis are very close about those sites,' she said and left it at that.

'Part your lips a little more, mademoiselle. Give us everything,' hissed the cylinder-spinner, Jean-Pierre, who had returned for some reason.

'I think there are to be a hundred of such sites in the north and all within range of England. Flying bombs, messieurs. Each site is first to be aimed at London.'

'When?' demanded the brewery foreman who had moved a little more to her left so as to block any attempt past the dentist.

'The late autumn perhaps. Who knows? But all the sites will fire on London at once—twenty . . . thirty . . . *Ah, mon Dieu, mes amis,* maybe forty flying bombs from each of them in one continuous barrage and each bomb of about a thousand kilos of high explosive.'

Ledieu let a breath escape and she thought, Now was her chance. Now she must leap at him—yes, him!

The muzzle of that revolver pushed its way among the hairs that were plastered to the back of her neck.

'The Sturmbannführer Kraus,' said someone, a reminder, but had they, too, come back from blocking an exit?

Allard nudged her head with that thing. Calming herself, she said, 'Berlin expect Kraus to make an example of Abbeville and yourselves.'

'He wants a parachutist that doesn't exist,' snorted Jean-Pierre.

'He wants Châlus, idiot! and the girl who came with him from Paris.'

'The novice,' muttered Ledieu, his mind racing perhaps over possible avenues of escape for him and his family.

'He will stop at nothing,' she insisted, and turning around left off her prayers to look desperately up at them. 'Please,' she begged. 'Let me join you. Only I can help you escape. I'll do it, yes, and then . . . then you can kill me.'

Questioningly Ledieu glanced at Allard and she saw that one attempt to nod all but imperceptibly. Her lips began to quiver, but she couldn't seem to stop them and began to recite the Hail Mary.

He lifted the Luger and pointed it at her head, the muzzle touching her right temple causing her to cry out inwardly, Hans . . . but Kraus was her only hope.

'Messieurs, I know where there is a Schmeisser and two hundred rounds, another thirty for that Luger you're about to use.'

'*Ah merde*, where?' bleated Ledieu.

Allard was impressed.

'In the place where I hid them. You see, messieurs, my lover, the Standartenführer Dirksen, is to be recalled to Berlin and replaced by the Sturmbannführer Kraus but this my lover most certainly doesn't want.'

She shrugged. She had about her the insolence of an alley cat in heat and would fling herself at any of them in order to get what she wanted. 'Go on,' said Allard. 'Empty your little can of worms.'

'So that you can go fishing? Yes . . . yes, please allow me to continue. But first, I must stand, I think. My knees. I haven't been on them like this for such a long, long time, they ache.'

'Then let them ache a little longer,' said the foreman, wanting to strangle her perhaps.

'Very well, my lips give only silence,' she said tartly. 'You've had your opportunity. The one solution to all your little problems is to do exactly what my lover wanted but you . . . you thirst only for revenge, yet are too ashamed of what you are doing here to conduct me to the altar.'

'Just tell us, mademoiselle,' said Ledieu.

They waited. They asked if she had given their names to this lover of hers and she rejoiced in their asking, was filled with hope. 'How could I have? He's forbidden to leave Paris. Oh for sure, maybe he has sent me a telex saying he has been recalled to Berlin earlier than he thought, maybe he has asked if I've done what he most wanted.'

They were all so nervous. 'I was to have killed Kraus for him and my lover knew I would, but you see, messieurs, I was to have made it look like a *Résistance* killing.'

A bloodbath would have followed but there had already been one. Was an example then not needed for all those who remained? A *Résistance* example?

'Killing Kraus could be my little gift to you,' she said.

'But not in return for your life,' said someone.

'Then let him get his hands on monsieur le maire, eh? That is all he needs, and believe me, Monsieur Ledieu, no matter how much you think it impossible for him to pry the names of these others from your lips, such things they are easy. He's a natural. A sadist. Instinctively he knows each person's weakest point. A wife, a son, a daughter, and all the while you are watching what is happening to them, a part of you is begging you to betray your friends.'

Someone made a move to intervene. 'She can't be trusted, and you know this,' said the foreman. 'The slut is just causing dissension among us. Kill her now and let's be done with it!'

'Dissension or not,' sighed Allard, 'I think we have to listen. None of us will be safe until Honoré is with Châlus and has gone into hiding.'

The room was dark and cold, and when she had somehow turned onto her back, Angélique found that breathing was still very painful.

She tried to swallow. Gingerly she probed her rib cage, now here, now there. Her left arm seemed useless to her and she wondered if it had been broken. She ached everywhere, was stiff and sore and feeling very weak.

I must sit up, she silently said to herself but found the effort too much.

Martin put a wet rag to her lips and gratefully she sucked on it and could swallow more easily. 'Can you talk?' he whispered in English.

'*Un peu,*' she said and immediately he reverted to French.

'They have taken Châlus upstairs again, from the next room. I have heard him moaning with such bitterness, Angélique. I whispered to him earlier through the crack that is beneath the door that connects us. I tried to get him to answer but he could say nothing.'

'Châlus . . . ? Anthony . . . Your father, Martin.'

'No. It's better if we know him by his new name. He's different now. He's not the same.'

'Where are we?'

'In Bagatelle Château, in the cellars.'

'The wine cellar?'

'A storage room. One of them guards the outer door always.'

'Sit me up.'

'Lie still. Rest for a little. I'm working on a plan.'

He left her then and she could hear him as he quietly rooted about in a far corner. He was pulling up the stones in the floor. He was digging. 'Martin . . . ?'

'*Shh!*'

She felt her left arm, felt how sticky it was and, probing further, found where the flesh had been torn open and still oozed.

She felt her left hand. It was so stiff. The ham of the thumb was swollen to twice or three times its normal size. The left side of her forehead and scalp had been bitten. There were lacerations, puncture wounds—her right calf, the thigh also. . . . 'Martin . . . Martin, find that rag for me again. We have to stop the bleeding.'

They came and they took her upstairs while leaving him all alone, and for a time he tried to follow her with his mind's eye.

'The kitchens,' he said softly. 'There the floor is of tile and easily cleaned, and the chairs can be replaced if necessary.'

Would they beat her again? Would they kill her this time? 'Angélique . . .' he started to call out but warned himself not to.

She wouldn't hear him anyway. The cellars were too deep.

Fortunately he hadn't been bitten and but for a few bad bruises, bumps and scrapes, he was in perfect condition, and once the stones in the floor were removed, he could dig his way under the wall and into the next room. The wall wasn't of stones but of boards, and equally fortunate, the Boches hadn't swept the room clean of a flat metal strap, a rusty bit of refuse they had missed.

'These old places,' he muttered under his breath as he worked. 'They might be beautiful but constantly damp mortar easily decays and the Boches should have thought of this.'

There was gravelly sand below the stones but digging through it was not difficult. An hour passed—was it two? he wondered. Suddenly he had to know why they were keeping Angélique away so long but he couldn't ask the guard. Not with the evidence heaped on the floor.

Lugging the heavy stones over to the door, he placed them behind it to slow their entry. If he could, he would pile up as many as possible.

He was in the next room where Châlus had been kept when he heard them coming for him. 'The boy . . . The boy . . .' the order rushed down the cellar stairs from guard to guard.

They would kill him if they found him, and if they didn't, they would soon set the dogs to looking for him but he had to try. He was their only hope.

The door to this room was open.

'THE PARACHUTIST!' shrieked Kraus. A fistful of her hair was grabbed. Her head flew back. Someone had her by the neck. Others had her by the arms, the legs . . .

'THERE ISN'T ONE!' managed Angélique, only to see the water rushing at her, to try to thrash her legs and arms and struggle to free herself. 'NO . . . NO . . . I CAN'T BREATHE!'

Her eyes bulged, her nostrils pinched. She struggled as her face was pushed against the bottom of the bathtub.

Vomiting—choking—panicking, she was yanked out, slapped hard, shaken and dumped onto the floor to double up and shiver uncontrollably, her mouth opening and closing as she tried desperately to breathe.

Walls of pain kept closing in on her. White hot and tear-ing . . . Her chest was on fire. Her lungs refused to expand.

They grabbed her by the hair and neck. Naked, she was upended and thrust under again to fill her lungs all but to the point of drowning, then yanked out to puke it up and blindly cough it out.

Evacuating herself, she received their curses, their punches, their kicks but wasn't really conscious of them. Was too ter-rified . . .

'Bring her round,' swore Kraus. The bitch had splashed the bathroom so much, he was drenched. Two of the Waffen-SS began to work on her. While one grabbed her round the waist and hoisted her from the floor, the other rammed his fingers into her mouth to pull out her tongue.

Draped over the arms, she yielded up more water. They shook her, slapped her cheeks and pounded her back.

'Cognac . . .' gasped one of them.'Give it to her.'

They forced the neck of the bottle between her jaws and tried to pour some down her throat. Bruised, cut, torn, bat-tered, she threw up again and again, dragging in a scant breath each time.

Her chest heaved and rattled. Her breasts were blotched with red and blackened blue, her arms, her neck. Blood rushed from wounds that had tried to close. Two molars had been lost and lay in the swill at her feet.

Kraus screamed into her ear, 'THE PARACHUTIST!'

She tried to tell him. She really did.

The door burst in. 'ENOUGH!' yelled someone, though she was hardly conscious of it. '*VERDAMMT*! HAVE I NOT ALREADY TOLD YOU NO OFFICER OF THE REICH SHOULD DO SUCH A THING?'

A silence came but only vaguely was she aware of this. Kraus threw the colonel a scathing look that said much. Armed Waffen-SS had crowded into the room behind the colonel.

Lautenschläger swore under his breath but said more calmly, 'Will you not listen? What she said was true. The boy simply drew the parachute after his name or instead of it. It was his way of telling himself—*himself*, Sturmbannführer—how he had come to be in France.'

'No parachutist . . . Is this what you're saying?'

'None. It was all a figment of his imagination.'

The oak stave that had leaned against the end of the bathtub but would normally have been used to bend the prisoner at each ducking, shot through the air. Her lower jaw dropped. Blood spurted from her nose. She gasped, tried to cry out—stiffened—tore at the floor with her fingernails, jerked once, twice and passed out.

'Now are you satisfied?' asked Lautenschläger with barely controlled fury. 'That woman and her son . . .'

'HE'S NOT HER SON!'

'The boy then. They were completely innocent. They didn't even know they were being used when they went to Paris.'

Kraus tossed his head. 'Arrest him. Take the colonel to his room and keep him under guard.'

Lautenschläger held up his hands to gain a moment's respite. 'Consider carefully what you do, Sturmbannführer. You invade my jurisdiction, you take command and issue orders without the proper authority. Arresting a colonel isn't wise. Believe me, the Oberkommando der Wehrmacht will take a very dim view of your actions. Instead of protecting the security of the Retaliatory Weapon sites, you have drawn immense attention to them.'

Kraus was livid. He'd been sweating profusely and now his hands shook so much, he fumbled for his cigarettes and barely got one alight. 'Continue,' he grated.

One of the men was holding a bottle of ammonia under the Bellecour woman's nose and each time she got a whiff, her head jerked back. They had thrown her into a chair.

'Very well, I will, Sturmbannführer. Did you think you could hush up the killing, the looting and burning? The news has spread like wildfire and can only work against us. Instead of the twenty-two you senselessly killed or had killed—murdered, you understand—it will be sixty or seventy. Who knows how large the number will become as word is passed? Instead of eighteen farms razed to the ground, their badly needed crops destroyed or left to rot, it will be fifty.'

'*That is what Reichsminister Himmler wishes!*'

'Then he has little understanding of the roots of the *Résis-tance* and its sympathizers. The Führer will hear of this, Sturmbannführer. If I'm arrested, there will, of necessity, have to be a court of enquiry. Do you really want this, you who have made such a total blunder?'

The Wehrmacht wasn't often soft on civilians. Indeed, they had atrocities of their own to account for, but men like Lautenschläger—wealthy Prussians of the landholding class—could sometimes be far too soft. 'The terrorists must be stamped out, Colonel. Their mayor is one of them. Already my men are looking for him, for he has much to tell us.'

'Like Châlus?'

'Exactly.'

'But that one, like the surveyor Doumier, I gather, told you nothing. Neither got a chance, did they?'

One of the men forced his way into the room to find the Sturmbannführer. Lautenschläger noted how agitated the young SS-Oberschütze was and that the salute he gave was clumsy.

He heard the acid of, '*Find him! Find the little bastard and bring him to me alive or dead!*'

Martin had escaped.

At dawn the rain had stopped. Now fog filled the Valley of the Somme and water dripped from every branch and leaf on the slopes above Bagatelle Château and it was cold—cold like the feeling one had always had moments before a final assault.

Hastily Ledieu crossed himself and, in uncertainty, wet his lips with the tip of his tongue. 'It's impossible, Théodore,' he whispered. 'There are far too many of them at the château.'

Camouflaged lorries were parked end to end on the metalled drive. The colonel's car was off to the left, next to the Sturmbannführer's. Winging in from the river, swans had come to forage the lawns, ducks too, and geese, and soon the sounds of them echoing in the fog were joined by the raucous threats of the peacocks.

Allard let his gaze sift slowly over the lorries. If only they could set them afire, if only they could put one of the cars out of action and steal the other.

'I wouldn't get far and you know it,' confided Ledieu, having read his mind. 'I might just as well go down there and give myself up.'

'And let them find out where your wife and family are in hiding, your grandchildren too?'

The family were downstream at one of the *hortillonnages* of Jean-Pierre's uncle. Ah! it wasn't good, it was terrible. 'Will the Sturmbannführer Kraus go to the de Fleury woman alone?'

This was critical. 'Probably not.' She was being held in the ruined hut on the slopes of the Monts de Caubert directly across the valley from them, and yes, she had led them there to a Schmeisser and two hundred rounds but . . . 'Why not wish me luck?'

'You'll need more than that. Frau Hössler may already have told Kraus it was your car that brought Angélique to us yesterday from the Kommandantur.'

'I talked my way around her. I said the terrorists had commandeered me and the car at gunpoint. I made heroes out of you all. Nicolas would have been proud of me.'

'Knowing Frau Hössler as I do, I can well believe she swallowed it but . . .'

'She did. She even gave me a telex to deliver.'

'Pardon?'

'A telex from the Standartenführer Dirksen to Kraus.' He ripped the envelope open and read it aloud. '"Vergès and concierge Hermé Lemoine arrested Paris 1600 hours. Book-seller Patouillard a paid Gestapo informant the terrorists attempted to finger. Am leaving for Berlin at dawn. Heil Hitler".'

'She'll be disappointed,' said Ledieu.

Allard ignored the wry humour. 'But not the Sturmbannführer. If what she told us is true, Honoré, this may be the thing that causes him to go to her alone.'

'Hope is far too fickle at such moments.'

Allard shrugged off the remark and gave him the envelope to burn but not the telex. 'Now I must play postman, eh? Already the mail has been delayed too long.'

What would he find, what would the day bring? *'Bonne chance*, then. *Au revoir, mon ami de la guerre secrète.'*

*'À toi aussi.'*

They shook hands and held on to each other as old soldiers would. Allard found his cigarettes and self-consciously stuffed them into Honoré's jacket pocket. 'Those are for all the ones I borrowed over the years and failed to repay.'

'They'll do. They're like gold.'

He left then. He went back up to the road to find his car and was soon lost from view. Their little *réseau* was so few in number and now dispersed over such a wide area. Two had stayed with the wife and family, two were guarding the infiltrator at the ruined hut. One kept the Kommandantur under surveillance. 'And I wait here while Théodore risks his life.'

It wasn't good. Ledieu watched the flames destroy the envelope, then checked the Lebel—the Luger had been necessary elsewhere. One by one he removed the black-powder cartridges they had had in the Great War, already damp then, by storage since the Franco-Prussian War, and one by one he replaced them. 'These old bullets,' he said, 'sometimes they misfire.'

The fog made sounds carry. It shut out the light of day and caused the dawn to grow but slowly. Still in her wet clothes and freezing, Marie-Hélène tried not to shiver. She had until noon. If Kraus didn't come to her, one of these two would have to kill her. A burst from the Schmeisser would be far too risky. Would he use a knife, his hands, or a boulder as she had with Véronique Dussart?

The two of them had left her alone in the darkness and now in that greyest of lights. Marchand, the foreman, was taciturn and ultracautious. It was he who had insisted her hands be tied behind her back, her mouth gagged and her ankles bound together. He, alone, held the Schmeisser and all attempts by the cylinder-spinner to get his hands on it had been refused. They seldom spoke. Occasionally they shared a cigarette but usually Jean-Pierre was sent to be lookout.

All the broken bottle glass and bits of rusty metal had been carefully removed from where she sat on the floor, leaning against the back wall. Marchand had even ripped the prostitute's photo from its nail and had destroyed it.

He'd kill her. He wouldn't leave it up to Jean-Pierre, knew his compatriot's failings far too well.

Kraus wouldn't come alone. If he came at all, he would bring so many, the three of them would be killed instantly.

The light grew a little and it revealed the rubbish that had been pushed aside, the bullet-dented helmet, the cartridge casings, empty tins, a water bottle, a cut-open boot, shreds of bloodstained gaiter and webbing.

They would kill her if she moved from where they had left her—Marchand had warned her of this and he'd do it too, no matter what. He didn't want to be here at all, thought it nothing but a huge mistake.

She had to do something but they often checked on her. The gag made her throat parched and when the foreman ducked in to look at her, she tried to tell him she was thirsty.

'Kraus hasn't come yet,' he said. There was no other expression but that of hatred and distrust.

She tried to speak, to beseech him with her eyes. 'Urinate in your clothes,' he grunted.

Violently she shook her head and nodded towards the thermos they had brought with them.

'Ah!' he said. 'It's empty.' She was trouble—Marchand felt it so strongly. She still had that look about her. Not of defeat, ah no, but of a wariness he didn't like.

'You have much to answer for,' he said. 'May God forgive you, but I doubt He will.'

Again he left her, and when, some twenty minutes later, Jean-Pierre ducked in, he grinned, but then he, too, left her but left a pair of scissors hanging on a nail beside the splintered door.

The scissors had opened widely because only one grip encircled the nail. They were old scissors, and in the growing light, the patina of their long usage grew and she thought they were those of a seamstress or tailor, and she wondered if the one who had guided her to the church last night hadn't been a sailor at all.

Shears . . . they're a tailor's shears, she told herself but couldn't touch her hair to feel it.

The parachute with its secret agent had been drawn in blood on the bathroom mirror. It had been drawn on the windows too, and when Martin wet his finger again, he drew it on the inside of the door.

'It's of dark blue silk,' he muttered softly. 'It has a great big yellow moon and brilliant stars so as to be invisible against the night sky, and you steer it by pulling or letting up on the straps.'

Angélique was no longer lying on the floor where she must have lain but they hadn't taken her clothes. Châlus wasn't here either, but some of their hair had been found floating in the bathtub—he had known the ones that were hers and had thought the others must be Châlus's. And for each he had glued hairs to the straps of his parachute.

'They have killed her,' he whispered as he added flying bombs to the picture on the door. 'They have killed the *résistant* Châlus also and now I'm the only one that is left.' The bombs were being dropped by himself but they had wings so that they could glide, and some were already exploding as they hit the ground. There were dead Boches everywhere, but he only made dots to represent those.

Hiding behind the bathtub had been easy—the soldiers had searched, had pulled out all of the towels. Bars of soap had been thrown aside. Soap, can you believe it? he asked himself, and tucking a cinnamon-scented bar into each pocket, prepared to leave. But why had he chosen the cinnamon kind? he wondered. 'It's exotic,' he softly said. 'It smells nice, and Angélique would have talked about it for years after it had all been used up.'

The Germans were downstairs, most of them. They thought he had run outside and now they searched the surrounding woods and the marshes next to the river, now they used the dogs, the three of them that were left.

When he hurried along the corridor, he heard urgent voices behind a closed door but had no time to listen. Soon he had found the servants' staircase, soon he had made it to the ground floor again but now the sound of harsh voices broke over him.

Darting into a room, he eased the door shut and tried to calm himself, but it was the strangest of rooms. Long spears were crossed over big shields made of lion and tiger skin and these were mounted on the walls between the heads of their victims and those, too, of the gazelle and antelope. There were zebra skins on the floor and on the armchairs too, and the curved tusks of an elephant made an arch over an ebony and glass-windowed cabinet in which there were guns, and in the drawers below, bullets for them. Those of the elephant gun were very heavy, those for the gazelle much lighter.

Four double-barrelled shotguns stood side by side. Gingerly he took one of them down and, after some fiddling, broke it open.

The number 12 cartridge fitted the chambers snugly. 'I will load this one,' he said, 'but first I must find out how the safety works. I can't have it on when I have to pull the triggers.'

Photographs showed the former owner of the château as a young man on safari. He stood with an arm draped over the shoulders of his gun bearer. In another photo, his wife lifted the head of a tiger she had just killed. With the elephant, they watched as the blacks butchered it and cut out the heart.

In a desk drawer there was a Mauser pistol in a worn leather holster and when Martin took it out, he didn't pull the trigger but whispered, 'I have everything I need. Now I, too, can go on safari.'

Bagatelle Château wasn't just teaming with armed SS, a crisis was in progress, but when the doors to the winter salon were closed, the sound of that was muffled.

'Well, what is it, Sous-préfet?' demanded Kraus.

Irritable, a danger at any time and with his left ear swathed in bandages, the Sturmbannführer was scowling. 'I have two messages for you from the Kommandantur,' said Allard, deferentially mopping the all but bald crown of his massive head with a handkerchief. 'Every Tuesday morning the colonel and I have a briefing and, as I was coming this way, Frau Hössler asked if I would deliver them.'

'Oh and did she now?' seethed Kraus as he looked him over. The widely set, large and dark brown eyes were far too wary—had he known there hadn't been a parachutist? *Had he?* wondered Kraus. 'Messages?' he asked, reaching for a cigarette.

The Gestapo Munk was with him. Both were sitting by a fire that had been allowed to go out. 'Yes, Sturmbannführer.'

A half-empty bottle of the colonel's Calvados and two glasses were to hand. The cigarette was lighted. 'Then come . . . come closer and let us hear what you have to say for yourself. We have been interrogating the terrorist Châlus and the Bellecour woman for hours, and apologize for our state of untidiness. Such things are never easy. You'll have heard, no doubt, of our little successes.'

The rampages, the murders.

Blood, and what could only be excrement, were spattered on the sleeves and collar of Kraus's brown shirt and open tunic. The black tie was missing. There was blood, too, on the Gestapo Munk.

Allard found the telex and extended it only to hear Kraus saying, 'Read it aloud and clearly. Please don't falter like a schoolboy—you did go to school with Ledieu, didn't you?'

*Ah merde*, what was this?

The nostrils of the sous-préfet's big, flat nose pinched as he drew in the breath of the condemned. The bayonet scar that ran from beneath the lower lip to the line of his jaw tightened.

As calmly as he could, Allard ignored the question and read the telex. Kraus smiled at the news it brought of Dirksen. 'That reading was very good, Sous-préfet, but had you practised, I wonder?'

The Gestapo Munk let his gaunt-eyed gaze sift over him, causing Allard to shudder.

'*Well?*' shot Kraus. 'As a police administrator, did you or did you not read it earlier?'

'I read it, yes.'

Had a little of that patriotic defiance not left him? wondered Kraus. 'Usually such things are placed in sealed envelopes but when I spoke to Frau Hössler but a few moments ago by telephone, she made no mention of this not having been done.'

Had he really talked to the woman? 'She was understandably very tired, Sturmbannführer. Indeed, I gather she hadn't left her post all night.'

How cautious of him. 'And she gave *you*, a Frenchman, confidential messages for *me* in unsealed envelopes?'

'Only one of them wasn't sealed. We were in a hurry. The failure to seal it was entirely my fault.'

Yet the envelope had vanished. '*Ach*, it's noble of you to take the blame so readily, Sous-préfet. Yes, that's good of you, but do you know what the terrorist Angélique Bellecour said of you?'

*Cher Jésus*, forgive that poor woman. Trapped, Allard stood in uncertainty, trying desperately to retain a modicum of composure. 'No, Sturmbannführer, I don't.'

'Châlus had words to say about your mayor. Abbeville holds a terrorist organization right in our midst. You and Father Nicolas and Ledieu have been close friends for a very long time, have you not?'

Châlus might or might not have said a thing, the same for Angélique Bellecour. 'Sturmbannführer, there were two messages for you. Both are very urgent. Time is . . .'

'ANSWER ME!'

The Gestapo Munk got up and reached for his gloves. There were two armed SS standing sentry just inside the doors to the salon. Escape was impossible. 'Very well, then, yes, we were schoolboys together. We were in the Great War also, Sturmbannführer, in the same unit from the start and until wounded.'

'And Ledieu is a terrorist—we have absolute proof of this.'

Did they only know that much and nothing more? demanded Allard of himself but said of Honoré, 'This I can't believe, Sturmbannführer. Too much is at stake—his town, his family, his grandchildren . . .'

Kraus snapped his fingers. The Gestapo Munk took a step closer and then another and another. 'The second message,' demanded Munk, and the two of them watched as Allard fumbled for the thing and finally managed to drag it from a pocket.

'Sealed,' said Munk, raking him with a scathing look and, turning to hand it to Kraus, swung back suddenly with a fist.

Allard felt blood bursting from his broken lips. Clutching

his stinging mouth and jaw, he swallowed hard and tearfully blurted, 'Sacré nom de nom, what was that for?'

'YOU'RE ALL TERRORISTS!' shrieked Kraus. 'You have the affront to come here to *me*, to demand answers? Then I will give them to you! The boy has escaped but will soon be apprehended and punished. The colonel is under house arrest. The terrorists Châlus and Bellecour are . . .'

Munk must have signalled that such irrationality of newsgiving deserved caution, for Kraus shut up and tore the envelope open to silently read the note from Marie-Hélène de Fleury.

> *I am waiting for you in a ruined hut on the slopes of the Monts de Caubert not far from the anti-aircraft batteries. There is a path from the Calvary to the viewpoint and then it is but a short climb to the hut. Come alone. Please don't break my cover. I have the names of all of them but must leave for Paris before it is too late.*

The peacocks cried, the geese honked. Seen through the fog, the dogs strained at their leads and in one curving sweep, the line of armed SS fanned out as it turned from the marshes towards the wooded slopes.

Ledieu gripped himself by the chin in thought. Should he leave while he could; should he stay? He was up the slope some distance—there was a good vantage point here. Théodore had not yet left the château. Had there been trouble?

There must have been, he said and, wetting his lips, touched them in thought. Was it all over? he asked and hated to think it, but one had to, and when Théodore came down the steps, he could barely see him but knew for certain two armed SS followed him.

The line of soldiers had all but crossed the lawns and were about to enter the formal gardens where statues stood grey in the grey of the fog. 'I must,' he said.

Théodore paused beside his little car to throw his friend a last look but the distance, it was too great. Perhaps he said, Run, Honoré. Forgive me for failing you. Perhaps he simply said, Retreat. Try to warn the others, but we're both realists, eh?

The two with the machine pistols also got into the car. One sat in the front passenger seat; the other directly behind Théodore.

They drove away. The line . . . the dogs had now reached the woods. Seldom calling to each other, the Boches advanced up the slope and soon were lost from sight.

Again Ledieu wet his lips in uncertainty. Leaning back against an oak, he said, 'Nicolas, are you there?'

And when he lay on the ground face down so as to silence the shot if possible, he said, 'Forgive me but I have no other choice if I am to protect them,' and put the muzzle of the revolver into his mouth.

*Doumier. Remember Henri-Paul. Keep him always in your thoughts.*
The SS-Unterscharführer, a young man of twenty perhaps, crumpled into a fist the rain-soaked card that had been tied to one of the bouquets of drenched red chrysanthemums.

Allard glanced doubtfully up at the heavily timbered cross with its crucified Christ. He had to give Joseph Marchand and Jean-Pierre all the time he could. They would have kept a lookout. They'd have seen them arrive.

The Calvary on the Monts de Caubert was not frequented much these days, not since the Defeat, and idly he wondered who had made the effort to leave these tributes.

Prodded, he gave the two SS a curt nod, then said, 'The hut is this way. Please follow me.' He had no other choice. Kraus had not yet had him arrested but had been suspicious and hadn't cared about the de Fleury woman's cover.

Following him, the SS stayed close but all too soon the path dipped below the edge of the escarpment and narrowed as it passed among the trees and underbrush. Angular blocks of mossy limestone caused it to narrow further, to be constricted so that one burst from the Schmeisser would hit all three. Why hadn't Joseph fired that thing? Why hadn't he?

*Ah merde*, one of the armed SS had vanished. Silently Allard cursed them. The other one, a stern-faced Stabsscharführer who had been awarded the Infanterie-Sturmabzeichen for hand-to-hand combat no doubt, and the silver Verwundeten-

Abzeichen for wounds incurred in the same, nodded for him to continue. 'We will take no chances,' he grunted.

Was it to end this way? wondered Allard but thought that yes, it might be more suitable. Perhaps Joseph and Jean-Pierre had left while they could, fading away into the woods but first killing the infiltrator.

In his heart of hearts he knew there was no hope for himself and he wondered then if he could at least deal with the Stabsscharführer before that one killed him.

Things outside the ruined hut were too quiet. Always in the past she had heard one or the other of them when they had come to check on her but they hadn't come in quite a while.

Cautiously Marie-Hélène brought her knees up to her chin and braced her back and bound hands against the wall behind her. Constantly she searched out the gaps in the door and walls—even in the roof—for some sign of what was happening.

Perhaps five more minutes passed, perhaps a little more. Then she heard a furtive step. A hand, an arm crept across the splintered door to ease it open slowly.

Another step was taken but these were not the steps of the one who was opening the door.

Tears filled her eyes and, terrified, she tried to stop them because they blurred her vision.

The one called Jean-Pierre ducked silently into the hut to reach for the shears and to flatten his back against that wall. Now he, too, waited. His hand was raised. The shears were gripped. There was a wariness and fear in his dark brown eyes she did not like.

He was young. Even younger than herself.

The door was eased open further by the toe of a well-greased jackboot that glistened with accumulated beads of water. The grey-green trousers were heavy, the leg strong, the Schmeisser gripped at the ready by thick-fingered hands.

She waited. The one with the shears waited. The armed SS saw her quite clearly—she was certain of this and violently shook her head to warn him, only to have him misunderstand.

He thought she meant she was alone. He went away. She tried to cry out to him and fought to clear the tears, but it was no use.

Satisfied that they were alone, if only for a moment, the one called Jean-Pierre lowered the shears and threw a last glance at the doorway. Then he stepped over to her but did not smile or try to fool around—things were far too desperate.

He crouched. He tried to get her to unlock her chin from her knees. He wanted to get at her chest.

'I *can't* stab you in the neck,' he managed. 'Please be reasonable.'

She refused. She balled herself up more tightly. Plucking at her shoulders, he began to pull her away from the wall but she pushed her back and hands against it more firmly.

'*Putain!*' he hissed and began to hack off her hair.

She ducked away. He grabbed a handful of hair. The shears tore at the roots. He was pulling, had caught a determined breath. She must kick him now—NOW! she cried out inwardly and pushed herself at him—kicked out hard, saw a startled look come into his eyes, saw blood rush from his gaping mouth and, as she toppled over onto her side, saw the armed SS release Jean-Pierre's throat and let the head fall back.

Butcher to him, the rawboned, blond, grey-eyed Unterscharführer wiped the blade of the knife on Jean-Pierre's shirt, then cut her ankles and wrists free.

He put a finger to his lips and cut the gag that had silenced her.

Cramped, Marie-Hélène tried to ease her wrists and move her fingers and toes.

He had no more time for her and, putting the knife away, swung the Schmeisser back into hand.

Shakily she teased the shears from Jean-Pierre's fingers and stood up. Kraus hadn't come. Kraus had sent this one and others to bring her in.

The Unterscharführer ducked out of the hut. One moment he was there before her, the next he was gone.

Now, again, she waited and strained to listen, only to realize she was breathing very rapidly.

Catching a breath, she tried to calm her racing pulse. Kraus wanted her on his terms, not hers and then . . . what, then? Up against the whitewashed execution post to guarantee her silence, was that what he'd do?

Or would he have her all to himself?

A burst from a Schmeisser came to her. It was short and sharp and she had the thought that it couldn't have been the foreman of the brewery who had fired it but one of the others.

Another burst came from off to her right. It was longer, harder, and yes, it had a reckless finality to it.

The smell of cordite was caught in her nostrils. Fog from the valley was seeping up the slope as it lifted and she felt the mizzle breaking against her cheeks and hands.

Stumbling, she went down hard among the mossy, angular talus. The shears shot from her hand. Crying out inwardly, she frantically strained to reach them, pulled herself forward and dug her right arm much deeper among the rocks.

At last she had them and had hooked her thumb and forefinger securely through the grips.

Some of her hair still clung to one of the blades. If only she could slip away unseen. If only she could meet Kraus on her own terms.

When she found the Unterscharführer, he was slumped against a ledge and his eyes were filled with disbelief. His stomach was a mass of blood and as he gripped it, he looked up at her in question and tried to speak but couldn't.

His Schmeisser had been taken.

Twice more she heard the sound of one of those things, sharp and hard and echoing through the fog.

Only then was there silence again and this lasted for far too long. Trembling—not knowing what to do—Marie-Hélène began to pick her way back to the hut and when she saw the Stabsscharführer grinning up at her, she fought for words and finally managed, 'Is it true? Am I safe at last? Those bastards were going to kill me.'

'They'll kill no more,' he said and, gathering the Schmeissers by their shoulder straps, told her they should leave while they could.

She picked her way down to him.

'A moment, please,' she said. 'Excuse me, but it's necessary.'

Again he grinned. He watched as she hiked her skirt and squatted to urinate and only then did he turn his back on her.

She leapt. She drove the shears deeply into the side of his neck. Startled—crying out in pain and rage—he grabbed his neck and fought for the shears.

Together, she clinging to him and fighting to use them, they rolled down over the rocks. Repeatedly she drove the shears into his neck and as blood spurted from his jugular, she sank the blades deeply into him and held on fiercely. Felt him jerk in spasm after spasm until at last his body was still.

Blood covered her hands and arms. Her shirt-blouse was soaked, her skirt too. '*Salaud!*' she swore and spat as she tried to wipe her mouth on a corner of his shirt. 'Did you need to bleed so much?'

Exhausted, she remained straddling him, her head bowed not in defeat but in despair, for what was she to do? Others might come running at any moment. Others . . .

Standing—calming herself as best she could—she went into the hut to hack away at what remained of her hair and to let it fall where they had kept her.

Jean-Pierre and he would have to appear as if they had died fighting. The body of the SS was almost too heavy for her, but when it lay on the floor, she took his knife and drove it into the small of Jean-Pierre's back. Then she sprinkled her hair over both of them and left the shears in Jean-Pierre's hand.

There was blood everywhere along the trail over which she had dragged the Stabsscharführer's body. Perhaps he had been wounded first. Perhaps the two of them had fought out here before dying on top of her.

It would have to do but somehow she would have to explain how it was she had managed to cut herself free.

Picking up the Schmeissers, she soon found the sous-préfet's body and took from it the keys to his car. Hans would have to help her. She would try to kill Kraus for him, would try to make it look as if the *Résistance* had done it, but then especially, help would be needed.

She was now a walking advertisement of all those she had betrayed and those she could still finger. If Ledieu, the mayor, didn't kill her, then one of the others would. For her, Abbeville was far too dangerous and the sooner she was away from it, the better.

But first she had to go to the Kommandantur. First she had to see if Hans had sent word from Paris. Hans couldn't let her down, not now, not after all that had happened.

It was Frau Hössler who told her where to find Kraus and that the Standartenführer Dirksen was on his way to Berlin.

'Please wash and find a change of clothes, yes? Here, I will help you.'

'No. No, it's all right. I'll go as I am but telephone ahead, would you, so that I'm shown right in to him and don't have to wait.'

'The boy is missing. The boy has escaped.'

'Martin . . . ? Ah! I'll watch out for him. He and I are old friends.'

The peacocks were making noises, the swans too, and as the soldiers dragged someone's body across the lawns by the heels, the ducks flew up and away.

The fog was everywhere. Martin wondered who had been killed in the woods. The dogs were following the body with their heads down as though ashamed of what they had done.

When the soldiers reached the circular drive, they left the body lying on the stones. 'It's monsieur le maire,' he said softly, and letting go of the drapes behind which he stood, remained silent in thought.

Had they killed or arrested all of them? he wondered. Had the Mademoiselle Isabelle betrayed the whole *réseau*?

He swallowed hard. He knew he mustn't cry—crying did no good at times like this. Angélique had to be rescued if she was still alive. And Châlus? he asked but answered, 'Châlus didn't say I was his son. He denied it.'

The door to the gun room opened onto the corridor near the summer salon, and from here he had a chance to look towards the main entrance. Kraus and the Gestapo Munk and some others were going out to see the body. Their backs were turned. There was no one on the main staircase.

Hurrying—carrying the double-barrelled shotgun and the Mauser pistol—Martin reached the foot of the stairs and was starting up them when someone decided to come down. It was the Oberst Lautenschläger and he was angrily shouting. '*Verdammt, Dummkopf!* House arrest? Shoot me if you wish but I must know who was killed!'

He, too, went outside and so did the SS who was supposed to be guarding him.

The bedroom door was open, and when he saw the shotgun pointed at him, the doctor who sat beside the bed hesitantly got to his feet and raised his hands. 'It's all right, Martin,' he said, throwing a questioning glance at the corridor. 'Keep calm. She'll live if she gets the help she needs.'

Moving across the room, the doctor sat down at a table next to the windows and indicated he would behave. 'It's not my quarrel. I know nothing of it, you understand, but the Sturmbannführer Kraus is very much in command and this you must consider.'

'I have. I'm going to kill him and her too.'

'Who, please?'

'You're just trying to get me to tell you things,' said Martin shrilly, but calmed himself. 'The Mademoiselle Isabelle. The infiltrator.'

'Ah, yes, the de Fleury woman.'

He sat so still, this doctor, as still as Angélique lay on the bed. Martin threw a glance at the door and decided to close it. 'There, that's better,' he said.

The doctor wasn't young and the jacket of the Wehrmacht uniform he wore was open. The sleeves of his shirt would still be rolled up. His glasses needed polishing and he asked if he might do this and take a cigarette case from his pocket. 'You're making me nervous,' he said and smiled. The accent was much like the colonel's, the French not so bad.

I'll give him a nod, said Martin to himself. Then I'll sit beside the bed in that chair he was using, and I'll point the shotgun at the door so as to take the colonel hostage.

'I won't kill either of you,' he said to the doctor. 'Not if I can avoid it.' And gingerly setting the pistol on the bed beside Angélique's bandaged right hand, sat down to face the door and wait.

'My name is Haeften, Martin—Alfred, if you like, and I have a son your age back home in Hamburg. We write from time to time but the mails aren't always so good. Because of the bomb damage, he's living in the countryside with his grandmother now.'

The doctor waited and waited and finally Martin knew he had to ask, 'What happened to his mother?'

'The incendiaries,' he said. Just that and nothing more, for he had lighted a cigarette and had taken to looking out the windows.

Half hidden in the fog, Bagatelle Château seemed empty. There were no sentries on the door, no camouflaged lorries parked in the drive. And when she stopped the car beside Ledieu's body, Marie-Hélène wondered where everyone had gone.

Hesitantly she swept her eyes over the French windows of the ground floor and then those of the first storey, the bull's-eye ones. A curtain was pushed aside. A figure stood at one of those upper windows, and when she got out to cross the drive, she saw that it was Martin Bellecour but that his back was to her.

A fist-size hole had been torn in the top of Ledieu's head and she asked, What's this? and understood he hadn't been killed by anyone but himself.

Again she swept her eyes over the château and then turned to questioningly search the grounds. The peacocks looked at her, the white swans did too. She had passed no lorries on the road in. Had they taken another route? Had they gone after her, gone to the ruins of that hut?

They must have.

Uncertain of what the château held, she reached into the car to take up one of the Schmeissers. This she kept at the ready.

There was no one downstairs—Châlus had been dragged down here and lay naked in the cellars. He had been beaten to death but she felt no relief, glanced uncertainly at the ceiling timbers above and then hesitantly went back up to the front entrance.

Still there was no sign of anyone. '*Ah merde*,' she sighed. 'What has happened?'

There were little dark brown hairs on the back of the Sturmbannführer's neck where it had been closely shaved, and these hairs, the muzzle of the shotgun pushed aside as it was pressed more firmly against them. Kraus sat in the chair beside the bed but facing the door. The Gestapo Munk stood between him and the door but to one side so as to give a clean shot.

The Oberst Lautenschläger, the doctor and the Hauptmann Scheel, who had carried the orders to the others, sat at the table by the windows.

'We're not interfering,' the colonel had said to Kraus. 'Might I remind you we have been placed under house arrest by yourself?'

The soldiers had gone to find Isabelle Moncontre; the Sturmbannführer Kraus had been furious with the colonel and the others and had accused them of being traitors and of not having tried to stop the little parachutist from taking him and the Gestapo Munk hostage too.

Now they all knew the infiltrator had arrived alone and that she was armed.

Angélique stirred but didn't awaken. Her breathing wasn't good. Her chest rattled. There was a bloodied froth on her lips. The bubbles grew as she exhaled but subsided with each new breath.

Martin braced his back against the wall because this was what the colonel had told him to do. I'm not to make the mistake of discharging both barrels at once, he reminded himself. This, too, the Oberst Lautenschläger had said, and yes, that one wanted the Sturmbannführer and the Gestapo Munk dead and out of the way so that he could again take command.

They each listened intently to the château. Not a one of them stirred. The visitor came on up the stairs, perhaps a step at a time—who could possibly tell? Carpets muffled the sound of her.

Angélique breathed in.

'Be reasonable, Colonel,' the Gestapo Munk had nervously begged. 'Let's not have an accident.'

'Accidents are common enough with shotguns,' the colonel had replied. 'We are all of us hostages and at risk.'

At last the doors were nudged open. Isabelle Moncontre—Marie-Hélène de Fleury—took them all in at a glance. She gasped and managed to say softly, 'Martin, what's this?'

Her hair had been hacked off with scissors. Blood made the white shirt-blouse cling to a shoulder, to a breast, an arm . . . There was blood smeared on her brow and cheeks and on the backs of her hands, on her skirt also.

'You . . .' began Martin only to find his eyes, they refused to obey and filled rapidly with tears. 'You lied to me! You betrayed us!'

The Gestapo Munk didn't turn to face her. The Oberst and the others sat so stiffly, she realized what was wanted of her and, finding voice enough, said, 'Martin, stand away from him. Go to your mother. Get on the other side of the bed. Please . . .'

A ten-year-old boy, the son of Raymond Châlus, she thought, but not of the woman whom Martin had called mother.

'Please,' she begged. 'It's over for me, Martin. Let me kill him for you. Me instead of you, *chéri*. Then maybe when this war is done you won't think so badly of me.'

'Mademoiselle . . .' said Lautenschläger in alarm.

Kraus glared at her. Finally he hissed, '*Kill them, idiot!*'

Martin felt his fingers tightening on the triggers. He heard her saying, 'No, Martin,' and even as the Sturmbannführer leapt at her and the Gestapo Munk turned swiftly towards her, he heard the Messerschmitts firing, heard the cannon shells exploding as they struck people and smashed things, saw the blood and brains being scattered everywhere. A froth of them.

Thrown back against the wall, dazed and unable to stand, he felt himself sliding to the floor. Angélique murmured and urgently reached out to him. She was trying to say his name . . .

The sound of the shotgun blast rushed in on him so loudly, it filled his head but then he heard a last burst chasing it.

'*Lieber Gott!*' swore Lautenschläger, leaping up from his chair to hesitate as did the others.

Blood and brains peppered the walls, the doors, the ceiling. Decapitated, Kraus lay near Munk who had tried to draw a pistol and had been hit both by the woman's Schmeisser and the shotgun.

Thrown back into the corridor and sitting, slumped against the wall, Marie-Hélène de Fleury tried to speak but couldn't.

There was no forehead, and when they reached her, she toppled over.

Snow fell softly and though it would make the streets of Paris even more miserable, in the Jardin du Luxembourg it made the children happy.

Angélique watched them chasing each other and throwing snowballs. With the littlest ones, there was that sense of wonder, of magic. They licked the snow and felt how cold it was on their tongues—their minds were so far from this lousy war and Occupation and yet they were caught up in it.

For months she had lain in hospital in Abbeville. No word—nothing. Martin gone from her like that, the Oberst Lautenschläger making sure she got well. But could anyone recover from such a thing? she asked herself. Just to be in Paris was enough. She had found a room nearby and each day, she tried to walk a little farther.

'But I do miss Martin,' she said to herself. 'He and I, we were at each other's throats half the time but companions otherwise.'

She sat a while on one of the benches near the pond where he had sailed a little boat and had lost monsieur le maire's pencil. She tried to remember, to recall how he would intuitively respond to her needs by reaching out to brush fingers against her cheek or take her by the hand.

She searched the faces of the children. Some watched the puppet shows; others slid on the ice of the pond. Mothers worried, as they always did. Fathers remained reserved or upset, depending on each child's actions.

Pulling off a glove, she hesitantly touched the scars on her forehead, nose and chin. She didn't know if she would ever be able to face people or be able to work again—ah! it was too early to think of such things. Her right eye was still not good.

Something distracted her. Some pigeons she thought and, turning to look at them, saw a boy striding through them towards her. The coat was dark blue and its collar was up. He wore a matching toque, and his hands were jammed into the pockets of the coat. A real urchin, a tough guy. 'Martin . . . ?' she managed. 'MARTIN!'

The little parachutist had been released from prison and had been sent to her.

# About the Author

J. Robert Janes (b. 1935) is a mystery author best known for writing historical thrillers. Born in Toronto, he holds degrees in mining and geology, and worked as an engineer, university professor, and textbook author before he started writing fiction. He began his career as a novelist by writing young adult books, starting with *The Odd-Lot Boys and the Tree-Fort War* (1976). He wrote his last young adult novel, *Murder in the Market*, in 1985, by which time he had begun writing for adults, starting with the four-novel Richard Hagen series.

In 1992, Janes published *Mayhem*, the first in the long-running St-Cyr and Kohler series, for which he is best known. These police procedurals set in Nazi-occupied France have been praised for the author's attention to historical detail, as well as their swift-moving plots. The sixteenth in the series, *Clandestine*, was published in 2015.

# J. ROBERT JANES

FROM MYSTERIOUSPRESS.COM
AND OPEN ROAD MEDIA

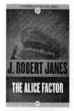

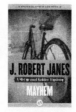
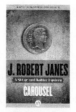
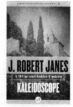

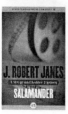
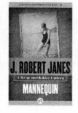
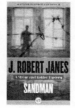
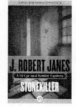
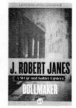

MYSTERIOUSPRESS.COM

OPEN ROAD
INTEGRATED MEDIA

MYSTERIOUSPRESS.COM

Otto Penzler, owner of the Mysterious Bookshop in Manhattan, founded the Mysterious Press in 1975. Penzler quickly became known for his outstanding selection of mystery, crime, and suspense books, both from his imprint and in his store. The imprint was devoted to printing the best books in these genres, using fine paper and top dust-jacket artists, as well as offering many limited, signed editions.

Now the Mysterious Press has gone digital, publishing ebooks through **MysteriousPress.com**.

**MysteriousPress.com** offers readers essential noir and suspense fiction, hard-boiled crime novels, and the latest thrillers from both debut authors and mystery masters. Discover classics and new voices, all from one legendary source.

FIND OUT MORE AT
WWW.MYSTERIOUSPRESS.COM

FOLLOW US:
@emysteries and Facebook.com/MysteriousPressCom

MysteriousPress.com is one of a select group of publishing partners of Open Road Integrated Media, Inc.

**THE MYSTERIOUS BOOKSHOP**, founded in 1979, is located in Manhattan's Tribeca neighborhood. It is the oldest and largest mystery-specialty bookstore in America.

The shop stocks the finest selection of new mystery hardcovers, paperbacks, and periodicals. It also features a superb collection of signed modern first editions, rare and collectable works, and Sherlock Holmes titles. The bookshop issues a free monthly newsletter highlighting its book clubs, new releases, events, and recently acquired books.

58 Warren Street
info@mysteriousbookshop.com
(212) 587-1011
Monday through Saturday
11:00 a.m. to 7:00 p.m.

## FIND OUT MORE AT:

www.mysteriousbookshop.com

## FOLLOW US:

@TheMysterious and Facebook.com/MysteriousBookshop

OPEN ROAD
INTEGRATED MEDIA

Find a full list of our authors and
titles at www.openroadmedia.com

FOLLOW US
@OpenRoadMedia

CPSIA information can be obtained at www.ICGtesting.com
Printed in the USA
BVOW02s1653260616

453428BV00002B/2/P